ANAM

ANAM

ANDRÉ DAO

PICADOR

First published 2023 by Hamish Hamilton
an imprint and division of Penguin Random House Australia

First published in the UK 2023 by Picador
an imprint of Pan Macmillan
The Smithson, 6 Briset Street, London EC1M 5NR
EU representative: Macmillan Publishers Ireland Ltd, 1st Floor,
The Liffey Trust Centre, 117–126 Sheriff Street Upper,
Dublin 1, D01 YC43
Associated companies throughout the world
www.panmacmillan.com

ISBN 978-1-5290-9469-5 HB
ISBN 978-1-5290-9470-1 TPB

1 3 5 7 9 8 6 4 2

A CIP catalogue record for this book is available from the British Library.

Printed and bound by CPI Group (UK) Ltd, Croydon, CR0 4YY

Visit **www.picador.com** to read more about all our books
and to buy them. You will also find features, author interviews and
news of any author events, and you can sign up for e-newsletters
so that you're always first to hear about our new releases.

For Ông Bà Nội

I. MICHAELMAS

C

(If I think of my grandparents now, after all this writing and reading and imagining and remembering, two couples are thrown into relief, their outlines like clay figures in the mud where so many others are failing to resist the ebb and flow of forgetting. Both couples are elderly and Vietnamese and live in an apartment outside Paris with their eldest daughter. Both couples have been together sixty years, through two wars, and many separations. Both speak to me in a mix of Vietnamese, French, and a smattering of English. But one couple speak to me of suffering, loss, exile, forgiveness and redemption, and the other couple do not. Instead they are always laughing, with each other and at me, pinching, touching, feeding me, looking at me, shaking their heads and chastising me, praising my plumpness and my height and my grades. This second couple is harder to write but easier to remember. I think of them as saying to me over and over again, We want you to be. And also, Why don't you marry that poor girl? And, When are you taking the bar exam? And always, Eat up, Why aren't you eating, Finished already? I've been trying for a long time to bring the two couples together in my mind, or at least to avoid having to choose between them. And just now, thinking of them, I remember the visit that my grandmother and I paid to my grandfather one late afternoon when he was on his deathbed. He was in a clean, beige room in a public hospital a train and a bus away from their daughter's apartment. He patted the side of the bed for my grandmother to come sit by him, and I asked them once again about the story, expecting them to tell me the usual things. Instead they chose to sing, something they had never done before, and would never do again, an old jazz standard: *I remember you* . . . But even as I was fumbling to record them on my phone, they were already finishing, lapsing into wrinkled smiles, so that the recording I have is nothing but silence.)

D

This will be the last time that I will have begun again – the last, because I will have learnt to see what I failed to see at the beginning. I will have learnt to see that a muddy swamp can be called a fen, that not knowing where you're going can be a virtue, and that walking is a kind of perfection. I will have learnt to see that the dilapidated rental we left behind in Footscray will always be the house where we first bathed our daughter, washing off the blood and muck with which she arrived, and I will have learnt that after Cambridge we will return to that house in Footscray after all, and that, in time, it will also be where we first bathe our son, washing off the blood and muck with which he arrives. I will have learnt that the robes we matriculated in at Cambridge, hired from the college's graduate student association, were actually cheap polyester, that most of the books in the many libraries in which I will have sat have never and will never be read, and that the past is no more a home than any of the string of place names with which my family is entangled could be a home: Hung-Xa, Hanoi, Saigon, Ho Chi Minh City, Laon, Paris, Boissy, Cambridge, Footscray. I will have learnt that we walk, as Paul said, by faith and not by sight. I will have learnt to stop stopping – that is, to stop waiting while stopped. I will have learnt, instead, to wait while walking, to walk without expectation of arriving and yet still be ready to arrive at any moment. In the end I will have learnt – or remembered, if there's any difference – how to live.

Or, at least, I will have learnt what we receive from our ancestors and what we pass on to our children – what we give them, even as we wash away the blood and muck with which they arrived.

1

We are walking in the meadows halfway between Cambridge and Grantchester. To our left, the river Cam, narrow and deep, winds its way towards town. It's a fine autumn day, six months after I'd nearly lost them both, and the scene is dreamily bucolic: a canoe or two travelling upriver, a birdwatcher with binoculars trained on some bird of prey – a windhover, probably – beating at the gentle currents with its great wings, a silver-haired walker in Hunters and country coat, all bathed in weak English sunshine. Edith is asleep in the carrier on my back, which is so well designed that I can forget for lengthy stretches that she is even there, as if it is just the two of us again – Lauren and me.

As we walk through the meadows in silence, I remember the crowd of doctors in scrubs that suddenly appeared in the delivery room, the way they stood around Edith's body – though she wasn't Edith yet – on the table in the corner as I dumbly held Lauren's hand; I remember the machine they wheeled in, a big plastic tube on wheels, the way the doctors spoke with quiet authority as they put not-yet-Edith inside and began to wheel her away; I remember the way the last doctor stopped at the door and looked back at me as if to say, Aren't you coming? I let go of Lauren's hand and followed, still mute.

I don't know how much of this she remembers. But maybe it's not so important to remember everything. Maybe there are reasons to forget.

As we enter the village of Grantchester, past a herd of grazing cows who pay us no mind, Lauren asks me if I've settled on a topic for my thesis.

At the beginning of term, Simons, my international law professor, told the class that in lieu of sitting the exam we could choose to submit a thesis. He meant a dissertation, an essay. A medium-length piece of writing duly researched and footnoted. He meant a very minor contribution to scholarship – a reappraisal of the doctrine of state responsibility for internationally wrongful acts as it appeared in the American–Mexican Claims Commission, or tracing the evolution of free-flow-of-data clauses in bilateral trade agreements. These are the kind of topics, I say to Lauren, that might tip the balance in my favour for a pupillage at one of the London chambers, or a traineeship at one of the international arbitration firms.

And that's what you want, says Lauren, somewhere between a statement and a question.

It's what everyone here wants, I say. The other students, they're all Australians, New Zealanders, South Africans, Canadians, Indians. The best the Commonwealth has to offer.

Back to the imperial bosom for validation, says Lauren.

And a golden ticket to stay on in the City, I say. Or clerk for a judge in the Hague.

Just so long as you don't return to whatever backwater you came from, right?

At a pub in Grantchester, as I eat my first ever Yorkshire pudding, Lauren asks again about the thesis. I don't respond right away, lost in a trailing thought about Wittgenstein – he'd completed this same walk many times to take tea with Bertrand Russell at the Orchard, a nearby tearoom. Beside us Edith sits in her high chair, squeezing a slice of avocado into a pulp in her fist.

A thesis, I say, is also a theory, an idea. And I have one of those, even if it isn't something that will get me a job:

Forgetting is complicity. Remembering is complicity. Making art is complicity. Living in the world, pursuing material gain, buying a house you can't afford: complicity. Starting a family, putting down roots is complicity; migration, travel, too. Hope is complicity, but so is despair. Asking, What is to be done? is complicity. Not asking is complicity. Being a human rights lawyer is complicity. Loving my daughter.

I imagine I am already hearing Lauren's response: Complicity in what? Complicit how? Why don't you just say what you mean? And why can't you say it without referencing someone else? But instead she says, Then what are we doing here?

2

Some people seem to do their best thinking while walking. Or at least, that's how a certain kind of writer writes themselves thinking: always on the move. They promenade, they perambulate. Materialising on the horizon are convenient prompts to their thinking: an advertising board or a stray word from a passing pedestrian reorients the train of their thoughts, until walk and thought together end at some fitting revelation. The magic of it is that we, the reader, move with them, through the pastoral landscape of Wiltshire, along the East Anglian coast, across Manhattan.

But it's a trick, isn't it? Perhaps the walking does animate their minds. Fresh air, visual stimulation. Maybe the gentle exertion of putting one foot in front of the other, all the thousands of micro-adjustments required to find sure footing, to maintain balance, to stay upright, to regulate your breathing, to watch out for danger – maybe all that keeps your animal brain occupied just enough that you have some room to think. But even then, the walking cannot be where the real thinking is happening, the thinking that is being recorded in the writing. Even if on your walk to Grantchester, say, you think very clearly and deeply about some problem that has been troubling you – the relationship, for example, between reason and desire – the thought that counts will be the one that you later record at your desk, at which point you will be recording not the thought you had while watching the sun set over the River Cam but your memory of that thought.

And it's there – hopefully in a quiet study, or an old library, though any flat surface will do – that you meaningfully pass through the meadows, thinking whatever it is you were thinking about.

So in the interests of accuracy, I will begin at a desk, a week or two into what I now think of as my new old life as a law student. Through the library window, I can see the great beech tree in the middle of the lawn, aflame in orange and red, the afternoon light glinting off the dormer windows of Clare College's dining hall, clouds floating past the spires of King's College Chapel, and the tourists on punts laden with blankets and cameras drifting under the bridges and looking up in wonder at the window where I am only pretending to study, imagining, no doubt, some conscientious scholar, oblivious to the true course of my mind, which moves not as a walker moves through the city – no matter how much the flaneur, still plodding along from a beginning to an end, one foot after the other – but rather as an idea moves through history, as in a game of snakes and ladders, climbing up and sliding down pathways that open and close seemingly at random, at the roll of a die. Which is to say that my mind moves not with the logic of the body but the illogic of the dream, or the nightmare.

Here is a map of this afternoon's thought: it begins with the tropical island of Manus, off the coast of Papua New Guinea. There, immigration officials have cut off water and electricity to the detention centre in a bid to force out the refugees who have been living there for over four years. The men are mounting a last, hopeless protest, collecting rainwater and smuggling in solar panels to charge their phones so they can broadcast their plight online. Some of the major news outlets, on a slow news day, will scrape the men's social media accounts for brief, generic articles that will receive a moderate number of clicks from those vehemently for or against the refugees' cause and will otherwise pass by unnoticed. At least until someone dies, which they do, every few months. And though I have never been to Manus, I have spent much of my time over the last few years imagining the different compounds:

the converted shipping containers of Delta compound, the disused World War II hangar of P-Block, the white-domed tents of Oscar compound. The subtropical rainforest all around, and the gentle ocean just nearby, beyond the cyclone fencing. Somewhere here, on this portion of the map, is a small triangle labelled Chauka. Although I've managed to fill in the other spaces in the centre – mostly with photos and videos sent to me by the men, or posted online, showing filthy portable toilets, or a warren of bunk beds hung with sheets and towels to create little privacy closets, or guards push-starting an ambulance carrying an attempted suicide out of the centre – I have never been able to fill out the small triangle called Chauka. All I know is that it is where some of the men were taken, the so-called ringleaders of the hunger strikes and the protests, to be beaten and broken. I know as well that, for some reason, someone decided to name that place after the chauka bird, a small white-and-brown honeyeater endemic to Manus, whose call can be heard throughout the island – a bird revered by the locals as a symbol of their home, a bird with magical powers, whose booming voice marks the island's time, announces the deaths of the island's inhabitants, and sits in judgment over their desires.

And it is there, in the blank space marked Chauka, that the map of my afternoon's thought produces a wormhole, for it is through that dark, fetid place that I move from Manus – my eyes still flicking over my news feed as I wait for updates on the men's protest – to a tiny apartment shared by my grandfather, my grandmother, and my aunt in a dull grey-pink building surrounded by busy, truck-laden highways that become so icy in winter that they are too dangerous for my grandmother to cross on her own to get to Boissy-Saint-Léger station, the end of the suburban RER A line, a typical Parisian outer banlieue dominated by a monolithic, modernist shopping centre in which half the shops are permanently shuttered behind heavy metal rollers and in whose central lobby, beneath the too-bright strip lighting, a muzzled German shepherd and boilersuited security guard cast sleepy eyes over the stream of African, Arab and Asian faces shopping for chocolate-coated chocolate-flavoured cereal, microwaveable croissants, and instant noodles; the scene, in other words, of four hundred years of French colonialism come home to roost.

3

Over the last decade, I have visited that apartment perhaps a dozen times. But I have thought about it so often that my memories of it, its rooms and its contents, and the stories I've heard in it, have begun to blur together. Sitting at my desk in the Jerwood Library above the River Cam, I am torn between remembering the literary and the ordinary: the bookshelf in my grandfather's room, crowded with icons – Christ on the Cross, a Mary-shaped bottle of Lourdes miracle water, Vietnamised Mary and Child, black-haired with dark, almond-shaped eyes, dressed in the flowing silk robes of pre-colonial, independent Vietnam – and religious pamphlets, meeting minutes for the Societas Peregrinus, pilgrimage itineraries, and the collection of books my grandfather taught himself English with (Fisher's *A History of Europe, The New Economics: Keynes' Influence on Theory and Public Policy, The English Constitution, The Morality of Law,* William Faulkner, Graham Greene and the Bible); the table where we ate banh cuon and pho ga, the plastic stool in the narrow shower, my grandmother's ointments and hair dyes, the washing hung out to dry in the bathroom, the fat round containers of fish oil capsules stacked by the front door, the galley kitchen where I stood a little over a month ago, pointing, for Lauren's benefit, through the window above the kitchen sink to the Eiffel Tower in the far distance, a little upright prick on the horizon, saying, See – we really are in Paris.

That visit, with Lauren and Edith, had been the first time I'd seen the apartment since my grandfather died. We were on our way to Cambridge, and we took the opportunity to bring Edith to meet her great-grandmother. As I bounced the baby on my knee in the living room – where I had formerly sat with a notebook and a voice recorder as my grandfather told his stories – and while my grandmother interrogated Lauren about her religious affiliations (it was, of course, as much a chance for my grandmother to meet this white woman I'd seen fit to have a baby with, but not to marry), I tried to reconcile the apartment-as-it-appeared-before-me with the fictitious space of my congealed memories. Where was the writing desk at which my grandfather had written lengthy letters to important Church men about the contribution of laypeople to the faith? Had they sold it off already? Or was the desk that I was thinking of – well worn and scuffed but ornate all the same – just a figment of my imagination? What if all along there had been nothing but this fold-out card table and an ancient Dell laptop? What if my grandfather wrote no letters, but only surfed the Catholic web for New Testament exegeses displayed in fluorescent Comic Sans? And what about the coffee table laden with careful, chronological stacks of *Le Canard Enchaîné*, *Le Monde*, *La Croix*, and *Time*? Had there never been any order, just this garage-sale mess? Cards from grandchildren jumbled up with sheet music for the piano no one ever played, photo albums of seventies Saigon mixed up with souvenirs from theme parks across three continents: a plastic Pluto mug from Euro Disney, a photo of my grandparents dressed as King and Queen at Medieval Times in Houston, a picture of me, age nine, between Batman and Robin at Warner Bros. Movie World on the Gold Coast?

A junkyard marks the heart of this map I have been drawing. A junkyard full of broken things, of unfinished projects, all to be fixed and completed in the future: my grandmother's silver handgun, my grandfather's correspondence, and a scale model of Chi Hoa Prison.

4

I have been imagining and reimagining Chi Hoa since I was a teenager, when I first found out that my grandfather had been imprisoned there by the Communist government. Actually, for the most part my thoughts were not focused on the place itself, but rather on what impressed people most when I told them about my grandfather – the time he spent in there: ten years.

There was something satisfying about the roundness of that number, the definitiveness of saying, My grandfather spent a decade in prison without being charged or tried. In my late teens and early twenties, as I finished school and entered university, it served as the anchor for my self-image. I was the son of refugees, the grandson of a political prisoner. There was an authoritative weight to that way of thinking and talking about myself that most of my classmates lacked. Especially the ones competing with me for internships and editorships, all of them as middle-class and well educated as me, but without that aura of authentic suffering. And so it proved when I got my first job out of law school. When the two interviewers, Anglo-Australians in their fifties, asked me why I wanted to work with refugees, I could run through what was by then a well-rehearsed story: my grandfather the social justice lawyer, his imprisonment, the intervention of Amnesty International, his release, and my inspiration to use my talents for the betterment of people just like him. By the end of this telling the interviewer to my left, a woman with spiky grey hair and red-rimmed glasses, was saying, Your grandfather sounds like an *incredible* person, while the man to my right nodded and wrote on his notepad: refugee family.

When I was fifteen I went on a school camp that, unlike previous years, had no rope courses, no overnight hikes or white-water rafting. Instead, the camp – dubbed a 'Christian Living Camp' – was focused on talking and personal development. We had been paired with a class from our sister school, so for the duration of the camp we attended co-ed talking sessions and art therapy workshops, at which we all spoke about our families, our insecurities, our dreams for the future. It was this camp that was, in many ways, the beginning of all this remembering. In the days leading up to the camp I had discovered what had never been a secret, and yet had also not been the subject of open conversation; I remember doing the calculations on an envelope – from the bank, a statement for one of my parents' accounts – and arriving at a number that was all I had to help me understand what my father had just told me: that his father, my grandfather, had spent 3653 days in a Communist prison – the three extra days being for the leap years in 1980, 1984 and 1988. It was that number – three six five three – that stayed with me throughout the school camp's seminars on family values, abstinence and trust, along with a vague sense of shame for not having known the number, for not having any idea that there was any history to which such a number could apply, for having never asked about the possibility of such a number.

So it was not really surprising that it all came tumbling out on the last day of the camp, when we sixty students gathered in the auditorium, which had been equipped with full stage lights to accommodate the theatre groups who often hired the centre for weekend workshops. A religious education teacher, whom I had seen the previous day with tears streaming down his face as we watched the scene in Mel Gibson's *The Passion of the Christ* in which Christ is whipped, had explained to us that we were to each, one by one, take to the stage, standing in the centre of the spotlight, which was, I would later find out for myself, so bright that the audience disappeared in a blaze of white, and there, lit up and alone, we were to share a story – any story that came to mind – that illustrated one lesson we had learnt from the camp. I was terrified. I could not bring my mind to the principles of Christian living we had supposedly been learning. All I could think about was that number.

Other students took to the stage to speak and – so it seemed to me – were finished in a flash. I didn't take in much of what they said. Too soon, I was making my way up the stage steps, to stand in the glare of the spotlight, blinking. For want of anything else to say, I started talking about my grandfather. How he'd been a lawyer in Vietnam, and a Catholic, how the Communists took over after the US had left, and how he'd been imprisoned without trial, for three thousand, six hundred and fifty-three days. I didn't know any more at the time, so that was all I said. Afterwards, a girl I had never spoken to approached me and said that my speech had been amazing, that my grandfather had been like Nelson Mandela.

In all those years of self-mythologising, Chi Hoa hardly figured at all. It was only later on that I started to think of Chi Hoa as a place – and even then, only as something like an Orientalist version of a prison from an American TV show. Or perhaps I thought of *The Bridge on the River Kwai,* and the POW camp in *The Deer Hunter.* But as my knowledge of Vietnamese prisons grew, so my imaginings of Chi Hoa acquired more – though possibly erroneous – depth.

Once, on our first overseas holiday, Lauren and I took a detour from our south-to-north itinerary of Vietnam to see Con Dao, a former prison island used first by the French colonial powers, then the South Vietnamese, to torture Communist revolutionaries in the infamous 'tiger cages', narrow concrete trenches with metal bars for ceilings. Today, Con Dao is known as a beach destination, and the prison is open as a tourist site. After an early-morning snorkelling

expedition, with a couple of hours to kill before a motorbike ride
to a hidden beach on the other side of the island, we walked along
the upper floor of the tiger cages, peering down at the life-size
mannequins installed inside, six or seven to a cage, each with one foot
manacled to the floor, sitting or lying in painful contortions. Whoever
had created the models had not spared any details – each mannequin
grimaced or shut his eyes in a different way. Some of the prisoners
were posed as though reaching their hands up to the guards patrolling
above, begging for water or mercy. In the next room we saw another
characteristic torture technique: the model, a woman this time, her
hands shackled behind her back and suspended by the manacles from
an iron hook in the ceiling. Later, when we were having sunset drinks
at a nearby resort, I tried to imagine my grandfather in one of those
tiger cages.

Then there was the museum at the Maison Centrale in Hanoi. This
time I was not in Vietnam for a holiday but for a writing residency, so
Lauren was back home in Melbourne. I was able to take my time in
the museum, jotting down detailed notes about the exhibits. It was,
admittedly, still the wrong city, and the wrong era – Communists
imprisoned and tortured by non-Communists was the inverse of
what I needed: Catholic intellectuals imprisoned and tortured by the
victorious Communists. But being at the museum by myself seemed
to increase my capacity for transposition. What impressed me was not
the manacles and the iron bars – though those were there again, this
time in a solitary cell in which the only source of light was a small square
window the size of my hand, three metres above the prisoner's head –
but the details of everyday prison life that I was able to glean: prisoners
tied their chopsticks together so as not to lose one; they bathed together
in a large, round concrete cistern in the middle of the prison yard; they
used pieces of charcoal to carry on their political writing, which they
hid in the roots of an almond tree; they wrote wooden, self-glorifying
poetry about the nation and sacrifice and the Maison Centrale itself,

which the Vietnamese prisoners referred to as Hoa Lo, the name of the village that was demolished to make way for the prison, a village that had been known for its earthenware kettles and stovetops.

At the museum, alongside some pottery characteristic of the lost village of Hoa Lo, instruments of torture were displayed behind glass like all the other sterile objects, with matter-of-fact, bilingual labels that gave no clue as to how they were used, for how long, what information was obtained or why punishment was meted out: electric wires, an electric engine, a bamboo cane, a metal barrel, a glass bottle, a jerry can, a wooden bench, a ladder and rope. Then, in a final room at the end of the tour, was a guillotine. It towered over me, four and a half metres tall, its angled blade – weighing 50 kilograms – raised and ready to fall. It was lit from below so that its long shadow stretched across the ceiling, and model heads were arranged in a basket at the guillotine's foot. Apparently the French had brought this particular guillotine out from the metropole and toured the provinces of colonial Tonkin (now northern Vietnam), dispensing justice to the enemies of the empire. There, at Maison Centrale, looking up at this machine of death, I understood for the first time why they had called its reign *la Terreur*.

I read somewhere that there had been a guillotine at Chi Hoa during the French years (1858–1954). It arrived in the colonies in 1917. After a distinguished career in the rural south, it was transferred to Chi Hoa in 1953, just a year before the French lost the war. There, its final victim was a famous Vietnamese revolutionary, a woman whose dedicated spying helped turn the war. She had been born to an aristocratic family, so the story goes, and received the best French education. But she fell in love with a young intellectual who had recently returned from France, where his head had been filled up with revolution. Of course, her parents disapproved of the connection, and the engagement was broken off. Unwilling to choose any of her very eligible suitors, she instead used her family standing and education to get a job in the offices of the French Transmissions Corps. It wasn't until eight years later – and only because a Viet Minh plane carrying decoded messages was shot down over the Central Highlands – that the French finally realised that she had been a spy all along. It had, apparently, all been planned: the breaking off of the engagement, the position with the Transmissions Corps. When the fighting ended, she was to be reunited with the young intellectual, who was by now a political commissar in the Viet Minh army. Instead, on 9 March 1954 – just a few days before the start of the Battle of Dien Bien Phu, which would mark the end of the war – the guillotine at Chi Hoa severed its final head.

A few weeks after my visit to the Maison Centrale, I made a trip down to Ho Chi Minh City, just to see if I could get closer to Chi Hoa itself. I nearly missed it altogether, hidden as it is behind a primary school, a street market, and a row of electrical goods wholesalers, whose fridges and karaoke systems spill out onto a busy road where the endless motorbikes buzz like angry flies. And there, in the middle of residential Saigon, down an unmarked alleyway: the outer wall of the most secure prison in Vietnam. I took some photos of the wall – four metres high, topped by barbed wire – and the guard post on the corner. I thought – half-hoped, really – that someone might stop me, ask me what I was doing, but nothing happened. The children continued to shriek in the school's playground, the thit nuong vendor fanned his charcoal grill, and I turned around, looking for a xe om to take me back to my hotel.

5

The fragments I could glean about Chi Hoa came from the stories my grandfather told me in that apartment, from what little I could find online, and from my own fantasies. I read somewhere about the 'movie theatre' – a large cell with no natural light, where troublemakers were thrown into pitch blackness. The men in the movie theatre got so used to the darkness that they developed super-sensitive hearing; later on, when some of them were released, they were able to describe the sounds they heard throughout the rest of the prison with such accuracy that forensic investigators could produce the first rough maps of the prison's layout.

I read somewhere else that there has only ever been one successful escape from Chi Hoa, in 1995, when the notorious armed robber and death-row inmate, Eight-Finger Phuoc, used a razor blade to file through his iron leg shackles, then used the shackles to bore a hole through a metre and a half of the concrete wall of his cell, before navigating the labyrinth of underground tunnels, undetected by any of the guards, to make it out of the sole entrance and exit to Chi Hoa, 'Death's Door', and away to freedom. Short-lived, as it turned out: a year later he was in Chi Hoa again, and this time there was no escaping the firing squad.

The only other thing I knew about Chi Hoa: it had been designed along the scientific principles of the panopticon, an ideal prison structure imagined by Jeremy Bentham as a way to use architecture to discipline and control human minds. For Bentham, our minds were as mechanical, and as susceptible to rational analysis, as our bodies, which he saw not as a sacred vessel but only as a tool, useful for a time and then, when useful no more, to be unceremoniously discarded – or, as in the case of his own body, to be bequeathed to his university to be disembowelled and dissected, and then put together again, preserved and dressed in his old clothes, to be useful once more as a display for the edification of students. This was at the new secular university in London, a place dedicated to free and rational thought in ways that Oxford and Cambridge – steeped in the Church – could never emulate, granting it a freedom that led to new and ingenious methods for making others less free – like the panopticon; roughly circular buildings with prison cells around the edge, their internal walls are transparent to a central viewing tower in which concealed guards might at any point be looking at any prisoner, so that over time the prisoner's mind opens itself up to the imagined watcher; once let in, there is no need for an actual watcher anymore – the prisoner will watch themselves. Nice in theory, but, like any ideal, Chi Hoa failed to take into account life-as-it-really-is. That seems odd, because Bentham was nothing if not an empiricist. But his empiricism had no time for the reality that exists in each human mind, which cannot help but bump up against the reality measured by Bentham's science, knocking things over and causing all kinds of trouble; the great flaw in the architecture of Chi Hoa was precisely that it failed to accommodate – or contain – the sovereign minds of the men and women imprisoned within it.

6

Imagine an octagonal structure. Each of the eight sides, named alphabetically from A to H, is in fact a long building, filled with cells. The inside wall of each lettered side is open – sealed with iron bars but otherwise transparent to the guards in the watchtower that stands in the centre of the octagon. A hyper-rationalist prison built by the hyper-rationalist colonial power.

But look closer. The French only completed the prison as it had been conceived by the Japanese. The true model for the prison's design is the *I Ching* – the famous Chinese *Book of Changes*. Look at the eight buildings that make up the octagon: each one is three storeys high. Each building, therefore, corresponds to one of the original eight trigrams, the bat quai, which, paired up, constitute the sixty-four hexagrams of the *I Ching*. Each floor is a line of the trigram and is either broken – yin – or unbroken – yang. In the architecture of the building, the break in the line is represented by a concrete wall that cuts the floor in two. So in what the French called Building A, on the north side of the prison, there are no dividing walls, because Building A corresponds to the trigram for Heaven: ☰. But in Building E – which sits opposite Building A, so on the south side of the prison – every floor is blocked by a concrete wall, so one cannot pass through E to get to D or F; E corresponds to the trigram for Earth: ☷.

I could see all this very clearly in the scale model of Chi Hoa in my grandparents' apartment. Its intricate detailing was astonishing.

It was mostly made of plaster, but painted to look like fading, weather-worn concrete. All the iron bars in the cells, and the ornamental gate at Death's Door, were made of real metal, hand cut and polished. The one-way windows in the watchtower were made of real glass. The Buddhist pagoda in the yard of Building C was carved out of balsa wood, and each of its seven floors was painted a different shade of yellow.

Most astonishing of all were the details inside the cells. Leaning in very closely, I could see through the iron bars of the wing where my grandfather had been imprisoned, Section FG, the buildings making up the south-west and west sides of the octagon. Tiny painted numbers, in red, identified the different cells; I always looked for Cell 6. Inside I could see a mass of twisted bodies – I knew from what my grandfather had told me that there were about fifty bodies in all, so small in this model that it was hard to tell where one ended and the next began. I could see the drop toilets at one end of the cell, at the other the thin mattresses for the trusties – prisoner-guards, like the concentration camp kapo – and their allies. I saw the bare concrete on which everyone else slept. With the aid of a magnifying glass I could see even more: the tiny chess sets with which they amused themselves, the lacquer bowls they ate rice from, fifty individual faces in the writhing mass.

Stepping back, I could see the tower in the middle of the octagon. The French believed the octagonal shape would allow their guards to see every prisoner at every waking moment, or at least give the impression to each prisoner that he or she was being watched at every moment. Meanwhile, adherents of feng shui believed the octagon was the source of the prison's spiritual power. But I could also see the one inconsistency in the design: unlike all the other buildings, which had sloping, tiled roofs, the roof of Heaven, ≡ – Building A – had been flattened, and was now a bare concrete surface.

It was to let out the ghosts, my grandfather once told me. We were in his room in the apartment in Boissy. Sitting hunched over on his hospital-style bed, coughing between short sentences, he looked like a ghost himself. Chi Hoa, he said, was too well designed; even the ghosts couldn't get out. At night, the noise in the yard got so loud that none of us could sleep, prisoners or guards. They were confused, looking for their ancestors, for their ancestral village. Where was the family temple? Instead all they saw were the eight walls of the prison. A very strong shape, very hard to break through. Only the strongest ghost could have broken out of that octagon. Even then he would need help: he would need a sorcerer, tools, money. But they didn't even have clothes or food. Who was going to burn paper offerings to them in Chi Hoa? So they wandered the yard at night, naked and sobbing. It was too much! The guards paid for a feng shui master to come in. He said, clear the path for these souls through Heaven. And that's what they did, levelling the sloping roof and replacing it with a flat, concrete patio – a single stair, they said, to Heaven.

Did the ghosts all leave? Well, I still remember the day they finished the work. The ghosts, still naked but calling out in happiness now, started climbing up the iron bars of the cells. Soon the whole side of the building was nothing but skinny bodies and bare buttocks. Ghosts used their feet to push off the heads of the ones below. Some slipped and fell to the floor of the yard. It was a stampede. But eventually everyone who wanted to get out did. And then the only ghosts left were the ones with nowhere better to be.

7

It was much more bearable in Chi Hoa once most of the ghosts had gone, said my grandfather. The ones that were left understood their ghostly duty, which was to quietly haunt corridors in underused parts of the prison, and to speak when spoken to about their ghostly memories. They were useful too, for contacting dead relatives, or for a game of chess. And they knew things, if you knew how to listen. Take the meaning of his section of Chi Hoa, Section FG. Everyone knew what the trigrams represented, said my grandfather. But it took a ghost for me to learn what they meant for me.

Building F corresponds to the trigram for thunder: ☳; building G corresponds to the trigram for fire: ☲. Together, these two trigrams form Hexagram 21 in the *I Ching*, fire over thunder, or Shih Ho – which, my grandfather was fond of telling me, is all about justice. Without justice there can be no harmony.

One day, said my grandfather, the men in my cell, we pooled our resources. My grandfather marked off the currency on his long, thin fingers: cigarettes, scraps of paper, contraband salt, food packages from family. In return, we got fifty yarrow stalks. We used the stalks to consult the oracle: what kind of justice were we receiving? The answer was inauspicious. Nine at the top. It meant that our necks were fastened in wooden stocks. Our ears had disappeared beneath the brace. What did it mean? It meant that we were deaf to counsel, and our punishment was just.

8

For a very long time, my grandfather told me, I could not accept the oracle's answer. Perhaps it was right about the other men in my cell. But not me. I was not guilty. Well – and here my grandfather grinned at me, as if we were sharing a great joke – I was not guilty of anything *they* could charge me for.

Then, one day, he met a ghost from Nghe An province. My grandfather had noticed him before – he had a sour demeanour, and had kept himself apart from the other ghosts. One of my grandfather's cellmates, a Chinaman named Tchen, had said that the sour ghost had been a legendary VC commando. He'd operated in the south, deep behind enemy lines – behind *our* lines, Tchen had said, correcting himself – for twenty-one years. He was only caught in the clean-up operation after the Tet Offensive. He lasted another six years in Chi Hoa. If he'd made it one more year, he'd have been liberated along with the other Viet Cong when Saigon fell. But dysentery got him – shat himself to death, Tchen had said. On the day of the great exodus over the levelled roof of Heaven, my grandfather remembered seeing the ghost's puckered face watching without interest from his seat on the edge of the concrete washing basin in the yard. The next day, the day my grandfather met him, that's where he was, sitting cross-legged on the side of the basin as fifty prisoners scrubbed themselves in the filthy water.

He smiled at me, said my grandfather. The effect was not exactly pleasant. Then he said, I come from Nghe An province. Cattle country.

Our bullocks fetched top prices with Hanoi butchers. I can tell you're a northerner. Perhaps you've had some of our beef in your pho, eh? I worked in an abattoir. It's not the dirty profession you think. There was a time when we butchered animals in the open air, on the street. They still do that in the hamlets. But you're a town boy, so what would you know about killing and flaying? You think of meat hooks, blood, knives. But do you think of the noise? And the smells – sweet blood mixed with excrement and bile and disinfectant – all wreathed in steam like mountain fog.

I'll tell you how it goes in there, because you're a town boy. There are two of us – it only takes two, if you know how. My partner throws a young bullock down and I tie his head to the ground with a rope. A strong blow breaks his skull. I use a large, sharp knife to open his throat; the steaming blood spills out in full, short bursts. We plunge our arms into the hot wet innards. A blowpipe inflates the carcass and gives it hideous shape. We take up our cleavers and chop off the legs. It's quick, precise. There is an art to really fine butchering.

I thought that that was how life would be, said the sour ghost – and he looked right at me, said my grandfather. A life more or less the same as my father's. But then came the floods. The dykes overflowed and the cattle starved. And sure enough, like locusts, the jauniers came calling. I will never forget the one who came to us: he wore a double-breasted suit, even in the heat. Somehow that impressed me. That he wore it buttoned up, his tie drawn up tight to that big Adam's apple. Even his assistant, formerly one of us, a native, was trussed up like a new bride, bright yellow bow tie and all.

That assistant, he looked at us like the dirt under his fingernails. But his master, the jaunier, offered us three-year contracts on fifteen piastres a month, with a ten-piastre advance! What choice did I have? I knew – I thought I knew – about the plantations. I was no fool. But the cattle were dead, washed away in the rains, and Father and Mother were well into their autumn. So I signed their contract.

The ink was barely dry when the assistant began abusing me, shoving me towards a truck they had ready. We were stripped, hosed down and scrubbed raw. The assistant told us that three piastres were being deducted from our advance to pay for the two sets of cotton pyjamas he handed us. A further two piastres were taken to cover the food on our journey south.

We drove to Vinh, where they loaded us onto a big ship. I don't know how long we sailed for – we were below decks the whole way, sleeping one on top of the other. We landed at Phan Rang, where we were put in trucks again and driven to the plantation, somewhere in the mountains south of Dalat. I was shown to my new home: a filthy bunk in an overcrowded dormitory. The next morning, before dawn, we began.

Every morning was the same, said the ghost to my grandfather, who was finished washing now, but stood by the basin, still dripping. We were like a ragged army, marching in a long thin line towards the trees as dawn approached. It's cold up there in the mountains. Growing up on the flood plains, I never knew cold like that. But the sap flowed best in the mornings, we were told. So we got up when the foremen knocked the door down, avoiding their fists and ignoring their insults.

They called us tappers. At each tree I would cut a diagonal half spiral around the outside. Inside the tree, the sap runs in spiral tubes to the right, so by cutting down and to the left we sliced as many of the tubes as possible. I had to be careful to not cut too deep – the sap is in the bark, and cutting into the tree itself would make it sick. All told, it took twenty seconds to tap a tree, if you knew what you were doing. On an average day I tapped maybe a thousand trees. At the end of the cut I stuck a small wooden spout that piped the sap into a coconut shell. The sap bled out as a sticky, milky-white latex. Le bois qui pleure. The tree that cries.

The sap bled out for four hours before it coagulated in the trees' veins. So when I'd tapped a thousand trees, I could return to the first one to collect its coconut shell. We worked as long as there was daylight – eleven, twelve hours – with a fifteen-minute break at noon. We sang as we worked.

> How beautiful are the rubber trees!
> Under each one, a worker is buried.
> The trees lead a happy life –
> when they are sick, they rest.
> Doctors, Eastern and Western, fuss over them,
> while we die of exhaustion.

The sour ghost's singing voice was not a strong one, but still, my grandfather said, I could imagine them among those trees, a choir of the living dead.

We never got our fifteen piastres. There was no kitchen in our dormitory. We had to take all our meals in the canteen, which was run by the wives of the foremen. When we were allowed to cook for ourselves, where were we to buy our provisions but from the plantation store – run by the same people as the canteen. If we got sick – and we were always sick – medicine was too expensive. All in all, we were lucky to save up one piastre each month.

The other prisoners had all dried themselves off and were now moving back towards their cells. My grandfather knew that a trusty would come by soon to sting his back with a rattan switch, but he felt that he couldn't move. The sour ghost continued his story, breaking the eye contact with my grandfather that up until now had never wavered, looking up at the sky instead.

One day, after the sun had fallen, we were told that we could prepare our own meals that night. The foremen and their wives who ran the canteen were celebrating a French holiday, for their warrior-lady, Saint Joan. As it happened, the plantation store had a bullock for sale, surplus to their feast-day requirements – a scrawny thing, underfed.

A bullock like that in Nghe An would be unsellable, we'd give him to the children to ride on, but on the plantation it seemed a blessing from the heavens. One woman – I won't say her name, even now – bargained with the foremen's wives to buy the bullock with some of our meagre savings. They must have been impatient to begin their revelry, because we got the bullock at something like a fair price.

I volunteered to butcher it. I knew how to do it safely, and with the least pain for the poor beast. The woman who'd done the bargaining asked if she could help, and I didn't know how to tell her about the steaming blood and viscera. I don't know that it would have made any difference. So the two of us walked the bullock away from the buildings, out to where the jungle had already begun to reclaim its territory. My tools were blunt, and not suited to the task, but her help made up for it. After it was done, and I was splattered with blood, she smiled at me. Ignoring the glossy red smears that ran up past my elbow and halfway to my shoulder, she put her hand on mine and held it, for a handful of heartbeats. Then we gathered up the butchered meat and bones and went back to the others. That night, we ate as well as I've ever eaten.

From then on I felt a buoyant, hopeful secret between me and her. She smiled at everyone, and she had gentle words for all, but she reserved something different for me. The thought of her kept me going, among the endless trees, which were planted in such straight rows that by the mid-morning heat I was lost, drowning in weeping trees. Some nights, we sat together in the canteen. We didn't talk very much, though I tried to tell her everything I could remember about Nghe An, home, my parents. She had little to say about herself, except that she hoped one day she could have children. That was the saddest thing about the plantation, she said. They didn't let workers bring their families. No little faces, no bright voices. Where she came from – though she never said exactly where – there were children everywhere, and the children were everyone's. They would wander in and out of neighbours' homes, she said, and you would turn around in the kitchen and find them standing naked in the doorway, watching you.

Not long before our contracts were due to finish, my secret happiness was taken away. It had been a normal, back-breaking day when we returned to the dormitories to find the plantation owner with the chief foreman. The owner was a sickly man who normally lived in Saigon – he found plantation living was no good for the water in his lungs; being so remote, we were at least a day away from the nearest doctor. As soon as we were in sight, the foreman began yelling and screaming, holding up a small bottle, about the size of a man's thumb. He ran among us, hitting out with a rubber truncheon, still yelling. We protected ourselves as best we could, covering our heads, our faces. A blow to my stomach had me doubled over when I heard her voice, saying, It's mine, it's mine. My vision was still blurry but I saw the foreman dragging her away by the hair, and now the other women were wailing and the men had finally found their voices. But the other foremen had arrived with their truncheons out, and some of them had run to grab guns.

The sickly plantation owner raised his hand for silence. She was on her knees, at his feet, thrown down there by the chief foreman. The hubbub started to die down when we saw the fleshy white hand raised aloft. When we had all fallen quiet, he said in his timorous voice that this woman at his feet had stolen a bottle of medicine from the plantation store. A woman next to me sobbed – the medicine had been for her. The plantation owner raised his hand again for silence. He said that a rider had been sent for the police commissaire, who would come tomorrow to dispense justice. The foremen started herding us into the dormitories. There would be no food tonight for anyone. Craning my neck, I could see them dragging her by her hair again, out towards the rubber trees.

That night, I snuck out of the dormitory. It was a big, low moon, so everything was lit up with a silver glow. I found her tied to a rubber tree in the first row. She looked exhausted but otherwise unhurt. When she saw me coming she gave me a tired smile, then slumped against the ropes again. I had nothing with which to cut her free, but I quickly saw that they had tied her quite simply – after all, who would be mad enough to free her?

But as my hands went to the knots, she shook her head. Where will I go, she asked. They will burn down any house that dares to take me in. If they don't find me, they will beat every one of you senseless. And if somehow I found my way home, it would already be in ruins, and Mother and Father would be in prison, or worse. This is my fate, Anh, as your fate is to walk away tonight, finish your contract, and then live again. We will meet again on the bank of some distant river.

I left her among the weeping trees. The next day we were given the morning off, to wait for the police commissaire. They lined us up in ranks to witness their justice. By noon they were done and we were back among the trees. The sap was like blood to me. When the foremen called an end to our work, we were finally able to untie her body. We pooled together enough money to buy new clothes at the canteen, some paper for the burning, and a small portion of rice. She is buried along with the others, on the far side of the dormitories – as far away from those trees as possible.

9

The men on Manus are being forced out. Their updates flash up on my phone: security forces are coming through and smashing the men's makeshift water tanks and solar panels, confiscating phones and tablets. It is no longer my job to reply, but I do anyway, writing the same messages I wrote before: I hope you're safe. I hope no one is hurt. And I get the same messages in reply: Thanks brother.

By now, the daytrippers have left and the river below me is quiet. In the library, undergraduates sit before great piles of books – on Roman history, molecular biology, the collected works of Philip Roth – which they ignore as they scroll through their news feeds. I still haven't done any of the reading I came to the library to do, and soon enough it will be time for me to go home. But I am too full of Chi Hoa to open my books.

Am I guilty, after all, of making the same mistake as Bentham did with his panopticon? Have I failed to take seriously the life of the mind? I had thought my grandfather's stories and images were a history of a place called Vietnam. But now I realise he was always speaking of some other place, not entirely coextensive with the thin, S-shaped spit of land between the sea and the mountains that bears that name on our maps.

I hesitate in assigning this other place a name: Gia Long, the Nguyen dynasty ruler who was the last man standing after thirty years of civil war, named his newly unified country Việt Nam. But that name – meaning South of the Viet – had been forced on him by the Chinese Emperor. It was a shock to me to read that the country running from the Red River Basin to the Mekong Delta was of such recent provenance – Gia Long had been a contemporary of Louis XVI, who welcomed Gia Long's eldest son, Prince Cảnh, to the doomed court in Versailles, where the seven-year-old boy became a sensation, and a plaything of Marie Antoinette.

Gia Long had wanted to call his new country Nam Việt: the Viet of the South. But that had sounded, to the august ear of the Manchu Son of Heaven, Emperor of the Middle Kingdom, like a claim to China's southern provinces. And as much as Gia Long styled himself on the great anti-Chinese warriors of the past, he was also a practical man, so Việt Nam it would be. In any case, the Chinese had their own name for this place: Annam. But that meant the Pacified South, and so was unacceptable to the inhabitants of the place, for obvious reasons. Gia Long's son and successor, Minh Mạng, called his kingdom Đại Nam, the Great South, but only after the bloody conquest of much of what we now call Cambodia and Laos.

Then there were the French names, which were even more recent, but in some ways the ones most familiar to my grandfather: Tonkin, Annam and Cochinchine, the three 'Vietnamese' partitions of colonial Indochine, alongside Kampuchea and Laos. Then, in an attempt to halt the progress of decolonisation – much too little, much too late – it was known as the Indochinese Federation, junior member of the French Union. Next, there were the two Vietnams (note the contraction, which was, I suspect, an anglicisation meant to appeal to the Americans), the Democratic Republic of Vietnam and the Republic of Vietnam, each laying claim to the whole S but in reality existing either side of the seventeenth parallel.

So the stories my grandfather told me were all part of a bigger history, a history of all of these places, and none of them: Vietnam, Nam Việt, Annam, Đại Nam, Tonkin, the DRV, Indochine and 'Nam.

And where these stories took place for me, once I'd heard them, well, that was somewhere else again – less populated than my grandfather's places, and less detailed. Flatter, like a map or a diorama, but one that more often than not appeared to me out of focus, as if fading away at the edges.

What, then, to call this place? It is a heavy responsibility. We had hesitated over naming Edith, deflecting the question from family and midwives for day after day in the hospital. Finally we wrote it down on a scrap of paper while she lay grizzling in the cot next to us – and only then, when it had been committed to paper, could we say it aloud to ourselves. In that ordinary – indeed, compulsory – parental act there is something of the arrogance of conquerors and explorers, and the false reverence of town planners.

Still, a place without a name is not a place at all. So I will call this place Anam – with one N – a place with a curious topography, bending as it does towards memory, and whose guiding principle is *anam*nesis, which, according to one's persuasion, might be the Ancient Greek belief that our eternal souls have forgotten all there is to know, or the Catholic act of salvation through worshipful remembrance.

Anam, I imagine remembering my grandfather saying, was raised on dragon's blood. An ancient governor, so the story goes, who was reckless in his desire to clear a path through the mountains, wounding the veins of the sacred monster and creating three rivers, the Clear, the Red, and the Black, which dump 105 million cubic yards of rich alluvial soil in the great northern delta every year, so that the reddish dirt rises twenty inches a century. From that rich loam, my grandfather might have said, sprang a peculiar race of men: the Anamites.

The Anamites are marked out by two exceptional traits: they are fecund, masters of all things procreative – fucking and conceiving, incubating and delivering – and thus are given to expansion and proliferation, first marching south and west from the northern delta to populate the lands of the less fecund, and then, more recently, taking to planes and boats to establish Little Saigons in Paris, San Jose, Parramatta and Footscray; and, secondly, they are masters of memory, so good at remembering that they remember things that never happened, and things that are best forgotten.

In these two ways, at least, my grandfather was a typical Anamite – and Chi Hoa prison a city-state of Anam. From his cell in solitary confinement – where he had been put for lingering too long to listen to ghosts – he heard the sound of children laughing. At first, my grandfather told me, he flinched at the sound. It had been many years since he'd heard children laughing at play – long enough to have forgotten that the sound children make when playing is more like shrieking, because their play is in deadly earnest, and together their many voices produce a kind of high-pitched keening that penetrates your thinking.

Here, in this tall, square concrete chamber, with his ankles in iron chains, and with the laughter-shrieking filtering in through the tiny rectangle three metres above his head, my grandfather populated his memories with his own children, with his sons, racing their trikes through the apartment on Rue Catinat, the best street in Saigon; he remembered the strange mixture of embarrassment and pride at the rude, unselfconscious life of his sons as they interrupted his brother-in-law and the other great men who would gather in the apartment to discuss matters of state. And he remembered how important that had always been to him, the life of the flesh, the feeling of the sun on his back as he stood on the diving board at the Cercle Sportif, posing for a photo to mark his entry to the most exclusive sporting club in wartime Saigon. He remembered his pleasure at his own tensing muscles as he dived in, the pleasant cooling rush of water that met him.

And here is the mystery of it, proof positive that Chi Hoa is the innermost citadel of Anam, a magic, perhaps even sacred place, as any place where so many souls have suffered and died must be:

then he populated his memories with me and my brothers, all of us
as yet unborn – unhoped for, even – but somehow he imagined us,
projecting his memories forward into the future, seeing us on a beach,
his Australian grandsons, who spoke English and no Vietnamese,
who played laughing-shrieking in the sun and the sand – yes, full
of that rude life – who knew nothing about Chi Hoa or prisons or
Communists, and who did not think very much about the stooped,
quiet old man wearing a three-piece suit in the forty-degree heat
on the sand behind them, a man whom my grandfather recognised, in
the trail of his thinking there in the solitary confinement cell, as some
future version of himself – albeit a frail, broken version, wraithlike –
and it was then, in the grips of that vision, that he knew that he would,
after all, survive Chi Hoa – that he would survive this cell and survive
Section FG, that he would even survive a journey over oceans to this
harsh, sunny beach, to stalk in silence after his offspring's offspring –
yes, he would survive, if that could be called survival.

10

The Cambridge University Library is a brick cathedral topped by a twelve-storey tower, a great thrusting phallus from which a steady plume of steam billows out, visible for miles around. Germaine Greer – thinking, no doubt, of the building's thirties' rationalist-fascist style – said that the library looked like the kind of place where books are burned rather than read. It's true that the entrance to the library is forbidding – the six-storey wings run north and south of the tower like fortress walls – but inside, through the pass card–activated turnstiles, the library opens itself up to the willing reader. Straight ahead, down a long corridor called Carnegie Hall, between two internal courtyards – concreted, grey, and uninviting – is the Main Reading Room, a vast, high-ceilinged chamber lined with shelves and divided by rows and rows of lamplit tables, at which studious figures can be found at any hour of the day hunched over books and computers.

I am more interested in the stacks, which can be explored in the much less capacious wings that form squares around the internal courtyards, running anti-clockwise from the entrance beneath the tower: North Front, North Wing, North Reading Room Corridor, the Main Reading Room, the Supplementary Catalogue Corridor, South Wing, South Front. Granted, the ground floor of each wing is more in keeping with the palatial dimensions of the Main Reading Room, but any sense of grandeur is absent on the upper five storeys. When I first ventured up the stairs of South Front, I had the impression of having entered the sort of labyrinth the ancients constructed to keep tomb raiders out, or else to keep something terrible in. There, the stacks are cheap metal shelves cramped too close together and barely fitting beneath the low ceilings. The aisles are narrow and poorly lit. Some wings have views to the outside, with small study desks pressed up against the wall, and at each can be found a lone reader, a pile of books before them, diligently turning pages. Elsewhere, the stacks are hidden in gloom, narrow slits allowing in only strips of natural light from the internal courtyards. There are no readers here, only the occasional searcher, who appears suddenly under the fluorescent lights and then disappears just as quickly towards Ancient East Asian Literature or New Institutional Economics.

To search the stacks feels like falling victim to an elaborate hoax, littered as they are with signs, printed out on sheets of A4 paper or even scrawled in highlighter on the back of some discarded printout, bearing instructions such as:

CASE 34 HAS NOW BEEN RELOCATED TO SOUTH WING FLOOR 2 OVERFLOW SHELVES

306.B.1.203–306.B.1.3218 CONTINUES ON FAR SIDE OF STAIRWELL

IF YOU CANNOT FIND THE BOOK YOU ARE LOOKING FOR, CHECK OVERFLOW TABLES

This last sign is crossed out in red pen, replaced by a new scribble that reads: PLEASE IGNORE, THIS IS A LIE.

The overflow tables are scattered throughout the wings, books stacked three rows deep. Sometimes the books spill down onto the floor, still in neat rows, and one is left with the impression that, in time, every surface will be covered in books: the corridors and the many stairwells, window ledges and fire-extinguisher cabinets, so that the books will have to be stacked one on top of the other until they begin to resemble row after row of self-propagating growths, a cancer of unread words.

But for now, there remains room to walk between the stacks, if not always enough light to see the way, and it is among these shelves, in the middle of Michaelmas term, that I am looking for Trần Đức Thảo's *Phénoménologie et matérialisme dialectique.*

11

I first came across Thảo's book in Paris, at a flea market at the Marché St Germain, one of those typically French stalls selling leather-bound editions of Mallarmé, Sartre, Pascal. I was with my father – we had both answered the summons to come to Paris. My grandfather, we were told, was on his deathbed. But then, some three weeks after our rushed arrivals – me from the writing residency in Hanoi, my father from early retirement in Melbourne – the urgency had dissipated, so my father and I spent our mornings in Paris before trekking back out to the suburbs for the evening visiting hours at the hospital in Créteil, where my grandfather lingered.

On this particular day we'd had a long lunch at a bistro in the sixth, where I had taken my father to see Sciences Po, the elite university I'd gone to on exchange. This was not at all a typical activity for my father and me, but it was possible to imagine, as we sat facing a mild autumn street in Paris, watching the suited waiter popping into the grocery store on the other side of the street for another demi-bouteille of the Sancerre for our table, that this was something we did regularly.

Walking off the wine, we came across the book stall in a kind of ersatz flea market for the wealthy widows of the Left Bank. It was my father, whose reading habits were strictly catechistic – or so I had always thought – who stopped to point out the Maupassant and the Balzac and the Gide, books of his youth, he said, growing up in wartime Saigon but imagining, nevertheless, the very streets we were walking along that day. And it was then, just as my father finished his surprising speech (we did not, as a rule, talk about literature), that I saw it.

The slim volume first caught my eye because at the time I affected an interest in phenomenology, knowing little about it except that I liked the general impression of ethical rigour that I derived from reading the odd paragraph of Emmanuel Levinas. From that patchy reading, my understanding of the French philosopher's work was that it primarily consisted of a fierce ethical commitment to the Other as the one who comes before the Self, whose recognition of the Self makes the Self possible.

This understanding crystallised for me, as it so often does, through biography and anecdote. A Lithuanian-born Jew, Levinas spent much of World War II as a prisoner of war in a camp near Hanover, where he wrote down in a notebook the fragmented thoughts that he would later turn into his book *De l'Existence à l'Existant*. During his captivity, not only the guards but the local women and children passing the camp looked at the prisoners as if they were subhuman. But when a stray dog began to visit them, barking in delight when they returned each day from their forced labour, Levinas realised that for the dog, at least, there was no doubt that he and his companions were human. This encounter, for Levinas, became exemplary of how the Self depends on recognition by the Other.

My encounters with Levinas had suggested to me the appealing possibility of great meaning and significance in our vulnerability to others – and great power, too, in our capacities for recognition. The paradox of his thinking, as I understood it, is that having been made possible by this recognition, my insistence on being, and on being recognised, displaces the Other that recognised me – I take the Other's place in the sun. For me, this is the first and most pressing problem: how to address this irresolvable tension between wanting to be and not wanting that being to displace, to exile, the Other. When I found the book at the flea market in St Germain, this was already a tension I faintly felt in the foundations of my relationship with my family, whose recognition of me had given licence to an intellectual life that was gradually erasing them.

I also noticed the book because of the telltale diacritics and the three-barrelled, three-syllable staccato that was the unvarying, unmistakable rhythm of a Vietnamese name. That, too, was a kind of recognition. There was solace, or validation, in seeing a name like that on a book like this. Still, I didn't buy the book – it seemed expensive – but, as my father and I stood on a crowded RER train out to Créteil, I felt the peculiar remorse that comes from the failure to buy a book you almost certainly would not have read.

It was a few more years before I came across the book again. I had been reading 'The Time of a Thesis', Jacques Derrida's doctoral defence. While I had affected an interest in phenomenology because of its air of ethicality, my interest in Derrida had always been different. He embodied everything I yearned for as a young man going to university, a yearning with many names: *critique* and *Continental*, postmodernism and poststructuralism, anything, really, with an air of scholarship, of intellectualism, of non-instrumental knowledge, the more useless the better. But of course I couldn't commit to uselessness, not fully, so I read law during the day and Derrida in the evenings.

Derrida's was not an ordinary defence – there was no thesis to be defended, so the work being examined was his extant published writing – which, by 1980, when he was giving his defence, was already considerable and undoubtedly significant: by then he was the world-famous deconstructionist, a kind of emblem for French post-structuralism.

A few pages in, as often happened, I interrupted my own reading to pursue tangential lines of research: in this case, to look up images of Derrida from that time. I wanted to see him as he would have been on the Sorbonne stage, defending his life's work before a jury of eminent professors, one of whom was Levinas. I found a clip from a film by Ken McMullen, *Ghost Dance*, that was shot in the same year. In the film Derrida is sitting at a disordered desk, smoking a pipe. His hair is shot through with grey, but it is not yet the shock of white that we know from his years as the world's most famous philosopher. He is asked if he believes in ghosts. As the camera slowly zooms in, Derrida replies by saying, You're asking a ghost if he believes in ghosts. He then embarks on an extended, improvised monologue about cinema, psychoanalysis, telecommunications and their relationship to ghosts. Some people think we left ghosts behind in the Feudal Age, he says, but these new technologies – of the image, of the telephone – have not diminished the realm of ghosts but rather enhanced their power to haunt us.

My grandfather, who at the time I was reading Derrida's thesis was still alive, exerted over me a kind of ghostly influence, as if I carried him around with me as I went about my work as a lawyer. I suppose in some ways I did – I had saved on my phone copies of the recordings I'd made of our conversations. Sometimes at lunch I would make the effort to walk to Flagstaff Gardens, put on my headphones and listen to one of those old conversations as I made a little circuit, up past the eponymous flag and back down to the city, past the lawn bowls and the netball. That familiar voice sounded a little distant, full of reverberations – a result of my low quality recorder – speaking slowly, deliberately, and always in whole sentences, a barrister's trick.

All this meant that I was only half paying attention when I read 'The Time of a Thesis', a narrative that charted Derrida's gradual estrangement from the university. And though most of his words passed by me, I could not fail to notice, and recognise – even without the diacritics – the name of Tran Duc Thao. This time, recognition came with a much stronger jolt. Never before had I seen a name like that in a book like this, unless it was to mention Ho Chi Minh (and even then, it was only ever in the context of American imperialism – no one, it seemed, even those who professed to hero-worship Uncle Ho, had read anything Ho had ever written). Yet here was Derrida, defending his life's work with a Vietnamese name, uttering it in the same breath as more famous European names – Sartre and Merleau-Ponty – citing Thảo as synonymous with phenomenology as a 'discipline of incomparable rigour'.

And for a few brief moments I thought that I had found satisfaction for a yearning I had barely admitted to myself existed. That I could finally say, we, too, have philosophers. But then I read on, to find that Derrida made it very clear that he was recalling an obscure work, a book which is no longer discussed today, a book whose merits can be very diversely evaluated, a book that was significant not for what it achieved but in what it failed to do; it was the stakes of what had been attempted, not the outcome of the attempt, that mattered. A glorious failure, then.

12

I finally find *Phenomenology and Dialectical Materialism* on the sixth level of the South Wing. I have that curious feeling that I sometimes get when something I have been thinking about for a long time finally happens – a kind of deflation, coupled with a conscious effort to be 'in the moment', to not let this point in time that I had been thinking of for so long slip away unnoticed, unremarked, but the effort of which makes it almost impossible to be 'in the moment', so that the whole thing feels like a waste of time – which, strictly speaking, it is, as I should be doing any number of things other than wandering among the stacks, looking for a book I don't have time to read and about which I hardly know a thing.

I do know that Thảo was only eight years older than my grandfather. I know that he, too, died in a public hospital in Paris. I had read somewhere that Thảo had gone to the best French school in Hanoi, the Lycée Albert Sarraut, and that he had been so immersed in the French language that he had only learnt to read and write quốc ngữ – the Vietnamese script alphabetised by Jesuit missionaries – after graduating with his baccalaureate. My grandfather had also gone to the best schools; he, too, had spoken more French than Vietnamese as a child.

But that is about as far as I can take it. And to be honest, I can see that they weren't really that similar. My grandfather was never an internationally renowned philosopher. Thảo was never a Catholic, not even a lapsed one. I know all that, but still: I can't get inside my grandfather's head. I have hours and hours of tape from our conversations in the tiny apartment in Boissy, and still I can't make him come alive. I've tried ventriloquising him, fictionalising him, verbatim transposition of his speech. None of it worked. That was years ago, before my own fatherhood, before law and human rights, before Manus. I had tried and failed to write what I told people would be the story of my grandfather.

So now I turn instead to the life of Thảo, a man who never met my grandfather, who took up the opposing side in the war that defined everything. But Thảo, at least, has left behind a body of writing of 'incomparable rigour' for me to read – even if it is no longer discussed today.

I read about how Thảo went to Paris after graduating from Albert Sarraut, how he studied there the work of Edmund Husserl, the father of phenomenology. Husserl wanted to solve the problem of radical doubt – what if everything, from numbers to ethics, is merely subjective?

The crux of his phenomenological method is counterintuitive: to get closer to objectivity, the phenomenologist retreats into a kind of total subjectivity. Let us assume, says Husserl, that the world we experience is real, and let that assumption be more than a thought experiment: the world we experience through our consciousness is the only world there is, and to question its reality is unnatural – a confusion introduced by philosophy itself. The job of the phenomenologist is to go back to the origin of the world-as-we-experience-it – otherwise known as the Lifeworld – to a moment before categories and classifications and philosophy distorted our perception, to describe phenomena as they appear to us with as much rigour and exactitude as possible.

Like everyone else at the elite École Normale Supérieure, Thảo was enthralled with the brilliance of Husserl's method. But unlike his master, Thảo became a Marxist, and then an anti-colonialist. At the end of World War II, after the liberation of Paris, de Gaulle's new government imprisoned Thảo for three months, describing him as a threat to the security of the nation. Upon release, he fell in with Sartre, Merleau-Ponty and the *Temps Moderne* crowd, becoming their most strident anti-colonial voice. Then, in 1951, he published his magnum opus, which I now hold in my hands.

In *Phenomenology and Dialectical Materialism*, Thảo attempted to synthesise the two intellectual currents not only of his life but of life at the ENS: phenomenology and Marxism. He began – and this is the part that caught Derrida's eye – with a brilliant critique of the very centrepiece of Husserlian thought, the phenomenological technique with which Husserl hoped to go back to the origin of the Lifeworld. Husserl, said Thảo, was caught in a contradiction. Standing at the origin of the Lifeworld, the phenomenologist is supposed to describe objects as they appear to his consciousness – that is, to his senses – free from the baggage of the world – culture, history, and so on. But even this prelapsarian moment of pure description is loaded with assumptions, chief among them the assumption that the phenomenologist can pick out, from the undifferentiated unity of all things, distinct objects to describe. Where, in other words, does the concept of distinct, describable objects come from, if all concepts have been bracketed out? The irony, for Thảo, was that at the very moment that Husserl thought himself on the sure road of science, he was in fact still lost in the woods of relativism.

Still, said Thảo, Husserl was right to argue that the life of the senses is the foundation of all truth. But the life of the senses is not a matter of immediate interaction with the environment. It is mediated by the material conditions of that life. Only the study of these material conditions could make phenomenological description truly objective. Applying this thinking to the struggle against the French, Thảo said that, for a Frenchman, an independent Vietnam was a mere possibility, an abstract hypothesis, so that all consideration of Vietnam was conducted through the lens of French intervention. For a Viet, however, a Vietnam as it would have been without colonialism – completely without French influence – is a project actually lived, the project even of his existence. Thus, the phenomenological horizon – the Lifeworld – of a Frenchman and a Viet are diametrically opposed, and apparently rational debates about the future of Indochina were bound to lead to radical misunderstandings: given the same facts and arguments, a Frenchman and a Viet would assimilate them into their incommensurable modes of existence.

Take the question of whether French colonialism had brought demonstrable benefits to the Vietnamese. Of course, Thảo, ever the materialist, said that the modernising influence of the French was irrefutable. But to leave the matter there was to remain within the French experiential horizon. What might the Vietnamese have accomplished as a free people if the West had come in the spirit of friendship and intellectual communion? That, an obvious, crucial question for a Viet, did not even occur to a Frenchman.

It was not long before people began to notice this brilliant young Vietnamese philosopher who combined his Marxism with the rigour of phenomenology. *Phénoménologie et matérialisme dialectique* was a hit. It should have made him a star. But, instead, it was his final act in Paris: that same year, he gave up the metropole for the colony – only it was no longer a colony. And for Thảo, at least, it was no longer the periphery but at the very heart of things, for by then Ho Chi Minh's revolution was half a decade old and he was coming back to do his duty – and to put his theories into practice.

Thảo took to re-education with relish. Like other intellectuals, he traded in his Western suit for the plain brown pyjamas of a peasant. At the re-education camp he slept without a mosquito net, all the better to train for the hard life of a revolutionary cadre. He caught malaria and collapsed, but survived. He became the dean of the Faculty of History at the new nation's first university. He worked on the Vietnamification of Vietnamese history.

Then tens of thousands of peasants and rural Communists – maybe hundreds of thousands, nobody knows – were purged in the botched land reforms of 1954. Disquiet about the direction of the revolution grew in the party rank and file. Elsewhere in the Communist world, Khrushchev denounced Stalin's cult of personality, and Mao called for artists and intellectuals to submit suggestions, even criticisms, of the Party, to 'let one hundred flowers bloom'. Reflecting the liberalising mood, Thảo commissioned for the university review a translation of the Chinese propaganda minister's speech promoting the Hundred Flowers campaign. He wrote two articles for the dissident journal *Nhân Văn*, appealing for the Party to respect democratic freedoms. The two *Nhân Văn* articles would be the last of his work published in Vietnam for over forty years, except for a confession and a self-criticism that appeared in the Party's *Nhân Dân* newspaper in 1958. He was all but erased from history. For thirty long years, Vietnam's greatest philosopher was silent in his own language, packed off to the provinces, where he practised his phenomenology in harmless obscurity.

13

There is very little documentary evidence about my grandfather's imprisonment in Chi Hoa. What there is, I keep in a green paper folder that travels with me – to Vietnam, to Cambridge. None of it reveals anything but the bare fact of his imprisonment. He was never charged, let alone tried. So the real evidence – the evidence about what it meant to be imprisoned in Chi Hoa throughout the eighties – is almost entirely contained in the memories of the men and women who were there, men and women who are now all dead, or soon will be. And when that happens, when all the forgotten prisoners from this forgotten prison have gone, what evidence will there be?

When I was a lawyer, some of my colleagues would tell their clients that the testimony they were giving would not only be crucial to winning their case but would also be on the record – for anyone and everyone to read and hear, for years to come. One day, some of them would say, there will be a royal commission. Then it will all come out, what they did to you.

I never made such claims. Not because I thought there would never be an investigation into what we had done in places like Manus and Nauru, but because I wasn't sure what the point of an investigation would be. Staying a deportation order, getting someone their visa back, getting a woman flown to Australia to have an abortion after she'd been raped in one of the camps – those were tangible victories, something I could tell myself was worth all the work, worth asking people to relive their trauma again and again. Anything less than that seemed abstract, an ideal. I had become a lawyer not to be an idealist but the opposite: a worker bee doing what I could to make the world a bit less degraded for the person sitting across from me in the client interview.

So why did you resign?

Lauren is at our kitchen table, with an open bottle of wine. I am still in my black robes and tuxedo, just back from a formal dinner. I don't know how to answer her. So instead I talk to her about an idea that I have been carrying with me for a long time, about a machine for perfect remembrance. I think of it as one of those early, fifties computers, I say. You sit at a console in a room, and the room itself – the walls surrounding you – is the computer. And sitting there you can type whatever questions about the past occur to you, and the machine will reply in lines of text that scroll across and down the screen like MS-DOS.

The machine runs off ghosts. As each person dies, their ghost is summoned to the machine, and there they tell the story of their life – like the most detailed oral history ever undertaken, told by someone with nowhere else to be, and no stake in the world that they are remembering. The machine listens with infinite patience. Not only that – the machine is truly egalitarian, listening to everyone, so that the memory of the world is parcelled out equally. With this machine there will be no more archival lotteries that see some genealogists (always with certain names, from certain places) finding treasure troves of municipal records, marriage certificates, electoral rolls, etc., while other genealogists (always with other names, from other places) hit dead ends one or two generations down.

I don't know who I am anymore, says Lauren. I don't have a job or a reason to be here. I don't know anyone. I spend all day in this house that's too big, with this baby I love more than anything, but that can't love me back, that doesn't give me any indication that she thinks of me when I'm out of the room.

It won't be forever, I say. We'll only be in this house for a few more months.

And then what? Another new place to be anonymous in?

London is such a big, busy place, I say. There's bound to be more people you can meet there. Other parents. We can find childcare there. Edith will make some friends, and you'll get some work. If my parents could move from Vietnam to the West in their thirties, then Melbourne to London at our age isn't so bad. We're still young enough to start our lives over.

Forgive me, Lauren says, if I'm not blown away by the conviction in your delivery. Since when have you used your parents as a yardstick for anything?

We finish the bottle and go upstairs to our room. As I lie next to her, tracing the lines of her shoulder blades with my fingers, I imagine a courtroom like the ones I sat in for so many hours – sleek, modern, nothing like the nineteenth-century grandeur of higher criminal courts. Places where efficiency is as highly valued as justice. I imagine a trial in that modern courtroom. The defendants are the guards and administrators of Chi Hoa. There is no dock in the new-age courtroom, so these defendants – there are dozens of them – sit in the first few rows of the gallery, seats covered in the soft, inoffensive upholstery of public-service waiting rooms.

One by one, the defendants are taken up to the witness box, where they swear their oaths and answer questions posed by a pencil-thin man in woollen robes with slicked-back hair and a wide flat nose. The man looks very much like the framed photo I see every time I visit my grandparents' apartment in Boissy. His questions for the guards are about the conditions in Chi Hoa, the frequency of the beatings and the meagreness of the rations, and his questions for the administrators are about the legal basis for imprisonment, the compatibility of indefinite detention without trial with international law, the whereabouts of countless letters sent by family members that were never received.

But the guards and the administrators alike are inarticulate. The guards because none of them have completed primary school and are, as my grandfather often told me, illiterate sons of farmers who supported generously extended families not on their pitiful government salaries but through the envelopes of cash that were passed to them by relatives of prisoners desperate to smuggle in cigarettes, gio lua, some mooncakes for Tet. The administrators are inarticulate for the opposite reason: they speak in bureaucratese – lengthy, circular sentences without subjects, sentences that unspool like false paths in a labyrinth, so that the lawyer who looks so much like my young grandfather has to interrupt them again and again with clarifying questions, their exchanges becoming more and more hostile as the administrators get defensive, answering questions with their own questions, or mock-sighing when their obtuse answers aren't understood.

Finally, there are only a handful of defendants left who have not yet testified. The first is Xuan Dieu, Vietnam's greatest romantic poet, the king of love poems, a disciple of Baudelaire and an admirer of Rimbaud and Verlaine. In 1939 he said, of the movement to give Vietnamese literature a Vietnamese character, to the exclusion of Western influences: Do we need to close all seaports, absolutely forbid all communications, shut off the entire country?! Preserving does not mean wandering around and around a stagnant pool of water. Yet in 1945 he wrote 'The National Flag' and 'The National Conference', poems glorifying Ho Chi Minh's August Revolution. How can it be, asks the man who looks so much like my grandfather, that a leader of the New Poetry could lend his prestige, his integrity – and, moreover, his artistry – to a regime that crushed free thought?

Next comes the poet To Huu, who brings with him the scent of late-blooming peach blossoms. He strides to the witness box as if it is the dais at the New Year's festivities, as if all day li xi envelopes have been passed from adults to children as gifts, as if later tonight there will be fireworks and raucous drinking. Indeed, before he can even be sworn in,

To Huu bursts out with the opening stanza of his ode to revolutionary fervour, that emotion which causes him to link his soul to 'all those suffering souls':

Since then, inside me, summer has blazed up –
The sun of truth has shone through my heart,
My soul's a garden full of leaves and flowers,
Rich in all scents, alive with all birds' songs.

Before he can continue, my grandfather interrupts him. Isn't it true that you became a censor for the new regime? That you played a part in the destruction of Trần Đức Thảo? That the love of all mankind can too easily justify the hatred of a particular man?

14

The anamnesis is a part of the Catholic mass, though I didn't know
what it was called when I suffered through that interminable hour
every Sunday with my parents and my brothers alongside me. The
suffering was entirely due to my failure to appreciate the subtlety
of the magic that was taking place before my eyes, preferring instead
the literal magic of fantasy novels, or the pornographic magic of the
magazines I bought from the Chinese owners of our local milk
bar, spending the hour turning those magics over in my mind until
I felt guilty enough to need – but also dirty enough to be sullying –
the Eucharist.

Later, as soon as I was old enough, I started skipping mass
altogether, telling my parents that, having slept in, I would go to the
afternoon mass on my own. Instead I went to the park opposite the
church and read books that seemed, at the time, to be magical firstly
because they were about other places, far away from the south-eastern
suburbs of Melbourne, and secondly because they connected me to
stories and ideas that promised to give weight to my otherwise too
light life. I never realised that these were books of lesser magic and
that the real thing was happening over the road, in the ugly seventies
brick church, where Father Peter was saying the anamnesis: repeating
Christ's words at the Last Supper, after breaking the bread and sharing
it with his disciples. This is my body, which is given for you; do this in
remembrance of me.

The mystery of it, the miracle, is that through this repetition of Christ's words and actions, and through the prayer that follows, memorialising Christ's sacrifice, the gathered congregation are not only remembering their Saviour but ushering in their own salvation; in this moment they do as much for their own redemption as Christ ever did. By remembering something we have forgotten – something eternal, and known already to our immortal souls – an impossible future is brought into being.

But then it's not at all clear that the anamnesis is a faithful memory at all. Though the words appear in Luke's Gospel, the other gospels that record the Last Supper make no mention of Christ's injunction to remember. And the relevant verse in Luke 22:19 – And he took bread, and gave thanks, and brake it, and gave unto them, saying, This is my body which is given for you: this do in remembrance of me – is itself suspect. Some scholars believe that the words 'which is given for you: this do in remembrance of me' are an interpolation added by some unknown author – or perhaps an imaginative scribe – many years after the original manuscript was written.

So where does that leave us? I suppose it is still a matter of faith: do I believe in the magic properties of remembering, whatever the provenance of the memories?

15

It sounds like you are looking for absolution. But a minor thesis is not a confession.

As he speaks, Professor Simons stares at the sheets of paper I handed him at the start of our supervision. Frankly, he says, I don't see how any of this relates to international law.

We are in Simons' art deco apartment, in a decrepit but elegant building at the back of Cambridge's oldest college. One of the quaint things about Cambridge is that the academics do not have their offices in their respective faculty buildings but are instead squirrelled away in and among the undergrads. Some, such as Simons, live 'in', too – though we are in the office of the apartment, I can see through the double doors behind him the messy quarters of a bachelor academic.

Simons shuffles through the pages again, as if some sense will emerge if they are handled with greater precision. You say that this Trần Đức Thảo was imprisoned by the Vichy government for his anti-colonialism.

Briefly, yes, I say.

And there he wrote an essay, 'On Indochina'. Simons trails off.

Which is where, I say, he explains that an individual's experiential horizons are materially determined by our communal pasts. In other words, history, economics, race – these forces shape the conditions of possibility of consciousness itself.

I did not know, says Simons, that Thảo was an influence on later anti-colonial thinkers, including Frantz Fanon and Aimé Césaire. Now that – Simons looks up at me – could be interesting. There could be some potential there. Because, of course, Fanon was very influential on many international lawyers working on decolonisation in the sixties and seventies – the Algerian struggle was, for many, as significant as Vietnam. Perhaps more so, in the Francophone world. Indochina was distant, but Algeria – Algeria was Europe's backyard. Simons looks again at my pages. You write that you wish your grandfather had read more Fanon – that you wish he was the kind of man who would have wanted the cleansing blood of the Frenchman to flow through the boulevards of Hanoi. Ah, I see – you are adapting Fanon's words from *The Wretched of the Earth*. Am I to understand by this that you wish your grandfather had been a man of violence?

Simons gets up and goes to one of his shelves and returns with a book – Aimé Césaire's *Cahier d'un Retour au Pays Natal*. You also say, he continues, that you wish he had been the kind of man who would have said to the colonial flunkies, after Césaire, Va-t'en – Beat it! Get away! It's an interesting question, theoretically. That is, the question of violence, and when it is justified. But then you say that your grandfather joined the nationalist army – that he fought both the French and the Viet Minh. So, after all, he *was* a man of violence, or at least a man willing to use violent means to achieve his political goals. Isn't your problem really with the goals, rather than the means? So really it seems to me the question you should be asking yourself is whether you wish your grandfather had been a Communist. Césaire, you know, ran on the Communist ticket in Martinique. And of course Fanon was his disciple . . . To put it another way: do you think your grandfather's beliefs put him on the wrong side of history?

Simons looks at his watch. Time for the next student, he says. Standing up, he gives me back my sheet of paper. This will be fine. Just make sure your focus is on violence and its role in the formation of the post-colonial state. You could take Algeria and Vietnam as your two case studies.

As I'm stepping out the door he says, Watch *The Battle of Algiers*. There's a good scene on the FLN's need to show the UN that there was broad support for independence. You can cut Thảo – Fanon can give you what you need, and he's much better known. And forget about complicity, all that hand-wringing about your grandfather. You have to believe in something – so, just ask yourself: what do you believe in?

16

My phone pings with a notification as I turn my bike off Storey's Way to cross over Madingley. I make my way down the path that runs past the Centre for Mathematical Sciences, whose glass and steel structures rise out of the Cambridge greenery like the biomes of the dystopias in the young-adult novels I devoured as a child. The bitter cold has already set in, and on mornings like this my woollen gloves can't keep my hands from feeling frozen to the handlebars. The notification, I guess, is from S, one of the men on Manus that I have stayed in touch with, even after I resigned as his lawyer.

Five minutes later, once I've locked my bike to the railing opposite the law faculty, I check my phone to see that my guess was right: S has sent me another voice message. The men have all been relocated, to new 'transit' centres around Lorengau. After the drama of the siege, when the outside world had at least been paying some attention to them, the men have more or less settled back into the anonymous, monotonous existence in which they are not officially detained, yet have nowhere to go.

When I was S's lawyer, our correspondence had been mostly over the phone. In the lead-up to hearings I would speak to him almost every day, asking him questions that must have seemed simple-minded in their specificity. What food was served for lunch today? Did they offer you a choice? How long did you wait in line?

Were there signs about hygiene and safety? What language were the signs in? Where did you eat the food? Was it hot, sitting in the sun?

After, when I was no longer his lawyer, we hardly ever spoke anymore, at least not in real time. Without a shared purpose I no longer knew what our relationship was; I had no more questions for him, specific or otherwise. But then he began to leave me voice messages, which began as short updates about what was happening, the rumours that were spreading – that the negative-assessment guys were going to be deported right away, that the US State Department people were coming in from Port Moresby to do more interviews, that a refugee had tried to kill himself by jumping out of a bus. Gradually, the voice messages became less detailed, until he hardly spoke at all – but at the same time, the messages were getting longer and longer. S would record himself cooking a fish curry for a friend (the *clunk-clunk* of a knife rapidly chopping, the soft splashing of ingredients falling into liquid); or he would record himself listening to his favourite music, Hindi love songs (he called it 'slow music'); or the sound of the insects at night when he couldn't sleep (a deafening, constant, multi-toned screaming). Once, he sent me a thirty-minute recording that was just him sitting on his balcony, smoking a cigarette (in the background the screeching and humming of the jungle, punctuated by the eerie call of the chauka, or an ashtray being pushed across a table by unsteady fingers).

Eventually, I came to expect these portals into his life on Manus, portals that opened up wherever I happened to be when a new message arrived – at the supermarket, in the library, at home in our lounge room as Edith played on a mat at my feet. I began listening to the recordings over and over again as I studied, so that even as I read about the International Court of Justice or the UN Security Council or any of the other institutions that constituted the web of power called global governance, I was also sitting with S as he waited for his laundry to finish, walking alongside him as he made his way through Lorengau market.

Walking up the stairs to the third floor of the law library, where the cavernous curved ceiling is reminiscent of the featureless, rootless immensity of an airport terminal – the architect, Norman Foster, also designed nearby Stansted airport – I listen to S's latest recording: him on the beach, listening to the waves, trying to relax. But as I take my place at one of the big tables on the third floor, I find that the sound of the waves is not relaxing me at all. Instead I can feel – but not stop – my jaw clenching, my whole body tensing, as I listen to the waves crashing against the shore, rushing back and building again, then crashing against the shore once more. Intellectually, I know that for many people the sound of waves is soothing, perhaps because it puts them in mind of a tropical holiday, or childhood summers when life seemed more simple and carefree. In the past, I, too, found this sound relaxing. But today the waves seem to me like the endless beating of a drum, the marking of time's remorseless, unsentimental progress.

My grandfather was already an old man when they put him in Chi Hoa. He must have suspected that his life's work was over – not only that, that it was a failure. Or is it only me who thinks so? Perhaps I am too beholden to comparisons, offered up by well-meaning friends, colleagues, editors, and audience members whenever I mention my grandfather. Who they compare him to varies according to political persuasion, from Aung San Suu Kyi to Rosa Luxembourg, Mahatma Gandhi, Saint Paul – and bestride them all, that colossus of transcendent incarceration: Nelson Mandela. The comparisons are meant, I suppose, to elevate my grandfather's suffering. He was no mere prisoner, they are saying, but a dissident. Yet I can't help but think that for each of these supposed analogues, imprisonment was not the end but a beginning: for these extraordinary prisoners, at least, the waves might be ceaseless, but their rhythm is not constant; there is a 'play of ebb and flow'. Could I imagine that the same might be true for my grandfather?

17

If nothing else, these luminaries spent their time in prison productively. They prepared for the revolution, they corresponded with allies on the outside, they read and they learnt from each other, and they wrote: novels, letters, memoirs, manifestos, poems, textbooks and wills.

Once, on a backpacking trip through Europe just after high school, I stumbled across hard evidence of this carceral productivity. Hungover, and with some hours still left to fill before I could start drinking again, I had followed some of the other travellers from my hostel to a prison-themed exhibition at a design fair. There I found a series of mock cells, each designed by a different architectural studio. The one I lingered in the longest was set up like a library, with a single shelf running along the cell walls at eye level. On the shelves were hundreds of books written in prison, arranged by length of incarceration, so that the collection began with a letter from Lilly John, who spent one day – her last – in Auschwitz, and ended with Danylo Shumuk's memoir *Life Sentence*, about his cumulative forty-two years in Soviet, Polish and Nazi prisons. According to the architects, the library was testament to the way spatial confinement and isolation could induce creative, imaginative, and spiritual production.

I remember wandering along that shelf until I found the spot where my grandfather's memoir would have been, if it existed: between the prison letters of George Jackson – given an indeterminate sentence of one year to life for robbing a gas station of seventy dollars when he was seventeen, and who later wrote that he met Marx, Engels, Lenin and Trotsky in prison, and that they redeemed him – and Antonio Gramsci, the founder of the Italian Communist Party and an enduring lodestar for revolutionaries everywhere.

Can I – should I – imagine my grandfather in their company? Would it transform his suffering to imagine something like the *Chi Hoa Diaries*?

First I would have to imagine that he had been able to procure pen and paper inside Chi Hoa. It's not so unlikely. He would not have had to go as far as Ngũgĩ wa Thiong'o, who scribbled *Devil on the Cross* on toilet paper while held in a postcolonial Kenyan prison. The guards at Chi Hoa were poorly paid, and very few of them were truly ideological, perhaps only the very highest ranking, and even then it was rare. What did it matter to them if a broken old man scribbled down his thoughts if it meant some extra cigarettes or another portion of salted pork?

But then, I shouldn't get carried away. Cell 6, Section FG, was no gentleman's garret. There were no privileges accorded to writers – no writing desks, no libraries. Precious little light to write by.

Perhaps I shouldn't fixate so much on the physical act, on the making of marks on paper. That's not what interests me, the existence or not of some notebook, some scraps of paper. Nor should I try to make him into a revolutionary – and certainly not a Marxist one. No, what I have always wondered – and what I have always wanted – is something for which there can be no definitive proof: what sort of man was he, to survive as long as he did in Chi Hoa? By which I mean that I have always wondered what his mental life was like over those ten years. Had he, too, thought about someone else in this way, tracing their mental pathways by following his own memories and sensations, extrapolating and inferring from his own experience of consciousness how this other person might perceive and encounter the world? And if he did do this, did he also find the boundaries of his own mind to be insurmountable? Did he discover that all extrapolations and inferences were invalid, the inner life of the other inaccessible and unimaginable?

We cannot transcend ourselves. Yet it is the promise of such transcendence that brings us back to literature.

In that tiny apartment in Boissy, my grandfather would often say to me matter-of-factly that he had forgiven the men who had imprisoned him. I accepted that statement, the same way I had accepted the things I was told about Catholicism as a child – that forgiving one's enemies, like Christ coming back from the dead, was at once utterly ordinary, unsurprising to anyone who knew even a little about anything, and at the same time completely mysterious, beyond all mortal comprehension. I believed that my grandfather had forgiven his captors the way a child believes in God: without question, and without interest.

But as I got older, such faith became harder and harder to maintain. Why should it be plausible, let alone expected, that a man, whether religious or not, should forgive the people who kept him from his family for ten years? Who cut short his career, took away his books and ruined his body? Why should he forgive the greedy and the stupid and the cruel? Who killed so many whom he loved? Who took away his country, which he loved most of all?

Revelation: I have suffered, these thirty years, from a chronic lack of imagination. I have failed to imagine things as they otherwise might have been, which has had the perverse effect that I do not fully understand what was. I have accepted, without wonder, the mysterious and the extraordinary, and in doing so I have made them commonplace.

For he might have been a bitter old man. Why not? I know of myself that I don't wear even condescension lightly, never mind crushing injustice. I carry slights around with me like fuel for a fire. So it would be more understandable, in many ways, if my grandfather had been one of those men still prosecuting the war thirty years after it ended. Maybe it would make for a better story, or at least a more comprehensible one, if the Boissy apartment had been festooned with Republic of Vietnam flags – the yellow field crossed by three horizontal red stripes. Well, then everything would have been different. I would have found in Boissy a Little Saigon, where my grandfather would have told me about how our country had been betrayed by all and sundry: by the Americans who had escalated the war only to abandon us when they couldn't control their home front; by the Western media who told lie after lie about the state of the fighting, the authorship of the atrocities, and the willingness of the people of Vietnam to fight off the scourge of Communism; by self-serving presidential generals who lined their own pockets and left the country to rot while they lived it up in America; and most of all by our own brothers and sisters who split the nationalist movement into bitter splinters, so that the people were tricked into following that fraud, whose name was as fake as his nationalism, Ho Chi Minh.

I had failed to imagine my grandfather as the kind of Vietnamese man who would put on his finest woollen suit and a tweed cap to go to any of the many events in that vast metropolis that might prove fertile ground for his memories: a writers' festival event about war photography, a local council's Lunar New Year celebration, the premiere of a short film about the European refugee crisis. I had failed to imagine him sitting attentively through the talk or the speech or the film, neither taking notes nor looking at his phone, just waiting for the programmed activity to finish and for the floor to be opened for questions, whereupon he would raise his hand and wait patiently once more, this time for the MC to motion towards him and say, The older gentleman in the first row, and for a roving microphone to be handed to him, and only then would he stand up at his seat, cap held between his hands, and say in his surprisingly loud, heavily accented voice: Did you know that in that famous photo by Eddie Adams, the man being executed by Brigadier General Nguyen Ngoc Loan was a Viet Cong terrorist who had, just prior to the photo being taken, been found at the scene of a grisly massacre, the home of an ARVN officer, whose wife and six children had been brutally murdered? Did you know that the Tet Offensive, widely reported in the Western media as proof that the war was an unwinnable stalemate, was in fact a comprehensive defeat for the Viet Cong, so devastating that they were rendered basically inoperative and had to rely on the North's regular army to keep fighting the war? Did you know that the largest-scale atrocity committed during the war was not at My Lai, nor was it perpetrated by Americans, but was actually at Hue, where the Communists tortured and killed six thousand civilians – men, women, children and infants – some of whom were buried alive in huge pits dug up around the city? Did you know that they arrested me in front of my children, that they stopped my wife from even visiting me, that they took away first my books and my notes, and then my health and finally my hope, my spirit, my dignity, until ten years later when it was safe to release me, when I was sick and broken, when I had finally decided it was better to die than to live – that that was when they let me go?

If I had imagined all that, I might have really understood the critical fact about him: he forgave his captors. He did not go to expat events. He did not speak to other old men about the mistakes and the betrayals of the wars. And if I could comprehend that – not just intellectually, but in my bones – then surely the rest would flow.

But I can't comprehend that. I don't have that spirit of forgiveness in me. And since I don't have a prison notebook to help me understand, I will have to imagine one. The *Chi Hoa Diaries* will begin – how else – with someone else's words: 'Elected Silence, sing to me.'

18

I came across that line a long time ago, during my first life as a student, before Cambridge. It is the first line of a poem by Gerard Manley Hopkins, 'The Habit of Perfection'. In it, Hopkins, himself a student – of Classics at Balliol College, Oxford – expresses his desire to give up worldly things by renouncing the senses for life as a mystic in his new-found faith, Roman Catholicism. In the opening stanza he gives up the sense of hearing, and its attendant pleasure of music. Now silence – but crucially, a *chosen* silence – will beat upon his ear.

At some point my grandfather must have made the same choice. Like Hopkins, my grandfather had lived a worldly life, full of music, sounds, words – and then there had been the silence of Chi Hoa. Not that Chi Hoa was ever silent, or even close to it. But it was a kind of silence, nevertheless, especially for a man who had spent his professional life speaking with judges, and much of his private life listening to the voices of the great writers of the past. The trick, then, must have been to take that awful silence – the cessation of the thinking and the speaking that had sustained him – and convert it into something chosen, an elected silence.

But how might one go about doing that, short of self-deception? Or is that the wrong question? What is the difference between faith and self-deception?

That's Lauren, who has come to meet me for lunch with Edith asleep in the pusher.

Do you mean, I say, why do I care about deceiving myself?

I mean, why are you so anxious to show that you have not deceived yourself? We all do it – why should you be different?

The Ancient Greeks had this idea, I say. Anamnesis. The Catholics borrowed it to describe their belief that salvation can be achieved through a certain kind of remembering. But originally it was the idea that all knowledge, everything we know or could know, is just a matter of remembering.

So all mistaken knowledge is a kind of self-deception?

Or all self-deception is just misremembering.

And how did we forget everything?

Socrates said it was from the trauma of being born. Entering the world, taking on material form, is so horrific that we forget all the eternal truths our souls already know.

Typical, says Lauren, rolling her eyes. He got it precisely the wrong way around. It's the giving birth that makes you forgetful.

I defer to her expertise on matters of birth, so she continues.

I still think it's awfully conceited of you. You know how I feel about genealogies, she says, almost apologetically. I've never understood the logic of it: so you uncover some new ancestral fact – can you really take pride in your ancestor's war heroics? Should you really be ashamed of a massacre you just found out about, committed by an ancestor you've only just discovered?

It's not really the same, though, is it, I say. I knew my grandfather. So it matters to me how he's remembered.

Okay, she concedes, so it's not exactly the same. But still – why do you feel as if you need to compare him to others? To the great and the famous? To writers and statesmen? What difference does it make to you, to your life, to your real living family in the here and now? It's just ego. Or a search for better fathers, which is the same thing.

If I could just make the comparison to Mandela stick somehow,

I say, if I could dig up the right scrap of writing, uncover some unknown bit of history —

— and then what? You'd be the grandson of Vietnam's answer to Mandela. Or whatever it is you think you want to be. But whatever greatness you think is yours, it doesn't need to be authorised by a family tree. If it's all a fantasy anyway, if you want to remember your grandfather a certain way, go ahead. But you can't justify it with an idea you don't believe in. We both know you have no faith – in eternal knowledge or anything else.

Not for want of trying.

Desire for faith is not faith itself.

But my grandfather had it – or found some, at any rate. He chose silence. I have to believe that, at least.

19

With all matters of faith, it's easier to be shown than to be told. Back inside the library, after lunch with Lauren, I remember my grandfather rummaging through the objects on his bookshelf and pulling out a small, square cardboard box. My friend, my grandfather said between rasping breaths, the Chinaman we called Romeo, he showed me how to make this. A chess set. Not Western, Vietnamese. Co tuong. Very, very difficult to make. A lot of patience, a lot of skill. He opened the box, and I could see a set of round, black pieces, each with a red or white Chinese-looking character carved into it.

Each piece, my grandfather said, took one month to make. He held up one of the pieces and said, haut prix. First we had to collect as much plastic as we could. Any plastic wrapping would do. Each sheet was washed and dried, then hidden away until there was enough to make a new piece. That was the easy part. Then we needed fire. But matches were absolutely forbidden. In good times, when we weren't being punished, a guard would come to our cell after each meal and light a match. One of us – always a trusty – would use it to light his own cigarette, and then the rest of us, or at least those of us on good terms with the trusties that day, would light our cigarettes off his. So we could smoke three times a day, at the appointed hour. My grandfather laughed and said, Of course, that wasn't nearly enough. We kept our own fire, for between meal times, and overnight. That was good – sleep was always difficult to come by, and that meant we could smoke away the early hours.

I remember, said my grandfather, before erupting into a series of long, raking coughs. I could hear the wet rattle in his lungs, and tried to think of something else. When the bout of coughing had subsided, my grandfather continued. I remember, he said, having to keep the flame alive overnight. We all took it in turns, except the trusties, who could get a lackey to cover for them. On nights when it was my turn, there was nothing to do but smoke, and even then I couldn't smoke all night, I would have run out of cigarettes. So I would look at the fire – often it was nothing more than a single flame travelling up a piece of paper – I would stare at it, for hours. It was so alive, the fire, in that dead place. I looked and waited and the fire burned. I fed it, too. But that seemed secondary to the watching, which I came to feel was what truly kept the fire alive – my attention.

Simone Weil, who is fashionable now for you young people – but remember, she was first and foremost a Catholic, and only then a philosopher, an activist – you think she starved herself to death for an idea? No, it was God, love for God. The love of a convert. Which, as I can well tell you, is all the greater for coming later in life, and coming consciously, a chosen love and a love that chooses you. Weil said that attention is the rarest and purest form of generosity. And I really understood that on those nights of watching, for it was my attention, and my attention only, that kept this life going, the only life present in that place, so that without my attention there would have been nothing living at all.

Later that afternoon, my grandfather told me the rest of the story about the chess set – how the plastic got melted and poured into a tin can as a mould, how they used black ink to dye the melted plastic, how the Chinaman called Romeo had a contraband knife, which he used to carve the necessary symbols into the chess pieces. But what I remember most about that conversation is the fire, and the image of my grandfather sitting before it, eyes focused, attention unwavering. There is something in that of an elected silence.

20

That very same image of my grandfather watching the fire recalls to me another line, a line also written by a Catholic priest, but a memoirist rather than a poet, and heavy with all the hubris that Hopkins was praying to be freed from with his chosen silence.

I came across this second line only a few days after my grandfather had shown me the chess set and entrusted it to my keeping. The little cardboard box – no bigger than my open palm – had felt heavy in my hands as I took it from him, and it was still weighing on my mind a few days later as I made my way up the narrow staircase at Shakespeare and Company. This bookstore had harboured Ginsberg, Baldwin and Nin, and I had once dreamed of sleeping in the narrow bunks set among the shelves, as apparently some ten thousand aspiring writers had done before me in return for stacking books. Today I was only interested in escaping from the crowds of tourists who blocked every footpath outside, and who stood downstairs taking photos of books but rarely made it upstairs, which was as quiet as one could hope for in a habitable space on the bank of the Seine.

Indeed, when I turned the corner into the nook which housed the out-of-tune upright piano, there was only the resident cat, her green eyes opening lazily to look at me from her position nestled into the corner chair. It was there that my eye caught on the spine of a book by my left arm: *Elected Silence* by Thomas Merton. I had never heard of the author, but the title set off a strong enough echo to make me pull the book off the shelf. It turned out to be the autobiography of an American Trappist monk. When it was published in 1948 as *The Seven Storey Mountain*, it had been a surprising success, touching a nerve with a Western world that saw faith in decline and consequently found something in this Augustinian confession for the twentieth century – written by a thirty-year-old fugitive from the literary world – that spoke to a need for spiritual sustenance in an increasingly material society.

I knew nothing of any of this as I leafed through the yellowed copy – probably a first edition – in Shakespeare and Co's reading library. Merton's parents, a New Zealand émigré father and an American Quaker mother, both painters, did not suffer from what he snobbishly called the little spooky prejudices of people who knew nothing but automobiles and movies and which neighbours were getting a divorce. By way of contrast, Merton described what he had inherited from them: a bit of his father's integrity, some of his mother's dissatisfaction with the mess the world was in, and from both, 'capacities for work and vision and enjoyment and expression that ought to have made me some kind of King, if the standards the world lives by were the real ones'.

I recognised right away in Merton's line the arrogance and moralism of youth, the disdain for a hypocritical world, and the solipsism, too, of assuming that the self's moral struggle is unique – that all others are as undisturbed as their surfaces suggest. But now I recognise something else, too: my grandfather should have been some kind of King. But this thought transforms Merton's line into something else entirely – I have lost its essential core of Catholicism and replaced it with the hollowness of my own atheism. For when Merton writes that the world does not live by the real standards, he says so not with bitterness but only with a melancholy hope. If this world does not live by the real standards, then at least there is a world to come that will. I have no such consolation, and so the thought of my grandfather's life, his imprisonment, his death – alone, in a public hospital in suburban Paris – can only appear to me as the most god-awful waste, and the failure of the world to save him, a world that professes to care about justice, a tragedy without remedy.

But here again, I must be wrong. The man who forgave his captors could not have been so despairing. Yes, he may well have thought, as he stared into the fire in Cell 6, Section FG, that he should have been some kind of King. Still, that he was not a King, but its opposite, was not a source of bitterness for him. If I am to ever understand him, I have to believe this: that on those nights, the loss of the kingdom that was rightfully his was not soul-shattering. The fire, and the fire's need for him – and him alone – was enough.

21

My grandfather answered the phone and the heaviness of his face lifted. He said, Ban, is that you?

It was an old prison friend, calling about the next Peregrine Society pilgrimage. My grandfather had tried to tell me many times about the Peregrines – the Societas Peregrinus, to be precise. They were pilgrims, mostly Catholic exiles from Communist countries, though some were in exile more figuratively than others. One member I had met, an Italian high-school teacher, had talked at length about how she had no home – nowhere to belong, no home for her soul, Rome was only a tomb – yes, she meant a *spiritual* home. She blushed at my grandfather.

Ban, my grandfather and the other exiles from Vietnam formed the core of the society, and they were real exiles – homeless both in spirit and by law. At a get-together at Ban's house in Lille to mark Don Bosco's day, a fusion feast, thit heo quay followed by gaufres, prepared by their wives, who preferred to stay out of the ruminating-on-exile business, they came up with the idea of walking together. Happy are those without a home, my grandfather was always telling me, for they settle in one city or another, knowing that no city of man can ever be the City of God. He who is forever walking is always looking, like the starving man casting about for bread. Only those who stop looking – who stop walking – are truly lost.

So they began planning yearly walks. To Lourdes, to Fátima. Along famous routes that I had not heard of. On the phone to Ban, my grandfather spoke of Saint-Jean-Pied-de-Port and St James. I thought that he might have been talking about the most famous pilgrimage of all, the Via de Compostela, to the cathedral in Santiago, in north-west Spain.

When he hung up the phone, my grandfather began telling me a story. When I first met Ban in Chi Hoa, he said, I thought he was a ghost. He was so fat! Only a ghost could be that fat in prison. Not even the guards were so plump. When I discovered he was a man after all – you will remember that the latrines were inside our cell, furthest from the trusties' mats, but not so far from where I lay, and, well, in such conditions it quickly becomes clear who is phantasmic and who is flesh.

I couldn't resist asking him for his secret. I've been watching you for some time now, I said. And I never see you with any more food than the rest of us, certainly less than the trusties and their lackeys. So why are you so round? Ban laughed and said that I had just reminded him of a wedding he had gone to as a young man, in the north, when the French were still around. The wedding was something of a sensation, said Ban, for the bride was the daughter of a wealthy merchant, whereas the groom was from a peasant family. Still, the food was excellent – the old merchant liked to boast that he had the best cook in the province, and he just might have been right. It was old-fashioned, a bit rustic, but done right – cha gio, ga luoc, served with their own rice wine. Strong stuff! Well, they had beds for all their guests, but I had to be in Hanoi in the morning – a business meeting – so I paid my respects to the newlyweds and to the old merchant, with whom I was hoping, in the near future, to strike a deal for a new leather contract, and got on my motorbike.

It was late and I was quite drunk, but I didn't mind riding through the dark countryside, the cold air on my face. Though I couldn't see the paddies either side of me, I thought about what my father had always said: we are, essentially, a rural people. A flock of white egrets, a naked boy riding a water buffalo, an emerald sea of rice stalks swaying like wavelets in the wind. That is the heart of the nation.

But even as I was thinking of this pleasant image, the road changed. I was winding up a mountain. And the darkness around me was changing – it pressed in on the road. It wasn't rice paddies anymore but jungle. I started taking the turns as hard as I could. I could almost hear the music in the wind as it whipped around me. By this point I was in some kind of trance – all I could think about was my racing line, pushing the bike right to the edge as I took each corner, even if there was nothing but sheer cliff beyond. I rounded another corner – and just as I was coming out of this beautiful turn I saw in my headlights something big and grey, and I was going too fast, there was no way I could brake or swerve, I was just going straight into the thing, and in the instant before impact I realised what it was: a water buffalo, and he wasn't moving, he was staring straight at me. And I remember thinking, death has come for me – and death is a fucking water buffalo!

Ban laughed and seemed to expect me to laugh as well, said my grandfather. But I only asked, So what happened? Ban stopped laughing and said, Nothing. Nothing at all. I went right through him. But he was there, real as you or me. He stared right at me. But I rode through him, and for some reason I kept thinking, *I've been spared*.

Ban grinned at me, said my grandfather, and whispered again, *I've been spared*. Why? God only knows. But I've always been lucky. Of course I was so surprised by my lucky escape that I forgot to take the next corner. Too late, I tried to turn, but it was no good – the bike slid out from under me, gone, over the edge of the cliff, and I was left on that mountain road, flat on my back, staring up at the stars.

22

I imagine my grandfather after this conversation with Ban, lying on the hard rattan mat spread over the concrete floor of Cell 6, Section FG, ignoring the sounds and smells of urination and defecation coming from the latrines, forgetting the daily power struggles between the guards, trusties and regular prisoners, forgetting even his wife and children, wherever they were and whatever they were doing – forgetting, in other words, the moment. But only for a moment. Suspending it, then. Deferring the inevitable return of the moment just long enough to exist in a state of something like grace, having forgotten just enough to memorise sentence after sentence of the stories he later told me in that tiny apartment, stories told with such deliberate care that they must, after all, have been chapters of a work to rival that of any of those other, more famous imprisoned writers, a work committed not to paper but to memory during those endless days in Chi Hoa and transmitted to me without fanfare or chronology or explanation, just a succession of stories, some lacking even the basic structure of a narrative and so more like an image, or a riddle, a torrent of words handed down to me, to – what? What am I supposed to do with his words? With stories like Ban's and the sour ghost's? What else but act as his amanuensis, reconstructing the book the fragments must once have been part of, if only in his imagination. Is that not why he told me what he did? Is it not my duty to read what he said, to piece it together? And yes, to translate and explain, to make his life and his words known to the world? And if, in doing so, I make my own life and words known to the world, that is hardly a criminal offence, is it?

23

When my grandfather arrived in France after Chi Hoa, he had not been able to speak. The doctors said it was severe depression. This is a wrinkle in my imagining – an inconvenient fact. Was it a continuation of his imprisoned silence? But if so, why would he elect for it, now that he was free? And if it was unchosen – what was so much worse about freedom in France than imprisonment in Chi Hoa?

Whatever it was, it lasted a decade – almost as if he needed to repeat his imprisonment, day for day. So when I was young there were no phone calls from my grandfather, no familiar, wise old voice that stirred something in me when I finally met him in person. Then, on the tenth anniversary of his release, he began speaking again. But he said nothing of significance – certainly nothing about Chi Hoa, or life before. He only thanked my grandmother for the food she put before him, prayed the rosary aloud with her, and kept up a running commentary as he watched football and tennis on the TV, which he began to do as often as he could.

Eventually, with Ban's encouragement, he spoke about pilgrimage routes, about the organisational needs of the Peregrines. But never, until I arrived, did he speak about the past. Which is unusual, because ghosts speak – that is what they do. They return to the living to say things that were left unsaid, or things that cannot or should not be said, but that nevertheless must be heard. Actually, it's more specific than that: ghosts always return so that someone or something – usually they themselves – can be remembered. Ancestral spirits crowd around the family altar to be remembered through nourishing offerings; if left unremembered, they become hungry ghosts, taking what they need from the living and thereby enforcing remembrance in the form of loss, haunting, catastrophe. The ghost of Hamlet's father returns to be remembered to his son in the form of bloody vengeance.

But the ghost who returned from Chi Hoa did not make it clear how he wanted to be remembered. At first, he did not speak. Then, when I showed up at the apartment in Boissy with my cheap voice recorder, it appeared for all the world as if my ghost had found his voice. But now, listening back to those tapes, it's as if he's played one last trick – like the apparition that won't appear on camera. I listen back and he's not really there – if the he is supposed to be a person, in the full sense of the word. Instead, there's just a trace of a man, a timbre, a way of arranging his sentences, a recurring exhortation for me to do – to be – what? I can't make it out. Good? Godly? More like him, or less?

24

There is, if you believe the psychologists, both healthy and unhealthy remembering. The technical term for healthy remembering is mourning. The mourner understands that the loved object has departed. Rather than keeping it alive, mourning preserves the image of the lost thing, much as Egyptians mummified their dead. Successful mourning honours the dead – at the same time, it is a second and final death. Remembering the ghost – doing what it asks – is also a way of dismissing the ghost: we speak of putting ghosts to rest, but we really mean burying them, deep enough that they can't get out again.

Some days, I think that my grandfather would have wanted me to be healthy – of course, what grandparent doesn't? Other days, like today, I'm not so sure. The technical term for unhealthy remembering is melancholy. In contrast to mourning, melancholy keeps the lost thing alive: the melancholic has not grasped that the loved object has really died. The emblematic melancholic, the one whose mad love goes beyond all reason, is Antigone, daughter of Oedipus, who defied King Creon's orders to leave the body of her brother Polynices, a traitor to Thebes, to rot outside the city walls. For her disobedience, Creon sentences Antigone to being buried alive. She says to the king:

Living in daily torment / As I do, who would not be glad to die? This punishment will not be any pain. Only if I had let my mother's son / Lie there unburied, then I could not have borne it. This I can bear.

This I can bear, says Antigone of being shut up in a stone tomb still living. I have often thought that there is a thread tying Antigone to the phrase 'to bear witness' – we talk as if testimony were an ordeal, a trauma.

And indeed it was for my grandfather, who spoke to me as if it had been something he'd had to bear, as one bears a cross. Every part of his body must have been asking him to stop. He was dying, when I was speaking with him, of pulmonary oedema – excess fluid in the lungs. He spoke to me through the constant sensation of drowning. How much easier it would have been to be silent, to focus on the intake of oxygen. Even the thought of that feeling – of breathlessness, of slow suffocation while sitting in one's favourite armchair – crippled me with anxiety, but for my grandfather, that was evidently a pain he could bear. The thing that he could not bear was to not remember. Without remembrance, the lost thing – Anam, and the Anamite he was, before Chi Hoa – would truly be dead. And for that purpose, simple mournful remembering was insufficient – he had to remember madly, beyond all reason. He had to keep Anam alive, or else be entombed within it.

25

Outside, winter has begun in earnest – the trees are bare, and the few punts that slide past my window are half-empty, carrying more blankets than tourists. But the skies are a clear, happy blue, and it is easy to be fooled, safely ensconced as I am in the heated library, by the bright sunlight bathing the college sandstone in a soft, romantic glow.

The work that I imagine my grandfather composed in his mind while in prison, which I imagine he then told me, word for word, in Boissy, and which I now imagine recalling in double translation – from the Vietnamese of his mind's composition to the French of our conversations to the English of my own thinking – as I sit under the sloped ceiling of the Jerwood's second floor – that was a work of mad love. But love of what? What was it that he could not bear to lose? One possibility: in those garbled tapes, in my imaginings of his perfectly composed stories, in my spectral dreams of him, he was trying to tell me about the Vietnamese concept of phuc duc – an untranslatable amalgamation of personal destiny, social status, your family's public standing and your place and role in the social orthodoxy. The source, in other words, of Vietnamese pride, which is derived not from who you *are*, as it is for a Westerner, but from how well you play your assigned part.

What would my grandfather have thought of my presence at Cambridge, an institution that had been home to men like Sir John Seeley, Regius Professor of Modern History? I pass the library named

after him whenever I go into the law school. In 1883 he wrote that
the elimination of native peoples from new English nations – like the
Australian race, who were so low on the ethnological scale that they
could never give the least trouble – was a matter for self-congratulation,
because their elimination meant that the English Empire was, on the
whole, free from the weakness that has brought down most empires:
the weakness of miscegenation. Despite this history – or because of
it? – the fact I am now a scholar in Cambridge would, I presume, be
a source of significant phuc duc. My parents seem to think so. They
would have preferred Harvard or Oxford, the two universities that
every overseas Viet has heard of, but once I explained that Cambridge
is generally considered on par with the very best institutions in the
world – thus the portmanteau 'Oxbridge' – they began telling friends
and family.

(My parents have even loaned me more money than they can
really afford, to cover what my savings from community lawyering
cannot – a loan made on the implicit basis that it will all pay off in
the end. Indeed, that is reason enough to go on to London when
my time at Cambridge is done. There I really could earn enough to
pay off the debt. But I am beginning to feel that I owe something
to my grandfather as well. He has loaned me something too, with
strict – if unclear – instructions to safeguard it, nurture it, mourn it,
bury it. Worse yet, whatever it is I am supposed to do with Anam, it
seems to me that it might not be compatible with a high-paying job
in London. Or at least, there are two versions of this story, one more
self-serving than the other. I could say that my grandfather wanted
me to remember him in a healthy way – that by becoming a lawyer I
was following in his footsteps. Not only that – by becoming a lawyer
I was making good my father's loss, my father who had been in training
to become a lawyer when Saigon fell. So repetition would be not only
homage, but healing and closure, too. In this version of the story,
I go to London to get my horsehair wig and silk robes and I pay off

both debts at once – the monetary one to my parents and the spiritual one to my grandfather, remembering him healthily, reasonably – all the while accumulating phuc duc – with every trip to court. But in the other version of the story, the one in which my inheritance is a mad love, beyond all reason, the two debts are not so easily reconciled. For the mad thing would be to try to live with Anam – to bring it into being. A quixotic endeavour, doomed and heroic. Not the kind of thing one can do from chambers in Holborn. Which would leave me doubly indebted, unable to pay off my parents and failing – however gloriously – to find salvation through remembrance. Well, what can I say? It's shameful, really, very bad phuc duc, having no clear path out of these debts. Which is the point, isn't it – how to get out from under everything you owe. Though really the shame only set in once Edith was born. I mean, it was shameful before, but I didn't feel it – what I owed was theoretical, always payable in a future that would come, some day, I was sure, but there was never any hurry. And now? You could say the bill is due.)

What I didn't say to my parents about Cambridge – but perhaps should have – is that they might want to withhold their approbation. The example of Ngo Vinh Long is instructive: the first Viet to go to Harvard, Long's path to America was extraordinary. He taught himself English with a bilingual dictionary and a copy of *Great Expectations*, which he memorised in its entirety. At fifteen he convinced American officers to hire him as a map-maker, going out into the countryside to measure heights, angles, distances and water levels, to give the Americans a better picture of the strategic hamlets into which they herded 'friendly' Vietnamese, all the better to starve and shoot and burn the 'hostile' ones in what remained of the defoliated jungles.

After that, Long received a full scholarship to Harvard – unheard of! Especially as Harvard at that time only admitted fifty foreign students each year, and none from non-English speaking countries. What phuc duc! Especially for a son from a long line of scholars.

Only one problem: Long did not arrive in Cambridge, Massachusetts, as the good native – on the contrary, as he got off the plane at Boston airport in October 1964, he said to the throng of reporters and photographers – over thirty in all – that he was both honoured and worried to be the first Vietnamese at Harvard. Why worried? Because all signs pointed to a full-blown war between America and Vietnam, far beyond the skirmishes that had broken out so far, and such a conflict would be detrimental to all.

Soon enough, Long was on the anti-war speaking circuit, both the token Viet and the main event, always speaking last after such luminaries as Howard Zinn and Noam Chomsky, because that way the audience was guaranteed to stay to the end, to see what a real-life Vietnamese had to say about the war. For his stance, Long earnt the lifetime enmity of much of the Vietnamese diaspora – Anamites all – including a 28-year-old former naval officer who in 1981 narrowly missed Long with a Molotov cocktail as he was leaving the East Asian Legal Studies Forum at the Harvard Science Center. Shortly before the attacker's trial, a leaflet from the Vietnamese Party to Exterminate the Communists and Restore the Nation (Anamites are many things, but pithy is not one) proclaimed: the shameless Ngo Vinh Long has been sentenced to death. One of our comrades threw a cocktail bomb at him, but unfortunately he escaped death. The naval officer was acquitted on grounds of temporary insanity.

Such is the complexity of phuc duc! As to whether Long himself is an Anamite, I cannot say. At least, I cannot tell from his writings whether he carries around with him the memories of a future home (I know, of course, that he carries with him memories of a home that has been lost, but that is quite a different thing). But there are other attributes that suggest a connection to Anam. There is, for instance, a passage of his book *Before the Revolution*, where the future professor of history recounts his days as a student in East Asian History and Far Eastern Languages at Harvard. In the preface, Long remembers being taught in the spring of 1967 by a professor who had recently returned from a fact-finding mission in Vietnam. The professor – whom Long describes as a future National Security Advisor and Secretary of State, and so could only be Henry Kissinger – cheerfully announced to his students that the US was winning the hearts and minds of the Vietnamese people, since the Vietnamese were Confucianists, and so always favoured the side with overwhelming force in any conflict, that being the side that clearly had the 'Mandate of Heaven'. The peasants were simple-minded people, said the professor, who mostly wanted to be left alone, and who answered his simple questions with epic poems. When the young Long tried to explain to the professor that his 'Mandate from Heaven' was little more than the Western concept of 'might is right' mixed with the American concept of 'jumping on the bandwagon', the professor dismissed Long's intervention as another epic poem, to the giggles of the Harvard classroom.

Ah, wounded pride. As a motivating force, Anamites share this with every other colonised people, every exile and émigré group that has ever existed. Those Harvard giggles may be substituted for the mocking grin of the blond boy who trips Ali La Pointe at the beginning of *The Battle of Algiers*, the sneers of the Desperance townsfolk at the Pricklebush mob in Alexis Wright's *Carpentaria*, every word from the white – and not a few of the black – speakers in Ralph Ellison's *Invisible Man*.

26

It pains me to admit it, but I suspect that I am more Kissinger than Long. For what is my grandfather's story to me but an epic poem – inscrutable, flowery, full of a mysterious self-regard (phuc duc)? My ghost finally spoke, and all I got was this lousy koan:

In the immemorial past, the Anamite race sprang from the rich loam of the northern delta. They fell under the yoke of the Middle Kingdom for ten long centuries. They fought off the invaders, established their own nation. Then priests came from the West, bringing with them the Good News. And then French gunboats came to protect the priests, bringing with them Modernity. In exchange, they took Raw Materials back home and manufactured them into more Modernity. They sold Modernity back to the Anamites (and Civilisation and Progress and Enlightenment) – at a premium, of course. All the while, they extracted more Raw Materials (and Natural Resources and Cheap Labour), to manufacture more Modernity, for seventy more years. A virtuous cycle.

Into this cycle, a second son was born to a minor bureaucrat in a provincial city on the Red River. Though the bureaucrat was no lover of the French – his household was run on the strict Confucian model – he knew better than to sail against the prevailing wind. So the second son learnt the language of Modernity (and Civilisation and Progress and Enlightenment). He played Modern sports and joined Progressive youth associations. He read Enlightened novels and digested Enlightened philosophy. He and his older brother were trained to follow their father into the colonial bureaucracy. But then war broke out around the world. Germany overran France, France handed over the Anamites to Japan, the Americans dropped not one but two atomic bombs on Japan, and the French were invited to return to their rightful place leading the Anamites to their glorious future – which just happened to be the same as the French past.

That ought to have been a good thing for the bureaucrat and his sons: their careers remained on track, their fortunes remained secure. And yet, that was not how things went. For somewhere in that chain of war–France–Japan–France–war, the brothers left home, filial piety be damned. Certainty be damned, too – they not only left home, they left home for the radical uncertainty of guerilla warfare as part of the Viet Minh, a minuscule, poorly equipped, poorly trained, Communist-dominated outfit hiding in the mountains along the Chinese border – as delusional a set of Anamites as you are ever likely to find.

So two brothers set off to fight a war they had no hope of winning. That is the first mystery. But at least they were together: brothers-in-arms. The second mystery is more vexing still: somehow, the brothers separated. Elder brother continued to the mountains and to the Communists. Second son got as far as Hanoi. There, the erstwhile revolutionary converted to Catholicism. Worse yet, he went on to work for the very regime he had been on his way to overthrow. In this, the second son exceeds even his father – while the minor functionary is always forgivable, useful even, the second son went beyond the pale, becoming an active agent.

So the two brothers found themselves on opposite sides of three decades of war. And the delusional band of Anamites did the most extraordinary thing: they kept on winning against imperialists old and new. And they kept on liquidating their rivals, their enemies. Eldest brother climbed the ranks until he was a General, and his comrade Anamites were no longer few, nor delusional. In fact, they pulled off the most extraordinary feat of all: they transcended their own imaginations – they made their Anam real by force of arms. And so, after forty years, the brothers met one last time. The General, who won, and the second son, who picked the wrong Anam, captive in the prison guarded by the General's own soldiers.

27

What to make of these mysteries? Why did my grandfather and his brother go to war? Why did they turn against each other? Like Kissinger, I am tempted to shrug my shoulders and say, Another epic poem. Of course, Kissinger's shrug licensed the dropping of two million tons of cluster bombs on Laos, to pick one war crime among many. I must do better than Henry Kissinger. Admittedly, a low bar – but I have to start somewhere.

Really, my problem is the same one identified by Trần Đức Thảo in his alchemical blending of Husserl's phenomenology and Marx's materialism. What appears to me as inscrutable, unreasonable, beyond the pale, is absolutely natural to the Anamite – necessary, even. That is because the Anamite's world of lived experience and possibilities constitutes the background against which perceived realities appear: it is this background that gives perception meaning. So there is no such thing as innocent or neutral perception – all perception is immediately situated within the horizon that defines one's existence. It is little wonder, then, that even though we perceive the same facts, the Anamite and I will draw contradictory conclusions: our horizons are radically different.

To correct this – to reach across the chasm that separates us – I must go back to beginnings. A kind of amateur phenomenology: I must go back to the moment when my horizon splits off from the Anamite's and take one step further back still – to the last moment of mutual understanding.

28

One such beginning would be the signs that marked the French-only carriages on the trains that pulled into the railway station my grandfather's father all but managed: signs that read, pas de chiens, pas de chinois. And always in that order, my grandfather would tell me. We were lower than dogs to them. And of course they did not bother to tell the difference between a Vietnamese and a Chinois. An alcoholic Frenchman was nominally the chef de gare, but he spent most of his time at the brothels by the canal, leaving my grandfather's father – the deputy manager – to do all the work.

Another beginning: the Renault Primaquatre – two-door convertible, four-cylinder engine, powder blue – squatting in the middle of the road, and the two French, a man and a woman, clambering out to check the chassis for damage. The woman's hair was bright blonde, pulled up into a bun beneath a cream-coloured scarf. The man was hatless, his light brown hair shiny with brilliantine. My grandfather remembered how young they seemed to be, hardly older than him and his brother Minh, the two boys running up the road to where their friend Cuong lay in the dust a few metres behind the Renault, whimpering like a whipped dog, his left leg twisted horribly beneath him. I felt the bile rushing up my throat like old coffee, my grandfather said to me, as I saw the grey thing that had punched a bloody hole through Cuong's trousers.

What happened next had been the subject of so much remembering that, for my grandfather, or so I now imagine, it was no longer a memory but a kind of comic strip, a series of emblematic images that, over the years, he had used for motivation, for absolution, and finally, in Cell 6, Section FG, for a kind of company – familiar, warm and silent.

The memory went like this: the young Frenchman covered the distance to Cuong in a few quick strides, his handsome face contorting in an ecstasy of rage, mouth agape, neck and cheeks blotched red. A well-booted foot making precise, brutal contact with Cuong's stomach. The Frenchman saying, Putain de merde, my brother's face a mirror of the Frenchman's, apoplectic, as if he couldn't breathe. The Frenchman's boot pulling back for another kick, driving forward, connecting with Cuong's skull. A dull sound like a faraway football. The blonde woman already back in the car, impatient to get going. The Frenchman pulling out a silk handkerchief, sky blue crisscrossed with white flowers. He wiped the sweat from his face. He looked down at Cuong's prone body, sniffing. He reached into his pockets and retrieved a five piastre note. He threw it on the ground and spat after it. He looked at me with his pale blue eyes, as if waiting for a response.

29

Such a beginning would make sense of the first of the koan's mysteries: my grandfather and his older brother Minh went to war because of wounded racial pride, because Cuong's eyes rolled up into the back of his head with that last kick, because of their hatred of those other, pale blue eyes.

And yet a different beginning gives a different meaning to their decision to leave: it was around Christmas, evidently, for my grandfather and Minh had gathered in the stone church for the nativity play. They were not Catholics, but had come, like many of the others, for the theatrical entertainment. The choir of angels – a motley crew of local boys, dressed up in white robes and chicken feathers – were singing Hallelujah! Hallelujah! They raised their paper trumpets to their lips and the blast from their false instruments rang like gunshots in the stone-walled church. Wait, the trumpets *were* gunshots – there were masked men on the stage, and they were armed, and they fired overhead and small puffs of stonework drifted down like thin clouds from the church ceiling. The three kings were kneeling before the infant Christ.

Three kings because there were three gifts, my grandfather told me, forgetting that I had gone to Catholic schools my whole life, and he listed them off on his long, slender fingers – gold, frankincense, and myrrh. Not kings, really, said my grandfather, but wise men, learned in the movement of the stars. And so the East came to the West.

The masked men unfurled a star of their own, he said, yellow and five-pointed on a red field. Mary, swathed in blue, began to cry. The four masked men, each wearing the face of a sacred animal – a Dragon, a Phoenix, a Tortoise and a Unicorn – began chanting something in unison, but my grandfather's hearing was gone, replaced by this terrible ringing like bells. Some of the crowd in the church chanted along with the men, including my grandfather's brother Minh. Their faces were ugly with passion and rage. Slowly, my grandfather's hearing returned, as if he had been underwater, swimming up to the surface. Finally, he could hear the chant:

Be devoted to God! Love the Fatherland! Death to all imperialists! Independence for Vietnam!

My grandfather felt giddy; he wanted to stand and shout too, but he was afraid. That is when he remembered the pale blue eyes. That is when he knew: when he did open his mouth, his voice would be like a bugle, louder even than their gunshots, louder than thunder, loudest of all.

30

Adventure, a sense of nationhood. Still mixed in with that hatred, which I feel, too – but only as an impulse. Never sustained enough to come to anything but imagined conversations, imagined violence. But it is that straightforward, undoubted sense of belonging – to a place and a people – that I find hardest to bring into my own horizon. And chanting in unison: I have never been able to open my mouth in time with others.

But adventure – and the adrenaline rush of fear, and following someone older, someone with some quality that I do not possess – that is not so far for me to go. Which, I suppose, is why I often think of my grandfather telling me how cool the dirt felt on his cheek as he lay prone in the open field, as he had been taught to do, while American B-52s crawled like ants across the sky.

As ever, I was initially disoriented. Which war were we in? B-52s had dropped bombs over northern Vietnam for most of my grandfather's life. (Which is to say nothing of Anam, where the bombs have never stopped falling. Even when the Anamite is remembering a rendezvous with a lover, or a favourite dance hall, the bombs are always falling – always about to fall – on his head.) It was only when he said that the field was a football pitch, and that, before the B-52s had appeared in the sky, he had been at football practice, that I understood that we were in World War II, that the B-52s were targeting Vichy French and Japanese infrastructure, that my grandfather was sixteen or seventeen, and that he was about to make the decision that would lead him onto the long road to Chi Hoa.

Next to my grandfather, his brother Minh was lying prone in the dirt too. They both watched as the bombers opened up and little white eggs began tumbling out of their yawning bellies. They kept watching as one of the bombers broke off from the others, trailing a thin plume of black smoke, sinking quickly.

Later, my grandfather and his brother would pedal their rusty bicycles to go see the downed plane, emerging from town into the open rice fields, riding single file along the dirt lanes on top of the dykes, eyes down on the dirt and the muddy paddy water on either side, swerving to avoid the many potholes, ignoring their sore elbows from the rattling journey and ignoring, too, the obvious sickness of the rice paddies, which at this time of year should have looked like the surface of a lake, with water stretching out like a smooth mirror dotted by rice stalks, rather than low and murky, full of stunted and locust-ravaged stalks, so he would not look, but would instead cycle on in silence until, after an hour, they would finally arrive at the site of the wreck, where the bomber lay shattered and smouldering in three pieces. My grandfather would see through the fuselage like an anatomical cross-section from one of his textbooks, or like a butchered carcass on display at the market, which he would have cause to think about again when they came across the body of a crew member thrown clear of the wreckage. And it would be while my grandfather stared at that mangled body that Minh would find the flight goggles, which he would loop around his left handlebar on the ride home, to be presented as a trophy to the other boys back home.

There would be time for all that – but for now both boys lay in the dirt, waiting for the remaining bombers to disappear. Minh said that he was going to change his name, to Son, the Chinese word for 'mountain', to show that he was reaching for the virtue of the Heavens. My grandfather knew what that meant: that Minh had chosen a nom de guerre, that he would go first to Hanoi, and from there on to southern China, or the mountains, and there join the revolutionaries led by another who had changed his name, Ho Chi Minh. And though there would be one last childish adventure together, to go see the downed bomber, it was in this moment, as my grandfather lay in the cool dirt beside his brother, that he grew up, for it was in this moment that he made the decision that I have been trying to understand: he said, I will go too.

31

Go where? To Hanoi? It was said that on cloudy afternoons, in every little hamlet across the country – from the river deltas to the mountain jungles – the people sat in their courtyards looking up at the sky in the hope of catching a blurry reflection of the old capital in the clouds. Or was my grandfather committing himself to something more – to travel on to southern China, to join the revolution, to kill or be killed? He had to have had more in his mind than adventure, more than tagging along with Minh-now-Son.

I have imagined him thinking of pale blue eyes and gunshots in stone churches. I imagine, too, conversations with Minh-now-Son, conversations away from eavesdroppers, about the glorious promises being made by the Viet Minh: independence, yes, revenge, of course, but also land reform and the end of all taxation, true social equality, universal education, and the international brotherhood of all mankind. Put that all together, and what do you get?

32

End of term, which only means that we have been assigned masses of reading for the break. Of all the anachronistic trappings of Cambridge, this is perhaps the most telling – they expect us to be able to sit and read hundreds of pages a day, day after day. Who still has such capacities for attention? Even if they have the discipline to sit in the library all day – as some of my classmates evidently do – no one I know can do so without constant, obsessive mental breaks on social media, on news websites, on online shopping.

Today I am in the law library again, at one of the top floor's long tables. Instead of doing my reading I am thinking again of the Christian Living Camp, and the first time I told my grandfather's story – not as a koan but as a straightforward narrative. And it occurs to me, thinking about it now, that that was the best rendition of my grandfather's story I have ever told – will ever tell. Because that rendition's paucity of detail ensured no one in the audience was alienated or confused. For them my grandfather was a blank but worthy space – an intellectual who had suffered terribly at the hands of a repressive regime. The story made sense like that. And really, what more does anyone have to know? The human side of it was covered, I now see, by the mere fact of me, his grandson, standing there on the stage and speaking about him. It implied a wife, children and grandchildren, a home – just enough, in other words, to give his suffering some heft.

So why complicate the story with more details? What good does it do to talk about my grandfather lying in the dirt next to Minh-now-Son? About the way he loved his older brother like a flower loves the sun? About fate and the Anamite mind? About complicity, and how the innocent, like my grandfather, rarely ever have clean hands?

What should we keep uppermost in our minds when translating the suffering of others? Should we let the people have what they want? Should we avoid inserting complexity between the audience and their desire for cleansing, edifying pathos? Should we let them *sympathise*?

I have considered leaving it at that. It would be easier, and more gratifying. But I cannot shake the nagging feeling that more is owed, even if it dampens sympathy. (Nor can I shake the less honourable feeling that giving the people what they want is somehow base – that taking the harder, more complicated path is superior. It's always possible, of course, that I just needlessly complicate things that are really quite simple.)

My grandfather was not just like me. Nor was he like you, dear reader, unless you are one of the very last of the Anamites, holed up in a hospital ward in Paris or Hanoi or Orange County. No, he was different from us, and I owe him more than whatever sympathy I can elicit on the false premise of like-mindedness. And, in any case, just-like-me is only another way of saying, I am not guilty.

Lauren, you asked me what we're doing here. What I think you meant to ask is why aren't we at home. Unlike everyone we know, you've never felt a need to travel. You didn't go backpacking after finishing school. You don't have a bucket list of places you need to visit, much less live in, but it's not as though you have some great attachment to Melbourne, or even Australia.

No, I don't think it's anywhere specific that you're missing, but a home – a settled place, a shelter, a hearth, your own place in the sun. A place you have every right to be, where you need not be embarrassed – because travel is embarrassing, and to be a tourist especially so. There's no getting around the essential frivolity of being a tourist, and being an immigrant is not much better – being a stranger is never comfortable. So you want a home: a place where you can be innocent. But that's just the thing – you and I can never be innocent in Australia. The only thing worse than a tourist or an immigrant is the coloniser, the stranger who insists: I have always been here.

What I keep coming back to is the way everyone around me was always proclaiming their innocence: it was the others who were guilty, the ones who weren't taking these cases, who weren't writing submissions, who weren't posting in solidarity, who weren't marching, who weren't boycotting, who didn't read the right things, or say the right phrases, or acknowledge Country, or pay the rent, who didn't care like they did. But I have long been haunted by one of Levinas's lines, which is itself a paraphrase of Dostoevsky: Each of us is guilty before everyone for everyone, and I more than the others.

Well, maybe there's power in proclaiming one's non-innocence. I don't know if this will satisfy you, but that is why I have brought us here. Because if it's *a* home you really need, then we could make one here as well as anywhere. The advantage of being strangers here is that we're under no illusion about our innocence, about true belonging, as we are tempted to believe back *there*. Here, at least, I can stop denying what I have always felt since that day when my father told me, matter-of-factly, that his father had been imprisoned for ten years: that I, more than the others, have been guilty. Guilty of the fact that, when I was born – the firstborn son of his firstborn son – my grandfather was still in Cell 6, Section FG, of Chi Hoa Prison, in District 10 of Ho Chi Minh City, in the Socialist Republic of Vietnam. Guilty from birth, and after too: guilty of not knowing, and not asking – and then, when I did ask, and when I finally knew, guilty of squandering that inheritance.

33

A telltale symptom of the guilty is their rush to judgment. I did it with To Huu when I first read his poem, 'Since Then'. When the poet wrote of linking 'what stirs my breast to everyman / so that my love may spread, go everywhere', I had understood the 'love' that he venerated to be nothing more than the mechanical – and thus hollow – love of an ideological position, the kind of love a certain type of intellectual thinks, rather than feels, for an empty category like 'all of mankind'. My judgment of To Huu was influenced, no doubt, by his subsequent political career, and his later role in destroying Trần Đức Thảo, both of which encouraged me to dismiss his love as cover for hateful violence.

But I realise now that that is not the only way to understand the love he writes of. For what is a love of all mankind if not an excessive love – mad, even? And just as his later life points to a totalitarian love – the kind of love shown to dissidents by secret police who watch them every minute of every day – so To Huu's early life shows a different side, a Romantic one, foolish, to be sure, but not totalising.

(It was only when I read about his early life that I realised I had been getting his name wrong all along, leaving off the diacritics: I should be thinking of him as Tố Hữu, not To Huu. The realisation is an uncomfortable one. Should I be thinking of Chi Hoa as Chí Hoà? Of Hanoi as Hà Nội? But then, when it comes down to it, Hà Nội is itself a nineteenth-century renaming of the ancient capital of Thăng Long, a name with a glorious thousand-year history. Then again, Thăng Long is only an alphabetisation of 昇龍, using an alphabet developed by Portuguese, Italian and French missionaries, who in 1651 adapted the orthography of their Romance languages – with liberal use of diacritics borrowed from Ancient Greek for the six tonal categories of vowels – to represent the phonemes of spoken Vietnamese. 昇龍, meanwhile, is only how the elite eleventh-century mandarins administering the Vietnamese state wrote the name of the new capital, the logographic characters incomprehensible to the vast majority of the 'Vietnamese' people who lived and died with no written language at all, and had only the barest notion of the state that ostensibly ruled them. So, after all, there is no true source script, no solid foundation that I can build on. When the idea of changing the name of Hà Nội to Thăng Long resurfaced in the nineties, Communist Party intellectuals opposed the idea on the basis that, despite Thăng Long's glorious history, it was the name Hà Nội that had become a symbol of anti-imperial resistance the world over. So the latter name – bland as it was, meaning only the city in the bend of the Red River – was retained. Every word of my forgotten mother tongue has a history as complicated as this one. Fidelity to diacritics cannot recuperate or articulate all that history; if anything, it will only make it seem as if I know more than I do. And, as my relatives are forever telling me, my wooden tongue mangles the language beyond recognition. Wouldn't it be more accurate, then, to leave off the tonal markings, when my own voice is so flat? But, having thought of all this now, leaving off these markings feels impossible.)

Tố Hữu had actually been born Nguyễn Kim Thành. He came to his pen name on a trip to Laos as an eighteen-year-old, where he met the old Confucian teacher Quang Bích, who chose the young poet's nom de plume after one of Confucius's sayings, in which Tố Hữu – 素有 – refers to the strength hiding within a man. But Tố Hữu, whose Han Chinese was evidently less than perfect, accepted the name on the mistaken understanding that 素有 was 素友, which refers to a man of purity.

Perhaps I have made a similar mistake – I have mistaken forms of love, not only in Tố Hữu's poem but in my grandfather's story. Not only have I substituted one form of love for another, I have failed to take love seriously – I found it easier to imagine hate, wounded racial pride, the pursuit of adventure, self-regard, a sense of nationhood. What could be more wasteful of an inheritance? To pass something on – isn't that itself an act of love? And if you don't take love seriously, how can you know how to receive such a gift? How can you even know that something has been given?

34

I have always tripped on the nuances of that word, love, on that phrase, I love you. I wonder, for instance, whether love, as my grandfather used it, carried with it any of the tenderness I remember observing as a child in my friends' families, but which was largely absent in my own: not for us the hugs and kisses and I-love-yous.

On the final day of the Christian Living Camp, the facilitators announced that they had, in preparing for the camp, asked our parents to write each of us a letter detailing what we meant to them. I remember thinking, absurdly, that there would be no letter for me at all – I simply couldn't imagine my parents putting their feelings into words, for me or for anyone else. But of course when the facilitator got to me I was handed an envelope like everyone else. The letter within was written on a sheet of notepaper with the logo of the bank my mother worked for. In the letter itself, co-signed by my parents but written in my mother's looping handwriting – handwriting that I now realise, at the age of thirty, I have been mimicking all these years – I read of their pride in my scholarly achievements, and their pride in my sense of social justice. The letter ended with that word that had no place in our familial lexicon: love.

I tried to reintroduce the word years later by inserting it as the closing of my emails to my mother – I never emailed my father – and to my surprise she started responding in kind: love, Mẹ. But in that correspondence, in which my mother emailed me articles about

Vietnam–China relations and the safety risks of charging your phone by your bedside, the word still stuck out awkwardly, as it had in that letter from the Christian Living Camp – too forced, too explicit.

Which isn't to say that there were never any tender moments in our family, though for some time I had thought that that was the case, as if we were living in the world of *Alphaville*, the Jean-Luc Godard film, in which tenderness is one of many illogical concepts to have been banned – or rather, it has simply disappeared altogether from the technocratic, totalitarian future. Along with tenderness, weeping, love and autumn light: other word-concepts that no longer exist. In a logical world such word-concepts are intolerable. I had thought, immature as I was, that this explained my family's tenderness deficit, but that was just a repetition of the old colonial lie about the cold, calculating, inscrutable Oriental. I should have recognised that my family differ from the world of *Alphaville* in one crucial respect: in that dystopian future, tenderness has disappeared because love is unthinkable. But my family are not loveless – far from it. If anything, they suffer from a surfeit of love, a superfluity that smothers tenderness in its cot.

Still, tenderness is there, struggling to get out from beneath that suffocating love, but only in flashes. I remember my grandfather saluting my grandmother as she came into the hospital room where he lay dying. An oddly stiff, formal motion. She fluttered her hand at him – he shouldn't be exerting himself like this. But they were both smiling broadly and he patted the bed for her to sit down by his side. In the room across from us a man screamed, À l'aide, for a nurse, with monotonous regularity. My grandmother took out a half lemon from her purse and started to clean my grandfather's fingernails with it. The citrus softened the nails, which made them easier to cut. My father stood in the corner with a little dyno-powered torch, which he shook up and down to charge; the fluorescent lights in the hospital ought to have been bright enough, but the light had a strange, dull quality that didn't get into nooks and crannies. My grandfather became listless again, staring up at the muted television, oblivious to the industrious family around him busily readying his still-living body for embalming.

Once the nails were cleaned and the torch was powered, the cutting began. My father held the torch steady, to make sure my grandmother didn't accidentally cut any flesh. If my grandfather started bleeding now, it wouldn't stop. My grandmother said he liked the lemon treatment, and the sharp smell of citrus did help to dispel the odour of mildew. Every now and again he spoke, but we mostly ignored him. When he breathed he blew out his lips a little bit, filling them with air and making him look like a monkey. When they were done with the hands they moved on to his feet.

The nurse came in and said, Oh, vous faîtes la beauté, and smiled at her own joke. We had to leave the room as she checked on his catheter and replaced the small plastic bag that held his bright orange urine. When she was done she came out whistling and smiled at us again. Then we all went back in and the pedicure continued as my father told my grandfather about my trip to Laon, where my grandmother had first lived with her children when they arrived in France. My grandfather smiled at that – a great big smile that lifted up his whole face. But he soon drifted off again, staring at his freshly cut fingernails in wonder.

Perhaps our tenderness only comes out in the presence of mortality. I can remember three flashes of tenderness from my father, who is otherwise a muttering, concerned presence in the background of our family life, always worried about our safety, or our grades, or our souls. First, when I was five or six, and my baby brother was in hospital for severe asthma. I can still hear his ragged breathing, like glass in his lungs. My father cradled him by a hospital window, his face turned down to the struggling little body in his arms. Then, twenty years later, I arrived at the hospital in Creteil to find my father already there, holding his own father's hand while the latter slept. And then a year ago, when we had finally been allowed to hold Edith, careful not to dislodge the cannula inserted into her left forearm that would leave a dark bruise that took weeks to fade, my father arrived with a strained and ashen face – in the three nights since Edith had been delivered, my mother told me, he had barely slept – and, ignoring the rest of us, he held on to the baby as if he meant to walk out of the hospital with her. Three flashes that, in the remembering, seem now like the one memory.

Tenderness is metonymic. Or at least, it works through the logic of metonymy, in which one thing stands in for something else: something concrete – a glance, a touch, a spoken word – is taken for something abstract – love, gratitude, desire. And yes, it is a logic – perhaps a surprising one, or a hidden one, but a logic nonetheless: the metonym must somehow be linked to that which it substitutes. Metonymy must, after all, drive at the truth, even as it is also always a lie.

There is something transformative in the logic of metonymy, for even in the most well-worn substitutes – the crown for the sovereign, the heart for human feeling – the metonym is never a perfect substitute. It is a form of magic, then, in which even something insignificant, banal, worldly, can be transformed – in the blink of an eye, or the stroke of a pen – into something beautiful, something grand. Water into wine, alchemy.

But who is doing the transforming? Not the one who makes the tender gesture but the one who perceives it. Not that metonymy is wholly subjective. It is constrained by an intersubjective, communal logic: what I take to be tender – whether I take a particular gesture to be an adequate substitute for love, gratitude, desire – is conditioned by the horizons of my experience: my family's language of tenderness, yes, but also the languages of tenderness I have seen on screen and page. All this, then, is contained in every tender moment: the transformation of the mundane into the sublime, made possible by a kernel of truth and a whole culture and community of substitution – or self-deception.

35

My grandfather loved his parents. It's so obvious that it feels redundant to even bother thinking it. He honoured them. And yet he left them, knowing that there was every chance he would never see them again. He left them even though doing so was bound to cause them untold pain, social stigma and loss of phúc đức.

I imagine that when my grandfather spoke of his love for his parents, he had in mind the instances when his mother – my great-grandmother – called him her little scholar-prince. The moments when she held the back of her small hand to his forehead when he was sick, when she watched him eat with hungry eyes, greedy for the life within him, as I am greedy for Edith – for the perfect tiny body, her bright eyes, her chubby thighs and round face.

His father was different. He bowed and scraped before the Frenchmen who passed through his train station. At home he was severe, enthralled by the past: ancestor-worshipper, Sinophile, the Old Way is the best way. But even then, I can imagine that it was his father who taught him how to fly a kite, one morning when he was not, for some reason, at the station, and instead had taken Minh and my grandfather down to the river, where they had run along the buffalo track pulling on the string and casting their faces up to the sky, laughing and shouting.

But such moments, such memories, are not the product of an Anamite mind. They come from a mind trained by a whole culture of sentimentality to seek out moments ripe for metonymic transformation.

I have been accused of such sentimentality before, when I first took on S as a client. It was a hopeless case – not because, as I had seen in other cases, he had a history of violence in detention, or because they did not believe his refugee claim, or because he had been secretly assessed as a danger to the community or a foreign agent, but because there was no case at all. No one could find it – the file that ought to have recorded his arrival, his first interview and his asylum claim. There were no identifying documents from the time before, and no acknowledgement of his existence, and therefore no acceptance of responsibility had been received from any of the five likeliest countries of origin.

To make matters worse, S was unable to remember the 'facts' of his own life. Which is not to say that he could not remember his own life – he could speak at length about his mother, about his childhood, about life in one camp after another. But he could not recall the proper names for those camps, nor the nominal side of invisible borders they fell on, nor the date of his birth. So as far as the file was concerned, it was as if he'd been born on the day the fishing boat he'd paid many thousands of dollars to take him to Australia had landed on the beach at Christmas Island. It was there that the file began – and then, as if to make up for lost time, the file had metastasised, overflowing with every minute detail of his life in detention: observations from case officers, surveillance reports from guards, requests to the private contractor running the centre for a second pair of trousers, complaints about the quality of the food, records of visitors, appointments with health workers, prescriptions for his headaches and his back, which was scarred as if he'd been whipped.

Neither the scars nor his vivid memories of how they were made were facts – memories that returned unbidden in the middle of the night, or the middle of a conversation. Only the date of the whipping or the name and rank of the whipper were facts, and he did not know those.

There were forms for participating in weekly activities and reports on his performance at those activities, memoranda noting room transfers, emails arranging for armed escorts to court appointments, decisions by tribunal members and judges lamenting his situation but concluding that their hands were tied, applications and defences filed by the government arguing in the most reasonable manner for him to be imprisoned forever because they did not know what else to do.

I had taken him on at the request of an acquaintance, a regular visitor to detention. Not to try to get him out, or even to try to locate his file – the real one that must exist somewhere, the one that mattered. That had all been tried before, by better and more experienced lawyers than me. Instead, I was running a novel – and very speculative – claim: essentially, that the government, having lost his file, had a positive duty to imagine this man's life – to imagine all that had brought him to Australia – and to imagine it as beneficially as possible. I appended to the application an example of such an imagining – on the off chance that it came across the desk of a bureaucrat with a heart. I filed the documents and waited for an official response.

After a few weeks, I got a call – not from the department, but from S. He said sorry, but he did not want me to go ahead with the application. He had read the appended imagining of his life – which had been based on my lengthy conversations with him. He said that I had taken his life, which was hard and unrelenting, and I had transformed it into something soft and beautiful. The problem was a metaphor I had used to structure the imagining – a labyrinthine metaphor drawn from Kafka, who was an obligatory reference in such cases. I had thought it would bring out the tragedy and absurdity of his situation, and the flimsiness and cruelty of the system that detained him. He said that he understood that I had my reasons for doing this, that no doubt I knew the heart of an Australian bureaucrat better than him, but even then, reading what I had written made him feel like his life had been stolen all over again.

Which is not to say that S was not sentimental. His preferred metaphors seemed to me mawkish and clichéd. But they were his. In the same way, the Anamite is not immune to the temptations of metonymy – quite the opposite. It is just that the Anamite metonym, while equally sentimental, functions through a different logic to mine.

36

Which brings me back to another epic poem – specifically, a story my grandfather told me. I didn't understand this story at the time, for it had seemed almost a caricature of Orientalism. Now, though, I wonder whether it might not have been an oblique answer to the second mystery of the koan – the mystery of why my grandfather, having left his parents, left his brother too, trading in revolution for Catholicism. I know, an epic poem to answer an epic poem – but what can you do?

We had been speaking of Ngô Đình Diệm, the Catholic president of South Vietnam propped up by the Americans as part of their Cold War politics, when my grandfather said, apropos of nothing, There is an old story about a young scholar, the son of a local magistrate. The young scholar had been away a long time at his studies, and he was now on the cusp of adulthood. Before entering the world, he travelled to the land of his ancestors, to visit his father. But as he was sailing down the river, a sudden gust of wind brought his boat to shore. It so happened that Prince T'eng, the youngest son of the Emperor, had just finished building a riverside palace at that very place. Even more fortunate, the young scholar had arrived just in time for the opening banquet.

To honour his host, the young scholar picked up a lute and called for quiet. Gradually the banquet hall fell into an easy, expectant silence. Into this void the young scholar played a single, vibrant chord, and composed an eight-line poem in the free style, celebrating the magnificent palace and the even more wonderful prince. The poem was an instant sensation. Prince T'eng called the young scholar up to a place of honour by his side and all the ladies of the court smiled shyly at him from behind their hands.

The young scholar, flushed with his success, stepped out into the warm night air to contemplate his good fortune. There, he saw a red leaf floating down a stream that ran out of the palace grounds. On a whim, he plucked the leaf out of the cool water and saw that there was a poem written on it, nearly washed away by the water. Written by a woman in the imperial harem, the poem told a sad tale. By day she dreamed of a constant lover, a stone and bronze man who would support her as the tree supports the vine. But every night she was the Emperor's captive in the green pavilion, a creature of clouds and rain, subject to a life of moon and flowers. Moved by this story, the young scholar composed a reply on the other side of the red leaf; though he had never met her, he declared that for her his heart now privately bore a vow of love etched in sight of streams and hills. He walked upstream to float the leaf back into the palace, then returned to the banquet with a hopeful heart.

In the morning it was time for him to travel onwards, to his native lands. It was to be a long journey, so he set off quickly, graciously refusing offers to extend his stay. But as he lost sight of the palace, a woman appeared among the willows on the riverbank and called out to him, Does your love ebb and flow such that you leave so soon? Startled, the young scholar tried to steer for the bank, but the river was too swift, and the woman was soon lost among the willows.

They say that every thirty years the vast sea turns into a field of mulberries, and the mulberry fields turn into the vast sea. Who knows why, but he who gets this, will lose that. The young scholar became a great and famous poet. He married well, and his family prospered. They say the wind that blew him ashore was the wind of good fortune.

But I prefer another version of the story, said my grandfather, in which a second gust of wind blew the young scholar ashore to the willows, and to the woman. In that version of the story, she is holding the red leaf. They marry, and two years later, the young scholar drowns at sea. Losses must always balance gains.

37

We are walking to Grantchester again. It is one of the only things that makes us happy here, this short but stimulating walk, even now that winter has settled in and made the path muddy, and, in places, frozen. It is early, and we are the only walkers on this grey morning. Edith is so much bigger now, much more active in the backpack carrier, chirping at the birds and grabbing at the bobble of my beanie.

Your problem, says Lauren, is you're fundamentally patriarchal.

At first I think she's joking. We often talk like that, as if political theory could explain away all the idiosyncrasies of our personalities – that she is so punctual because of a deep-down sympathy for fascism, that my messy eating habits are really an expression of my misogyny. But her tone today is different.

You're so fixated on your grandfather, she says, that firstborn, đích tôn stuff. You've never really thought about the women in his life – his wife, his daughters. It's your grandmother who's the real hero. Raising seven kids more or less on her own. Fleeing south, and then fleeing again to France. Having to remake her life over and over again, with none of the compensating glory that your grandfather received. That's the story that no one hears.

Lauren has never met my grandfather, though he had been a background presence in our relationship. We had been together for a couple of years when I made my three-month-long research trip to Hà Nôi, immediately followed by that unscheduled visit to Paris to

sit by his deathbed, where I stayed for six weeks. And there had also
been the evenings and weekends I spent reading books and searching
the internet, trying to understand the Anamite mind. For her, he must
always have been a spectre, even when he was alive – a spectre who
made me absent-minded, who encouraged me to give up my stable
job, who made me restless and dissatisfied.

    In contrast, Lauren had actually met my grandmother, in the
apartment in Boissy, which Lauren must think of as my grandmother's
apartment. Either way, if she ever thinks of it at all, it must be that
she recalls an apartment habitually – perpetually, now – free of my
grandfather. And it is a flesh and blood woman that Lauren would recall
when she thinks of my grandmother: tiny, shorter even than Lauren,
thinning hair dyed jet black, warm and fussing over us endlessly, still
cooking in the galley kitchen even though her body was well past the
exertions, vain about her jewellery and her appearance and diligent and
devout with her prayers, a lover of the murder mysteries that played on
the television all day – her only company when my aunt was at work –
lost in memory much of the time or else swiping across social media
on the tablet one of her daughters had bought for her, keeping tabs on
her grandchildren, or her old friends from a lifetime ago in the
glory days of Hà Nội, now scattered across the world. Courteous and
refined, but also given to a vulgar joke from time to time, insisting on
cooking us traditional dishes from the rolling office chair she used to
get around the kitchen and then watching us eat as she waited for her
own council-provided meals-on-wheels food, which was invariably
mushy and flavourless. Forgetful, tired, bone-sore and sick-at-soul,
ready and waiting to die, ready always to pinch Edith too hard on
the cheeks, asking whether Edith had been baptised so often that
we began to suspect she might spirit the baby away for a clandestine
baptism. Full of stories about the old, useless objects that cluttered
the apartment – her father's opium pipe, a century old, the triptych
of a traditional landscape that had belonged to her mother's father –

stories full of the pride in her family's former wealth and prestige that was so strong it was like another object in the tiny apartment, sitting alongside her shame at that pride, shame at its unseemliness, and for the fact that it put her on the wrong side of history. When Lauren thinks of my grandmother, she is able to draw on all this and more – the weight of my grandmother's hand on her back when she guided Lauren to sit and eat, the too-sweet fragrance of the laundry liquid my grandmother used, which got onto Edith's clothes. The way my grandmother covered her face with both wrinkled hands when she laughed.

We reach the turn in the path to Grantchester but take the left fork instead of the right, descending down towards the river, where a herd of cows stands huddled under a tree.

I think of the way Lauren smiled when we used to play tennis, at the sheer joy of using her body. I think of the way she slipped her arm through my own when we went for early morning walks through Princes Park. I think of her pallid face when I returned from the intensive care ward, where Edith lay alone in her perspex box, and the way she waited in tired silence for the midwife to finish with the stitches. I remember leading her by the hand through the hushed hospital corridors, past the unmanned night desk, and into the intensive care unit. I remember her voice, thin and fragile, asking me which one was her baby.

There are some things the refugees told me that there's just no space for in Australia, I say as we pass the cows and go on through a kissing gate into a wide flat meadow that runs between the town and the river. No one wants to hear it. Stuff about sex, and women, and love. Like finding a quiet spot in the detention centre to masturbate. Or falling in love with the Aussie women who contact them through social media. Or starting relationships with some of the local women on Manus. Or starting a relationship with another man, a fellow detainee, and how good their sex is – and how afraid they are of being discovered by locals. There was one guy, I said, a 22-year-old Iraqi, whom I was interviewing for a class action about life in detention. He said, Everyone wants to know about the conditions, the size of my room, the way the guards treat me, how much food I get, how long I have to wait to go to the toilet, things like that. No one ever asks me about love, or sex. I have the most vivid dreams. You wouldn't believe it, brother. Crazy stuff. Some days, that's all I do, think about those dreams. 'Cause we're still human, you know?

Beside me, Lauren nods. What research has established, she says, can be modified by remembrance. I wrote an essay on Walter Benjamin in undergrad. I don't remember the essay anymore, but I remember that line. We stop in the middle of the meadow for Lauren to adjust Edith's hat, which was hand-knitted by Lauren's mother. You're not as tied down by the past as you think, she says when we get going again. Guilt is all well and good, as long as it gets you somewhere. But don't get lost down there – don't get stuck doing elegy. There's something very seductive about it. It lets you paint a pretty picture, elicit some deep-seeming emotion, without really saying anything. A mournful, meaningless moment. She makes a motion with her hands as if pushing away the air in front of her, out and around like a kind of breaststroke. But the elegiac moment is apolitical, she says. It sucks the air out of the anger and righteousness you need to change things. It makes a useful thing – a memory of injustice – into a pretty bauble.

38

On the shelves in the hallway of the apartment in Boissy, beside my grandmother's cheap paperback murder mysteries, was an old leather-bound photo album. The photos are all poor quality, about the size of the palm of my hand, in black and white. In one of the photos, my grandparents stand side by side, my grandfather smiling in a double-breasted suit, while my grandmother holds a large bouquet. She is wearing an elegant black áo dài. She isn't smiling – she doesn't smile in any of these photos. Not in the one where they are in the same pose but also flanked by men in suits like my grandfather's and women in áo dài like my grandmother's (though none are in black like her). Not in the one where she and my grandfather are mid-stride towards the camera, walking through the gates of the church, led by my grandmother's father, the only other person dressed all in black, a shadow passing out of frame to the right of the picture – a thin man with sunken cheeks and round spectacles whose gaze catches the camera just as the shutters are closing. Not in the one where the photographer snaps my grandparents standing at the back of the church, a relaxed moment before the ceremony begins, with children swivelling in their seats to look at the couple and my grandfather smiling at the camera. Not in the one where they both sit in huge, uncomfortable-looking wooden chairs, hands clasped in their laps, eyes to the front, where the priest is holding mass. Not in the one where my grandmother is surrounded by women, all of whom are like her, stony faced.

39

Later, at a table in the ground-floor reading room of the Jerwood, I think about this most recent walk to Grantchester – remember it and modify it in my mind, so that it better relates to the next thought that is already forming, primordially, about the relationship between documentary evidence and truth-telling, a thought that takes a surprising turn when I find myself thinking about a plane suspended somewhere between Bangkok and Karachi in December 1989. Onboard, about halfway down the aisle, a passenger in the window seat is so absorbed in the view of billowing white clouds that the flight attendant has to wave the in-flight menu up and down a few times to get his attention. When he finally notices her, he turns away from the window and looks up in mild surprise.

Le menu, she says, offering the small card to him with her friendly, professional smile.

His face cracks open, beaming, and he responds in flawless French, thanking her and taking the menu.

As the flight attendant moves down the aisle, the image of the frail old man staring intently down at the cheap card, as if it were a great work of literature, stays with her. It is an image – seen from the flight attendant's perspective – that stays with me too, for it is the clearest picture of my grandfather I've found in all my research. Everything before this flight – the gunshots in the stone church, the hateful pale blue eyes, the cool dirt against his cheek, the ghosts and magic of

Chí Hoà – seems unreal to me, like a fable. And after the flight – well, that starts to get a little too close to home, for by that time I will have appeared in the story.

It is only on the plane, suspended between past and future, 30,000 feet up, that I can see him clearly. And it is only through the flight attendant's eyes, grey-green like Lauren's, the disinterested eyes of a stranger – eyes that are as close as I can imagine to God's eyes, far above the fray, looking impartially at brown bodies struggling in the mud – only through those eyes can I imagine the possibilities of what happened next, possibilities kept open only by her detachment. How I have longed to see through eyes such as these! But after all, why not? Why can't I pretend that my eyes are a different colour, that my gaze has a different intensity?

Try it, now: does he grab her wrist and speak to her in urgent, hurried tones? Can I imagine, against all probability and the rules of social interaction, against the pressing needs of the other 523 passengers on board the plane, against the chasm of their cultures and ages – he, a colonial subject of an empire that no longer exists, a forgotten ghost of an already embarrassing past, and she, young and unread, but global and connected in ways he can't possibly understand – that against all that, they nevertheless speak?

And what do they talk about? Perhaps the giant sable antelope, which adorns the menu he is reading so intently, about which there is information printed on the back cover of the menu: discovered in 1913, the *Hippotragus niger variani* distinguishes itself from other subspecies by the majestic curve of its immense horns, which measure over one-and-a-half metres. Now confined to the Luanda reserve in Angola, the population of this antelope, decimated by hunters, is only five hundred animals.

Looking at the drawing on the front cover, they might speak about how it seems a rather fantastical creature, its ribbed horns curving round to sharp points over its back like the very devil. It has the pointed ears of a donkey and an equine face, but the dainty legs of a deer.

The information on the back of the in-flight menu is followed by a single imperative in dark bold type. CARE FOR NATURE. Below that instruction is a small black and white logo, a panda, and the letters WWF. Then a Parisian address.

It must seem impossibly exotic to my grandfather that he is on a plane to a city where an organisation that exhorts him to CARE FOR NATURE could exist. Perhaps that is what he says to the flight attendant. That he could not have imagined, from his rattan mat in Cell 6, Section FG, that nature needed saving, or that humanity would have the time or inclination to save it. To which the flight attendant – who is an environmentalist, of course, like all of her friends, feeling as they do that it is easier to care about animals (what could be more innocent, after all) than to pick a side in a Cold War that in any case is about to end – might say that the giant sable antelope numbered in the thousands as late as the sixties. That, along with hunting, the antelope has been decimated by the long civil war in Angola, a proxy war between the Cubans and Soviets on one side and the Americans on the other, a conflict that continues to this day, and which the antelope has only survived, in minuscule numbers, because of its symbolic importance to the Angolan people, symbolising as it does vivacity, velocity, and beauty. Ah, I imagine my grandfather saying, smiling already at his own joke. So he – pointing to the antelope on the cover of the menu – he and I are the victims of the same struggle.

What I like most about seeing my grandfather through a stranger's eyes is that her indifference is not cold. On the contrary, it is her disinterest that allows her to look at my grandfather the way she does when she hands him the menu. For her, nothing is at stake. And so it is a look of undisguised sympathy – of tenderness, even – which is a feeling he has forgotten, among many others, during the long night of his captivity.

Not that he is the only forgetful one, nor the only one startled by the flight attendant's gaze. In all my forensic research, across decades and continents, have I ever looked as tenderly at my grandfather as she does on that plane?

So let me turn now, with a tender eye, to the ghost in seat 17A. First things first – he is not really a ghost, or a phantom, some haunting apparition, but a very skinny man. He is beginning to feel very hungry. He does not linger long on the giant sable antelope; the inner contents of the menu are of more interest to him. They were served a small appetiser on the short flight from Sài Gòn (Ho Chi Minh Ville on the menu) to Bangkok – some stiff cheese and dry crackers – but on the longer flight from Bangkok to Karachi he is looking forward to a more substantial meal. They have already been served an apéritif – he chose a glass of diluted Pastis, the sweet anise-flavoured liqueur reminding him of colonial Hà Nội – and soon, according to the menu, they will be served a dinner of smoked fillet of fish, grilled tournedos in green peppercorn sauce, roasted potatoes in butter, a fresh garden salad and cheese, followed by Tosca cake and Colombian coffee. On the even longer flight from Karachi to Paris – eight hours and fifteen minutes, according to the menu – he can expect a breakfast of orange juice, his choice of coffee, tea or hot chocolate, grapefruit, white cheese with fruits and cereal, garnished omelette, grilled beef sausage, and a brioche toasted bread roll with butter and jam. It is, he thinks, quite the feast after the famine.

Then, a few moments later – and here I am on firmer epistemological ground, possessing as I do not only documentary but *material* evidence – the stewardess hands him an Air France branded pen in striped tricolore of blue, white and red, and, closing the menu, he carefully begins to write in the white space on the menu's front cover, between the antelope's horns and its back: Air France. J est 8/12/89. En souvenir de mon passage de la mort à la vie.

And then, thinking perhaps of the one-year-old grandson living in Australia, he writes in English: Recalled to life!

I know, beyond all doubts, that this happened, or something very much like it, because as I sit in the Jerwood thinking about it, the menu is even now on the living-room shelf in our house. Which means that I know for sure that the words were in French and English, not Vietnamese; that his handwriting was small and neat – not shaky. He may have looked frail, but he was no mere wisp. He was substantial. That was the point. He had, after all, just come back to life. How often have I looked at the menu and wondered, what kind of man writes something like that? In memory of my journey from death to life. The phrase throws back my tender gaze: it's too grand, too much like something the chorus would say in a Greek tragedy. And recalled to life – wasn't that Dickens?

But if my grandfather is to speak to the flight attendant, it cannot be in the language of fatalism – of which Anamese is a dialect – which is utterly foreign to her. How, then, can we imagine the scene? We will have to suspend our disbelief, just as he is suspended in the sky, midway between Vietnam and Paris. Now, in our suspended state, we see him asking the flight attendant for the pen, see her watching him as he writes on the menu. Imagine her, out of politeness and curiosity, asking him what it is he is writing. And imagine now his reply, not in epic or tragic or fatalistic form, but translated, so that she might understand.

A love story, then. What could be more universal? And, well – why not? Is it so improbable that he might tell her his life story as a love story? Isn't there a family waiting for him at Charles de Gaulle, a wife, who hasn't seen him in ten years? And even if it seems unlikely that he should speak about love, that's the thing about miracles – they're a mystery. And isn't love always, at heart, miraculous? 'The heart has its reasons of which reason knows nothing' (Pascal). So let us imagine that it is the power of love that brings him back, resurrected, as it were, from the dead. That it is love he is thinking about as he writes in the menu. That it has always been a story of love, from the dirt field through the thirty years in-between, to Chí Hoà and beyond. We need to believe in something, so why not believe this? That love, like winged arrows of desire, can fly across time and across continents to set a man free.

Well – at least that'd make for a nice story, wouldn't it?

II. LENT

1

The first flakes of snow make us giddy with excitement. Lauren spots them first, floating past the kitchen window to settle on the low fence that borders the right of way that runs between our house and the neighbours'. I grab Edith and all three of us go out to the backyard, barefoot and bareheaded, to stand in the grey dusk and watch the flakes falling around us. It is hardly snowing – we know that – but it doesn't stop us from looking up at the sky and then down again, smiling with wonder. At one point, our neighbour, coming home from work and wheeling her bike down the right of way, laughs with us, the Australians marvelling at this not-quite snowfall.

When it really begins to snow, over the next two days, even the locals share our joy. I am in the college library when it begins in earnest – one minute, there is only a smattering of lazy flakes, evaporating almost instantly on lawn or tree. And then, suddenly, the view outside my window is swept away – all I can see is a pelting grey-whiteness. After fifteen minutes, when it lets up to a gentle shower again, the college grounds are completely, fantastically snow-laden. Students emerge from the dorms to take photos. Some build a snowman beneath the leafless beech tree, while others make angels. A group of undergrads gather up snow balls, and I hear delighted screams from the river as punters are ambushed from the bridge and the red brick walls overhanging the water. After trying, and failing, to do more of my reading, I find my bike in the quad, dust off the snow that lies on it like a mantle, and ride home along the Backs, which have been transformed into a Narnian landscape.

I get home in time for Edith's bath. It has become a routine: after a long day in the library, I take her from her high chair in the kitchen, where she has just finished her dinner, and take her upstairs to the bathroom. Now, as I undress her, pulling her cotton undershirt up over her head, I think of something I read that day, before the snowfall. In the midst of a lengthy passage on the Rights of Man in *The Origins of Totalitarianism*, Hannah Arendt had begun speaking about the great and incalculable grace of love, which she described, taking after Augustine, as the act of saying, Volo ut sis, I want you to be, without being capable of giving any particular justification for such a supreme and unsurpassable affirmation.

It made me think of Edith, and now, as I lift her naked body into the warm bath, of how it is impossible to give a reason for our having wanted her to be, how it is still impossible to give a reason for our wanting her to continue to be. I want you to be is not the same as I want you to be happy, or even I want you to be good – I want you to be happy immediately becomes, you must be happy, you must be good, or, worse still, you must be happy in ways that make me happy, you must be good in ways that I believe are good. You must not be unhappy, or happy in ways that make me unhappy. The only injunction within I want you to be is: you must be. You must not not be. An injunction and a promise: I will not let you not be.

Amo: volo ut sis. I love you: I want you to be. Heidegger, the Nazi, wrote that in a letter to Arendt, the Jew. Apparently it was a phrase he recycled for other lovers: a phenomenologist's pick-up line. Still, it has the ring of truth for me when I turn my mind to Edith, especially when she is before me – as she is now, pouring water from a cup back into the bath – but also when I behold her in my mind, smiling up at me from the floor or smearing yoghurt across her bib. Even – or especially – when I think of the manic, comic episodes that seem to be inevitable when travelling with a baby: catastrophic nappy failures, trying to time an expensive lunch around her nap, endlessly refining sleep routines to try to make up for dragging her halfway around the world. And yet it is also true that I mostly do not think about her during the day, when I am in class and at the library, when I speak with Lauren or ride my bike, or even when she, Edith, is with me, toddling from our living room into the kitchen – whereas Lauren's mind is constantly burdened with thoughts of our daughter, about her meals, her naps, or else simply thoughts of how overwhelming her love for Edith is – it is like a background hum, Lauren once told me. A hum I myself cannot – choose not to – hear.

Even now, as Edith plays with some farmyard animal puppets that lie facedown in the water, I am too full of Chí Hoà to play with her properly, too occupied with thoughts of how I should not be thinking about prisons, or about Vietnam, or even about my grandfather – but here I am, crouching by the bathtub, ready to catch my daughter should she fall as she slaps the water with her open palms, shrieking with delight, and I am thinking not about her but about the stack of documents I packed at the bottom of my suitcase without telling Lauren, and flew here from Melbourne, to sit on a shelf downstairs, unopened.

I think in particular about a black and white photocopy of an Amnesty International (French Section) newsletter from May 1983. Here is another genesis: it was this photocopy that I found in a drawer in an upstairs room of our suburban home, which I had been so sure could contain nothing of any literary interest, and it was this unexpected discovery that precipitated my father's explanation, a few days before I'd left for Christian Living Camp.

The newsletter's title was a mouthful: Chronique d'informations internationalise sur les droits de l'homme, les prisonniers d'opinion, la torture, la peine de mort. Down the right-hand side of the front page was the newsletter's contents – a snapshot of what was wrong with the world in 1983: the disappeared in Argentina, the dubious confession of Eamonn Kelly in Ireland, abusive internments in the USSR, tortured and murdered civilians in Zimbabwe, imprisonment for having long hair in Swaziland, enemies of the people in Libya, acquitted police officers in South Africa, torture in Turkey, military prisons in Bangladesh, torture and disappearances in Uruguay, executions in Singapore, secret trials in Guatemala, the extradition of Klaus Barbie, butcher of Lyon; it had astounded me, as a sixteen-year-old, that all that suffering could be placed under the one, all-encompassing logo, the candle behind the barbed wire. It had been this story – the discovery of the Amnesty International newsletter at the same time as the revelation about my grandfather's imprisonment – that I had told as the first chapter of my Bildungsroman during interviews for human rights internships and jobs.

At the bottom of the newsletter's front cover, below the contents list, were the appeals for May 1: 'two detainees among thousands' in Vietnam, Nguyễn Hữu Thời, deputy opposition leader under the ancien régime, in re-education since 1976, and ——, my grandfather, intellectuelle non-communiste, in prison since 1979. To the left sat two portraits, one of Nguyễn Hữu Thời – bespectacled, moon-faced – and the other of my grandfather – big-eared and flat-nosed, a long thin face and small, clear eyes. He looked out at me from the page as he had looked at me in life, in the tiny apartment: steadily, without hysterics or reproach; in a word, calmly, as if he had all the time in the world to say what he needed to say.

Inside the newsletter, on page 12, were three short paragraphs about him:

Born on 1 January 192–, —— graduated in law from the University of Saigon and worked as a lawyer at the Saigon Court of Appeal. After 30 April 1975 he stopped work and lived at home, looking after his children while his wife worked as a hospital nurse.

On 10 June 1978, —— was arrested at home by Public Security officials. He was held for several months by the police before finally being transferred to his present place of detention, cell 6, section FG, Chí Hoà Prison, in March 1979. He has neither been charged or tried.

Amnesty International believes his arrest to be due to his position as a non-communist intellectual and has adopted him as a prisoner of conscience.

I had never before considered the last sentence of that first paragraph. But now, as Edith pushes a small blue boat through the shallow water of her bath, I wonder for the first time at both its inclusion and its meaning. Who had written that line, and who had given it to Amnesty? Lived at home, looking after his children. Why include that information? Was it to make us more sympathetic, to underscore how little threat he posed to the regime? And what did it look like, this childcare?

It didn't fit with anything else I'd ever heard about him. It was never like this for us, an aunt told me. We all – the extended family – were laughing and eating around the long dining table in my father's younger sister's house, in Champigny, a few stops city-wards on the RER from Boissy. It was, during those gatherings, easy to imagine that this warmth – so characteristic of big migrant families, at least as they are generally depicted, or as I have most noticed them being depicted, hungry for what I didn't have – would have been commonplace for me too, if I had grown up here in France. That had been the plan, after all, when my father arrived here with my grandmother. But fate intervened: my mother's refugee boat had landed on the Malaysian island of Pulau Bidong, where her application for resettlement was accepted by Australia rather than France. Had it been the other way around, then we'd be French, and my weekends would have been spent around this table.

As it is, I have to make do with a family lunch once every few years, where I learn what I ought to have learnt in childhood. Such as the fact that, back in Vietnam, before the fall of Sài Gòn, mealtimes had been quiet, orderly affairs. We children didn't speak unless spoken to, said my aunt, not when your grandfather was at the head of the table. He was not a man to joke or play with his children. As she spoke, I looked over to him, sat apart from us on his own fold-out card table, eating his council-provided food, bland and textureless, but which he had come to prefer to the Vietnamese feast food we were eating so happily together. Eating on his own, he almost seemed to be waiting for me to finish with the others, to come back over with my notebook and recorder.

My many visits to the Boissy apartment didn't give me any more clarity about what the alleged childcare might have looked like. He never spoke to me about how he felt – though he had spoken about humility and patriotism and grace, and I suppose those are feelings of a sort, though not really recognisable to me as such. He never said anything like, I missed my family so much when I was in Chí Hoà. Or, I would have given anything just to see my children for an hour. Or, I was not there to see your aunts grow up – when they took me away, your aunts were little girls. When I finally saw them again, they were grown women, like strangers to me. Instead, he never spoke about them at all.

2

After he'd finished his council meal, my grandfather sat in his armchair while the rest of us started on coffees and dessert. And as my aunts teased me about taking my coffee with milk – Comme les anglais, they said – I watched my grandfather as he sat, neither dozing nor fully awake, but kept in a kind of weary watchfulness as he tried to coax his lungs into breathing. Later that day I wrote a list headed, Possible (Metaphorical) Explanations for My Grandfather's Illness:

As poetic logic – the disease fits the patient's phúc đức – in which fate and worthiness are intertwined – pulmonary oedema, excess fluid in the lungs – caused by a weak heart – a failure to take blood through the lungs – he had been well known for his public speaking – a booming voice – a successful lawyer and spokesman for his brother-in-law, the ex-governor – now there were no more cases to be argued – no more great causes to espouse – his lungs were failing him.

As an expression of character – an excess of feeling – after Kafka, who wrote in his diary: the infection in your lungs is only a symbol, a symbol of a wound whose inflammation is called Felice – but if that were so, for whom was that excess of feeling held, and how was it expressed?

As an expression of character – a deficiency of feeling – the virile, the bold, the great lovers, die from swords and bullets, from nooses and pills – they do not die from a weak heart.

As supernatural punishment – in Chí Hoà, despite his Catholicism, my grandfather had consulted the number Oracle – that is, the

Book of Changes, the *I Ching* – perhaps because the prison's design had been based on the *I Ching* and such a correlation was simply too much for an Anamite mind to ignore – and the Oracle had told him that he was being justly punished – Shih Ho, fire over thunder – the same hexagram that corresponded with Section FG – so all the signs pointed to a punishment for some transgression. And now, the heavens having willed it so, his pain is a match for any man's: he has such difficulty breathing that he can't lie down flat, so that his hospital bed has to be inclined forward – he hangs on to a plastic grip above his head as he coughs – I can hear the soft tissue in his lungs being torn apart.

As a failure of will – wellness and sickness are both manifestations of one's strength of mind – I was used to thinking of him as a man of great mental fortitude – in contrast to both my father and me – yet it was my grandfather who was lying in bed, too weak even to read the newspaper.

A weak heart – there's no part of the human body more susceptible to metonymy – the heart is just a fleshy muscle – but it is also the thing that *is* me – it is also a place with*in* me – the place that bruises.

I had written that list before Edith was born – before I had imagined that there could be an Edith. Now I find myself arriving at yet another interpretation, still metonymic, as all interpretation must be. I am thinking again about tenderness. But not about gestures, about being tender towards someone or something, but tenderness as an attribute – as a synonym for being bruised, beaten, chewed up. I am thinking about how tender one's heart must be after so much suffering. A black-and-blue, swollen lump.

Or am I thinking about both kinds of tenderness? Tenderness as gesture, and tenderness as bruised heart. Perhaps that is how I should think about the person – an aunt, I guess – composing on a borrowed typewriter the short notice that was sent to Amnesty International for their newsletter; both an act of tenderness, and a symptom of it.

3

The night porter says there is an hour to wait – at least – for a taxi. Busy night, he says, pointing out the glass door of the porter's lodge. Back in the main hall I had been at a Brexit-themed college dinner, where the after-dinner speeches were given by an ex-Tory peer and a Cambridge economist, the former against and the latter for Britain leaving the European Union. As we sat in the medieval dining hall, beneath the college's marquee tapestry, depicting its prized plate collection, listening to the economist talk about taking back Britain's sovereignty and all but saying that it had been Polish migrants who had ruined his beloved nation, the snow fell so heavily that by the time we began to filter out, the four front-court lawns were perfect white squares. I wander in search of a cab down the laneway that runs past the college and the Old Schools. A trickle of people in twos and threes amble along the cobblestones, gazing up at the snow-lined gargoyles and rooftops. For a moment I feel as if Lauren is here beside me, seeing what I see – but she's at home, with Edith.

There are no cabs in Market Square, just a line of students and townsfolk, a motley assortment of black gowns, miniskirts and peacoats, all waiting for chips and kebabs from the takeaway van in the middle of the square. So I decide to walk home, over the little bridge to cross the river, along the Backs, and up Madingley Road, around the corner past Lucy Cavendish, and then down the road towards Girton, a thirty-minute walk that just about covers the extent of my physical world at the moment, and which tonight covers also the breadth of my conceptual world – a half-hour in which my thoughts range through a landscape as familiar as the College Backs.

When I get to our terrace house, Lauren and Edith are both asleep. The house is dark and quiet, and warm too – the solidity of English homes is a welcome point of difference to Australia, where we were used to draughty Edwardian weatherboards – and, still buzzing with the thoughts that occurred to me on my walk home, I pour myself a tumbler of the Aldi whiskey we got on special, and, thinking of how a quiet house and a calm world allow a reader to become their book, and how, at the same time, it is the act of solitary reading that produces that quietness and the calmness, and how, at the same time, it is the reader's desire to be a model reader, their desire for quietness and for calmness, that makes it so – thinking of that, I sit down at the dining table in the living room and try to remember the thoughts I had on my walk home – as if thoughts can be possessed, rather than experienced; as if my thoughts are a book that I can lean into, to which I can be true, and through such trueness of reading make order, quiet and calm where before there was none.

4

It is on Garret Hostel Bridge, shivering a bit from the cold, and looking in at the empty Jerwood, ablaze with light because whoever left last hadn't turned off the lights, that I think of Laon, a small town an hour and a half north of Paris by the TER train. The town, exposed as it is on the Aisne plateau, is subject to just such a cold as I am feeling now. Whoever had written to Amnesty must have done so from Laon – it was where my grandmother and her children had first settled in France after fleeing Sài Gòn. They had secured safe passage through my grandmother's brother, the ex-governor, who still had, despite everything, a certain amount of sway with some people who mattered. In truth, they might – my grandmother and her children – have got on a plane much earlier, before my grandfather had been arrested, perhaps even before Sài Gòn had fallen, and then they all – my grandfather included – would have been in France together. But my grandfather, like his brother-in-law, had refused to flee – they had not yet learnt to separate Anam from Vietnam, or memory from place. Sài Gòn was home, and that was the end of the story.

Only it hadn't been the end of it. The family, sans patriarch, had left Sài Gòn after all, and settled in Laon. During my visit to Paris, when my grandfather was in the hospital, my grandmother mentioned that I had actually lived in Laon for six months when I was four; my parents had moved there with me from Melbourne. If things had worked out differently, she said, if the phone call offering your father a job hadn't come a week after he'd already given up and gone back to Australia, then Laon might have been your home. As it was, during those six months, my parents and I had lived as if it were going to be our home. You even went to maternelle, said my grandmother. You sang, Isabelle à les yeux bleus.

I think, as I walk down the lamplit lane to the left of Trinity's backs, of another trip to Laon, not as a child but as a young man, when I had left off visiting my grandfather in hospital for a day in order to catch the train north. Laon was really two separate towns, I discovered: Laon-en-bas and Haut-Laon. En bas, where the train from Paris pulled in, was, literally, the low town, where the majority of Laonnois – including my family – actually lived and worked. But it was Haut-Laon that drew the eye, a medieval fortified village perched high up on the butte, looking down over the station and the rest of Laon-en-bas. And though my family had never lived up there, it was to Haut-Laon that I went first, on an old single-carriage monorail system that took me up over the desolate train yards. Up on the butte it was very cold, and along the ramparts of the town walls the wind cut right through me, so I walked along the cobblestone gutters of twisting laneways into the heart of town, until I reached the square and the cathedral, where I met Monsieur Braems.

He had been sitting at a table on the terrace of a café in the square, in the shadow of the cathedral. A heavy-set, balding Belgian man, he was a former agricultural engineer who had been something between an uncle and an older brother to my family when they'd arrived at the centre sociale, a miniature housing estate, in 1983. A man of faith, he had been a deacon at the nearest Catholic church. He was halfway through a glass of Amstel, though it was sometime before noon. He recognised me right away – I had seen no other Asian faces since leaving Paris – and he greeted me like family, a hug and three kisses on alternating cheeks.

Braems was delighted that I had come to Laon, that I was interested in writing something about my family. Incredible people, he told me. Like saints, he said, crossing himself. It continued like that as he finished his Amstel and as we made our way to his car. What M— went through, he said, using my grandmother's adopted French name, which made it hard for me to remember that it was her he was referring to and not some French woman. I never met someone who suffered so much and yet carried herself with such dignity. And the children. They were all studying so hard, some in Paris, and then in the evenings they were writing letters, to try to get your grandfather out of prison. Such incredible people, he said again.

In his car, we wound our way back down the butte to Laon-en-bas, passing by the warehouse supermarkets on the edge of town and out into open countryside. Finally, after ten minutes of driving, we arrived at the centre sociale, a seventies toilet block of a building, painted a garish, pastel blue. It's on the very edge of the municipality, said Braems. I mean it quite literally, he said, pointing to a big ditch cutting through the field next to the centre. You see – that is the border of the municipality. On the other side, it's Mons-en-Laonnois. I used to drive your family to church in Mons. But there wasn't enough room, so the boys had to walk. He paused, then said, So you see – they could not have put the refugees any further from the rest of us.

That, he said, indicating a long squat building at the back of the centre, is the salle de réunion. We had Christmas there that year, when they first arrived, my family and fifty Vietnamese refugees. Only your family could speak French, so they translated for us. Well, they tried their best. Everybody was talking at once, telling stories about home – you can imagine.

I had tried to imagine them, that first winter in France. But, when I was growing up, we had not been a part of the large Vietnamese community in Melbourne – much less the Anamite one. Unlike so many other kids of the diaspora, my childhood was not marked by overheard conversations about the war, about the homeland. There was no escaping our Vietnameseness – there was no possibility of our being mistaken for Australians – but in their refusal to talk about the past, my parents were certainly not Anamites. Then again, they might only have been conforming to the place and time in which they had found themselves – the outer northern suburbs of Melbourne in the nineties, the fields of forgetting where former green wedges became house-and-land packages, where Tamil refugees and Singhalese migrants could buy neighbouring neo-Georgian mansions, and the Italian Croatian Slovenian Greek Macedonian Turkish Iranian boys at school all played wog-ball together, where the English Protestants and Irish Catholics were both just skips, where no one said a word about the Wurundjeri Woiwurrung.

Our own neighbours, an older Australian couple – Australian, in that time and place, meant white, of course – were, I discovered later, exemplary of that amnesia. At the time I only knew them as our kindly guardians during the school holidays, when my parents would leave me and my brothers home alone, with a strict schedule modelled on the school timetable and a box set of VHS tapes from a mail-order home-tutoring program with corresponding exercise books so that we could work on our Maths and English. While I was in charge of home school, as we called it – marshalling my brothers out of our bedroom and into the lounge room at the school 'bell' and then overseeing our respective tasks – meals and snacks for 'recess' and 'lunch' were supervised by our neighbours over at their place, once we'd trooped down our driveway and back up theirs.

It was really only Elisabeth who watched over us – Martin, her husband, rarely ventured into their kitchen while we sat at the bench to eat our vegemite sandwiches. In fact, we would hardly have been aware of him at all except as a vague presence in their bedroom, or as a nest of white hair passing along the fence line, but for the larger than life portrait that hung in their living room: Martin, in full dress uniform, standing to attention with brightly coloured war medals on his chest. Of course, Elisabeth never told us anything of Martin's army career, and my only reference for war came from watching *The Longest Day* and *A Bridge Too Far* over and over again – the only videos we had apart from the home school tutorials, and bootleg copies of *Paris by Night* – so naturally I assumed that he'd been in World War II, probably fighting Nazis. Evidently, I didn't have much of a grasp of time or age, either.

It wasn't until long after Martin had died – a heart attack: we watched from our front window as the paramedics wheeled out the trolley, covered in a white sheet, and though we had lived next door to him for as long as we could remember I felt rather disconnected from whatever was under that sheet, as if it had nothing to do with me, which is to say that I did not really feel anything at all – it was only then that I learnt, almost by accident, that he'd been a Vietnam War vet. And it was later still that I learnt that he'd been the wake-up-screaming-in-the-night, drink-a-bottle-of-whiskey-by-day type of vet.

None of this had been spoken about, not by my parents nor by Elisabeth, not when my parents had their few friends over, trekking out to the suburbs from Richmond and Collingwood, and not when they came home from work to pick us up from next door, where we'd be watching *Wheel of Fortune* – home school having finished at 3.30, like the real thing. There was an occasional trade in recipes – my mother's *Women's Weekly* recipes were all from Elisabeth, while the dishes that went back over the fence were, I realise now, surprisingly funky, not the kind that most suburban Aussies back then would eat, let alone make – unless, of course, they were already acculturated through multiple combat tours.

The only other cross-cultural exchange had occurred before I was born, when Martin had counselled my mother to give the son in her belly an Anglo name. Heeding his advice, but unaware of the linguistic and geographic subtleties, my parents settled on something sufficiently French to be character-building at my local primary school. Even their tiny South Vietnamese flags, gathered in clusters throughout the kitchen and lounge room in little terracotta pots, were carefully balanced with Australian ones: an each-way bet on remembering and forgetting.

So whether it came from a conscious refusal of Anam or merely from a disposition to go with the amnesiac flow, my parents did not provide me with a model for that gathering of Anamites in the salle de réunion in Laon on Christmas Eve 1983 – and without a model, a precedent, or an analogy – in the total absence of Anamite feeling – all I could think, as I shivered in the wind that whipped across the open fields around the centre, was that they must have been cold at that Christmas gathering, and I think it again as I pull my robes tighter around me and cross the roundabout to get off Queens Road and onto Madingley.

As I was taking photos of the centre, a white woman came out of the main building, looking at me suspiciously. It was only after Braems said to her that I was a writer that her suspicion gave way to enthusiasm. The mairie have forgotten we exist, she said. You wouldn't believe the state of the rooms here. There are no refugees here anymore, explained Braems, the whole centre is used for regular social housing now. You wouldn't treat your dog like this, said the woman. Her voice dropped to a stage whisper. There are Africans – she said négres – who come over here and the government puts them up in five-star hotels. But here the mairie leaves French citizens to rot in this place. This is where they put people to be forgotten.

5

Sitting at the dining table in our rented Victorian terrace in Cambridge – built in 1888, according to the plaque on the whitewashed facade – I imagine a novel called *The Crowned Mountain*, written by a white author, someone from New York. I imagine a cover for it: an Impressionist landscape in the middle of which, seemingly thrust up out of the bowels of the earth, is a looming mountain topped by what looks like an old, crumbling citadel. I imagine a blurb too:

Just outside Paris, in the old town of Laon, the aftershocks of Vietnam's half-century of war still reverberate. Over the course of a single day, 31 January 1984, the members of a family of refugees go about their daily lives. But the past looms over them like the shadow of the cathedral atop Haut-Laon. *The Crowned Mountain* is a lyrical meditation on loss, guilt and the possibility of redemption.

The author has some connection with Vietnam – a war veteran, a diplomat or, better yet, a hard-nosed foreign correspondent. Someone who knew my family in Sài Gòn in the sixties, someone who went home and still thought, from his Brooklyn apartment, about the war, and the rice paddies, and the language that he thought sounded like 'bird song'. Someone who wrote a couple of war novels, widely praised for their unflinching portrayal of the horrors and absurdity of the war, of all wars. The inhumanity of man towards man, and so on. Someone who then decided to turn his talents to remembering the beautiful people – saints, really – that he'd left behind in 1975.

So I imagine a puff quote beneath the blurb:

'——'s achievement is stunning: he has succeeded in truly humanising the Vietnamese.' – *New York Review of Books*

And another:

'Remarkable . . . for how beautifully it achieves its daring project of making the Vietnamese real.' – *The Times*

I imagine finding this book on my grandfather's bookshelf in his apartment, squeezed between *Light in August* and a Vietnamese translation of *Don Quixote*. I imagine a cheap paperback, spine almost completely unstuck, the corners of the cover curled up as if they were the leaves of some wilted, sun-battered plant.

6

The Crowned Mountain begins, I imagine, with an intimate scene – one that will best show off the author's knowledge. It begins with my grandmother, a Vietnamese woman in her fifties, on her hands and knees on the floor of their apartment in the centre sociale, sweeping the floor with a dustpan and brush, thinking of the dust as moulting human remains: dead skin, wilted hair and God knows what else. The children would be up soon and then there would be no time for anything, let the house rot as it may.

This is not the familiarity of a vet or an old newshound, it's the familiarity of a man who has married into the family, and it is from her – his Vietnamese wife, who is perhaps even a covert Anamite, forever telling him about the old country, complaining to him about diaspora politics, cooking for him dishes from the Mekong or Quy Nhơn or Nam Định – that he is able to see my grandmother's morbidity, her servitude, her motherhood. He sees her all at once, in a single easy glance – stooping, prematurely aged, self-consciously well dressed, even now, even with as little money as they have, lost in memories of the grand old house on Boulevard Gambetta in thirties Hà Nội, which had seen white tablecloths every evening, polished silver on the table, guests coming and going at all hours, and – most special of all – spotless, clean in a way that no Vietnamese house had any right to be. My grandmother is bewildered by these memories and the reversal in her life now, unable or unwilling to understand how it was that her Vietnamese home had been more civilised than this French centre sociale, that France – which she had always thought of as the centre of all things, fashion and power, and the home of Christ and the Virgin Mary, who had never been Israelites in her mind but French, just as Jerusalem and Galilee were part of a wider French empire and Jésus himself (never Giesu, as the Vietnamese spelt it) was blue-eyed and brown-haired – France was actually grey and dirty, dreary and unread, racist and poor. Even the French they spoke on the street was a mocking, bastardised version of the language she'd proudly made her children learn.

He sees my grandmother's raw nerves, how those nerves make everything shimmer, how they make the world's foundations insecure. And he would see, no doubt, my own raw nerves, if it ever interested him to look in this direction, at my own raw phúc đức, that could move me to this long and fruitless exercise of imagination in which I have worked myself up into a state of confected outrage and indignation – and all the while, my original aim of thinking clearly about my grandmother recedes.

7

The stars were shining – I only realise it now that I am back at my desk. As I started up the hill past Lucy Cavendish College, my eyes caught the faint pinpricks of light just visible in the penumbra on the horizon between the orange light pollution of town and the night sky. My gaze continued upwards as I stopped walking, until thoughts of Laon and imagined books were dispelled for a moment as I looked straight up at the sky, heavy with stars.

There, in the street and the snow, my thoughts were no thoughts. But now, retracing them, rethinking them, I find that I can give shape to their absence, sound to their silence. Thinking of it now, I can imagine the crunch of snow under my dress shoes, or the occasional car passing. I can hear Edith's voice, and see myself standing in the middle of the street gazing up at the stars, her voice singing, Up above the – or, to be more precise, singing the first four notes of that line – sol-sol, fa-fa – blurring the words together and mixing up her consonants, but the timeless melody comes through, bright and clear.

A while passed in which I did nothing but look up – and thinking about that, listening to my mind reproducing Edith's voice, I begin to feel that unbearable lightness in which everything is being pulled loose, unanchored, floating away. I might have been having an epiphany right then, standing in the snow in my robes staring at the starry sky. Or not. It was too cold to get my hands out of my pockets to fumble with my phone to try to snatch something lasting, something productive, from this maybe epiphany. So by the time I get home it – whatever it was – is gone, and all that is left is that sense of vertiginous inconsequence, and Edith's voice. But from that memory I make for myself an epiphany – if such a thing can be done.

8

Sitting at my desk, I imagine that it was there in the snow outside the college – a far more picturesque setting for an epiphany than a makeshift desk in a rented house – that I realised how I would start *The Crowned Mountain*, had I written it and not some Pulitzer winner: not with my grandmother on her hands and knees, cleaning, but with her voice. Because for me, she is her voice, more than any other thing – over the years, it has been her voice that has remained the same. At first, she had been only a voice: a scratchy voice on the phone from Paris to Melbourne, speaking rapid Vietnamese. And even after she became a body, my grandmother was first and foremost a voice, for the body was bent and frail, while her voice chided and cajoled, giggled like a schoolgirl, turned complaining into a literary form.

It was the voice that thanked God for everything, that told me stories I did not really understand – stories that showed the chasm of unfamiliarity between us, like the one she told me the first time I saw her after my grandfather's death, a death I had waited for but in the end missed: he'd lingered too long in that hospital bed, and so I'd returned to Melbourne before the end had come. My grandmother now spent her days alone in that apartment in Boissy, waiting for my aunt Thi to come home from work. The next time I visited, it was only the two of us – Lauren and Edith did not come this first afternoon, but stayed instead in the apartment we'd rented for the week in Paris proper. We sat at the table where once the three of us, my grandparents and I, had looked through their black and white photo albums as I'd asked them about life in the fifties and sixties for the book that I did not write.

My grandmother told me a little about the funeral – someone had read out a few short paragraphs that I, as the supposed writer in the family, had been commissioned to write from Australia, the sum total of my public output from years of interviewing and researching. Then she suddenly changed the topic.

9

I tell you, my grandmother said that afternoon, there are so many injustices in this world. So much suffering, I can hardly bear it. See – my knees are so weak, no cartilage left, just bone on bone. Grinding down, all that weight. Yes – all that weight, she said, pointing down at her belly, laughing and shaking her head at the same time. I was going to become a nun. I was only sixteen, seventeen. I thought, Father in Heaven, take from me this body and this soul and make them into your things; leave of me only this taking itself, this exile.

I had got my notebook out, something that occurred so often during family conversations with me that it hardly interrupted the flow of words. I furiously translated and transcribed. You see, said my grandmother, my soul was transfixed by a face – the face of a dead man outside our house. His throat had been slit wide open, an ugly flap that ought to have been too obscene for the morning light. His eyes were open too, and his shirt had been torn. On his chest they had carved, người phản bội: collaborator. His body was just outside our side gate that morning, but we didn't know him – it had nothing to do with us.

This image transfixed me because it was such a contrast to the smell of that morning, the sweet smell of the frangipanis from our garden, drifting across this obscenity like a cloak of perfume. Father forbade us from seeing the body, so naturally we all found a way. I saw the body from Eldest Brother's room, upstairs. He looked small from that high angle, and absurd, like a just-butchered pig.

It wasn't until later that I got close enough to really see his face. The men from the Sûreté had come and taken a statement from Father, who was now in his room, where I knew from the bitter, chocolate smell wafting from under his door that he was stretched out on his back, pipe on the stand by his bed. So I slipped out to the side gate.

He was covered by a white sheet, but it would be a few hours before someone could come by to collect the body: there were too many bodies to be collected in those days. Covered, he might have been a street vendor's wares, ready to be unveiled. I could see the outline of his face through the sheet – a blank face, a sketch that still needed to be filled out: the line of a nose, the faint impression of lips, hollows for eyes. It was unbearable, that blankness, so I pulled back the sheet to see his real face – it was young, a boy's face, not much older than mine, still contorted in shock at finding death. I liked him immediately.

Already by then the neighbours had gone back inside, and passers-by hardly looked twice; it was common enough in those days and everyone had their own affairs to worry about. Only one man took any notice of me as I stood with the sheet lifted in my hand. He called out, I wouldn't do that if I were you, Little Sister. He might come back to haunt you.

I retreated back into our house veiled in frangipanis – a good French house on the best street in Hà Nội. I walked around the house in a daze. My grandmother smiled, and for a second I could see her, a little wisp of a girl, wandering through that cavernous home. That face, she said, her smile still lingering, called out to me. I felt his pain so keenly, I cried out and clutched my throat. Father, now out of bed and shuffling through the house to his customary place in the first room, saw my tears. He said again that it had nothing to do with us. But, I thought, it has everything to do with me.

I found some paper in the house and started to make offerings. A bowl for him to eat from. Paper clothes to wear. A paper wife and paper children. I made him a paper cross, though I didn't know if he was Catholic. I took three coins from Mother's purse. Then, as the heat of the day was beginning to set in, I burnt the paper by his body in the street, and put the three coins in his mouth. I said a prayer.

I thought his face looked a little less contorted, a little more at peace. But then I thought about what would happen in just a few hours. A municipal worker would come by, pushing an awful cart meant for sacks of rice. The cart would already be loaded with bodies. The worker would pick up this new body – his body, the body of this beautiful boy – and toss it onto the cart with all the others, as if it were just another carcass. When the cart was full, the worker would pull the cart to the trenches that had been dug on the outskirts of the city and filled with limescale, for all the dead that had been appearing in Hà Nội for weeks now, as if it really were the end of days, which I thought it must be, though Eldest Brother said it was not God's work but the Japanese, who had hoarded all the rice for their war machine, and the French, who had done nothing to stop them, and the Americans, who had bombed the trains and ships carrying relief rice from the South. But I did not understand such things, and I preferred instead to think that the dead littering the streets – even our street, Boulevard Gambetta – were a sign that the final revelation was at hand.

Revelation or not, I could not leave *his* body to be tossed onto a cart by some callous undertaker, to be deposited like rubbish in a mass grave. Still – what could I do? I knew that Father would not approve of my getting involved. We shouldn't get mixed up in all these goings on, he was always saying, especially to Eldest Brother. Obey the law, he would say, and everything will be okay. Which law, Eldest Brother would reply. Which side? But Father had an answer for that too: All the laws, all the sides – French, nationalist, Japanese – it didn't matter. You obey the law of whichever soldier is standing in front of your door.

My grandmother shook her head and waved her hand, as if to dismiss me from the room. But it was not as if I cared about *him* because of which side he was on, she said. How could I? I didn't know anything about what was going on. I was just a silly little girl who wanted to be a nun. I thought that the world wasn't important to me. No, the love I felt for that dead youth was like the love I felt for a brother. And who would leave a brother like that on the street? Who would let a brother be thrown onto a cart by some creature hoping to earn a few piastres from the municipality? I could not bear it.

I went and stood outside our side gate, just a few metres from his body. His face was covered again. I prayed for this new brother of mine. I closed my eyes and all I could smell was frangipanis. It was so hot, I could hardly breathe. I thought about the mornings when I would sneak out when the world was still grey and unmoving, before the world had found its colours. It was the only bad thing I did in those days. I would walk to the park, where the gardens were still asleep, dreaming of a time without people. I loved that grey garden that had not yet known humanity. Later, when the colours arrived, green, pink, and orange, it looked gaudy, like a cheap painting. And, sure enough, people came too, following the colours, and I would sneak back home once I'd felt the chill air on my bare skin. When I opened my eyes, the street was empty, and the body was gone.

10

Not long after, said my grandmother, I begged Mother to let me become a nun. I understood already that a woman's fate in this world is very hard. I understood, too, that there is a certain freedom in giving yourself entirely, for your whole life. A true sacrifice is always freely given. Sacrifice – hy sinh – must be the guiding principle of any woman.

Mother cried when I told her. I was her baby, her favourite. So she did what mothers have always done: she asked me to defer my decision, to postpone, to wait a year. How could I refuse? It was only a year, and I had a whole life ahead of me to sacrifice. So I said yes.

I felt like the condemned prisoner who receives a stream of visitors all telling them to confess – confess and your sentence will be commuted, from death to life. But what had I to do with life anymore? You're mad, Eldest Sister would say to me. She came and sat in my room and tried to talk to me about the world, to entice me back to life. Why are you burying yourself alive, she said. You who love Tino Rossi, and dancing the paso doble. She quoted Verlaine at me: You with the eyes of a young fool – what will you look at, walled up inside your tomb?

But it was not what my sister said, nor what Mother said, that finally convinced me to be selfish. It was books. I always knew that if it weren't for books, I would have been good. Even from a very young age, it had been my only vice. I always had my head stuck in a book, and if I wasn't praying I was thinking about those stories of tragic love, of a woman's hard fate. Mother and Father, who were normally so strict about our moral education, allowed me to have this little pleasure. They thought it was harmless enough. But it was to my books that I turned in that year of waiting – there was, after all, nothing else to do.

And as I re-read these stories of romance and chivalry, I found that I was forgetting *his* face, the face of the dead boy outside our house.

It's strange, but around the same time your grandfather appeared in our house. He was one of Eldest Brother's followers. I liked his hands. They were big hands, with long slender fingers. The hands of a scholar, an artist.

One day, he tried to speak to me, but I just turned away and walked up the stairs to my room. My year of waiting was nearly over. Downstairs, someone explained to your grandfather that I would soon be leaving for a nunnery.

He started to write me letters, letters I didn't reply to. You see, I had already decided to be selfish. It was the books, said my grandmother again, and she pointed through the glass door to the narrow corridor, which led to the Boissy apartment's two bedrooms, and was lined from floor to ceiling with cheap paperback novels. Well, she continued, the year passed and I did not go to the nunnery. But I kept him waiting – she laughed, covering her mouth with her hand – I kept him waiting five years!

The day I said yes, I thought I had chosen life. We were married a year later in the Big Church in Hà Nội. I remember clutching the bouquet to my chest, as Father walked ten paces before me. We were both dressed in black. My sisters and sisters-in-law flanked me in white. Children were ducking in and out of the crowd.

I remember everyone telling me that morning that I looked beautiful; my hair was curled in short waves. But I already felt old – as if I'd spent my entire youth on being transfixed by that face. I had a premonition then, as they sat me down next to your grandfather in matching heavy wooden chairs to stage a mocking repetition of that first yes – I suddenly felt that I had not said yes to life after all, but only to more waiting.

But the premonition faded. I had Thi, then your father. They made Eldest Brother governor, and your grandfather was his trusted advisor, spokesman, lawyer. If I ever thought about *his* face it was only as an image that haunted the corners of my vision – it no longer called out to me.

11

My grandmother got up then, heavily and with much sighing, and made her way to the galley kitchen. I followed her, notebook in hand. There, she sat on her wheeled chair and rolled herself between the cupboards and the stovetop, where a stockpot of phở gà had been simmering while we talked. Neither of us spoke as she ladled the soup into a bowl and topped it off with fresh herbs. Only when I was sitting at the narrow table on a plastic stool, soup spoon in one hand and pen in the other, did she go on.

Then came the first separation, she said. The French were leaving. Eldest Brother had hired an American plane to take us to Sài Gòn – me, Thi and your father, still a babe in my arms. Eldest Brother and your grandfather did not come – they still had political work to finish.

So I flew south in an American warplane. My ark was a plane made to deal out death. I was sick on that flight – my first ever. I thought at the time that it was the new baby in my belly, or the strangeness of flying. I didn't know then that the body has its own ways of marking an absence.

When we got to Sài Gòn, we were put up in the Hotel Majestic. JFK had just been staying there, on his fact-finding mission. He was only a senator then – but still, you get the idea. No expense spared for the little sister of monsieur le gouverneur. Now Eldest Brother was a delegate for North Vietnam. We soon heard that he was off in Geneva, playing politics again. But your grandfather had not flown with him. And now the border was closed.

I waited for him. I knew practically no one in Sài Gòn. I already thought the city was crawling with Americans – I had no idea of what was coming. They seemed to be tall and brutish compared with the French. I couldn't understand their language.

I waited; once Thi and your father were asleep, I sat at the Majestic's rooftop bar and watched ships coming and going along the river, feeling my belly and imagining, against all reason, that your grandfather was on one of those ships. I walked the kilometre down the Rue Catinat to the Pink Cathedral and prayed. I walked past the yellow Sûreté building opposite the cathedral and, being as ignorant as I was, imagined that they were on my side – that if all else failed, I could turn to them to find your grandfather. I walked to the post office, more violently pink than even the cathedral, and looked for letters I did not believe would arrive. No letters, but we did get news that the Communists had shot the priests at Phát Diệm. I walked along the river and thought that all the activity on the docks meant that life would be strong enough to survive here, that these southerners with their fishmongers' voices must be survivors. I walked, and I waited.

Our neighbour in the hotel, an old colonel, had a map with the new line drawn across it in thick black marker. I liked looking at the map as I waited. I liked having the colonel tell me that the line was only a line on a map. The real border was the Bến Hải River, wide and fast and deep. Cross the river and you were safe. But the bridge over the river was closed. The colonel told me that the northern half of the bridge had been painted red, the southern half yellow.

Waiting on the roof of the Majestic, the sunsets seemed quite profound. In Hà Nội I had loved the grey world before dawn, the way the world slept on without me. But here in Sài Gòn I came to love the sunset, the way it faded so quickly and left the city cloaked in its own night-time haze. I remember electric lights were appearing in the downtown districts then, so that the stars had to fight to be seen. The sunset never waited – not when I spent too long seeing to Thi and your father, not when I lay in my room too sick to move – and I liked it for that, that it had the strength not to wait.

And then, all of a sudden, like the last burst of light over the horizon, my waiting was over. Your grandfather had been delayed, trying to find his parents. He had not seen them for eight years, not since he had left home for Hà Nội. It took him weeks to find them. Everything was so chaotic, you can't imagine. They were no longer in Vinh. After weeks of searching, every day getting more and more dangerous for him, he finally found them closer to Hà Nội, in Nam Định. His parents had eight children, but they were alone now. Your grandfather's brother, Minh, had left home at the same time he had, but Minh had not stopped in Hà Nội. Minh had gone further north. Maybe he had joined the Communists after all – no one had heard from him. And your grandfather's sisters, they had all left, one by one, to join the Communists too. Some of them were married now, to Communist cadres. Others were in Hà Nội, working for the new government.

Your grandfather gave his parents money – almost everything we had. He gave them the key to our small house on Hàng Đào, full of the things I had had to leave behind before I got on my American warplane: the piano, our bicycles, my father's pipe, your grand-father's books, a Chinese landscape painting that had belonged to Mother's father, and much else besides. Your grandfather said goodbye to his parents, knowing he would never see them again.

Then he crept his way south, sleeping rough all the way to the Bến Hải River. He swam the river in the dark, the strong current pulling at him as he made his way across, waiting for the gunshots. None came. He returned to me, whole and healthy enough. We moved out of the Majestic and into a chic apartment on the Rue Catinat. I had thought then that the waiting was over – that my life could finally begin.

12

Aunt Thi came home in a whirl of shopping bags and kisses. When the groceries had been put away, she looked over at the table where my notebook lay alongside the black and white photos that had been plucked from the album and said, That's enough of that. She began tidying up. We can't wear Mamie out, can we? My grandmother made a show of protesting, but I could see that she was tired. On my way out of the apartment, Aunt Thi asked, And when will we get to read this famous book?

13

The next day – a Saturday – I returned with Lauren and Edith. We set Edith on the floor before my grandmother, who entertained the baby with her rosary beads, twirling them above her head like a mobile. Aunt Thi asked when we were going to baptise Edith. Lauren and I looked at each other nervously. We thought, I said, that we might leave it for her to decide.

Decide what, exactly?

To decide if she – I looked at Lauren, but getting no assistance there, I forged on – to decide if she believes.

Aunt Thi sighed. You mean, to decide whether you believe. But this is not how faith works. It is not a buffet. You can't pick and choose. You believe or you don't. And if you believe, if you have faith, then you must raise the child in that faith.

I remembered then that Aunt Thi was going to theology night school on the Rue de Bac, attending classes after her day job as a lab scientist. On the weekends, when there were no visitors, she worked on her dissertation – a treatise on love, faith, and walking in the works of St Augustine.

It's not that you cannot have doubts, she continued. Indeed, you must have doubts – a faith that is too certain is not faith but fanaticism. But this letting the child choose nonsense – that is not healthy doubt. That is abdicating your responsibility to decide.

A sudden outburst of crying from Edith spared us having to reply.

We fussed over the baby while my grandmother and Aunt Thi prepared lunch. Soon afterwards, Aunt Hương arrived, cooing, Where is the baby? as soon as she stepped through the door. After examining Edith from head to toe – just to remind us, I supposed, that she was the *medical* doctor in the family – and pronouncing the baby to be a picture of health, Aunt Hương slapped me on the back and said, Ah, the writer! But when can we read the book?

She waved away my mumbling about a work in progress and said, Now tell me. What kind of book is it? Who is it for? And is that why you are going to England, to work on it?

No, not really, I said. Feeling Lauren's eyes on me, I went on. I'm actually going over there to do another law degree. A master's.

What, more law? You had better watch out – you might end up studying even longer than me.

Uncle Quang, who must have come in while Aunt Hương was examining Edith, said, Sounds expensive. I laughed nervously – and affirmatively – but he didn't let me off the hook. So, how much is it? A few thousand euros?

I told him, and he let out a whistle. I could see my grandmother behind him, in the galley kitchen, shaking her head. Even Aunt Thi and Aunt Hương looked appalled. And you borrowed all that from your parents, said Uncle Quang. I knew that they were living the good life in Australia, but really, to come up with that much cash – not bad, not bad.

You know, said Aunt Thi, your father was very clever too. He was studying law when the Communists took over. He was going to be just like Father, but they put an end to that. And your mother was even cleverer. That's where they met, studying law. We all used to say how brilliant they would be.

And instead he became a postman, said Aunt Hương. And she works in a bank.

My father, a spectral presence on a red Honda, riding through the Boissy apartment in his Australia Post uniform, trying to deliver dead letters, muttering inaudibly to himself. My mother, an iron spectre, marching ahead of him, adding up the accounts. Everyone, it seemed, was terminally in the red.

Not that we should be defined by our jobs, said Uncle Quang.

Aunt Hương shook her head. It's not that – I'm not being judgmental, Brother. It's just the wasted potential. Which is why we're so proud of our nephew. Getting into Oxford – even if it is a *little* expensive – what a star!

I tried not to catch Lauren's laughing eye as Aunt Hương asked, And what does that mean for your book? It must be all finished, then. She put her arm around my grandmother, who was just then putting a plate of steaming bánh cuốn on the dining table. I hope you showed how strong Mamie has been. She kept us together all these years!

My grandmother broke away from the embrace to fetch more food, muttering about her airheaded daughters. We all laughed. Finally, as we sat down to eat, Aunt Phương came in, cheeks flushed from rushing, apologising as she flew around the crowded room to give everyone kisses. Lauren slipped away with Edith to feed her in the room where the hospital bed for my grandfather had once been.

Aunt Thi ladled me some nước mắm onto my plate. It is true, she said, that Mamie was our rock. And it would be so wonderful if you could write that down. It would give us – the whole family – something for the pain of that time.

It would redeem the past, said Aunt Hương.

But that's exactly the problem, said Uncle Quang. The very fact that you know that the past needs redeeming means that any redemption is going to be false. Sure, you can tell a nice story years later. But the truth is, and he looked right at me then, the truth is – we were waiting for Father for ten years, and never in those ten years did we know that he would come back to us. We spent ten years waiting for something we could not know would happen – that we could have no expectation of happening. And nothing you write now can bring back even a day, even a second of those ten years. Now he looked at Aunt Hương. You say that Mamie kept us together – well, I'm sorry, I'm sorry, Mamie, but it's just not true. We weren't together. We each suffered alone. We waited alone.

I don't remember it quite like that, said Aunt Phương.

You were a kid, said Uncle Quang. It was different for those of us who had to go out into the world.

But I agree with you, said Aunt Phương, even if my memories of the waiting are a little different – as you say, I was young. But still, I agree: we were waiting. How is Nephew going to write about that? We didn't do anything. Nothing happened. Life was suspended. Oh, of course he can show us waiting, show us putting off big decisions, avoiding relationships. But he can't redeem the waiting simply by showing that the event we were waiting for came to pass. That would be too anachronistic. It would make our waiting expectant, when it was anything but.

So why write it down then, if it's not to redeem it, asked Aunt Thi. Is it to honour your grandfather? Or to honour yourself? And if it's the latter, I am not criticising you. You would not be the first. Just as lacking faith is not a personal fault – but you must own up to it. You must be honest.

Father used to say, said Aunt Phương, that Marx was wrong about a lot of things, but that he was right when he said that men make their own history – just not as they please. We are all enslaved by our circumstances. That's what he would tell me when I got upset about his clients, who sometimes came to the apartment on the Rue Catinat – upset that there was nothing that could be done for them. I think he was trying to tell me that we have to wait for justice. That we do what we can in our own time, and that is enough. Justice will come, he'd say, but not right now.

I remember, once, a young mother came to the apartment. I must have been so small, Father probably thought I was still napping, but I was hiding behind the door to the room where visitors were received. I heard Father telling this woman that there was nothing he could do for her son, who had some kind of mental disability. I didn't really understand what the case was about, but I heard the woman's deep sobs as he spoke. I heard her telling him about her misery, and her shame, at her son's condition, and Father explaining to her again that there was nothing he could do for the boy. But he went on, saying that he did not mean he wasn't going to take on the case. He would, because it was important that the government be held accountable. He even had some hope that the government might be persuaded to change its ways. But any such change would come too late for her son. If change did come, it would be for someone else's son, someone else's daughter. And was she willing to go through a gruelling process, for that kind of justice?

Aunt Hương looked at me with shining eyes. Oh, Nephew, she said. You see how much you are like him? Warriors for justice! Kind hearts, that's what it is. You simply can't bear to see another soul suffering.

I hope, said Uncle Quang, that you at least remember to charge for your work. I, too, remember clients coming to the apartment. I remember their empty hands – or, worse, clutching a box of mangoes or some other ridiculous gift. As if we were still in the village, and Father was the village headman. He always said yes to these beggars. One or two charity cases, I can understand. But this was an open door. And this from a man who had no time for us, his children. Always busy, always reading. A kind heart? I wouldn't call it that.

I tried to explain, then, that I had not written a hagiography of my grandfather – I had not really written anything at all. Just fragments of his stories. I tried to explain that I didn't know about kind hearts and fighting for justice and all that. Mostly, I tried to say, I did the human rights work because I could not imagine doing anything else – because when I tried to do other things they felt hollow and unimportant, unreal – and that helping a client, even if I was not really helping, even if I was just patiently explaining that no help was possible, that all there was to do was to wait without expectation for change – even then, that felt real, that felt solid – or at least, more real than anything else. And that's what those fragments meant for me too, I tried to say, they gave me something to hold on to. Tiny handholds on an otherwise sheer cliff face. Which is why I carried those fragments around with me, even when I was no longer working on them.

That, at least, is what I tried to say. But it didn't come out right. When Lauren emerged with Edith, she found me surrounded by my aunts and uncle, all trying to get a word in. You can't borrow someone else's moral seriousness, Aunt Thi was saying, to cover up the lack of your own. Who pays the bills, Uncle Quang was saying, someone has to, someone is always paying – whether you realise it or not. You're too humble, Aunt Hương was saying, just like Father! Like rocks to weigh you down, Aunt Phương was saying, to keep you from floating to the surface.

14

When I finally get to our front door, my fingertips are frozen. My socks are wet through my leather shoes from trudging through the snow. Tomorrow, according to the forecast, it is going to rain, and then all this white will go grey and brown, turn to sludge and melt away. Before I go to the kitchen to pour myself that whiskey, and before I sit down at the dining table to try to take advantage of the quiet home, I stand in the dark hallway beside the landlord's cheap full-length mirror and open up S's latest recording from Manus on my phone.

He is listening to music – a classic Singhalese song. He sings along to the lyrics in his gentle, rasping voice, coughing every few seconds. I know that he's been sick all week, that there are hardly any medical staff left for the men on the island, and that as a result he has been waiting for three weeks to see a doctor. I stand in the hallway and listen to him listening, and I wonder if he thought it was worth it, leaving behind his wife and two daughters, his parents – in fact, his father had died the year before, and he had not been able to go to the funeral, something he mentions to me over and over again, how it is a great shame (and he meant here not just a mild sense of regret, but the deep world-shattering feeling that comes with failing to live up to your own sense of dignity) – all to end up languishing on Manus for four years and counting.

I've never asked him about his reason for fleeing Sri Lanka – best not to, in case what he tells me doesn't match with what he told

Immigration – so I don't know what danger he'd been escaping. Was he at risk of being arbitrarily detained? Tortured? Murdered? I know from reading country reports that all that is possible, especially in the remoter parts of the north. But they were only possibilities, and the four years on Manus are a certainty: how to weigh one against the other, an abstract risk and a concrete suffering? Even if he got off the island after four years, managed to start a new life somewhere, in a place where he would have to learn a new language, a new culture, find a new job, begin to send money home, and only then – after many more years, presumably – would he be able to see them again, his mother if she was still alive, his wife and two daughters. They would be different people by then, the girls especially – they would have grown up without him, knowing him only as a pixelated image on video calls and as the bedtime story their mother told them for years about the handsome young man who had braved many dangers and boarded a tiny boat to get across the vast, swarming sea, all to find a better life for them, his daughters. By then he would no longer resemble such a fairytale, if he ever did. And I wonder, would he say, then, that the waiting had been worth it? Or would he tell me that he should have stayed – come what may?

15

We can't redeem the past for those who lived through it. With that melancholy thought I sit down at my desk after my walk through the snow and return to my primary sources: the digital recordings of my conversations with my grandparents in the Boissy apartment, conversations that happened years ago now, and whose paths are so well trodden, backtracked and re-laid in my mind that to return to them now – to actually listen once again to their voices, to their actual words and the silences between their words, to the whirrings and clickings of the appliances in the apartment, to the monotonous babble of the television that was always on in the background – is like returning to a childhood home to discover that the memory of a pivotal joy or trauma is in some essential way false – because the bedroom window does not, in fact, look out to the neighbours' backyard; because my youngest brother could not have been there that day after all. Which is to say that, as I sit at my cluttered desk and listen to one of the handful of recordings that bear my grandmother's name, among the dozens and dozens I named after my grandfather, I feel the hollow vertigo – falling but somehow numb, deadened – of realising that once again I have imagined her all wrong. I have failed to imagine her as an Anamite. Or, more accurately, I both did and did not know that she was an Anamite.

Looking back on the pages that I had imagined for *The Crowned Mountain*, I see that I modelled my grandmother – the self-sacrifice,

being led astray by books, the excessive love, the waiting, entombed –
on Teresa of Avila and Antigone, patron saints of Anam. And in doing
that I recognised, however subconsciously, the Anamite strain in her
voice. For it is not only Catholic practice to model oneself on the
saints, but an Anamite one too: to believe that one can learn how to
live from our dead. But she is not an Anamite like my grandfather
was an Anamite. That is clear when I listen to her recorded voice,
which has none of the coherence that I attributed to her, and none
of that forward momentum. That was my grandfather's way of being
an Anamite, because for him Anam was a glorious battlefield, or a
cemetery for heroes. For my grandmother Anam is not something to
be recovered, it is something in which you are submerged, into which
you sink – are buried. For her, all her pasts are present, overlapping.

She says: I keep thinking of my mother laid out in her bed, in
her best áo dài, her hands arranged over her belly and wrapped up
in rosary beads, and her mouth has fallen open a little, from what
I don't know, the heat, maybe, and your father is staring at her, arms
folded across his chest as if they could protect him, and he stays there
longer than he wants to, he is a favourite of hers after all, he sits with
her in the afternoons, after his nap, still full of sleep, and she tells him
such stories, stories I didn't know she knew, stories she would have
laughed at when I was a child, stories she would have said were for
người nhà quê —

— your father is three and the light of my life, he is so beautiful, but
I can never say it, I can hardly even think it, it is such a sin, so prideful,
but all the same he is, you can't imagine, so beautiful that I can still see
him now – the brightest thing, running all over the apartment on the
Rue Catinat with that perfect toddler's body, compact and powerful,
squealing with delight —

— your aunts take me to the Louvre, I've been in France for twenty
years and finally someone thinks to take me, and all I can think is that
if a woman made any of this there would be more toddlers, naked

toddler bodies in marble and acrylic, but they only have babies there, and even then only cherubs, who have none of the power, none of the muscle of the toddler —

— the nanny is out, which is why I'm chasing him, watching some dreadful American cowboy movie, and though I'm shouting at your father to stop, I'm really too full of love for the way his shoulder blades move under his soft skin, the way his belly makes a taut round drum, so full that I'm thinking, wondering, how could this have come from me, what God am I to have made such a thing, oh yes, I think such blasphemous things, but you can't imagine what he looks like, with his back to me, head turned up and staring out the window at the heavy rain outside, stretching out a little hand to catch some of it on his fingers —

— your father always claps his hands in delight at her stories, for all he cares about are the happy endings, he doesn't understand that the suffering that led up to the happiness is not undone by the ending, it is still there, it comes back every time the story is told —

— how does such a bright thing fade, and could I have done something to stop the fading, oh, it was easy, then, to make the sun come back out, but then they get older and older and the right thing to

do gets harder and harder to see, until your grandfather is in prison and then it is gone forever, I never see it again, not even in flashes, which makes me feel sorry for you, because I wonder whether you have ever seen it, his brightness, or if you only know the shadow —

— it doesn't start with your grandfather's imprisonment, no, it's much earlier than that, when your father is still just a little boy, when my mother dies and there is a huge funeral where the mourners go as far as you can see down the street, they are there for my brother, not for her, but still, you've never seen anything like it, they stop the traffic for the procession to the Pink Cathedral, they load her body in its oak casket, imported from France, into a carriage fit for a European queen, horse-drawn and covered in gold, topped by a crucifix and driven by a man in livery, and men and women in white walk behind, and a dozen rickshaws in front bear flowers from such important people, and out in front is your father, holding up a picture of her, and it is so hot that I drape a handkerchief over his bare head to keep the sun off him, because his hands are busy with the photo frame, which is as big as his torso, and I am sure he is still thinking, as he trudges along, about my mother's body, which he saw as it was laid out in her bed, in state for family and friends and important people to come and see, and because we have to wait for all the arrangements for the grand funeral to be finished she lies in the bed for too long in the hot weather, the apartment is full of her smell and the children are already scared of her room even before we make them line up and shuffle in to look at her body while the photographer takes the photo, the children with their arms crossed and their heads bowed, and I am sure your father is still thinking of that moment because, afterwards, he wakes from nightmares and I hold him, and after that, after the funeral, he is never the same, never as bright as he had been when he was running through beams of sunlight in our apartment, though truth be told I already knew, I'd always known, that he would be an unhappy child, I am so full of dread even when I am nursing him, when he is just a little lamb, and there is no one else in the grand house in Hà Nội but his sister and me, because your grandfather is away again and everyone else has already gone south, and we are only waiting for my brother to arrange the plane so that we can go too, even then, I feel such dread while he suckles at me, he has his father's ears, and the family nose, and I know he is going to be unhappy, that he is going to have an unhappy life like his father, which is why, when you are born, I ask him on the phone, does he have your ears, does he have the family nose, and when he says no, and then he says yes, I think, one out of two is not bad —

— as long as you understand that happiness can only be a rest, not a destination, that the bright perfect child who smiles when you sing 'Kìa con bướm vàng' will not always be that happy, that life will not always be walking down Rue Catinat to Sunday mass in the Pink Cathedral, family trips to Đà Lạt, taking your father to the Cercle Sportif as a special treat, watching from the shaded seats by the pool as he walks between your grandfather and my brother, holding their hands, ready to swim in the pool where all the great men of the nation swim —

— one out of two means a chance at happiness, however temporary, and obviously Australia is a happy place, though when your father tells me that he's leaving us for Australia I think, what is Australia, what is in Australia that can make you leave me like this, when your brother and sisters need you, when your father is still in prison, and it's like he's a little boy again when he tells me, Maman, I am leaving, Maman, I am sorry, and I don't feel like being a mother right then, I am so tired, that's what I want to say, that's what I've always wanted to say, I'm tired, tired of waiting, tired of answering my children's questions, why why why, that is your father, all day long, he says that you are the same, when he calls us from Australia, he says your đích tôn is a motormouth, that you don't stop speaking, but when you get on the phone you hardly say anything, why would you, you don't know my voice, we've never met, I'm just an old woman on the other side of the world, and now you're here, asking me questions, why why why, and I tell you, I am tired, and —

— how I wish you could see him, your father, at the Cercle Sportif, in the water with your grandfather and my brother, then you would understand what I am talking about, how under the surface of every perfect happiness, suffering is ready to break out, fear and uncertainty too, as when your grandfather pushes your father across the water to my brother, only the distance is a bit further than they had meant it to be, and my brother has his back to the poolside tables where I am sitting so I can see directly your father's face widening with fear, his eyes bulging and his arms clawing at water and air, his body sinking down into the water, and in a second or two it is over, as my brother steps forward and lifts your father out of the water, and he is already laughing nervously at his moment of shock, but I am still thinking about his eyes, which looked past my brother and straight up to me, confused, pleading —

16

The next night there is no college dinner to attend, no long walk home through the snow. As forecast, it rains all day, and the white wonderland gives way to a dull, dreary greyness. A scheduled call with Lauren's parents has been cancelled – they have confused the time zones – so we are left to fill in the day, and get on each other's nerves, without interruption; me trying to study, her doing the housework and looking after Edith.

Around six we begin the night-time routine. Edith has her dinner – chicken meatballs and sweet chilli sauce – at her high chair in the kitchen. Then she plays with her plastic cups in the bath while I pour the warm water over her tiny back, which is both muscled and fat, both complete – a human back in miniature – and completely underdeveloped, incapable of the entire range of motions available to a fully grown adult.

After Edith's bath I carry her to her room, where Lauren has prepared a bottle of cow's milk. I pick out a book – *Spot Can Count* – and begin to read as Edith pulls at the flaps and moos at the cows and quacks at the ducks. When we are finished, I kiss her on her head and lay her down in her cot, where she will grizzle and sing softly to herself before finally turning onto her belly to fall into her toddler's sleep.

Downstairs, I clear away enough of the papers and books on the dining table to make a space for the bowl of chilli Lauren hands me, and I sit down to read and eat while she eats on the couch, watching a TV show about neighbourhood disputes between Kensington billionaires. This is what most of our evenings are like, once Edith is in bed.

I am supposed to be reading about the Hart–Radbruch debate. Are there any 'necessary connections' between law and morality? It is a question of analytical precision. I am supposed to strip away everything I know about the world and see whether the two concepts are connected as a matter of logic. But I wonder whether I have the cognitive firepower to do this sort of thing – whether I once did but have now lost it – to hold a concept and turn it around, examining it from different angles, to see how the light of other ideas appears on its revolving surface. Instead, I think about my experiences as a lawyer – a critical misstep for a legal philosopher, to slip from theory into practice – and of one client in particular, M, an Iraqi refugee with a long scar from his mouth to his left eye, who had come to Australia as an eight-year-old boy in the late nineties. His parents had divorced soon after, and he didn't much like school. He fell in with the wrong crowd, and his teenage years descended into a series of minor offences – cannabis possession, shoplifting, drink driving. Then, in his early twenties, on a night out at the casino, he punched another young man, who fell to the pavement. As the young man lay on the ground, M raised his right foot – wearing a size-10 Blundstone work boot – and stomped down on the man's face. One witness said she had heard the cracking of bones from ten metres away. M pleaded guilty to assault causing grievous bodily harm and was sentenced to three years in prison.

That was all before he'd become my client – I first met him, in the windowless interview room, when he was released on parole. The day he got out, he said, they handed him a letter from Immigration, which said that the minister was thinking about cancelling his refugee visa on character grounds. M had never thought about getting Australian citizenship – it had never occurred to him, and his parents didn't think much about those kinds of things. Now Immigration wanted to send him back to Iraq. I don't know anything about the place, he told me, his knee bouncing so hard that our cheap floor rocked along with him. I can barely speak Arabic, he said. I've got a kid here too. What's going to happen to her? He had tattoos down both arms and wore a large gold crucifix over his t-shirt. I converted, he said, when I was inside. The guy who came and spoke to us – the prison had an anger management and violence prevention program, often staffed by Christians – he was, you know. And no Muslim ever helped me, so –

Over the next few days I prepared a submission for the minister. I wrote fifty pages about M's history – how his family had got out after M's uncle had been disappeared; how M had trauma counselling throughout high school; how his parents had divorced after a long period of domestic violence; how he'd completed three behavioural programs in prison, all with very promising feedback from the instructors; how M had been remorseful about his actions, something acknowledged by the sentencing judge; how his daughter, an Australian citizen, would grow up without a father if M was deported. I attached letters from a priest, from M's current employer, from the mother of his daughter.

The minister's response was perfunctory and formulaic. He'd considered the best interests of M's Australian daughter. He'd considered the advice that M's prospects of rehabilitation were good to excellent. He'd considered the fact that M no longer knew anyone in Iraq, that his prospects there were less than promising. Nevertheless, the minister was persuaded that M posed an unacceptable risk to the Australian community . . .

I had read these lines dozens of times before, copy and pasted from one rejection to another by a twenty-something staffer, to be presented to the minister for his signature. The last time I spoke to M, he was in the detention centre on Christmas Island. By then, we'd gone through all available appeals and now he was just waiting for the knock on his door, when he would be given fifteen minutes to pack his things before getting on the plane where he would sit, handcuffed, flanked by two Serco security guards, first to Dubai, and then on to Baghdad.

17

Even when I do think about Hart and Radbruch, as I'm supposed to, I think about the wrong things. I think about how Gustav Radbruch, bald, moustachioed, a brilliant German law professor in the early twentieth century, had been so spectacularly successful as a scholar that he was drafted in to serve as Minister of Justice during the Weimar Republic; how he was the first professor fired by the Nazis after Hitler seized power; how he would later say that being fired was the greatest honour of his life; how he lost both his children in the war – his son at the battle of Stalingrad, his daughter in a skiing accident; how he later collected the legal maxims and epigrams he'd sent his son over the years in a book posthumously published in 1954 as *Kleines Rechts-brevier*; how, in 1941, he decided to finish writing the thesis his daughter had been working on when she died.

None of that is supposed to be of concern to me as a student of jurisprudence. In fact, it is not the Radbruch of those years that I am supposed to be reading about but the postwar Radbruch, the Dean of the newly reopened law faculty at Heidelberg, the Radbruch who launched a ferocious assault on the legal positivism of German lawyers – the doctrine that there are no necessary connections between law and morality. Radbruch said that it was this idea, that a law is a law if it has been enacted in the correct manner, regardless of its content, that had made the legal profession – the supposed defenders of the rule of law and the rights of man – supine lackeys of state power.

To which HLA Hart, Oxford Don, replied: how foolish to think that an idea – in an obscure discipline like legal philosophy, no less – would have made a skerrick of difference to the rise of the Third Reich. Do we really think a theory of law could have encouraged a German judge in July 1934 to strike down the law that retrospectively sanctioned the Night of the Long Knives?

No – that does seem like high-minded foolishness. But then, isn't it just as foolish for Radbruch, in the middle of the war – at the zenith of Nazi military power, when the thousand-year Reich looked more likely than not – to spend his time, and his undoubted intellect, on completing his dead daughter's thesis about the history of German farmers? Or to put it another way, what if that posthumous thesis and his own *Kleines Rechts-brevier* were not the extent of Radbruch's mourning? What if we were to think of all his postwar work – the attack on positivism, the debate with Hart – what if all that was not, as everyone presumes, a scholarly engagement with law and politics, but rather his own way of honouring his dead? There is something in that – that a man like Radruch might spend his remaining lifeforce on tearing down the laws that his children lived and died under, on saying that those laws were no laws at all. But as much as the idea appeals to me, I do not think that it will find favour with Professor Simons – at least, not enough to anchor my own thesis on it.

18

Giving up on Radbruch and Hart, I think instead of Melville's 'Bartleby, the Scrivener', in which the eponymous character is hired to copy, laboriously, the words of his employer, a Wall Street lawyer, from one page to another. From the beginning, I think, Bartleby's employment is engineered to make him spectral: the lawyer erects a screen in his office so that Bartleby may be out of sight but still responsive to his employer's voice, a voice gilded with the smug satisfaction of being ensconced among rich men's bonds and mortgages and title deeds. He calls out to Bartleby, his best employee, who responds, like a very ghost, agreeably to the laws of magical invocation.

But then, one day, when the lawyer calls to his servant as usual, Bartleby responds by saying: I would prefer not to. For the rest of the story, Bartleby repeats this formula in the face of increasing pressure and destitution. I would prefer not to. He loses his job, then is evicted from the lawyer's offices. He is taken to debtor's prison, where he prefers not to eat. And finally he is a wasted body, huddled at the base of a prison wall.

I had once imagined that there was a kind of utopian – even a millenarian – hope in the story of Bartleby, to be found in his curious formula: I would prefer not to. As an undergraduate, I had thought that Bartleby's preference not to work, not to respond to his master's voice, suggested some hope, forlorn or otherwise, in the potential of a life without waged labour.

Then I'd graduated from university, and got my first law job, as a paralegal working on the class action about conditions in immigration detention, a case so complex and unwieldy that it was still trudging along years later when I returned to it as a lawyer, conducting interviews with detainees. But as a paralegal I worked on discovery, trawling through the three million documents the government had handed over to our firm – emails, memos, spreadsheets, calendar items, reports, web pages, receipts, letters, photos, media releases, newspaper articles, phone logs, metadata – and tagging them as irrelevant, relevant, or highly relevant. In some ways, it was these documents that would form the backbone of the case. The interviews the lawyers conducted with detainees, including the ones I conducted in the following years, functioned more like guides for what to keep an eye out for – complaint forms about the lack of suitable clothes for a detained baby, the notes made by the private medical contractors about self-harm – rather than being evidence of anything much in their own right. People are – well, people: fallible, with corroding memories, warped by emotions and politics; only hard documents could substantiate their testimony.

Despite its importance, it was numbing work. I sat at my desk, looking at the documents in a bespoke program that had been designed by a wunderkind who, when he dropped in to the firm once a week to see how the paralegals were getting along with his latest tweaks, would always stay and chat about how he had done a law degree too, but that he'd seen the writing on the wall. There's nothing a lawyer can do that an algorithm can't, he was always saying. Instead of getting admitted to legal practice, he had begun his start-up, which he said was now doing really well, employed four people, full-time, had an office in Fitzroy in a converted brothel, had secured some pretty significant investment from a firm in San Fran, and that was all before the start-up had really even achieved its major goal, which was to develop a fully automated discovery program that would do away with the need for human paralegals, who, it had to be admitted, often mis-tagged documents, missed relevant information, took too long on lunch breaks, or – as was the case with me – simply got too bored, too overwhelmed by the sheer number of the documents that they had to review. By mid-afternoon I inevitably had to leave my desk and walk quickly through the open-plan cubicles to the lifts that would take me down to street level, then through the busy lobby and out into open air for fifty metres, where I stepped into a convenience store and ordered a lukewarm sausage roll, to be eaten as quickly as possible on the unstable metal seats lining the street-facing window, hoping that none of the lawyers from the firm would walk past and see me brushing flakes of dry, crumbling pastry off my only suit.

Soon, I imagine, there will be machines to sit at desks in Cambridge, with algorithms to read what they're supposed to read and produce the research they're supposed to produce. Machines to complete abandoned family histories, to write bespoke versions of every book for every reader: finally, no one can complain of being overlooked. Algorithms to remember everything for us so we can get on with forgetting.

Getting ready for school, and the ghost of my father had not stirred from his room. What, I might have wondered, is the difference between resistance and apathy? When is refusal merely torpor, paralysis? I waited in vain for the spectre to appear on the battlements, to tell me what to do – to tell me how to avenge him, how to redeem the past. I wait for him to deliver me a letter marked, For my heir. Finally, it was time to go – school was about to begin. Waiting no longer, I started walking.

A colleague of mine had once worked for one of the international criminal tribunals, prosecuting senior government and military figures for war crimes and crimes against humanity. The tribunal operated in the normal way of courts: witnesses appeared in a witness box, swore to tell the truth, and gave evidence about what they remembered. Sometimes witnesses could give evidence in a closed court, where no journalists were allowed, where even the alleged perpetrators were not allowed to be present – though they could read the transcript of proceedings. Sometimes witnesses gave evidence from remote locations by video link so that they wouldn't have to be confronted by faces – sympathetic, inquisitive, adversarial or otherwise – as they recounted the murder of their families, their rape by uniformed soldiers. But even then, the tribunal had the impression that witnesses were leaving things out. So they granted witnesses an additional option of testifying a second time, in an empty room, where the testimony would be recorded. Then, after fifty years, unless the witness at some point decided they wanted the recording released, it would be destroyed – without anyone having heard it. The idea, my former colleague had said, was that many of the witnesses might have more to say, things they would not or could not say before another person, but that not saying these things was only going to compound their suffering. Some experts thought that it could do them real psychological harm. So the tribunal decided that it should create a space for people to speak. And – well, you must see, my colleague said, it was not the same as speaking to no one. The room was not completely empty. There was a recording device in there. The machine was listening.

19

It is past midnight now, and I have hardly got through any of the reading for the morning's classes. A familiar panic begins to set in, about the money I borrowed from my parents to come here, the job I quit in order to return to study, about Lauren, asleep upstairs, still jobless and friendless after five months here. It is the panic of squandering an inheritance, of foreclosing the future.

Closing my computer, and giving up even the pretence of any further productivity tonight, I go to the suitcase that is still only half unpacked on the living-room floor and retrieve my copy of 'Bartleby, the Scrivener', the one non-school book I'd allowed myself to bring over. I read again the story's end, in which the lawyer recalls the rumour that Bartleby had previously been employed as a subordinate clerk in the Dead Letter Office in Washington, a place where Bartleby, or so the lawyer imagined, handled dead letter after dead letter – letters without destinations, rubbish to be burned. Letters that contained, in the lawyer's imagination, rings for now-dead brides, banknotes for now-starved paupers, letters on errands of life that now sped towards death.

I read all that again and I think about the letter my grandmother had sent to Mme Mitterand, the wife of the then President of France. The letter was written as an appeal, from woman to woman, from wife to wife, for one husband – the President – to help the other husband – the political prisoner. An errand of life that, we can assume, reached its destination, unlike Bartleby's dead letters, for it prompted a reply, typed out on the official letterhead of the First Lady, and hand signed by her, too. The reply arrived on a most auspicious day at the centre sociale outside of Laon, being 31 January 1984, the feast day of St John Bosco, the patron saint of editors and publishers, and the saint-name of my grandfather, who was at that very moment four years into his ten-year imprisonment – so expectations were high when my grandmother opened the reply at their too-small kitchen table, laden with a meagre celebration for the Feast Day, while her children crowded around her, my father among them, and read it out in a clear voice – the reply expressed the most heartfelt condolences for my grandmother's situation, hoped with the utmost fervour for my grandfather's release, and regretted, immensely, that there was nothing the First Lady could do.

20

That night when I go upstairs to bed I realise that Lauren is not asleep, as I had supposed, but lying in bed with her bedside lamp on.

You should at least try to read, I say, pointing to the little pile of books beside her. You've got to finish *Carpentaria*, at least.

I can't, she says. I can't keep my focus on anything new. I can only read things I've read before. The words have to be familiar or else I can't stick with it. I don't know what it is. A tired mind.

She does look tired, drawn and pinched at the corners of her eyes. She has lately had a way of getting lost in the middle of things too, stopping halfway up the stairs and asking herself what it was she had been going to do.

You know, she says, when you leave each day for class or the library, I have to try to find a way to fill in the next five, six hours? I leave the house, even though I have nowhere to go. First I have to put Edith in her warm clothes, because it's so cold outside. Sometimes that goes smoothly enough – she'll lie there on the floor of her room. But often it's a struggle. She tries to crawl away, she cries when I pull clothes over her head. Fresh nappy, then an undersuit. The closed-toe leggings, a cotton t-shirt. A woollen jumper, her beanie. And then I bundle her into that Nordic snowsuit we got at the baby shower. Then I have to dress myself. The same jeans I wear every day. A thermal top, then the black turtleneck jumper – again, that I've been wearing every day for three months. The padded coat from the charity shop near the Grafton centre. My beanie. I put her into the pusher and we go through the park, or down Huntingdon past the surgery, or down Victoria Road and through the cemetery – it doesn't really matter, because we always end up in the same place, in town, at the café opposite the Round Church.

For the walk down the hill I'll listen to an audiobook, but it has to be something I've read a dozen times. *Jane Eyre*, or *Middlemarch*. Edith sleeps in the pusher, and I walk and barely even listen to whatever book it is I'm listening to. It's like white noise. I'm not really thinking, either. I'm just on hold, waiting for the baby to wake up. If she hasn't woken up by the time we cross the river, I'll go to the children's book section of Heffers, or have a look around the M&S Foodhall, or wander along the market stalls in the square. But I always end up at the café. There isn't room inside for the pusher, so we sit outside, on the little bench facing the street. The double-decker buses turn down there. They're too big for Cambridge. I'll be thinking that the town is a bit picturesque after all, and then another bus will roar past.

Because I'm there every day – did you know that, that I'm there every day – the barista knows my order. He brings the flat white out to me and we speak a little, about the weather. But we don't really say much. To him I'm just a mum. What does a young guy like him have to say to a mum? Sometimes he waves at Edith; she's usually awake by then. But he's just being polite – you can always tell when they're just being polite. Then I pay, and there's still three or four hours to fill.

Do you remember, I say, when we first got together, you always told me you wanted to have a baby before you were thirty. And when I asked you what you'd do if it turned out, for whatever reason, that we couldn't have kids —

I said I'd have to rethink my whole life plan, she says.

Become prime minister.

Or an artist. The thing is, she says, I can't even think beyond June. You finish your exams, you hand in your thesis – then what? I can't picture it. Okay, so we'll live in London – but what does that look like? Live in London – it's just a phrase, a string of words that people like us say. Edith, growing up in London. I can't even begin to imagine it. I can't place her there.

So is it something specific about London? Because we don't have to —

No, it's not London. Or maybe it is, but not just London. It makes it harder, sure – whenever we're there I feel lost, the city, the way it spreads out, the way you move through it, it doesn't make sense to me. But it's more than that – I can't imagine us *anywhere*.

It's strange to hear you say that. Because I spend all day projecting us into all sorts of places, all sorts of futures.

You mean projecting yourself.

Not just myself. I daydream about us constantly – about where we'll be living, about our lives in twenty years. True – I'm also imagining conversations I'll have with future colleagues, lectures I'll give one day.

And I don't daydream at all. I'm thinking about Edith's next meal, about our next meal, about our grocery list.

For a long time, I say, I've been trying to put my finger on why it felt so oppressive when my dad would disappear into his room. Why was his non-presence so —

— present?

Exactly. And I wonder now if part of it was anger – that we weren't enough. That our future together wasn't enough to snap him out of the past.

He would prefer not to. And you wanted him to say, Yes.

I wanted him to say something – anything. To plan for the day, or dream about the decade to come. Anyway, my point was – you had your baby by thirty.

Just.

So you have it all – your greatest dream, fulfilled. And still plenty of time to become PM.

She laughs, and turns off the lamp. We lie there for a while, not speaking. Then we begin to touch each other, like teenagers fumbling in the dark. I try not to think about how long it has been – since well before the birth, during her happy second trimester – and think instead of how strange it is that knowledge of this sort – the knowledge of another body, that I had thought I knew so well, how to move it, how to make it respond – can be lost, that I can spend so much time with her, go through so much together, and still be reduced in this moment to being a stranger, wondering aloud whether it is this that she wants, or this – here, or there.

21

The problem with *The Crowned Mountain*, says Simons, is that it is not really rooted in a place. It is nominally set in Laon, but the truth is your grandmother's voice is unmoored from any specific place – certainly, she does not belong in that provincial French town, which so clearly wishes her presence away. Simons furrows a brow. I believe that it was the great Vietnamese nationalist Phan Bội Châu who said that, for a human being, the greatest suffering comes from losing one's country. There is an echo there, is there not, with Simone Weil, who said that the methods of European colonialism produced a terrible uprootedness that was like a sickness of the soul. Perhaps she was thinking of the Vietnamese she knew from her work with dissidents – including Vietnamese nationalists – imprisoned by the Vichy regime. Vietnamese who, like Trần Đức Thảo, had travelled to the metropole to complete their Western educations, only to find that those Sorbonne halls were not for them, that their place was the country they had left behind, and that this realisation had come too late, that the country that had been theirs was already lost. Simons looks at me carefully, apparently gauging my response to his speech. Perhaps, he goes on, you had hoped that by speaking with your grandparents, by writing things down, you might secure for you and your family a country. It's not as if your grandmother doesn't speak of many places. The home veiled in frangipanis on Boulevard Gambetta. The easy luxury of thirties Hà Nội. The glamour and danger of Sài Gòn in the sixties.

Grey, decaying Laon. But which of these places is her place? Which of these times is her time?

There is the apartment in Boissy too, I say. Either a sanctuary or a tomb, depending on how you look at it.

Simons puts down my pages. Don't take this the wrong way, he says, but there is something surprisingly cold about your writing. I did not think I would detect the lawyer once your thesis took this personal turn. I had expected that by deciding to go personal you would – well, get more personal. But instead I'm left wondering what your grandmother's predicament really means for you. Perhaps that is a poor choice of words. Not what it means for you – if meaning is conceptual or intellectual – but instead, what does it feel like for you?

Isn't that the point, though, I say. Unlike Phan Bội Châu or my grandmother, I did not lose my country. I simply didn't have one to begin with. How can you miss what you never had?

So any sadness for you is at one level of remove?

It's not even that it's vicarious. It's confected. I have to work myself up to it. I have to do all this listening and reading and writing, to try to make this loss real for myself.

And do you succeed?

It reminds me, I say, of Alexis Wright's provocation, about the swan that strays into brolga country. She is writing about the impact of dispossession on a people's capacity to sustain a vision. Can culture survive intergenerational tragedy? And if so, does it get stronger or weaker with each tragedy? Wright has in mind the accumulation of loss upon loss, of colonisation followed by genocide followed by racist assimilation followed by neglect followed by catastrophic climate change. Swans, she says, are on the move, appearing in places where they have never been seen before. What happens, she writes, when there is no story for swans in the places where they are now migrating to? When you have no cultural story that fixes you to a place – how do you take the ancient spiritual law stories that belonged to you when you move to another place?

My own sense of loss is like a shadow of that loss – my culture was not destroyed, only warped and made subservient. It was my connection to it that was destroyed. But that destruction happened before I became conscious. Ironically, no one really understands that – I am free to claim a connection that doesn't exist. In fact, between my face and my name, that connection is pretty much assumed. So you see, I'm free to write as if I were still in swan country. It's only when someone reads closely, as you have done, that the illusion falls away. Now you see me for what I am – someone who cannot feel his own loss. So I appropriate another's loss as my own.

Because —?

Because my own loss is too minor. It's trivial, in the grand scheme of suffering.

Yes, I see. Simons leans back in his chair and speaks to the ceiling, which I now see is covered in water stains. Or, he says, can you not feel your loss because it is so total? So total that your feelings are conditioned by that original loss – the primordial loss gives you your language and therefore sets the limit of your world?

If that were the case – if the loss of connection, of country, constituted my consciousness – I could hardly know that, could I? There is no position outside such a loss from which I can view myself. Perhaps you could say instead that the place I have been imagining is constituted by that loss, and that is why my imagined place is so different to my grandfather's, or my grandmother's: we are reading from different founding documents. Which would be why my Anam – for that is what it is, isn't it? – was unrecognisable, until now, as a version of Anam at all.

You know, before I was a law professor, says Simons, I was, if you can believe it, a music journalist, in London. I was a young father too – I guess that is why I've thought of it. I was mostly an appendage of the music industry public-relations leviathan, polishing up press releases and publishing them as reviews. But I had a grand ambition – I was going to write the definitive account of London in 1977. You can guess how that turned out. But what I'm trying to say is that you should write what you need to write, and I'll mark it on its own terms. Simons looks at his watch. Ah, time for the faculty meeting.

It's not just a sense of place, I say, getting up from the chaise longue. Wright talks about writing in a way that makes all times equally important. For Wright, time and place are one thing. Country and time immemorial aren't separate concepts. Country *is* time immemorial, the beyond-memory root of everything. And time immemorial *is* Country, is the ongoing and never-ending relationship of responsibility; to belong to Country is not only to belong to a place – that is a Western way of looking at it. To belong to Country is also to belong to time immemorial, to epic story, and to that relationship of responsibility – it is as much a question of what one belongs to as where. So it follows that, if my grandmother is a no-place woman, then she is a no-time woman too. What connection does she have, in her too-small apartment in Boissy, to time immemorial? To an ancient storytelling tradition? To epic time? No – she lives in the eternal, ever-more-compressed present. All her pasts – thirties Hà Nội, sixties Sài Gòn, eighties Laon, today in Boissy – are now. Her bones have always ground up against each other like mortar against pestle. She has always been just about to enter the nunnery. She has always been – is still – waiting for my grandfather.

22

All diasporic peoples belong to the same time-place. It is part memory-place, part here-and-now, part Babylon, or Zion. Different peoples have different names for it. Or, if you prefer, different peoples belong to different provinces of this same time-place. My family and I belong to the time-place called Anam.

23

In Anam, my grandmother is always waiting. And my grandfather is always in prison, in the DMZ, or, as he is in this time-place, in hiding, along with other former presidential advisors, for having dared to criticise the president's brother and spymaster, Nhu. She is waiting in her apartment in Sài Gòn, with a gun in her handbag, wearing her best áo dài – cream embroidered with silver fleurs-de-lis – waiting for a car that might be a black Citroën or a blue Renault or a yellow Peugeot, a car that will stop just opposite her apartment, outside the Hotel Le Grande on Tự Do Street, which she has always and will always think of as Rue Catinat. The driver will start smoking a Gauloise, which will be the signal for her to kiss the children goodbye, put on her aviators and walk down the five flights of stairs to the street, where everyone looks at everyone else from behind averted eyes, spying and watching for spies, because this is Ngô Đình Diệm's (Republic of) Vietnam, and though this republic will be remembered fondly – fanatically – by much of the diaspora in the coming decades, the order of the day is paranoia, and corruption, and the virtual exile of former advisors. Which is why my grandmother is waiting for a car to ferry her safely through the streets of Sài Gòn, teeming with Nhu's agents, to the mountains around Đà Lạt, where my grandfather is hiding. It's why she carries a gun in her handbag, which she will describe to me fifty years later as a very pretty silver handgun, and I will still, all those years later, detect the reflected glamour in her voice as she speaks.

A glamour and danger belied by the housecoat she wears as she waits in the cramped galley kitchen for my grandfather and me, in the living room, to finish speaking about my grandmother's brother, who had at one time been Diệm's Minister of Information and Propaganda and, prior to that, the last governor of the French protectorate of Tonkin. He had co-ordinated the evacuation of a million refugees fleeing from North to South before the partition, an operation codenamed Operation Passage to Freedom by the US Navy. All that was before the Manifesto of the Eighteen, and the press conference at the Caravelle, and the November coup attempt, and the arrests, and the flight to the mountains.

But for once my grandmother can't wait any longer and she interrupts us from the kitchen to talk about the pretty little silver gun, and how the car for which she is waiting – whichever one arrives – always smells of cigarettes and sticky leather, and how she jumps in without speaking to the driver but instead turns around to look through the back window to see if they are being followed. All she sees is the sea of grim faces on Hondas and bicycles, weaving in and out, chatting, eating, drinking, smoking, honking – a moving feast – with eyes flickering at the car driving erratically in their midst, suddenly turning down an alley, or stopping outside the market, where my grandmother runs out of the car, plunging into the crowd, to meet the car again on some other corner, all the while waiting for a hand to grab her arm, or for her way to be blocked by some thug in a suit, so that she holds her handbag tight to her body and feels the reassuring weight of that gun inside. Or she plunges into the crowd and finds a xe ôm to take her to a hamlet just outside Sài Gòn where the man with the Gauloise is waiting for her. Or Aunt Thi wears her own cream áo dài and mother and daughter get out of the car together, walking briskly through the market in opposite directions. Or the car just turns back, having spotted a tail, to drop my grandmother back at the apartment, rather than leading the spies to my grandfather's hiding place, only for her to find a tall thin fellow in the apartment already, playing with my father, and looking up to smirk at my grandmother as she opens the door, as if to say, we can get to you and your family whenever we like. That feeling has never left anyone in my family, the feeling that catastrophe – in the form of a man in a suit bearing orders, written or unwritten – is always just around the corner, about to knock on the door, so that our waiting – for reunions, for results, for the rapture – is always also a deferral of the dreaded catastrophe: as long as we're waiting, then the worst thing has not happened. And so as she waits, my grandmother thinks, if he was dead, I would know it. If they'd caught him, someone would have told me. All the while feeling, if not thinking: if I don't know, then he can't die, if no one tells me, then he can't be caught; if I close my eyes and ears and wait, then all will be well.

24

To get to the Cambridge municipal library, Edith and I have to make our way past the shiny shopfronts of the Grand Arcade, past the Apple store and Jamaica Blue and into the lifts outside John Lewis, and then back across the upper floor of the shopping centre, past the bench where teenagers in school uniforms go to kiss, and on to the library's entrance. The library is spread over three floors, and is filled, in the way of public libraries, with a representative sample of Cambridge's unwaged and unproductive: some of the town's many homeless men at the free PCs, high-school students in clusters around the tables that are noticeably – and deliberately – missing from the shopping centre, and young parents like me, looking for a space out of the weather where our children can roam.

Having got some more proofreading work from her old employer in Melbourne, Lauren is now in the college library, while I try to fill the morning with Edith. I park the pusher in a corner of the children's book section, alongside four or five others. Edith totters her way towards the shelves, where she will pull book after book onto the carpeted floor. Nearby, a girl – perhaps seven or eight years old – sits on a beanbag, absorbed in a battered copy of *The Dark is Rising*, while her brother, a couple of years older, flicks popcorn at her.

Last night I'd gone to bed late, trying to follow an idea about defining Anam according to the criteria for statehood set out in the Montevideo Convention, an idea that had seemed so promising that I'd had to get up from the table as I thought it. The thrill of it – flashing through my mind fully formed but beyond language – was too exciting, too perfect to try to set down in words that would immediately fall short, which of course was exactly what happened when I finally did sit down and try to write it out. But rather than giving up, I had chased it – that inarticulable concept – until I had wrung all the joy and life out of it, and only then could I see how limp, how trite, it had always been – at which point Edith woke, screaming, something she hadn't done for nearly a fortnight, long enough for us to have been lulled into thinking a corner had been turned, long enough for me to stay up late following fruitless thoughts, and for me to spend two long beats frozen in my chair listening to her screaming, momentarily disoriented, before the adrenaline rushed in, clearing away the sleepiness that had been clouding my thinking about populations and territories and recognition.

I found myself rushing up the stairs to Edith's room, ready to pick up her body, which I knew would be stiff with bewildered rage, back arched and legs straining, to shush that guttural screaming, but before I reached her I remembered that we were sleep training, that I was not to go into her room but was instead to stand outside the door, set my phone's timer to ten minutes, and wait for her to stop screaming, which she didn't, or for the timer to go off, which it did, and then I went in and picked her up and sang in that private singing voice only my children will ever hear, and when she started up again the ten minutes started again too, and Lauren passed me in the hallway to sit in the kitchen downstairs, to be as far away from the screaming as possible, because the sound of it made her heart ache and her breasts leak, whereas I had found a way to go inside the sound, to inhabit it so that I was neither listening to it nor ignoring it, but rather my mind went blank with it for ten minutes at a time as I sat waiting with my back against the cold hallway wall.

So as Edith unravels a library display made of multicoloured ribbons, apparently unaffected by the previous night's screaming,

I wonder if I'm falling into an old family trap. What if the waiting –
whether dread-laden or expectant – is not waiting at all? What if the
waiting is life itself? Pulling Edith away from the ribbons, I deposit her
on the wooden train that is also a bookshelf, where several other babies
and toddlers are climbing and falling. Rather than following another
thought, or picking up a book, I try to stay with her as she grips the side
of the locomotive with white-knuckled determination.

I try to stay with her as she watches the older kids climbing up and
down at will, and I think I sense a kind of greed in her watching.

I try to stay with her as she looks back over her shoulder at me and
shoves her free fist into her open mouth.

I try to stay with her as she reverts to all fours and begins rounding
the train with a textbook crawling action, legs and arms in rhythm.

I try to stay with her as I fetch a tissue from the baby bag slung off
the back of the pusher to wipe away the snot that is threatening to
dribble down into her mouth.

I try to stay with her as she clutches a book – a Wibbly Pig – with
both hands and whacks it with scientific interest against the train.

I try to stay with her as I give her a pouch of pureed vegetables,
which she sucks on without pausing, like a lost traveller at an oasis, then
drops on the ground without a second thought.

25

The self is not self-forming. I think that as Edith gurgles something that sounds like Dada. Da da, dar dar. Dadada. We come into a world that is already formed. We're born into a language that speaks us before we speak. No one – not the greatest artist who ever lived nor Christ himself – is autopoietic.

In one of my earliest memories, I am sitting up in my bed. My father is sitting next to me, reading from a book that I now know was an illustrated children's Bible. He is reading the story of the good thief and the bad thief. I remember feeling confused. How could one thief be good and the other thief bad? And why was the other man, the one who hung between them, also hanging from my bedroom wall?

Another early memory: my father explaining to me why I am not allowed to go for a sleepover with my friend. We don't know his family, my father says. You have plenty of time to play with your friends at school. Years later, during an argument about staying out late with my friends, I bring it up: You never even let me have a sleepover. You've always tried to stop me from having friends. He says, It's for your own good. Friends will always let you down. Only family – you can only rely on family.

26

I met Lauren as an undergrad, in English literature. We didn't start dating right away. We were both in relationships, but there were a couple of hours between the lecture and our tutorial, so we spent our Wednesday afternoons talking about Milton. Then we started seeing each other at parties, and we had more to talk about than Milton. From my sharehouse room – a tiny square box with a window out to a gloomy hallway – I sent her instant messages about the movie I was watching. She complained to me about her housemates finishing her tinned tomatoes. We met for dinner and didn't get home until the morning. She fell asleep in my bed after watching YouTube videos all night. We talked for years, through two break-ups and two more relationships. The first time I told her I loved her she laughed, then said, Oh shit, then cried. We spent a few more months like that, talking and crying. The day we decided to be together, she moved into my room – not the square box anymore, but a room with a little balcony that hosted warbling magpies in the morning.

Now when she lies awake in bed, unable to sleep, I tell her the story of Edith's birth. I roll over and put my arm across her, like some kind of safety rail, and start whispering into the dark: your contractions woke you up around three in the morning – about the same time as it is now. We didn't know if this was it, or a false alarm. You went out into the lounge room where you dozed on the couch between contractions. You tried to eat – we'd prepared every kind of snack, in case you had a particular craving – but you didn't want any of them. I waited until five-thirty before I called your parents, so your mum could meet us at the hospital.

After we got the green light from the hospital, I put you in the back seat of the car and drove us through morning commuter traffic. By then, your contractions were deep and painful – you'd let out long low moans and then you were silent until the next one. At the hospital they said you'd gone into ketosis – your body had run out of carbohydrates to burn for energy so it was eating itself. In the maternity suite, things went to plan at first. You were in the bathtub, and I was spraying your back with warm water while you clutched the gas mask. But after a few hours the pain was too much and you got out of the tub. You were on all fours on the floor of the suite, completely naked. When a midwife tried to cover you with a hospital gown, you gasped that you didn't give a shit. She backed off. You were making animal sounds then – deep, secret guttural sounds. In between contractions you were sobbing, begging for it to stop. I can't, you kept saying, over and over again. I can't. But you kept going, for hours and hours.

The whole day passed. It was night outside. Nearly there, said the midwife. But she looked worried. More staff came in, a doctor came and went. It was taking too long, and they didn't like some of the readings. We could see the crown of the baby's head, but you didn't have the energy to push anymore. So they cut you open, two quick snips, and they pulled the baby out with the forceps – stainless-steel tongs clamped on her tiny grey head. There was the sharp metallic smell of blood. More staff came, someone called some kind of code. A midwife held the baby against you for a heartbeat – one of those extra-fast infant ones. They opened the resuscitation cupboard and the baby was there in another heartbeat, and we watched the backs of the medical staff in their green and blue scrubs gathering over her.

This is where I usually stop the story, before they wheeled the baby away down the corridor, before I followed them. Instead of going on with the story, I tell Lauren, It was the most amazing thing I've ever seen. And then we lie in the dark, listening to her breaths, which are measured now. I'll know it's over once she asks for my phone, to look once again at the album named, Edith – birth.

27

In Anam, while my grandmother waits, her mind is always full of stories – some from her cheap paperbacks, love stories that are really stories about death and betrayal, others from life, though no less melodramatic. As she waits on the French bureaucracy to confirm safe passage for her and her children – as she waits to be granted permission to abandon her husband in prison, her country in defeat – she thinks about her son, my father, who has been courting the smartest girl in class. He follows her hopelessly on his Honda, not daring to speak to her, until one day she catches him out – turning around to say, I know you've been following me. She laughs at him. That is when my grandmother knows that she will have a daughter-in-law – but not yet. The young lovers have much waiting and separation to get through first. She – my grandmother – doesn't tell her son this, when he finally comes home, twelve months after the laughter, to announce that he is engaged. Our children have to live these things for themselves. And anyway, the letter from the French government will arrive any day now: time enough for their tearful adieu then.

Even when my grandmother is in the back of the car driven by the man with the Gauloises, on her way to see my grandfather in his monastery hideaway, her mind is full of stories. Of her brother, in love with a married American diplomat. Of her own husband's voice, before he was her husband, a voice given to saying absurd things like, A fish disappears in the immense river, but if you and I are destined for each other then I will wait for you for one thousand years. He'd said that to her the very first time they were alone together, standing on the red wooden bridge that crossed onto Tortoise Island in Le Petit Lac. It was where all the young lovers in Hà Nội went, to look out on the water where the pleasant green of the trees bordering the lake was reflected back like a mirror. She laughed (it seems that the men in my family are always being laughed at by the women we love) and said, You don't mean that. It's just something you got from one of your books.

It was true. He had read it in one of his many books. But it was hardly fair for my grandmother, who herself had been led astray by books, to accuse him of living by another's words. Perhaps it was that injustice that prompted my grandfather to say, a little more defensively than he had intended, What do you read, then? They continued over the bridge onto the small island, turning left to walk around the edge of the temple, finally coming out onto a stone platform. A series of steps climbed down into the shallow water. Couples milled around, hoping that one of the ancient and giant tortoises that gave the island its name might surface, blessing their union. But no tortoises had been seen for years.

Oh, my grandmother said, trying to be airy, nothing like the serious books you read. But what had been meant lightly came out cold. A nearby couple made their way around the edge of the island, hand in hand. Later, a cyclo deposited my grandparents just out of sight of the grand house on Boulevard Gambetta. My grandmother wondered what his hand would feel like in hers. She imagined wearing a white camellia, as a token of her availability. But he did not take her hand. Instead, he said stiffly, Au revoir. But his provincial accent made it sound like ohvore, and she was reminded that, for all his reading, he was still a boy from Nam Định.

These are the things that fill my grandmother's mind as she sits in the back of the car. White camellias and a provincial accent.

28

When all the spies have been shaken off and the car actually arrives at the monastery near Đà Lạt, my grandfather is still teaching. My grandmother slips into the back of the classroom. The students are all young men, from sixteen to about twenty-five years old. Catholics whose families have fallen out of favour with this most Catholic of presidents. So now they are hiding in a monastery, being lectured by my grandfather on love – or, more precisely, what love is not.

Beware the illusions of love, says my grandfather. Love is not the same thing as promoting the welfare of another. There is more to love than that. It is absurd to say that I seek to promote the welfare of God. Yet surely I love Him. Beneficence implies that we strive for some purpose or goal. But love has no goal except recognition. Can I recognise the tendency towards perfection in my beloved? Can I differentiate between doing good deeds for the benefit of my beloved and usurping their freedom to reach that perfection for themselves?

Sitting behind the young men, she seeks his eyes. But my grandfather's eyes are wide and bright as he speaks, and he sees nothing. Beware the illusion of love based on resentment, he says. This is the illusion that the good is that which costs much. The deluded think to themselves, I have invested so much time and energy and feeling in this person, it must be love. Or they may say, I cannot live without this person – but that is really only the inability to be alone.

Beware the illusion of love based on desire. We see this illusion in sentimental Western novels. It must be remembered: love is not desire. Love can and often does lead to desire, to romantic yearning. But desire and yearning fade away when their object is attained, whereas love does not fade – love is eternal. I do not mean that love cannot end. People stop loving each other every day. But love, unlike desire, cannot be satisfied. That is because the object of love, the beloved, cannot be possessed or attained. But perhaps you are thinking, in those Western novels, is desire not portrayed as unquenchable? Perhaps you are thinking of the many Don Juans in Western literature, whose lustful desire remains unsatisfied despite each new conquest. But here we see that they have it the wrong way around. Desire is mechanical. It can be mechanically, predictably satiated. Not so love. For it is love that endures, and it is love – and its dissatisfaction – that drives the Don Juans of the world to endless torment.

My grandfather writes three names on the blackboard behind him. Max Scheler. Bishop Wojtyla of Kraków. Blaise Pascal. After writing the third name, he continues, The heart has its reasons, of which reason knows nothing. In love, there is a split between the who and the what. Reason seeks reasons: I love her because she is beautiful, because she is clever, because she is kind. And so on. But these reasons are insufficient to explain love's intensity and love's particularity. There are others who are beautiful, who are clever, who are kind. But it is not any one of these attributes that you love, nor even their sum total. They are only rationalisations, after the fact. You love her first, the *who*, and you find reasons – the what – to justify yourself. But the beloved is reason enough.

A few minutes later, they are in his room and he is holding her in his arms. She feels absolutely safe there, because time has stopped, and the whole world – the war, and the children, and those stories flying around her head – all that is held at a distance. Lying there as evening falls, they tell each other about all that has happened since they last saw each other, about her work at the hospital, the politics of the monastery. They talk about their parents, and about things they remember from their childhoods, a time so rich that even now they are discovering new things about each other's past, like my grandmother's passion for the tamarind trees on the Boulevard Carnot in Hà Nội, where lovers walked the famously wide footpath, passing Parisian-style cafés, their cane chairs and round tables set to face the street, beneath the double row of tamarind trees, whose sour fruit teams of youths from the provinces risked life and limb to harvest, shimmying up the tall trees without harness or rope. In autumn, their golden leaves lined the ground, and my grandmother would stop to buy candied tamarind fruit, which smeared her hands and gums with sticky, sour-sweet juice.

They talk about the future, about what they want for the children, about what they will do when the war is over. And the magic of their embrace is that their words are enchanted – they say what they mean, and they understand each other. There are no prohibitions on their words, no topics are off limits. She tells him how scared she is, all the time. He tells her about collecting the dead in Hà Nội during the famine, how he had wondered what it was about him – what was wrong or right – that meant he hadn't died like the rest. They whisper a prayer together, a deal: let us have one thousand days of autumn for just one more perfect day of summer.

29

It's a relief when I meet Lauren outside the porters' lodge with Edith in the pusher, ready to swap over. It isn't that Edith has been difficult – after the library we went down to the University Centre by the river to have lunch in their big dining hall, watched over by portraits of some of the university's famous alumni, like John Milton and Stephen Fry. Then we walked back up Trumpington Street, passing a demonstration outside Senate House about changes to the academic pension scheme, and arrived outside Trinity Hall without much in the way of fuss or drama. But it is nevertheless a weight lifted from my nerves as I watch Lauren wheeling the pusher away towards the Backs. The relief is tinged with guilt, but even so, as I walk through Front Court on my way to the Jerwood, the guilt ebbs away.

The library is getting fuller by the day. Now that it is March, the end-of-year exams that seemed so far away in February are suddenly much more real, exams that, in a single three-hour sitting, will determine the success or failure of an entire year. All those thousands and thousands of words read and written, the hours spent in libraries, the tens of thousands of pounds spent on tuition and accommodation – it all comes down to an exercise of memory. And already I can see that the easygoing socialising in the library lobby, or in front of the library on Latham Lawn, has given way to solitary scholars at their desks, swaddled in the blankets provided by library staff, no longer engaged in the wide-ranging, peripatetic reading of Michaelmas term but moving on to the purposeful preparation of memory aids, flashcards, flowcharts and mind maps.

Seeing those students' nervousness, and hearing their transparent attempts to disavow that nervousness, makes me glad that my year is not going to be solely defined by exams. Instead of fretting about June, I can at least work on my thesis. Thinking of Simons' comments, I write: My grandparents' prayer was answered – of course, it was answered a little too well. They had much more than one more perfect day of summer. The brutal murder of Ngô Đình Diệm and his brother by US-backed coup d'étatists meant that my grandfather could come home from the monastery to the chic apartment on the Rue Catinat. Sure, the coup marked the turn to military dictatorship, the suspension of free speech and free thought in the name of fighting the freedom-hating reds, the theft of the national wealth into overseas bank accounts and domestic morgues, and the endless escalation of high-tech, asymmetrical killing – but what did that matter, so long as the summer stretched on even as the war dragged. Perhaps if they had not been so softened by their good fortune they would have seen that their happiness was linked to that god-awful war – that as soon as the war ended, so would summer. And so it was: finally, after four more children and his ascension to the rank of public intellectual, after a more glorious summer than they could ever have hoped for, came the autumn, and not just one thousand days of it either, but 3653.

That is a pretty way of thinking of it: evoking as it does orange and yellow leaves falling gracefully to the ground (and not the cell filthy with excrement and urine, nor my grandmother's morning vomit every day she was in France without my grandfather; bearing in mind that Sài Gòn has a Fall but no autumn, so any pretty images of leaves turning must stay just that – imagined). Even if you can't redeem the past, you can at least make it beautiful. You can at least make it an epic poem. And if it has to be ugly, you can at least make it exquisitely ugly. If you can't redeem the past, you can at least make it *useful*.

30

Pascal said that we are imperfect beings in an imperfect world. Yet we can imagine utopia, the perfect world. How can this be? Because we remember that which we cannot remember. We remember a life before life: heaven.

31

So it's not just mystical Orientals who are prone to epic poems. Remembering heaven! It's clever: cloak your desires in the authority of history, dress up your dreams with the sanctity of the immemorial past. And who is better at this game of making useful history than the nationalist? Beautiful when it needs to inspire, ugly when it needs to enrage. History that is neither mundane nor true.

As we all know, the beautiful and the ugly have their uses, especially when it comes to building a state. Simons would have me look at South Vietnam's various attempts at a constitution, or the structure of the military junta, or the means and modes of clamping down on press freedoms. When it comes to developing, in a nation's subjects, the necessary bonds of affection for the abstract – and, let's face it, absurd – construct of the state, nothing compares to the manufacturing of the beautiful and the ugly. Beauty, especially, is its own reward, its own justification. Ernest Renan said: the essence of a nation is that everyone remembers many things in common and also that they are obliged to have already forgotten many things in common too.

So it is with Anam, perhaps more so than any other nation-state, lacking as it does those more stolid and staid procedures of inclusion and exclusion: constitutions, passports, the bureaucratic apparatus for certifying births, marriages, deaths. And what better technology is there for useful remembering-forgetting – better even than poetry, epic or otherwise – than the novel? Because the novel, like the newspaper, spreads across the territory. Like the newspaper, it presents to the reader a mirror in which that which must be remembered is remembered and that which must be forgotten doesn't appear at all. Like the newspaper, the novel marks out a shared time for its readers – but unlike the newspaper, that shared time is more expansive. It marks out shared pasts, presents and futures. One is so much more loyal to the imaginative power of a novel than that of a newspaper.

Which is why every country, legal or imagined – if there's any difference – needs a Great Novel. This is the only permissible function of art: to make real a people's longing for a home. Well – not quite. But any other function of art does not need *permission* – not from the nation, or the state, anyway. The Great Novel, on the other hand, is licensed by a polity; in return, if it lives up to its greatness, the Novel becomes a kind of commons for the polity, terra imaginaria from which to dream of unity.

Can I imagine another version of *The Crowned Mountain*, not as a little empathy machine but as the Great Anamite Novel? A novel intended not for voyeurs but for fellow travellers: a novel written by an Anamite for Anamites.

Surrounded by the anxious sounds of study – turning pages, keys typing, pens scratching – I begin to write down a fragment of that book, a fragment that will not redeem but will, instead, be useful:

Aunt Thi says: I am a gossamer sheet blowing in the wind. I float up in a gentle breath of air, on a bed of sighs. Our suffering makes us light – makes us into light, beams of the Godhead, reflected brilliance of the sun on the face of the moon.

My father says: The stone floor of this thirteenth-century church is freezing against my knees. I'm stiff all over from prayer. I can hear the crows cawing from their roost in the rafters. Monsieur Braems prays and watches us praying. He will take us back to the centre sociale when we're finished, and he will say as he always says that it makes him happy to see such a pious family. But he is only right about Thi, who is as much a saint as the rest of us are pretenders. There is M Braems now, smiling indulgently at us, not knowing that I am not here at all. He is only smiling at a ghost.

Aunt Phương says: Will I always remember this moment, forever and ever? I try to fix it in my mind so that I will not forget: my brother Minh kneeling beside me, head bowed, lips moving softly. The cold of the stone floor and the whistle of the winter wind outside. None of this is memorable enough. Without more, this moment will fade. I have tried this trick before, of thinking to myself, remember this moment. And the thought is always so clear – like a bright, crisp winter morning – that it seems impossible that the trick wouldn't work. But thinking alone is never enough. I try to see the way a painter would. I try to see the way the light falls through the stained glass onto the empty altar. I would need soft hands to paint this light – the softest touch, like a caress. I am afraid of forgetting, though I do not have a bad memory. I can remember the usual things that people remember. Dates and names and events. History as a chronology. But I am afraid of forgetting details. Like the doll I was playing with when they came for my father, an American doll I'd been given by Mme Hutchinson, Uncle's lover, the doll whose blonde hair I had been carefully brushing when I heard someone crying – later I found out that it was Vương, an elderly neighbour – and the raised voices of two or three men – the neighbourhood watchmen, who were upset that an undesirable like father had been living in their quarter all along. Just think, I remember them saying, what this will do to our Party standing. You could have told us something, they said, it's the least you could have done. But that can't be right – I don't remember them saying anything at all. I wasn't there. I stayed in the room I shared with my sisters, alone because the others were all at school or work. I carefully brushed all the knots out of doll's hair.

M Braems says: It makes my heart lighter to see them, young people in the church like this. And tonight their lightness will fill our home. Before they started settling the refugees at the centre sociale,

I was the only one younger than fifty who came here. It gives me hope to see them, especially the little one, Phương, eyes closed, such a look of concentration and devotion on her face. Even Quang, who comes across so gruff, full of anger – he looks almost gentle, sitting there, elbows on the pew in front, hands clasped together.

Uncle Quang says: My buttocks feel as wooden as the cold pews that I must endure for another fifteen minutes. But at least I am not on my knees. I stamp my feet against the floor, hoping the movement will get my blood flowing again. My stamps echo through the church, startling the pigeons in the rafters, who flutter and coo above me.

My father says: The others are getting up to go with M Braems, back to the centre sociale, or on to Haut-Laon, or even, as Hương will do, on to Paris. I, too, should be getting up – I must go to Haut-Laon, and walk from business to business, looking for work. I know they will all say no, because they always say no, but still I have to ask. I have to glide, invisible, past the other jobless young men – white, brown, black and yellow. The others are loitering at the church's heavy wooden doors now, waiting for me before they let in the cold. But still I linger. What am I waiting for? I am waiting for this Christ to come down off His wooden cross, so that I can ask him, Why? And, How long must I wait? And, What should I do? I imagine it: Him pulling His bloody hands off the nails, uncrossing His legs and stepping down like a captain off a ship. I imagine myself blinded by the brilliant light coming from His body. I am struck by awe and terror. The little speech I prepared evaporates. I am deaf and mute.

Aunt Thi says: It is heartening to see Minh lingering among the pews. Even as I watch him, his face, normally contorted with all the pressures of this halfway life, and by the loves that stretch him across the globe, that face which is almost always twisting, now slackens. I see peace settling upon his closed eyelids, his nose, his mouth. I want to reach out to him, to feel for myself the grace that has come down to him. But I leave him be.

Aunt Hương says: The fields outside the car window look desolate. Are we late? First, M Braems will stop at the centre sociale, Phương and Thi will get out, and by then the train for Paris may already have left the station at Laons-en-Bas. It would be easier if I could just go straight to the station in the morning. I know that it is important to pray for Father's release. But – and I am afraid to even think it – we have to live our lives here in Laon. How, though, to stop a thought that has been thought? It's impossible. We have to get jobs. I have to pass the entrance exams at the Sorbonne. And there will be time enough to remember Father at dinner tonight. Phương and Thi get out of the car at the centre sociale. Good. It is not yet seven. I will make my train. Dawn will arrive as the train pulls into Gare du Nord. Now, in the dark, as I step out of M Braems' car to hurry up the station steps, I am free.

My grandmother says: I grip the plastic bag tightly as the POMA winds its way up the hill to Haut-Laon. We pass rooftops where people string their washing out on lines, underwear visible to anyone with eyes to see. We rattle through the fog and I can feel it coming on already, a kind of morning sickness. But there is nothing in my belly, no happiness that I am waiting for. Though it is true: I am waiting. Not for a happiness, but for him. It is for him that I feel this nausea that makes my head spin. I must try to push it away. I look at the people on the POMA. A young woman in smart business clothes, presumably on her way to the Mairie. An old man, his belly pushing out from under his khaki woollen jumper. He breathes with his mouth open, showing his yellow, gap-filled teeth. I can taste the bile coming up the back of my throat. Four months in Laon today, and every morning is like this. I wake up alone, in the dark. I listen for the sound of my children breathing, something I used to do when they were babies and their breaths came in short, sharp sighs. Now they are grown and it is harder to hear them.

My grandfather says: She is wearing borrowed clothes. A heavy black coat, a thick scarf. I hardly recognised her, sitting at the bus stop, by the side of a country lane that runs through bare fields. It was only when she stood up at the sound of the approaching bus that I saw: it was her, after all. Now she sits on a tram that shudders up the big hill, holding a plastic bag in front of her as if she were begging for money.

Aunt Phương says: Thi has gone up to the apartment in the centre sociale, to look over old letters again. I say that I am going for a walk, even though it is so cold that my mind hurts, and my mind's eye is frozen over, so that everything seems to move slowly: the occasional car on a distant lane, my feet plodding across frozen mud, even the bird of prey riding the buffeting winds above me. I am on a path now that runs straight as an arrow between empty fields before disappearing into a point in the distance. In one of the letters Thi is always reading, rewriting, and resending, there is a quote from Hương, about the day they came for Father. I don't know how the quote came about – whether Hương ever said those words to Thi. But even if she did once say something like it, Thi's never-ending revisions mean that the words in the letter are completely different now. So who knows if the memory in the letter is real or not. As I walk along the path, the point in the distance is beginning to resolve into greater detail. I think I can see a man up ahead, leaning against a fence post, smoking. The memory in the letter is not very different from what I remember about the arrest. Except that in my remembering, Hương is not there. I am home alone with my father, brushing my doll's hair. In Thi's letter, she says she remembers our father asking to be allowed to go quietly, without handcuffs. I don't remember that. For a second, the figure up ahead looks familiar, like an Asian man in a double-breasted suit. Then I see – it is only a twisted tree, beaten down and bent by the winds.

Aunt Thi says: The whipping, cold wind is nearly enough to convince me that I still have a body. It is not far to M Braems' house, but the way is very open – the wind will tear these letters from my hands and scatter them across the fields. Perhaps it would be better that way. If I still had a body, my body would be remembering right now the cold winds in the Netherlands, when I studied there on exchange. My body would be remembering the frozen fingers after bicycle rides, the stinging face, the feeling of being completely permeable to the wind. That thin, frail body had not been made for Dutch winters – it had been made for slipping between bodies and stalls in the Sài Gòn markets, for the sweaty, sticky heat that turned Europeans into slow-moving slugs. That body had been useful then: I used it to duck under tables and around slower bodies, clutching a bag of black-market medicines as clumsy police pushed their way after me. My body had a use, and now it doesn't. So the body fades away. Stepping into M Braems' house, I am only the spirit of the times, dragging in history in the shape of formal, typewritten letters.

M Braems says: Thi is already in my dining room when I get back from dropping Hương and the boys off at Laons-en-Bas. The place is a mess – it always is. I know she doesn't mind, but I smile at her anyway. I tell her we'll move it all to the bedrooms before the dinner, but she waves me off, as I knew she would. She says the last thing she wants to do is put me to any trouble. But what trouble is it to host such a family? Anyway, before any clearing, there is work to be done. Thi puts the letters on the small square of open table and we begin to read.

Aunt Hương says: Here is Marianne, looking through the book stands on the boulevard. She moves with an easy grace that I want to eat up. We start walking up the hill together and I am proud to be next to her. The way people look at her, at us. I am hungry for their looking. I straighten my posture, relax my shoulders. I note the way she is wearing her scarf. The streetlights are still on and everything glistens wetly. In class, we sit in the very first row.

My father says: How can I look Maman in the face and tell her that I am going to leave? A black cat stands watching me from the other end of the cobblestone laneway. It arches its back as I approach and then scurries past me, leaning in to the old stone wall as much as possible. The post office is just ahead. I will say, I cannot live without her. And the family will get on fine without me. I have hardly contributed anything since coming here anyway. Just another mouth to feed.

My grandfather says: You are the oldest son. It is your duty to look after your mother, your siblings.

My father says: Inside, the post office is wreathed in smoke from the customers waiting to be served by the single attendant. It reminds me of Father's office, where the smoke settled on everything. All day long, he sat at his desk, enveloped in the middle of that fog, never without a cigarette dangling from the corner of his mouth as he read over legal documents and dispensed wisdom. As a boy I had sat and listened to the voice coming from the clouds, a voice that spoke of everything, and always of self-sacrifice.

My grandmother says: If he was dead, I would know. The POMA arrives at Haut-Laon, and finally I am sick. The other two passengers scuttle away. I am alone for one, two retches. There is little to throw up, just bile and saliva. I would know, if he was dead. There would be no sickness in my stomach, no tenderness where the bile has peeled off the lining to travel up my throat, burning as it goes. This sickness is hope, I know. Like a bird caught inside me, fluttering – beating – its wings. When hope dies there will be nothing, no movement. Just a lifeless bird in the pit of me.

Aunt Thi says: I am the angel of history. Is that blasphemous? Perhaps: the angel of history sits on my shoulder, watching over the pages as I read. That's better. Beside me, M Braems reads too, but he can't keep at it. Every few minutes he stops, looks up, and says something about the mess in the room. He says that Mme Braems decided over the weekend to reorganise their memorabilia – keepsakes from their pilgrimages over the years. There are mail-order catalogues among the icons, for the holy water of Lourdes, for engravings of the Blessed Mother at Fatima. M Braems picks out one engraving in particular, of a curly-haired European man. Saint Don Bosco –

father's patron saint. His feast day is today. M Braems is talking about Torino, about Rome. He tells me that I must see the Basilica one day. The Sistine Chapel, too. A memory flashes: my father, sitting at the head of the table, lecturing us. Don Bosco is the patron of editors and publishers, he says. That's why I chose him.

My grandfather says: When did you become so thin? When did you become so serious? You used to read like that at home, sitting in the spare chair by my desk, eyebrows furrowed. But that had only been an act – you couldn't even read. And your serious lips always threatened to break into a smile. It was only the thrill of being near me while I worked that kept you quiet. It must have been sometime after that that you stopped pretending, that your seriousness stopped being an act. When did that happen? I didn't notice.

My father says: I am alone on a mountaintop, shrouded in fog. Alone, I know what I will say to Maman. I will say, I can feel the warm weight of my son in my arms as I rock him to sleep in the sickly blue twilight of a winter's evening in Reservoir. That is a suburb in Melbourne, in Australia. I am rocking my son to sleep and singing to him in the small room I share with my wife. It is my brother-in-law's house. We live here with him and two of her sisters. There is a shed at the back where the three women sew clothes for a man who pays them in cash, while I sit with my son in my arms in the sun-bathed backyard, between the house and the shed, next to the cải làn and the ngò gai and the kale my brother-in-law grows. This vision calls me, I will tell Maman. The weight of my unborn, barely hoped for son. I have to go, I will say. You understand.

Aunt Phương says: No one is home. I am sore and stiff from my walk. After the Communists took over, I exercised with all the other kids my age in our block. Every morning we met and touched our toes and wiggled our hips. It was like a group dance. We even sang as we exercised. Happy songs about summer finally arriving. I liked it. But after Father was arrested, I didn't go back. I said no. I stayed home – from group exercise, from youth group meetings, even from school, eventually. I stayed home and imagined other houses we might be living in. At first the houses I imagined were all like the apartment on Rue Catinat, where we lived before the Communists. I imagined apartments with fine wooden furniture and clean windows overlooking busy city streets. Then I imagined the many-roomed houses in the French novels I loved. I imagined the people who lived in those houses – always lounging on day beds, drinking wine, and talking about money. At first everyone tried to make me go back – Maman, my siblings, the neighbourhood watchmen. But then they gave up, or forgot about me – even Maman – and so I stayed home, alone, imagining. Now I sit at the kitchen table pressed up against the bare wall in our foyer apartment, and I think of houses again. The houses I imagine now have fewer rooms than the houses I dreamed of in Sài Gòn. They're modest houses, with a place for an easel and brushes. In such houses I would try to paint the image that has followed me from Sài Gòn to Laon: a young woman stands at the window of an empty house, looking out at cold, barren fields.

My grandmother says: There isn't so much difference between an old, dying Viet and an old, dying European. Their needs are the same, really. They smell the same. When I check their cannulas, their skin feels the same – slack, papery. There is the same torpor, the same complaints. Sometimes the French patients say something about my yellow fingers staining the bedsheets. In Vietnam, they tried to break the rules – to smuggle in street food – and then they called me names when I took the food away. I check a list of drugs administered this morning against an inventory, and all the things that need buying get in the way of my checking: after diazepam come bread, milk, rice, fruit, onions, lettuces, beef mince, tampons, detergent, and after morphine come new shoes for the boys and a new dress for Phương, who has not had a new one the whole time we have been here, and after memantine come gifts for M et Mme Braems, international newspapers to be combed for the dwindling news reports about Vietnam, coffee, textbooks for Hương, new sponges, soap, shampoo, some minimal make-up so the other nurses can stop offering to let me borrow theirs. And he had not wanted me to become a nurse in the first place! But he was not practical, he did not think about the things that needed to be bought. His clients paid however they could. Once, a crate of pineapples arrived at our door. Minh is the same – no practical mind at all. Neither of them would eat if I didn't put a plate in front of them. And it had been *his* insistence that we not leave for America, after the Fall. How can we leave again, he'd said. One upheaval, from North to South, is enough. And there is nothing for people like me in America. But that was not practical thinking. A lawyer can think like that – a nurse doesn't have the luxury. I can't dream on this job – I have to tell Yves about the broken ventilator in room B3, I have to replace the old butcher's catheter. I can't afford to dream – but still I remember – though America might have been nothing for us, still, I remember – the garden parties at their embassy, the way the lights were strung out over our heads like stars, the way the serious young men all stood up as I sat down at a table – it's not so practical, but I remember feeling young at these parties, though I was nearly forty, a mother – I felt young in a way I had not felt when I was young – it was the music, I still hear it – *I remember you . . .* – I sing it now, as I check the charts outside the rooms in my corridor, because there will be no singing tonight, only prayer, and I wonder whether – if only he had been a little more practical – mightn't we be together now, in Houston or Orange County? Mightn't we be warm?

Aunt Thi says: First, I write out the words longhand. The pen slows me down, but the slowness keeps me going. I feel a flow of words, imperfect words, words and sentences that get crossed out, moved around by thin black arrows, words that do not quite capture everything I mean to say. The words do not look on the page like the Spirit of History, more like thin, miserly scratchings. But the words come, and that is the important thing. When I have enough words, I start typing on M Braems' typewriter – a turquoise Olivetti – and I correct and refine as I write. My fingers remember certain phrases on their own. My father, the prisoner of conscience. We have had no communication with him since his arrest. If nothing else, please remember him in your prayers. The others – Quang especially – do not agree with that line. Quang says that it gives them a way out. Perhaps he is right. When they reply – if they reply – they always throw that line back at us. They are sorry they can do nothing practical, but they will pray for him, and us. I understand why that makes Quang so angry. But he is wrong when he says that words are cheap. Words take time, they take ink and paper, they take muscles to write and type. He thinks words are nothing, immaterial. That remembering is just an idea. And prayers are worse than words. But that is what *they* want us to think – *they* want us to forget Father. And forgetting is not nothing. Forgetting is progress, forgetting is moving on, forgetting is living. So remembering is not nothing either. It is making whole that which has been smashed. It is turning your back on progress, it is refusing to move on. From the Catechism, which I learnt by heart: What is meant by praying with recollection? It means remembering that we are speaking to God. So it is with every one of these letters: I remember him, and he is remembered to them, for at least as long as it takes to type out a response, and to say a prayer. And then he is remembered to Him, is he not? I feel the angel of history on my shoulder as I keep writing, like a great hunting bird, squeezing her talons in sympathy, firm and sharp.

M Braems says: I open another bottle of the Côtes du Rhône and pour it into as many glasses as I can reach, ignoring the flurry of polite hands trying to cover their vessels – but, óp la, too late. The table is still overflowing with food, a wonderful mix of cultures – spring rolls side by side with moules-frites – and I tell the boys to eat up. The girls dote on their mother – it is wonderful to see. A wonderful family. Hương is telling me about the Sorbonne, the packed lectures, the all-important first-year exams. Anyone can come to the first-year lectures, she says, but only a few will pass into second year. It all sounds wonderful, I say. So clever, so hardworking. Minh is quiet, as usual. My wife is speaking to him about something – I can't make it out over the happy sounds of cutlery and chatter – and Minh is nodding politely. But I can see him glancing over at his mother, checking that she is not wanting for anything, as an eldest son should. She is a wonderful woman, truly. Hardly home from the clinic and she was straight over here, elegant and sombre as usual. Soon I will stand and raise my glass. I won't make a speech, but someone has to say something. I hear Thi saying something to her mother. There is a letter from Mme Mitterand – from the President's wife herself! We must open it – she will do it, that wonderful woman, and read it to us. But first I will raise a glass and propose a toast: to Don Bosco, to your father, to freedom, to France.

III. EASTER

1

Edith is sick again, nose running like a tap and a cough that keeps us up all night. It's the third time this month, probably another virus picked up from a baby rhyme-time session at the library or the play group at the Anglican church – and, as with the other times, the virus has wormed its way around our household. Fortunately, there is no teaching in Easter term, only a revision class for each subject, and then a seemingly endless amount of time in which to read, fret, and procrastinate. These days the Jerwood is too full of panicked undergraduates, and the law library is too full of classmates who want to cross-reference their notes with mine, and the University Library is too full of distractions – dead ends and red herrings – so I have found a new place in which to pretend to study, in the Centre for Mathematical Sciences. The building is a marvel – perfectly circular, the desks on each level are arranged along the windows that make up the circumference of the circle, so that sitting there – or, better yet, standing at one of the many standing desks – one feels like the pilot of some spaceship landing on a green, leafy planet.

Or a prisoner in a panopticon. Each scholar, arranged as we are on the outside of the circle, is surveillable from the glass elevator that runs up the middle of the circular building. Actually – that's not right, is it? Bentham's panopticon relied on a careful calibration of opacity as well as transparency, and this building is transparent all the way through. This is one of my problems – getting carried away. I am not, however much I think about Chí Hòa, a scholar–prisoner, but just another procrastinating student. And in the detention system, I was never, however much I pretended otherwise, a friend, someone who really *understood*, but rather just one in a long sequence of professionals to come through its revolving doors – lawyers, nurses, social workers, psychologists – doing a job, and moving on. For S and the others, I was not even there, on the island with them. Just a voice calling periodically to ask repetitive, detailed questions.

Sometimes, when I thought that it might help, I would mention Chí Hoà and my grandfather – trying to demonstrate a kind of understanding-by-proxy. It felt like – it was – a performance, leading, at best, to a shallow intimacy. I don't know if my white colleagues tried, in their own ways, anything similar. I suppose they must have. Whether they talked about football or food or a visit to Syria before the war – there has to be an element of reciprocity, even if it is only a performance. Usually, I would just run through the bare facts: grandfather, ten years, Vietnam. Often, if I was speaking to someone who'd been detained on Christmas Island or one of the mainland centres, they'd tell me about a Vietnamese detainee. A really good guy, they might say. And there would be a kind of complicity between us: that, at least, someone who looked like me could be detained too.

On the few occasions I had a Vietnamese client, the gulf between us was all too obvious – in fact, it was worse, in the way a disappointed expectation is worse than having no expectation at all. In such cases it is tempting to swing to the other extreme – from false identification to total non-identification – by retreating into a role. To play the disinterested lawyer. That, too, seems like a mistake. It is a survival mechanism: to get lost in references, in research. As the psychoanalyst Dori Laub put it, to let a flood of awe and fear intercede between me, the interviewer, and the traumatised subject, prevents me from truly absorbing the account of the traumatic event.

And the problem is, it works. One reference among many: Tran Van Mai, a well-educated, well-off youth who saw the great famine of 1945 firsthand, struggled to evoke in himself the requisite sense of horror. I looked at the other people, wrote Mai, and then thought about myself. I was not moved as much as I wanted to be. I tried to take control of my mind, to kindle a flicker of humanity in my bronze-cold heart.

Lauren often says the same about me, but instead of bronze-cold, she says that my heart is flinty. It's not a criticism, she says. It's just a fact: that's how you do the work you do.

2

That famine, which Tran Van Mai tried, and failed, to rouse his
humanity for, was also a site of failure for me. At first, it was simply
a failure to hear – to receive what was being given. The first time my
grandfather told me about the streets full of the dead, and the cart he'd
pulled stacked with their bodies, we were sitting in our customary spots
by the television in the Boissy apartment. He had been talking about
history in that bloodless way that he had, and I had been diligently
writing down his words in my leather-bound notebook, words that
had the tone and temperament of a high-school text, complete with
headings like The Long Arc of the Vietnamese People, A Thousand
Years of Chinese Occupation, Vietnamese Patriots Past and Present,
and 9 March 1945: the Japanese Coup, so that I had a vague sense
of history unfolding, distant and inexorable, as if he had somehow
transmogrified my question about his life story into *A Complete
History of Modern Vietnam* from which he himself was all but excised.
So perhaps it's not surprising that it was only after I had written down
several pages about rice hoarding, and crop failures, and whole families
dying together in their beds, that I thought to stop and ask, What
famine are you talking about? To which he only smiled and shook his
head and said, as he so often did during our conversations, Did no one
tell you? Knowing, of course, that I knew nothing, that no one had
ever told me anything – because I had never asked – he called out to
my grandmother, who sat in her office chair in the kitchen, peeling a

mountain of carrots for pickling, separated from us by a thin, opaque glass door: He doesn't even know about the famine.

Since then, that first failure of reception has repeated itself as a failure of representation. Imagining the famine proved more difficult even than imagining Chí Hoà – at least for the latter I had a model in Manus, however imperfect the transposition. But famine – that seemed Biblical to me, and just as unreal. And while there are countless prison books, I struggle to think of famine books. Not just books where people are hungry, or even starve – I mean a catastrophic collapse of a national food system. Perhaps because, at the ground level, at the level of an individual, there is little to be done once a famine sets in – the tipping point, if there even is something as discrete as that, happens months before the actual starvation. Anyone likely to starve during a famine is unlikely to know when this point is reached: they have been condemned to death, but they do not know it. When the time does come, there is none of the spectacular violence of execution or warfare. It's a slow-motion disaster. Worse still – from a narrative perspective – it is quintessentially systemic, its causes wickedly complex. Easier to say it was God's will and be done with it.

And yet – how can I leave it out? An event that kills one in ten people – over a million all told – should leave a trace. Looking out at the indifferent greenery beyond the windows of the Centre for Mathematical Sciences, I hunt now for those traces – I try to remember, from my grandfather's *Complete History*, some detail that might serve as a leitmotif, a bridge across the chasm.

3

The faint hint of frangipanis wafts into the library on some unknown, possibly quite imaginary, draught. Yes, that will do. That scent – sickly sweet, like overripe fruit – had a double association for my grandfather. The first with the famine, with the dying, with the collection of corpses, and the second with love. One association, as it happened, leading to the other.

4

For some reason, the starving thought that they would be better off in Hà Nội. But, once in the city, they discovered that there was nothing to do but complete the destiny that had been ordained a year ago by the typhoons that devastated the rice crop. (Or earlier, when the Imperial Japanese Army occupied French Indochina, or even earlier than that, when the French Third Republic established its colonial administration over its new territories in Tonkin, or – and so on.)

My grandfather had preceded this influx of the famished by a few months, when he left home with Minh-now-Sơn. It made all the difference. They arrived in a city buzzing with anticipation of the war's end. All around the world, the Axis powers were being pushed back. The Americans had landed in the Philippines. Paris had been liberated. No one knew what authority the isolated colonial administration still had. The city's working assumption was that the French would soon be gone, the only question was who would replace them. Minh-now-Sơn favoured pushing on, to the limestone caves at Pác Bó on the Chinese border, where the real revolution was being planned. On the way, they could join the peasants marching on rice silos – at that time, the hunger in the countryside was still only a rumour in the city. But my grandfather thought that Hà Nội was the place to be – soon, he thought, they would be tearing down statues in the capital. He wanted to be there to see it when it happened, and to make sure the replacements were Vietnamese, not Japanese.

So the brothers made a pact. Minh-now-Sơn would join the liberation army, while my grandfather would stay in Hà Nội, making contacts, getting ready. Then, when the revolution came, they would meet again.

5

The famine arrived in the capital before the revolution. No time to contact the clandestine networks, to infiltrate the colonial administration, to get ready for his brother's triumphant return. Time only to find work, to feed himself while others starved. The municipality was hiring corpse collectors, paid per body. So my grandfather spent his days in the French Quarter, where the starving were making their way from gated household to gated household to beg for scraps, and more often than not dying there, too. Those walled gardens were crowned by white and yellow flowers. Thus my grandfather came to associate his work with the scent of frangipanis.

6

The scent had a veiling effect. For instance, when he later thinks of my grandmother's house on the Boulevard Gambetta – one of the villas in the French Quarter where the corpses-in-waiting gathered, hoping for alms – he thinks of it as the house veiled in frangipanis. Thinking of it that way kept the veiled thing – the house, my grandmother, his declared love for her – secret, sacred. It is easier to love through a veil, because the beloved remains mysterious, unknown. Kept close, but at bay, reality cannot dispel one's illusions. It was the same with the famine, with the work of gathering the bodies of the famished: by veiling the dead in frangipanis, he warded off their stench and covered up their sores.

(Let me be honest here: the only one warding off stenches and covering up sores here is me. After all, I might have asked for those details, there in the Boissy apartment, when my grandfather had said, He doesn't even know about the famine. I might have asked: What do I need to know, to know about the famine? I might have torn apart the veil, demanded direct access to the divine, and asked, What did the bodies look like? How heavy were they? How much did you get for each one? Did you slice off ears, as proof of collection, as some men did? How did you do it – how did you come back each day? Instead, I let the flood of awe and fear get between us.)

By veiling the bodies, he could link death to love, and in so doing he could transform death from banality, from horror, from the end of all meaning, into the scene of love, into the seriousness that gives love gravitas. And why not? Remember that I had left him suspended between Bangkok and Karachi, speeding across the world, on an errand of life. What if I rejoined him now, the man who had written en souvenir de mon passage de la mort à la vie on an in-flight menu? Who, citing Dickens of all people, wrote, Recalled to life! Yes, what else could my grandfather have been thinking of on that flight to France after his release from Chí Hoà but love – in particular, of love's first scene, veiled in frangipanis?

7

Imagine, then, along with my grandfather-suspended-in-the-sky: early morning, and a skinny teenager is struggling to pull bodies onto his wooden cart. He is in the French Quarter, by a house that smells as sweet as freshly cut peaches. Looking up from his task, he sees a girl kneeling before a body covered in a white sheet. Her eyes are closed, and paper offerings burn between her and the body. She looks as if she is waiting for life to begin.

Then, imagine that it is now late afternoon, and the skinny teenager is at the quicklime pit, pulling bodies off his cart and tipping them in. He is losing his balance, his foot slipping – preoccupied, perhaps, by the image of the kneeling girl – and all of a sudden he is falling among the corpses, he is thrashing about uselessly like a fish on the deck of a boat, ignored by the other collectors and the gravediggers, until a man in his thirties spots the flailing boy, so alive against the dead, and directs, for the love of God, someone pull him out, and bring some water. The man is a budding politician; he is visiting the mass graves in order to write an eyewitness account denouncing the authorities' public health response to the famine. Finally, after looking the boy over, still pale with shock, he decides to take him home to the house on the Boulevard Gambetta, where the frangipanis are flowering and the smell is almost overpowering. There, gathering fallen blossoms in the garden to float in the pond on this hot and lazy day, is the politician's kid sister, the girl who looks as if she is waiting for life to begin.

8

Months pass. The Japanese make a move on the French. The Americans drop two atomic bombs on the Japanese. My grandfather has become something of a project for his rescuer, the ambitious young politician who is the de facto master of the house on the Boulevard Gambetta. The politician has wagered his career on the promise of young Vietnamese manhood – properly harnessed to Catholic ideals, of course – driving the nation to independence and glory. And what better way to prove his point than to take this half-dead boy found at the mass graves on the outskirts of Hà Nội – I could hardly tell whether he was client or collector, was the latter-day joke – and take him home, to feed his body *and* his soul, and show the world just what a little instruction – properly done – could achieve.

The project is proving even more successful than the politician predicted. My grandfather is capable and loyal, and in time becomes not only a believer but a zealot. For his part, the great man – for whom my grandfather would do almost anything – will, in time, become the last ever governor of North Vietnam. And so it is that the two of them get out of the cyclo. They are glad to be back in Hà Nội after a secret conference with their allies among the priests of Phát Diệm, and glad most of all to be here, at the entrance to the white-walled villa with all its comforts. The great man leads the way, setting all the servants into a bother at his return.

In the waiting room, my grandfather hangs back as the servants fuss and call for their mistress. He takes off his hat and holds it stiffly in his hands as the great man's mother, a regal-looking woman dressed in the old Imperial style, comes down the stairs. The father is in the smoking room, my grandfather guesses, laid out next to an empty pipe.

He is still thinking about opium – the vast sums that are being made off the illicit trade, and its particular allure for Orientals – when my grandmother comes downstairs to greet her brother. All through the long journey from Phát Diệm, first by canal boat, then train, and finally cyclo, my grandfather has been preparing himself for this very moment. But now that she is before him, his schemes and resolutions, his rehearsed speeches and immutable convictions, they all desert him. Instead, a poem – Vietnamese rather than French, which augurs, what, exactly? – comes to him, about two young lovers, who spend all their time together, looking at each other out of the tails of their eyes, casting shy, amorous glances at each other. But their love cannot be consummated; they must both marry another. Finally, thirty years later, they meet again, and now they look at each other face to face – but too late.

He is staring – he knows it – but can do nothing about it. He searches her face and her body, trying to understand what it is that ties him so irrevocably to her. She wears a very plain áo dài, she avoids his gaze as she stands waiting for her mother and brother to finish their greeting. He feels like a child taking apart a watch to find out what time is: what was it that kept him awake in the night during these long months of separation? His eyes take her apart – he feels coolly detached from her, and from his desire for her, as if he is a scientist, or a medical student, calmly dissecting a corpse. He looks at her thin, arched eyebrows, her long eyelashes, her unpainted nails, the roots of her hair, the shape of her beneath her áo dài, her small, slippered feet, the expression of patient waiting on her face, and the hint – he thinks – of her determination to not look at him.

Still with the cold logic of the vivisectionist, he splits himself into two, the one who searches her body for signs and explanations, and another who looks at him looking. For he regards himself now with some surprise, so serene when he thought he would be afire, tranquil when he ought to be in an ecstasy of hope and despair.

And then she moves, and his two selves collapse back into one unthinking, uncontrollable, unknowable self. She is smiling demurely at the much revered, much adored eldest brother, the politician escaping the attentions of his mother and moving forward to embrace his sister. And in that movement, the dissected parts of her cohere again into a living whole. He is burning with desire for this shimmering apparition, which still does not look at him except, perhaps, from the tail of her eye.

9

If I was to remember only one date from my grandfather's *Complete History* then he would have wished for it to be 2 September 1945, when Hồ Chí Minh took to the stage in the newly renamed Ba Đình Square and declared, on behalf of the entire Vietnamese people, the overthrow of the centuries-old monarchic regime, the breaking off of all relations of a colonial character with France, and the establishment of a democratic republican regime. He declared the existence of an independent Vietnam, whose territory was coterminous with three separate French colonies.

Oh, bravura Anamite fantasy! How many cadres did Hồ command when he took to that stage? With what authority could he claim to speak for an entire people? The Indochinese Communist Party was minuscule, and Hồ's united front, the Việt Minh, were hardly more widespread. True, they had seized government buildings in Hà Nội, but his Liberation Army had a grand total of two hundred soldiers in the capital. In the countryside, the revolution was running ahead of the revolutionaries, as revolutions do. Japan's unconditional surrender had opened the floodgates: in the provinces, bands of youths took it upon themselves to break open granaries, evict landlords, burn tax records, and lynch counter-revolutionaries. Others used the chaos to settle old scores, or took to soapboxes, declaring the end of all exploitation. Some were more organised, but not by the Việt Minh – there were, it seemed, innumerable revolutionary parties manoeuvring for power: the Greater Viet National Socialist Party, the Greater Viet Nationalist Party, the Trotskyist Struggle Party, the Vietnam Revolutionary League, not to mention sundry religious communities, including some 1.6 million Catholics, many of whom were, somewhat surprisingly, fervently anti-colonial. The political insurrectionists led by Hồ threw a map over the top of all this social revolution, blood-letting and profiteering, and called it the Democratic Republic of Vietnam.

And yet the force of Hồ's vision held it all together – even those who knew about, and opposed, Hồ's Communism, were swept along, even if only for a day. But what a day! A hot, clear Sunday – the Catholic Feast of Vietnamese Martyrs, no less, commemorating those who had died for their faith. So while some cleaned their homes and burned incense at their altars as if it were Tết, my grandfather and the politician attended mass at St Joseph's Cathedral. When the service was done, the priest led the congregation out of the Gothic church into the bright sunlight, joining the half million or so Anamites – Buddhists spilling from their temples, schoolteachers and pupils singing revolutionary songs, peasants carrying the new bright-red national flag, ethnic minorities in traditional garb – thronging past colonial villas whose iron gates had borne witness, just months prior, to a similar stream, then of the dying, and now of the joyously, revolutionary living, who sang and shouted their way to the square, where a mysterious man dressed in a faded Sun Yat-sen tunic, wispy hair and beard blowing gently in the breeze, stepped forward to the microphone on the high stage and declared his Anam real. And there, in that square, the people – they were one people in that moment, perhaps only for that moment – loved him for it. He paused. He asked: Countrymen, can you hear me clearly? The people answered, as one: Clearly!

Hồ had begun, as any good Anamite does, with a reference. In fact, not just one, but two: he quoted verbatim, as undeniable truths

about the equality of men, the Declaration of Independence of
the United States of America and the French Declaration of the
Rights of Man and the Citizen. He burnished his own Anam
with those past glories. He remembered, summarily, the violence
and plunder of eighty years of French protection. And he forgot,
as all Anamites must do, what ought to be forgotten. He forgot to
mention the security apparatus that had been the Việt Minh's first
order of business upon seizing power. He forgot to mention that this
apparatus was already detaining, torturing and executing its enemies.
He forgot to mention the intrigue and outright competition between
Communists and nationalists in the long years of their mutual exile
in southern China.

What felt the Catholic politician and his protégé?

My grandfather: pure ecstasy, dissolution of the ego in the crowd.
Even the politician, standing beside him, felt elated. Along with
the others in their procession, they shouted, For Christ! For the
Fatherland!

What caused this surfeit of feeling?

They believed because they wanted to believe. They forgot because
they wanted to forget.

What effect had this believing, and this forgetting?

Because they believed, and they forgot, they hoped. Hoped that
this fragile coalition might last. That the Communist-dominated
Democratic Republic of Vietnam would share power, appointing
nationalists and Catholics as ministers. My grandfather, in particular,
hoped that the vision would hold because it would mean that his pact
with Minh-now-Sơn – whom he had been looking for since the Việt
Minh came to power – would be kept, after all. That they had found
their separate paths to the same revolution.

What separate paths?

For Minh-now-Sơn, the classic Leninist-Stalinist path. His
Liberation Army unit had not travelled to the capital for the

Independence Day celebrations. Instead, they trained for the inevitable war: already, that same day, there had been clashes between patriots and returning French forces in Sài Gòn as crowds gathered to hear Hồ's speech broadcast through loudspeakers in Norodom Square. Minh-now-Sơn and his comrades had been taught well by Giáp, the Liberation Army's founding commander: they knew that 1945 was not the end of war but only an interregnum. For my grandfather, the less travelled path of Catholic nationalism, whose shibboleth was Third Force-ism – anti-colonialism *and* anti-Communism.

When did the grandfather become a Catholic?

Sometime between arriving in Hà Nội and attending the rally on Independence Day.

Can the moment of conversion be determined with more precision?

No. There was no Damascene moment, no instant of conversion. There was a baptism, of course, in St Joseph's, sponsored by the politician and attended by the politician's sister. But that was only the outward recognition of something that had occurred internally some time before. Everything important that happens happens inside our minds.

Why, then, the return – over and over again – to scenes? If interiority – dreams and fears, choices and deferrals – is what matters, then why stage them as scenes?

Because representation has not, after all, withered away. Scenes are the best approximation I have. And because I get carried away, and scenes are excellent vessels to bear one away.

Such as?

A scene of conversion: my grandfather sitting in a window seat in the house veiled in frangipanis, reading the Catechism of Pope Pius X. Perhaps he agreed to read it only out of gratitude to the politician who had saved his life. Or because he hoped, if he could not convince the politician's sister to choose life, that he could at least learn to understand her waiting. However it began, one must imagine that at some point, as he read through question and answer after question and answer, something extraordinary happened: he began to believe.

Do the brothers' paths converge?

No, never.

So was the pact between them broken?

It was.

Did the grandfather have names for what was thus lost?

He did.

Recite them.

Blood brother, bosom brother, first brother, playmate, idol, bully, friend, rival, lodestar.

Did the grandfather have names for what was thus gained?

Yes.

Recite them.

Brother-in-law, brother-in-Christ, mentor, master, Monsieur le Gouverneur, life's purpose, morality's measure, her brother, love's brother.

10

Five years later, and my grandmother is still waiting (in the other room, for the father of the household is very traditional – the two sexes eat separately before rejoining for digéstifs). My grandfather is lost in reverie as the servants clear away the entrées. He is imagining taking her chin in his hands, sliding his magnetised fingers up to her ears like a barber. He will no longer wait for love – he will demand it.

But his fingers don't feel magnetised. And how exactly is he to take her chin in his hands? He can't quite picture it – does he cup her chin, as if he were trying to hold water? Or is it more like holding an apple? Perhaps her brother is right: too much Proust, not enough propaganda. That, incidentally, is why he is here at this dinner – to listen to men more important than himself talk about the war, to remember their praise of de Lattre and denunciation of Giáp – known derisively in these circles only as the high-school teacher – for later dissemination. But as their chatter moves on to French politics – yet another change of prime minister, the sixth in four years – my grandfather keeps looking up at the ceiling, imagining the girl sitting in her room, waiting to be called down. He is still wandering through his own thoughts as the dinner service is cleared away and the men begin moving towards the covered courtyard to smoke. Then, as they pass through the ornate double doors out into the courtyard, the many women of the household file in for their meal. Before he has had time to register her presence, she is already passing him. She doesn't look at him but it doesn't matter, because an electric thrill is running up his forearm – she brushed against him, the slightest touch of her soft arm against his, an accidental contact, it seems, as she skirted an untucked chair.

He carries that electric touch out with him into the humid summer air, intoxicated. She touched him! He felt her skin on his – feels it still. But what does it mean? For a moment he holds on to the idea that it was an accident, mere chance, only to discard it: it could not have been an accident – there is no such thing as an accident. Fate, not chance. Destiny, not chaos. He understood this even as a young boy, when he found himself to be the brightest boy in his class. Others talked of his luck or his hard work, but he'd known it was neither. It was simply his fate to be clever, to have the gift of persuasive speech. To be rescued by a great man who happened to be in need of a skilled speechmaker. And through this great man he has learnt to put a name to this fate – God, Jehovah, Lord the Almighty.

11

The Hmông, says her brother, are extraordinary people, truly. It's a shame the northern mountains are not safe – it would be good for you to see them as they are in the mountains.

My grandfather and the politician he hopes to make his brother-in-law both take long drags on their cigarettes. A kerosene lamp set behind them throws their giant shadows across the surface of the lake, but even their enlarged selves cannot reach across to the other shore. Beyond the reach of the lamp, the water is a smooth black expanse, impenetrable. And beyond that is Hà Nội, which at night is only a few dull glows in the distance. The older man stares out over the water while my grandfather thinks of those mountains and wonders if his other brother, Minh-now-Sơn, is there right now, with Giáp and Hồ. Or is he one of those insurgents who comes out when the sun goes down to claim French watchtowers, French roads and French towns, then melts away again in the morning?

Really, says the politician, we Viets should not have ignored the minority peoples for so long. It's easy to think that they are simple, primitive even. But the French thought the same about us.

The night is stifling, oppressive, as if all the pressures of the last few years – the war, the rationing, the constant political manoeuvring, and the great man's sister, who continues to refuse all advances – have come together and settled in the air around them. My grandfather tries to imagine Hà Nội as one of the world's great cities – a Paris, the city of lights, or a New York, all gleaming steel and glass. He has read about and seen photos of these cities, but he can't imagine Hà Nội changing, especially not now that the French have lost. Who knows what the Communists will build – but it will not light up the night sky like the capitals of the West.

Take the market in C——, says the politician. They call it the Love Market. By day it is just like any other market. It's in the middle of the town, a small covered square selling fish, chickens, spices. Just like in any other village in the nation, except, of course, that the women are dressed very colourfully, in bright reds and yellows, not just the brown pyjamas our peasants wear. But on one night, in certain months, this ordinary market is transformed. On that night, men and women from the surrounding countryside leave their homes, their families – their husbands and wives – and gather under the banana leaves. Who are these men and women? Old lovers, separated by the river of time.

The great man stands up and starts unbuttoning his shirt. Come, he says, let's get out of the heat. Soon they are both naked, splashing into the water. My grandfather dives under the surface and swims three strokes down into the blackness. The water is cool on his skin, and for the first time in days he feels less heavy – a feeling approaching freedom. When he comes up for air, the politician is off to his right, a little dark head bobbing on the surface.

These old lovers, he says, as if there has been no interruption in his monologue, were once moonfaced youngsters. Perhaps they came from incompatible families, or the boy had to go to war, or their fates were simply unaligned. And so, after a brief passion, they did their duties, marrying the men and women their families had chosen for them. They had children, and looked after their parents. When these old lovers pass each other during the day – and in those small mountain villages, can it be doubted that over twenty or thirty years such chance meetings are rather common? – there is no sign of recognition, no smile or nod, except perhaps the faintest flicker in the tails of their eyes. But on that one rare night, those glances become embraces.

Looking at the stars, which form a brilliant canvas above him, my grandfather imagines the world turned on its head; he is falling *up*, into the stars.

12

Not long after the conversation in the lake, my grandfather sits down to write a letter. It is a plea, a promise, a pitch, a proposal. After all the misrecognitions of their face-to-face meetings, it is this letter that convinces my grandmother to say yes. In the letter, my grandfather describes what he saw when he first arrived at the house on the Boulevard Gambetta: a girl with peach blossoms in her hair waiting for life to begin. He writes about old lovers looking at each other from the tails of their eyes. He writes about missed rendezvous and stars crossing. He writes that he has resolved to lose no more opportunities. This letter, he writes, is an invitation, a summons: let us begin life, together, now.

13

Half a lifetime later, my grandfather tried to repeat the trick – this time as a ghostwriter for Tchen, the fellow inmate in Chí Hoà who had helped make the chess set that my grandfather entrusted to me. Tchen – whom everyone called Romeo – whispered his predicament to my grandfather as they both stood in line with the other residents of Cell 6, Section FG, waiting for their turn to bathe in the communal bath. Romeo's whispered story was generic – aren't they all – a glimpse of a slender beauty, love at first sight. In this case, through the bars separating section FG from section GH, the women's section of the prison. Still, my grandfather agreed to help the young would-be lover. With Romeo taking dictation, my grandfather composed a love letter. Then, with a few cigarettes traded here, an extra portion of rice bartered there, the letter made its way along the tangled personal web that bound Chí Hoà together.

After that, there was nothing to do but wait, first for four days, until the proposed hour, in the corridor between the kitchen and Section FG – a corridor that also happened to share a wall with the women's showers. (The women, on public-morality grounds, were not required to use the communal bath.) As the four days passed, Romeo's nerves began to fray. Had his Juliet received the message? Would she be there when the time came? And if she was – what then? In another time, and another place, the boy's fretting might have amused my grandfather. But instead, it was all he could do to avoid saying, What do you know about waiting?

At noon on the fourth day, the reply came: as Romeo waited in the corridor, he heard Juliet's gentle voice, humming to herself the tune to 'Ai về sông Tương'. The answer was yes.

14

Leaving the story there – suspending it, as I left my grandfather suspended somewhere between Bangkok and Karachi – is tempting. It would allow me to imagine that word of Juliet's yes travelled back along the web of the prison. That hearing of it, my grandfather resolved himself once again. That this resolve carried him through the years in Chí Hoà and onto the plane. And now, he is the letter, the promise, the summons: recalled to life!

Believing in the success of his ghostwritten love letter, a man might well have written on an in-flight menu, En souvenir de mon passage de la mort à la vie. But my grandfather knew better – and so do I. After Juliet's yes came the happiest period of Romeo's life, of which there is very little to say, except that it lasted eight months, the remainder of her sentence. Then she was released. The two lovers made all the promises that are made at such times. Two years later, Romeo himself was released. By then, Juliet had got on one of the fishing boats bound for Malaysia. From there she went on to the US, to California. Of course, Romeo set off in search of her. He got on a boat of his own, though this one was bound for Hong Kong. He was detained there for a year before escaping. Then another boat, a refugee camp in Thailand. And finally an arrival in LA. Where he promptly found Juliet – looked her up in the phone book. She was happily married to a retired ARVN major. She had a baby, a daughter. No, she didn't want to meet him. My grandfather found all this out in a letter that made it past the censors to Cell 6, Section FG.

So he knows, on that Air France flight, that the letter does not always arrive at its destination, or, if it does, then it arrives with blank pages. Errands of life frequently go astray. Which is another way of saying that sometimes the body survives but the mind – and the soul – does not. Whatever resources he still has while suspended in the air – the resources it takes to inscribe the in-flight menu with those words of hope – have evaporated by the time he lands in Paris. The man who gets off the plane is exhausted of words – he doesn't speak to the family who have gathered at Charles de Gaulle to greet him. He goes to bed before he can taste the cake they've prepared to mark the occasion, a simple chocolate cake with a word iced on top: bienvenue. In the morning, the first of his new life, when the family think that he might have recovered from the shock of freedom, he still does not speak. They blame it on the jet lag. But after a week, and then a month, and finally a whole year – they begin to suspect that something is wrong. Of course, they say. Only now that he is a broken old man have they released him.

15

When my grandfather finally died, I was back in Melbourne. There was only so much time I could take off from work. I had stayed in Paris long enough to see him given the last rites, one day when his breathing had seemed too difficult to continue. A French priest had come to give the rites – he was a family friend, and a historian, who wrote books about the lives of the saints. We had stood around my grandfather's bed – my grandmother, my father, my uncle and aunts, and me – as the priest said the words. And then my grandmother had turned to me and asked that I, as the eldest son of the eldest son, lead them all in the Lord's Prayer. After a moment of panic, the words had come, like the cliché about riding a bike.

It turned out that the ceremony had been premature. He survived the night, and the emergency footing we were all on eased, little by little. When the end did come, my grandfather was alone. It wasn't visiting hours. By then, even my father had come home. He had only been in Melbourne a few days before getting back on a plane to Paris. Later, I heard that at the funeral he had fallen on the coffin as it was being readied for the grave, sobbing and apologising.

16

Before he died, when I first started showing an interest in the family story, my grandfather wrote me a letter in Vietnamese. At the time, my reading comprehension was so poor that I could barely get beyond the salutation – he said something about me being his dear đích tôn, the eldest son of his eldest son. Without reading the letter, I scanned its pages into my computer, with the result that the files sat on successive hard drives over the years, before eventually being transferred to the cloud, so that his words were pulled apart and scattered all over the world, stored in whatever combination of servers suited the computational, economic, legal and physical needs of my online storage provider from moment to moment. Even then, in that obliterated, dematerialised form, they remained unread. Even when I moved to Hà Nội to take up a writing residency offered by an Australian arts organisation beguiled by the family story; even when I moved into the top-floor room of Hà Nội's only multilingual second-hand bookstore, where I was surrounded by English-to-Vietnamese and Vietnamese-to-English dictionaries and translations, a treasure trove of linguistic learning materials. Even when my great-uncle – my grandfather's brother, not Minh-now-Sơn but a younger brother, a former journalist – began giving me Vietnamese lessons, using his background as an official Communist Party radio broadcaster to teach me the proper, six-tone diction of a true Hanoian, which, in his estimation, was the only true Vietnamese, the central and southern dialects, with their four or five tones, being mere corruptions of the original. Even when I started my one day a week at a government-run publishing house, as I was obliged to do by the terms of my residency agreement – a publishing house that produced propagandistic histories of Vietnam and where I spent my obligated day a week correcting the English in translations of books like a military history of Võ Nguyên Giáp's greatest victories, or a compendium of Hồ Chí Minh Thought, or a treatise on the compatibility of Vietnamese Communism with international foreign investment – even after all that, which saw my Vietnamese improve immeasurably, I failed to read the letter.

The longer it went unread, the more significant it became, so that by the time I came home from Hà Nội the letter was like a charm worn to ward off the evil eye, insurance against the inevitable failure of my research – no matter how far an interview with my grandfather would meander, or if I were denied access to the archives at the National Library in Hà Nội, or if I was simply unable to imagine Chí Hoà, there was always still the letter, the letter that on any given day would reveal whatever it was I needed to know, but which could perform that trick one time only, for once read its contents would be fixed forever and then my failures would be final; unread, there remained always the possibility – however distant – of redemption. Then my grandfather died, and there didn't seem to be any point in keeping up the charade. I read the letter a few days before we were due to leave Melbourne for Cambridge.

It was three or four in the morning. Edith was going through a sleep regression, waking up every two hours, and Lauren was so drained – of energy, but also literally, of milk – that the only thing to do was to hold the baby and try to eke out another thirty minutes of quiet. I opened the letter on my laptop and read while Edith's head nestled against my neck, stooping every now and again to tap the down button on my keyboard.

The letter began with a disavowal. I am not Rousseau, he wrote. I will not be writing an autobiography. I lack the necessary good faith, and the courage, to tell the whole truth about myself and my character. Even if I were to hire someone to write my biography, I would be left with the feeling of praising myself by another's pen. Instead I will write down my memories as they come to me, in no particular order – they come like ocean waves, steady and never-ending.

The letter was punctuated by interruptions. My grandmother was feeling nauseated, or the home-visit nurse had arrived for my grandfather's injections. About a dozen pages in, my grandfather wrote, I am telling you all this so that you don't become a Communist. I see myself in you, the same love of justice, the same weakness for poetry. He quoted Tố Hữu: I've linked what stirs my breast to everyman / so that my love may spread, go everywhere, / so that my soul and all those suffering souls / grow close and strengthen each other's lives.

I worry, he wrote, that you will be just like me.

17

The ebb and flow of my grandfather's memories brought tantalising fragments to shore. As a young man, he went to poetry-writing competitions where the poems had to be burnt afterwards because they contained too many dangerous words – nation, revolution, the people. After the Fall, he read banned books until they came to take him to Chí Hoà. One of the books was *Gone with the Wind*. The last time my grandfather saw his own parents was in 1954. They travelled 500 kilometres through a live war zone to get to Hà Nội before he left for the South. He had always been his mother's favourite, her scholar prince. He gave them the keys to his house, some gold and his bicycle, and said goodbye. They both died while he was in Chí Hoà. Later, when he was released and about to board the plane that would take him to Paris, the officials stamped his passport with a mark that said: never to return.

Finishing the letter was a blow. None of these fragments ever developed into anything substantial. There was nothing there to save my project. And now he was gone, and there would be no more meandering conversations. Only some illegible notes and poorly recorded tapes. And my memories.

18

We remember to give shape to our forgetting. Even the most assiduous of record keepers will excise something. How can you accurately record all of life without that record itself becoming life? No, memory is necessarily a reduction. How little of experience is amenable to recollection!

When I turn my mind to a particular subject – speaking to my grandfather in that cramped apartment, waiting in the hospital – I have to push myself to remember details, to do more than provide a bare sketch of the scene. But then, there are other moments when I am overwhelmed by a random memory – walking through a park when suddenly the sight of a fallen gum tree takes me wholly to a different park, twenty years ago. And this unconscious and undirected memory is of a completely different order to the cold researches I conduct into the past – these unbidden memories are not only full of sights and sounds and smells but full of feeling, too, so that seeing the fallen gum somehow turns me into a frightened child again, lost and looking for home.

Outside the windows of the maths library, spring has finally come. It means that Lauren and Edith will be out in the long garden of our house, where there is only a low wire fence between the neighbouring yards, so that we can sit under the blooming apple tree and feel as if we are in a wide, private park. Our neighbours on the right, a middle-aged lesbian couple, are keen gardeners, and the work they have been putting in – persevering even through the Beast from the East, an unseasonal blast of Arctic air from Siberia that has prolonged the end of winter – is now paying off, as their narrow strip is bursting with tulips, foxgloves, and hydrangeas. And even though the weather is still rather cold compared to what we are used to back home, Lauren has discovered that as long as it is sunny, she can happily lie in the sun and close her eyes as Edith plays with the pebbles that make up the right of way our neighbours use to access their gardens. I imagine that is what they are doing now: mum on her back, the surprisingly warm sun on her face, daughter grabbing at the neighbour's cow-parsley, which pokes through the wire fence.

It won't be long now before I can join them, exams done and thesis handed in, and then we will have a couple of weeks of spring-turning-into-summer, when it will finally become apparent why our landlord returns every year for July and August – it is not only for the summer conference season but also for the garden parties and the lush lawns that will finally be used, the long mild evenings and the gentle upturn in pleasant conversations among the English people around us, who have so far scowled their way around our pusher. And still we do not know what our lives will look like then – in just a couple of months – nor even where we will be living. Will we stay long enough to enjoy this long-awaited summer? In fact, it is not even a matter of not knowing: Lauren said that she could not *imagine* the coming months and years. Uncertainty is one thing, the absence of all potential quite another. How terrible has my pursuit of the past been, if it has led to the total occlusion of the future?

I think again about my grandfather, the living ghost who came back to silently haunt the family. He sat in his chair and stared out the window. It went on for years. Eventually, he began to live again, but he did not speak about *that*. Until I came along, so many years later. He spoke to me. But what did he say? And what did I hear?

19

During my residency in Hà Nội, when I was supposed to be writing a book about my grandfather – having deferred for six months the offer to become a trainee lawyer at the community legal centre – I attended a gathering with my extended family. On the rooftop of my great uncle's house in Hà Nội, the one who tried to teach me how to speak like a true Hanoian, I found myself looking at a peacock, which seemed to me a little forlorn up there among the discarded furniture and crates of old junk. Its tail feathers, compact for the moment, brushed against the dusty concrete floor. Isn't he beautiful, said Great Uncle. They're very hard to raise. Extremely difficult.

As if to prove his point, the peacock turned away from us and stood facing the low wall that bordered the rooftop. Very expensive to buy as well, said Great Uncle as he got down on his knees. Can't just go down to the market – you have to know who to buy from, you see. From his position on the ground, Great Uncle started to make a high-pitched whooping noise at the peacock, moving forward slowly on his knees, his hands tucked into his armpits. The peacock turned around from the wall for a moment to look at him, then turned back again, uninterested.

I'm trying to imitate a peahen, said Great Uncle. It's the only way to get him to show you his tail feathers.

He started making the whooping sounds again, bobbing his head up and down as he approached the peacock. I was wondering how often the neighbours had to put up with this pantomime mating ritual when the peacock suddenly turned around with its tail flared out, a great arc of colour taking up most of my field of vision. The rooftop felt very small and narrow.

Isn't he beautiful? said Great Uncle again.

Downstairs, the rest of the extended family were gathered around a pair of low wooden tables loaded with fruit platters. Great Uncle's house was small, and dinner had been cramped, all of us crowding onto each other. And yet I had felt quite comfortable, despite the elbows aimed at my forehead as I ate. I'd even begun to enjoy this distant family circus, sketching out all the different threads and relationships; the family dynamic – loud and bombastic, with what seemed like a constant flow of jokes and bad puns – starting to feel a little less intimidating and a little warmer, even cosy.

Things seemed to quieten down as everyone settled into an after-dinner semi-slumber. Eldest Great Aunt, seeing us descending the stairs, told her younger brother to play me The Video.

Without further introduction, a space was squeezed out of the middle of the couch in front of the television and I was told to watch. Great Uncle slid an ancient-looking VHS tape into the player below the TV.

After a few moments of black and white noise, the screen resolved into fuzzy focus. Everyone, already quietened by their full bellies, sank into silence as the video played.

The title card was written in texta on a white sheet of paper, *Có một lần trở lại* – which, in my own amateur translation, is *A fairytale return* – followed by the credits: cameraman, director, sound and composer – Great Uncle.

Scene One: My grandfather, leaning heavily on a walking stick, wearing a plain white shirt and black trousers. This is the first time he has been in Hà Nội for thirty-five years, says the narrator (who else but Great Uncle). After ten years in prison, our brother has come back to us. The camera zooms out to reveal the big white gates leading to Tortoise Island in Hoàn Kiếm Lake. There are more trees around the lake than there are today, no high rises looming in the background. My grandfather looks at everything with keen interest. His eyes see things that the camera does not. Crossing the red bridge over to the island, he looks hollowed out, as if beneath the white shirt there is only a void. A sentimental piano tune starts up and the camera pans over to the right, where a group of men are swimming in the lake, splashing water at each other. No wonder he didn't see a tortoise that day, said Eldest Great Aunt, swimming right there, they must have scared the tortoises right out of the lake! Then the camera pans left again as my grandfather continues to hobble over to the island.

Scene Two: My grandfather is skeletal, his skin stretched tight over the sharp ridges of his skull. The video shows him in someone's living room. That's my old house, said Great Uncle, very small, tiny, we were all very poor in those days. My grandfather is pouring beer into small glasses set out on a coffee table laden with food. In pride of place is an unopened bottle of Mackinlay's Whisky. On the screen, Great Uncle explains that he bought the whisky at a hotel in Moscow. It probably doesn't look like much to you, he says, but that's very hard to come by around here. My grandfather tries to open the bottle, but his hands are too weak. Great Uncle has to do it for him. Children squirm in the laps of the adults gathered in the living room, and I started to recognise the other faces. That's me, said Eldest Great Aunt. How young I look! And I recognised, too, the timbre of my grandfather's voice, though he speaks very slowly, as if each word costs him too much effort. The cameraman shares his focus across everyone at the gathering, panning from side to side and zooming in on each face in turn. But my eyes only wanted my grandfather, the way he slumps in his chair, as if his back can no longer support his meagre weight.

Scene Three: The camera zooms in on two photographs of an old Vietnamese couple, so Oriental they look like caricatures. Father and

Mother, said Eldest Great Aunt, setting off a lamentation among the older women, who all reeled off quick prayers of remembrance to the Heavens. A hand lights the incense sticks sitting in front of the photos. The video cuts to a cemetery. My grandfather squats in front of a gravestone, one hand holding an umbrella over his head, the other balled into a fist and propped against his cheek. He stares at the gravestone without moving, even as the other family members move in and out of shot. This time the cameraman doesn't share his attention around but stays locked on my grandfather. Eldest Great Aunt appears in shot wearing a conical hat and brown pyjamas to place a bottle of spirits on the grave. Behind my grandfather are the many feet of the assembled family, a few paces away, waiting for him. Older Brother pays his respects to his parents, says the narrator. The camera zooms in on my grandfather's face and we see the twin rivulets of tears streaming down his face, which is otherwise expressionless, blank and immovable, like a face carved from stone.

As the video faded out to the sound of more sentimental piano music, Eldest Great Aunt said to me, Your grandfather should have left in '75. He should have gone with the Americans. That would have saved everyone a lot of pain.

Great Uncle shook his head.

But Eldest Great Aunt would not be discouraged. I told him, when he got out of prison. I said to him, You should have left in '75. Why did he stay? I loved your grandfather – I was his favourite sister, after all – but he made so many foolish decisions. For what?

20

It was the walking that brought him back to us. That line – and the memory surrounding it – bubbles up to the surface as I stand at my desk in the Centre for Mathematical Sciences: we were in the hall attached to the back of the fourteenth-century church in Boissy. The hall was new – low-ceilinged but opening up, through double-glazed doors, to a rectangle of lawn surrounded by old, crumbling walls. It was the reception for an adult baptism – a middle-aged Senegalese woman whose entry into the Church Aunt Thi had sponsored. The hall was busy with happy chatter. A heavy-set man, whom I'd seen making his way from table to table – one of the few who moved easily between the newly baptised woman's Senegalese relatives, the many Viets and the smattering of older white French – suddenly made a beeline for me. The grandson, he said, his voice verging on laughter. The writer! And then he did laugh, a big boom of a sound. I'm an old prison friend of your grandfather's, he said, God rest his soul. My name is Bạn – I'm sure you've heard of me. And he laughed again.

Later in the evening, I overheard Bạn telling someone about his daughter, who now lived in Houston. She was a Tea Party candidate for the Texas legislature, running on an anti-immigration platform. Too many Mexicans crossing the border, said Bạn. Thinking of children walking across the desert, I asked him about the Peregrines. Is it true that it was your idea? He laughed again. It was all a bit of a joke, he said. You know when your grandfather got out of prison, he barely spoke a word. He sat in his chair in that apartment – yes, the black one, with the armrests – he sat there all day, saying nothing. When I saw him, I thought, God, it's a ghost, not a man. You know I was released a long time before him – I was only in Chí Hoà for two years. And I believe you have to get on with life. Get living! That's what I say. So it started off as a little joke, about your grandfather being tired from his pilgrimage – you know, the big holy man come down from the mountain, exhausted. But now I don't know if it was a great prank or something else. Your grandmother says it was a miracle. That it was the walking that brought him back to us. He laughed, and I found that the repeated booming was making me feel uncomfortable, even queasy.

A miracle! Well, it got him talking, anyway. I'd been to Rome, you know, Lourdes. I described them to him, often over the phone. He asked so many questions – where did I stay, how long did I wait outside the Basilica. Trivial things. Then it became a habit – something to talk about when I called him. Ah, look at your face! What, you think we really did all that walking? Look at me! That damned laugh again.

And think of his condition. We wouldn't have lasted a day. The Via de Compostela is over 800 kilometres, through the desert. No, we didn't walk. But we did our research. We read about the routes and looked over maps. Every pilgrim is a fantasist anyway, so we just cut to the chase. Really, we were just following tradition. They say that the pilgrims on the Via de Compostela carried stones on their way, to be added to the end of the road. In the depths of their pilgrimage, when they were starving and thought they could walk no longer, they imagined the golden stones they held to be golden loaves of bread. In Chí Hoà, we did that too: we made the bowl of rice we were given each day into a whole feast. Each bite of plain rice, we imagined a different dish, and we thanked God for each one. Eventually, your grandfather came up with the name for our little society: the Societas Peregrinus. Well – he liked his Latin, didn't he. And why not indulge in a little fantasy? It passed the time. And, after all, life goes on.

21

The beginning of a story that is always a kind of falsehood: I remember. And yet, I remember – I remember him in hospital, wheezing, absent-minded. I remember his voice in the tiny apartment, slow and considered, explaining the history of Vietnam to me. I remember feeling the distance between us, separated by language and years, but also by my own self-consciousness. I remember listening to him and, at the same time, listening to myself listen: the whirring of my own thoughts so loud that I could hardly hear him speak, working double-time to create a layer of interpretation – meaning, justification, misrecognition – between myself and him, so that I was always I and he always he, and we never quite came together.

22

I remember going to church in the deep eastern suburbs of Melbourne with my grandparents. They were visiting from Paris; it was their first and only visit to Australia. A newish church, constructed out of red bricks in the seventies. No stones or vaulted ceilings, just a big colourful tapestry of Christ aflame, alpha and omega stitched in white on either side of Him. The crucifix behind the altar was less gory than the ones I later saw in France, like the one that hung in the living room of the apartment in Boissy. Where the French preferred the sadomasochism of Christ on Cavalry, our post-Vatican II suburban church wanted the cleansing fire of Pentecostal Christ.

My memory of my grandparents at our church is so clear, the clarity itself a sign of how the image has been reworked and redeployed for various purposes over the years: they stood throughout the service, even when the rest of the congregation was sitting or kneeling. They stood for the whole hour despite their age and frailty, in their formal clothes, while the rest of us wore t-shirts and shorts, thongs and dresses. I remember my embarrassment, that everyone could see them doing the wrong thing. Among the congregation were the families of my schoolmates, and it was with a sense of appalled shame that I imagined them looking at these know-nothing people who, everyone could now see, were somehow connected to me.

23

I remember the way the thunder rattled the window panes. The way my neighbours threw open their windows, doors and shutters in anticipation. The way all the neighbourhood dogs were barking. Then the rain came, a deluge. The sound of it on the rooftops was deafening.

I went down to the kitchen, on the ground floor of the bookshop, tucked away behind a folding screen. The screen hardly seemed necessary – in all the time I lived there, it was a surprise if more than one customer showed up in a day. Most days, Thich opened the front door around ten, then spent his day looking for books that appeared on his handwritten stock list but weren't where they were supposed to be. At seven he closed up and retreated to his bedroom, which was really just a day bed wedged between bookshelves on the third floor. I had no idea how Thich paid the rent – the amount I paid for my room was too cheap for that part of Hà Nội, so close to Tây Hồ, where expats working for multinationals tended to live in semi-gated comfort – but he never seemed too worried about the lack of business. Perhaps he owned the building, but that would have made him a multimillionaire.

His daily search for missing books was no trivial task: the bookstore took up the first three and a half floors of the building (my room was the other half of the top floor) and every available space was filled with books – on shelves, and in stacks on the floor, old and new, rare leather-bound first editions next to pulp paperbacks, arranged by a haphazard logic – by spine colour here and alphabetically by surname there,

by genre, by relevance to Vietnam, South-East Asia, France, and each
continent, by year of publication, by format, by awards, by Now a Major
Motion Picture covers, by recommended reading age, by likelihood
to be sold (the other room on my floor was home to Gnostic texts
and histories of forgotten peoples), by subject matter, by language –
there were books in English, French, Vietnamese, German, Spanish,
Mandarin, Russian, a few in Thai, Japanese, Arabic, Korean, and a set
of ancient-looking Bibles in Portuguese – old maps and atlases were
on the third floor, arranged chronologically so that as you flipped
through them you could see the white man's progress into the heart
of darkness – coffee table books were in the nice room on the ground
floor, displayed so that their photos of cities, people, food, nudes, old
sepia days, paintings and artefacts all showed. All were noted down on
Thich's list, which itself spilled into countless notebooks, post-it notes,
loose sheets of paper and the occasional napkin.

The presence of all these books was having an adverse effect on
the book about my grandfather – the project that had brought me
to Vietnam in the first place. Interesting as it was to chase up every
obscure reference in my notebooks – and there were many such
references, ranging from Eastern mysticism to twentieth-century
Western intellectual Communism, William Faulkner and Graham
Greene, the Bible and the *I Ching* – the weight of all those books was
beginning to bear down on me; all those words sitting there unread,
ideas forgotten, put me in mind of a graveyard.

So on the day of that deluge, I went downstairs to make myself a
coffee, and to gain five minutes' relief from my notebooks. I remember
standing there on the tiled floor as the kettle boiled and the rain
thundered on, and the neighbours' children dashed, screaming in
delight, back and forth across the open courtyard. I couldn't get this
one line out of my head: the again and again of a failure. I didn't
know where the line had come from, but I knew what it meant. It
was the first time, there in the half-kitchen of Thich's bookstore,

that I knew for sure – that I allowed myself to know – that the manuscript sitting on my computer upstairs – a family history, filled with research, verbatim speech, fact upon fact, a work of duty but not imagination, of labour but not risk – was a failure.

Later, coffee in hand, I sat at the desk facing the narrow lane outside the bookstore and tried to think through what I had realised down in the kitchen. The act of remembering, I thought, is like ploughing a fallow field. It is the 'again and again of a failure'. We are always trying to fasten ourselves to a fixed point in the immemorial past, to anchor our sense of self on something solid – the story of an ancestor's heroic struggle, a mythic homeland, the inherited memory of a certain landscape. Such attempts to establish an origin are doomed to failure. Gospel truths are revealed to be interpolations, and the unmoored past slips by again.

24

In his letter to me, my grandfather apologised for not being able to leave me with anything useful – no money, no house, no introductions to district attorneys or senators. Worst of all, no home. No hearth place. No graveyard to bury my loved ones in and, in turn, to be buried in myself. Instead, his legacy for me would be nothing more than these memories. What good is an ancestor if they can't leave you a homeland?

For the remainder of my time in Hà Nội, having given up on my manuscript, I went through the motions of my residency, including my placement with the government-run publisher. The highlight of my days there was the canteen lunch we took in a neighbouring building, along with staff from several other enterprises. The food was simple, home-style fare. My conversations there were usually simple too – comparing notes on school, on festive days, on marriage and the relation between the sexes – the usual topics of polite cultural exchange. In that way I was no different from the steady stream of foreign interns who came through their office.

Only once did our conversation stray into less comfortable territory. It began with Khanh, a burly, brusque man about my father's age. He was rarely in the office, and his role when he did come in was unclear. On this day we'd brought our metal trays back from the buffet – mine laden with an extra serving of chả giò – and were settling down at a table when Khanh joined us, having apparently spent the morning elsewhere. He immediately started in on Việt Kiều like my parents. I remember, he said, when people started leaving. As soon as the war ended – everyone was talking about it, how to get to the coast, how to buy a place on a boat. About what life was like in America, Canada, and all the rest. But I thought, the war is finally over, why leave? So tell me, nephew, how did it go for them over there? They're coming back now, aren't they? I knew they wouldn't be able to stay away. It's not right, to leave one's Fatherland. Look at you – not even born here, but you feel the pull, don't you.

It's strange, I said, how things turn out. When I was young, the most important fact about us wasn't so much that we were Vietnamese but that my parents were refugees. It meant that when I was a teenager, and boat people were once again in the news, I felt predisposed to take their side. Especially because my parents tried to argue that this new wave, mostly Muslims, was different from their wave, which was mostly Catholics. Of course, teenagers are especially sensitive to any hint of parental hypocrisy. Anyway, that position on refugees put me on the left side of politics, or at least it did in Australia. I know the alignments are a little different here.

Ngọc, one of the younger editors, and a native Hanoian, asked, In the West, it was the left who opposed the war, wasn't it? At least, that's what I've read.

Exactly, I said. I was drawn to the left in the first place because of my family – but that led me to a position that was completely at odds with them. I mean, my friends idolised Fidel Castro, Che Guevara, Mao Zedong. For them, Hồ Chí Minh was yet another hero in the revolutionary pantheon. So of course by the time I gave it any serious thought, I decided, retrospectively, to be against the war. It was aesthetic as much as anything – you have to understand that, in the West, almost every important cultural figure was anti-war. There are no war poets! No songs – or none worth noting – urging young men to join the fight.

I always thought that all Việt Kiều hated Bác Hồ, said Khanh.

Most do, I said. To Ngọc, who looked appalled, I said, They don't really know much about him. Or at least, that's the way with my family. He just represents everything that forced them out. The face of the civil war. So of course they hate him.

But then they hate Việt Nam – they hate us, said Ngọc.

Maybe they did once, I said. But if they did, they've forgotten now. Or they're beginning to forget. It's like you say, Khanh – they're all coming back these days.

It doesn't sound like you've been so good at forgetting, said Ngọc. My generation – we don't think about it, we don't think about Việt Kiều or any of that. We're worried about China. We want to work in Korea or Japan. We think about the future! It's not even that we've moved on – for us there is nothing to move on from, it all happened so long ago, before we were born. Sorry Uncle, she said to Khanh. But it's true. Việt Nam is a young country.

I have noticed that, I said, living here. It hasn't been what I expected. Mostly, no one really cares about the past. Not even when I told you about my grandfather – you shrugged your shoulders. He was an enemy of the state! Someone once thought he was important enough to imprison for ten years – but I haven't met them, or anyone like them. What was it all for? Even your secret police – I don't know if I can call them that, they didn't introduce themselves – I didn't tell you, but they paid me a visit at the bookstore when I first arrived. But they didn't care about my grandfather, or the book I am supposedly writing about him. They only came to intimidate me because of my work back home – because some of the clients at the community legal centre there are Vietnamese asylum seekers. They wanted to make sure I wasn't getting in contact with any dissidents while I'm here. Even they are concerned only with the here and now.

And yet, I can't forget. You see, this is the funny part – the not-forgetting, I got that from my grandfather. Just as I will go home to

Melbourne and become a lawyer, the kind that often ends up doing work for free – that is inherited from him, too. And it's precisely this, whatever it is that I received from him – a sensibility, a politics – that makes me want to remember rather than forget. And that means remembering which side he chose, remembering that he believed in the revolution before he turned his back on it, that he collaborated with the French and then the Americans – and that he wasn't just a passenger, either, but an active propagandist, he told stories – another thing I inherited from him – to prop up the regime, the war and – I paused, but thought, why not, these are strangers, I will never see them again – and, I said, I am using his own politics, his own sensibility, and my only inheritance – I am using what he gave me, as well as what I took from him, thinking that it would help me understand him – I am using all that not to understand him at all but to judge him.

25

Just now, an envelope arrives from the National Library of Australia, delivered through the slot in the front door of our house in Cambridge and landing with a soft thud on the floor of the vestibule. Inside is a jewel case, and inside that a CD-ROM, on which is saved the audio from my interview for someone else's project, an oral history of second-generation Vietnamese in Australia.

I met the interviewer, an academic, at the Vietnamese Community Centre in Footscray, a dilapidated building opposite the train tracks. It was hot that day, and the air-conditioning wasn't working in the airless upstairs meeting room where I waited for the interviewer. She was late, and flustered by the heat. I felt a professional interest keeping me at a distance from her as I wondered about the equipment she was using, the wording of the disclosure agreement she handed me, what her opening questions would be. My coolness stiffened as the interview proceeded. Why had I agreed to this? I didn't want to be on the record, to give a definitive account of myself, or anything else. Perhaps that is why I never finished the manuscript about my grandfather, and instead revised the same fragments over and over: to avoid committing anything to posterity; to avoid committing *to* anything at all.

I found myself giving increasingly fantastical answers to her questions. Every word I spoke rang false in my ears. She wanted to know about my parents – where they were born, when they became Catholics, what they remembered of the Fall of Sài Gòn, when they had arrived in Australia. And to my astonishment I found that, despite all the years I had been trying to write a 'family story', these simplest details eluded me. I knew none of the facts that an oral historian wished to know.

I invented backstories and dates. Outside the stuffy meeting room, in the office space crammed with cheap desks and phones, community centre volunteers and employees kept up a constant, murmuring hum in Vietnamese. Finally, the interviewer asked whether, for me, Australia was home. I said no. She didn't seem convinced. She pressed me: But you were born here, you grew up here, didn't you? Your family live here. Your daughter was born here. How can you say Australia isn't home for you? Haven't you had a good education here? Haven't you prospered here? If Australia isn't your home, then what is it? A playground, or a marketplace from which you grabbed what you needed? And now you're off to England, to Cambridge. Will that be home? Or will you wander the earth like – she stretched for the right words – like a rootless thing, like one with no place to rest?

I might have answered (but didn't): Like a cosmopolitan, like a coloniser, like a transplanted native elite – like the Pondicherrans and the Corsicans who proudly administered French Indochina?

Recalling all this, I know that I will never listen to the CD myself. But one day Edith might listen to this interview. She might, after all, want to know what she has inherited from her father. She might want to know where her home is, where she belongs. She might want to know what I sounded like, as a young man. The words I used.

She might – who knows. But the recording has no power over me. I know now that if there had ever been any truth in my answers, it was a contingent kind of truth – contingent on the stifling heat of that day, the dead air in that meeting room, which was half taken up by empty cardboard boxes for computer equipment that was all ten years old, the anxious ticking of compressed time I always carried around with me in the weeks and months since Edith had been born, which had been exacerbated by the interviewer's lateness and the work I was not doing

to be there, the specific content of the interviewer's questions and the
framework through which I heard the questions and discerned what
I thought was the subtext – the nostalgic politics of South Vietnam –
and my too late realisation that the interviewer assumed that this was
a shared nostalgia, hers firsthand and mine transmitted, inherited.

It was a moment-to-moment kind of truth: when I said that
Australia wasn't home, that was true, insofar as I was truthfully
answering what seemed to me – harried and overheated and paranoid
as I was – a loaded question. I was also telling the truth when I said
that I had realised after my residency in Hà Nội that Vietnam wasn't
home either, could never be home so long as I was marked by my
wooden tongue and too large body as a Việt Kiều – I was thinking of
an encounter with a cab driver who had sized me up and, not believing
that I was Vietnamese, gestured at his own body, saying, We're a
small people, not fully developed. How could we be? We never had
enough food growing up. We were always hungry. I was born during
the war and, on more days than not, my parents came home and there
was nothing to eat. We suffered. But now, you Việt Kiều, you've had
meat and milk your whole life. You're tall and fat, like an American.
Laughing, he said: I hope my children will grow up to look like you.

Nostalgia is the longing for a home that no longer exists or has
never existed. So no, I did not have a home, but only in the sense that
I was refusing her invitation to be nostalgic.

Does that mean I am not an Anamite? For what is more
Anamese than nostalgia? But when I said, no, Australia is not home,
nor is Vietnam, I was not refusing all nostalgia, just hers. When we
compared crimes – me, the 1945 famine caused, I said, by French
and Japanese and American imperial policies, her, the kangaroo
courts and summary executions of landlords and wealthy peasants
and the socially unpopular during the mid-fifties land reforms in the
Communist DRV, me, the Agent Orange and the millions of tons of
bombs dropped on Vietnam, Laos and Cambodia, her, the massacre

at Huế during the Tết Offensive, me, Lieutenant William Calley and Mỹ Lai, her, the re-education camps and prisons like Chí Hoà where for years and years men and women, including my grandfather, rotted away (a mistake, that, to use the cliché about rotting – it made it so much easier for me not to hear, not to feel, the sting in her words) – when we compared crimes like that, we were really trying to interrupt the other's nostos, their return home. We did that because we knew, instinctively, that the other's idea of home threatened our own.

Rival Anams, then. Mutually exclusive. Deep down, she knew that the South Vietnam she longed for no longer existed – never had – and certainly I knew that, whatever it was I longed for, its non-existence made it fragile. Something to be cared for, protected from the wrong kinds of nostalgia. In a way, then, the failure of that conversation marked a kind of success – or at least, my re-remembering of it now marks a kind of success: if our shadow conversation had really been about rival Anams, then didn't that make me as much an Anamite as her? And wouldn't that mean that I have, in my own way, shifted or transcended my experiential horizon – that I have finally understood my grandfather by rejecting his Anam for my own?

Not that Edith could possibly get any of this from listening to the recording on the CD. There she would only hear the bare words uttered – she wouldn't hear anything about Huế or Mỹ Lai, she wouldn't know that what she was listening to wasn't true but only a recording of a conversation that, if it had any truth in it at all, was contained in what was left unsaid and so unrecorded – pauses or tilts of our heads or grimaces or smiles that meant, What about Chí Hoà, What about the famine?

And so I begin to worry about what will happen one day, when Edith is older and herself nostalgic – what will she hear, what kind of home will she be seeking? I worry that she will trust too wholeheartedly in my speech – beguiled, as so many are, by the voice. I want her to know: trust what I write, not what I say.

26

Dear Edith,

You're too young to remember today – a perfect spring day. We rode our bicycles with you in the trailer behind me, all the way to Anglesey Abbey. I am sorry that this day will not be part of what I leave to you, except for what you read here, which is not the same thing. I worry that you will also have been too young to remember summer holidays in Australia, a carefree childhood, koalas in the wild. What will our dry continent look like in twenty, thirty years? I worry that my legacy to you is a future without possibility. So I want to return possibility to your past, even if it seems cruel to remind you of what you would otherwise never know you had lost.

So – there are flowers in the garden I do not know the names of. Some I do know, like the peonies. One of the bulbs has unfurled itself, ruffled next to its smooth siblings. You have a salad spinner filled with water and a plastic cup, and that is enough. You turn the bright green plastic colander inside the spinner and catch water in your cup and pour it back in. There is sun, at last. It is 17 degrees, and that is enough too.

Your mother is lying on the picnic rug behind you, reading Maggie Nelson's *Bluets*. She curls and uncurls her toes as she reads.

I have been trying to imagine a past for you, a past that could be like a home. This is one slice of that past – you should remember that we were very often very happy. And that that happiness was simple.

Is that enough? Could you dwell in a house made of such light material? I suspect not. Or at least, if you can, then you will have no need for this letter.

But if you are anything like me, then you will be looking for something more – a house of many rooms. I saw a house like that once, when I was living in Hà Nội. I lived above a bookshop, and had almost nothing to do with my days except read and write, so of course I mostly rode my motorbike through the busy streets, guided by an online map of the city's best street food. I ate my way from district to district, discovering phở gà trộn on Lãn Ông, bánh xèo on Đội Cấn, bún chả on Hàng Mành, grilled banana and sweetened condensed milk on the corner of Mã Mây and Đào Duy Từ, chả cá on Thănh Long, coffee on Nguyễn Huy Tự, bánh cuốn on Bà Triệu, bún ốc on Hòe Nhai, phở bò with quầy opposite Hoàn Kiếm, phở gà on Quán Thánh, xoi on Nguyễn Hữu. (I list all this in the hope that you will be interested, perhaps even that the world will still be such that you might be able to retrace my meals.)

It took me a while to make it to the French Quarter – not much street food there – but finally I was lured there by a fusion restaurant doing Nguyễn imperial dishes with a nouvelle cuisine twist. The food was terrible – tacky and overcomplicated and somehow, at the same time, strangely bland. But after my meal I started walking around the neighbourhood, passing the old Indochinese-style public buildings that covered up their mustard-yellow facades and French shutters with billboards and noticeboards, until I found myself on Trần Hưng Đạo, that wide boulevard that had once been known as Boulevard Gambetta.

That's where I saw it: the house with many rooms. It was streaked with grime – soot from all the motorbike exhaust – but once it would have gleamed white behind its sky-blue gate. You have to imagine it as it would have been in its glory days: shrouded by flowering frangipanis. Imagine there, in the house that smelt like freshly cut peaches, your great-grandmother – your Bà Cố – gathering fallen blossoms in the garden to float in the pond. The morning is already sticky hot and your great-grandfather – your Ông Cố – is leaning against the cool bark of one of the trees, watching. The two of them are not yet your Ông Bà Cố – that is how you will refer to them, one day, when you talk about your paternal great-grandparents – but a girl who wants to be a nun and a boy who nearly drowned in the mud of a makeshift mass grave.

On a whim, the girl puts one of the fallen blossoms in her hair, a splash of white and yellow against the black. The crooked stems of the frangipani tree cast hazy shadows so that it seems to the boy that she is shimmering as she walks. The girl is intoxicated by the perfume coming from the blossoms in her hands and above her ear, and the early heat presses down on her, and the city outside the garden walls is still quiet, and the last of the stars are still shining against the coming day, and perhaps that is why she is turning now, still shimmering, to the strange boy her brother saved from the mud.

Ah yes – the mud. Let me tell you about the mud. This house, with its many rooms, its fine silver and French shutters, it sits on borrowed land. I mean that Hà Nội is a swamp. The city between the rivers – that's one way of translating Hà Nội. But really they built the city on lakes, filled in with silt from the Red River to make 'reclaimed land'. Like a lotus flower blooming up out of the muck and the excrement beneath the water's surface, it's all pretty enough, like a postcard, but in the end it will sink back into the miasma. It's already sinking, even now, as the shimmering girl and languid boy look at each other. That's why there are so many dead in the streets. This city is floundering, but its citizens don't even know enough to try to flee. Worse, people keep coming from all over the countryside, dragging themselves down dirt roads, to die here in a swamp, far away from home, abandoning their paddy fields and their family temples. They come here not only to die, but to be buried by a stranger, to have their ears cut off as a token of payment for the Sanitation Department and to be thrown into the mire with thousands of other bodies, to feed the bog. But there is no satiating the swamp, it's got bigger plans: it's coming for the whole city, from the makeshift slum houses in the Phố Cổ to the whitewashed mansions in the French Quarter. It's been waiting nine hundred years for this, ever since the first dyke was put in – ever since the fool king saw a dragon flying up the Red River, a vision that convinced him to build on the quagmire.

A false vision of fame and glory. That's what brought your Ông Cổ to Hà Nội too. For him it was a vision of utopia. Some men in masks broke up a nativity play, promised a world of brotherhood and justice, and that was enough. Well, that's one way of seeing it. The acrid smell of their gunpowder also promised adventure. False visions brought me to Hanoi as well (I didn't know enough to think of it as Hà Nội). I wanted to be a writer, but I had nothing to write about – I had not lived a very interesting life. Even worse, I did not know very interesting people, just a series of A students who became lawyers, doctors, consultants, journalists, teachers – you get the idea. And then at some point I realised that I had something interesting all along – the story, my story, that would make my name – and that story, or at least a part of it, was to be found in Hà Nội. There was also, I guess, the chance to find something out about myself, about who I came from, and so on. But the truth is that was only ever a secondary motivation. What I really wanted was to be famous – not even that, just recognised, appreciated. I wanted to satisfy my ego. I don't necessarily mean that pejoratively, either – perhaps you too are reading this letter to close up the wounds that make your self less whole. Okay, so that's a dodge – making oneself whole and projecting oneself into the lives and minds of others, these are not the same thing. But still, the point is this: like your Ông Cổ, like the inaugural king of the city, I followed a vision to Hà Nội and found myself sinking into the mud.

I was supposed to be fostering international links, spreading soft power, or having soft power spread on me. That, at least, was the justification for my residency. Instead, when I wasn't on my motorbike looking for new food, I spent most of my time wallowing in my room above Hà Nội's most obscure bookshop. The problem was that your mother had not yet told me, as she would on one of our walks to Grantchester, about Walter Benjamin's dictum: What research has established can be modified by remembrance. On the contrary, the advice I'd been given by so many people over the years ran in the opposite direction – that meticulous research would allow me to remember what I didn't remember, that it would allow me to reconstruct my grandfather's world. One of those people was Quinn Wharton, an American Quaker who'd first come to Vietnam during the American War as an aid worker, the first to operate in Communist-controlled areas. I don't care if the people I'm helping are VC or DRV, she told journalists at the time, they could be Hồ Chì Minh himself – I'm just here to help people who need medical attention. She'd split her time between Vietnam and Massachusetts ever since.

She was a legend in the expat circles of Hà Nội during my residency. A generous, forceful sprite of an old woman, still getting about Hà Nội on her own despite being the other side of seventy. It seemed to me that she knew more about Vietnam than the Vietnamese. We met in the café of the Institut Français du Vietnam on Tràng Tiền, between the lake and the opera house.

We spoke for a while about her time on Pulau Bidong, the Malaysian island that became the overcrowded refugee camp where my mother – your Bà Nội – had stayed for six months before coming to Australia. (I hope that that story, at least, you will have heard from your Bà Nội yourself.) A plastic city, Quinn said, blue plastic-tarp roofs spread over plastic-sheet floors, plastic buckets for collecting rainwater, plastic wrappers for ration food and plastic bottles, all washed down into the sea . . . She showed me photos of the refugees arriving on fishing boats, the crowds of already-there refugees swarming the rudimentary pier to see if their loved ones were on board. I wondered if one of those faces was my mother, your Bà Nội. But the faces were all so small and grainy, and anyway I could only imagine my mother's face as it appears in all the photos of her that I (and you) have ever seen – her straight-at-the-camera stare, unsmiling, solemn-lipped, a this-is-how-to-take-a-dignified-photo expression – and the faces in the photos of the arriving refugees were always looking at the shore with such hope and exhaustion.

When I told Quinn about my own project, she nodded enthusiastically. Then she fixed me with her piercing blue eyes and said, The details matter. The whole edifice of your story can come crumbling down if you put the wrong style of chair in the wrong apartment, if you put a southern word in a northern mouth. Anyone who knows anything will immediately hear the off note, and the whole thing will be swept away.

I bought half a library trying to heed that advice – many of those books directly from Thich's bookstore, where I was living. Sometimes I thought I might have been his only paying customer. Books on history, books on culture, omnibus editions of pre-colonial and post-colonial literature, the collected speeches of Hồ Chí Minh, an essay on the essentially peasant nature of the Vietnamese psyche, short story collections from the Đổi Mới era, architectural sketches of significant ironwork adornments in twentieth-century Hà Nội, black and white photographs of the Sài Gòn cityscape through the ages, a Paris Musée de l'Armée exhibition publication on military dress in the colonial era, novels from the diaspora, plays from the Nguyễn dynasty, témoignage of Vietnamese political prisoners tortured by the French, témoignage of French political prisoners tortured by the Vietnamese, témoignage of Vietnamese political prisoners tortured by the Americans, témoignage of American political prisoners tortured by the Vietnamese, témoignage of Vietnamese political prisoners tortured by the Vietnamese.

But in all those pages I only found the memory-industrial complex. Living in Vietnam was not much help either. Imagine – trying to find Vietnam, in Vietnam!

Perhaps you can already see the mud. I don't think I could at the time. I thought the mud was material. I thought that way even when I was working at a government-run publisher, which was really a local branch of the memory-industrial complex, housed in a dilapidated colonial building, where the memory workers arrived each day at ten, napped for two hours over lunch, and left again at four.

My job there was mind-numbingly repetitive: I trawled through a poor translation of the official Party annals of Võ Nguyên Giáp's battles – the great commander of the Revolution, the man who defeated the French and then the Americans – correcting spelling and grammar. The histories were absurd – they skipped over the battles themselves, the people involved and the wider context of why each battle was fought, focusing instead only on how every one of Giáp's battlefield decisions was a vindication of Marxist-Leninist principles; why the ambush at Lạng Sơn was a perfect illustration of Hồ Chí Minh Thought. History, after all, was scientific – and so memory unfolded like a chemical formula.

Worse yet, the government had recently outlawed criticism of national heroes. I imagined a committee of old, nearly senile men determining who these heroes would be, and how they should be remembered. It fell on my colleagues to put their edicts into practice. One of them – Thành or Ngọc – would rush over and tell me that there was a new file to work on, that some lieutenant or major had been deemed heroic or unheroic, and that the manuscript had been altered accordingly.

But what those old Politburo types didn't realise, what their political science left out, was that no law can prevent forgetting. At four, when I left the office along with the others, history receded to irrelevance – to a joke. I rode my motorbike through streets spilling over with consumer goods, past crowds of the young lining up for new restaurants, for new phones.

Once, I went from the publisher straight to the home of my relatives – your relatives, too, though I'm sure that this letter will be the first time you have heard of them. They were the children of another famous Communist general, and a giant bronze bust of the man dominated the end of the room – two metres tall, with rectangular shoulders, a large forehead that seemed to take up half the face, thick eyebrows and a stern expression. The bust's shoulders sported military epaulettes, and at least a quarter of the people present were dressed in the deep olive green of the People's Army of Vietnam. Despite that – and despite the fact that we were gathered to commemorate the anniversary of the General's death – the mood was very festive.

The General was your Ông Cố's older brother, whose name had once been Minh, but later became Sơn – a man who never got stuck in any mud. He had, by then, been dead more than ten years. We were eating at the home of one of his sons, who'd become one of Hà Nội's richest men as an army businessman. No one explained to me what being an army businessman entailed. A nearby table of senior-looking army men were all out of their seats, shot glasses outstretched to clink together over the middle of the table, shouting a drinking chant. (One, two, three, in, one, two, three, in, one two DRINK.) The food came stacked on stainless-steel serving trays: chả giò, gà luộc, tôm chiên cốm, rau muống xào tỏi, mì hoành thánh and chè thái. Everything came with its own small dish of dipping sauce – purplish mắm tôm, tương chấm, xì dầu ớt, muối tiêu chanh, differing concentrations of nước chấm.

After we ate, the General's son took me on a tour. An internal elevator took us to the rooftop patio, from which we had a sweeping view of Hà Nội, including the Ministry of Defence and its helipad, a few hundred metres away to the west. Descending, we entered a double-storey penthouse which was home to the General's son, his wife and her mother. Flat-screen TVs seemed to adorn every surface, and a huge chandelier hung from the ceiling. Their two children each got a floor to themselves; floors two and three were the living space, kitchen and entertaining area, complete with a professional-level karaoke system.

As part of the tour, the General's son took me back up to the penthouse, to see the family altar. There were more pictures of the General in the altar room, but from when he was a young revolutionary, his hair slicked back with brilliantine, almost handsome, before two decades of fighting in swamps and jungles.

Along with the photos, a framed letter hung in pride of place. Seeing my interest, the General's son cleared his throat and read the letter out aloud in the accentuated tones of formal Vietnamese. The letter commended the General's bravery, his strength, his sincerity and his devotion to the Revolution and to the People. The General had been one of the first to join Hồ Chí Minh when the latter returned to the country in the forties. He'd served loyally for forty-three years, across three wars; he'd been awarded the Hồ Chí Minh Medal.

Once, before the battle of Cao Bằng, the General and the letter-writer had lain belly-down in a muddy rice paddy for four hours as they waited to see if their plan for overwhelming a French watchtower would work. They had lain in the dark as the French machine-gun fired wildly into the night. Their own soldiers had not made a sound, not until the whole watchtower exploded like a Tết firework display. The flickering orange fire reflected in the paddy water had made them both look like monsters as they smiled at each other. The Frenchmen died screaming. That was when they knew that they would be victorious in the end, for the French suffered from the persistent delusion that they were safest behind the fortifications that were, in fact, traps of their own making. The culmination of that night would not come for seven more years, at Điện Biên Phủ, but the seed had been propagated in that muddy field near Cao Bằng.

The letter-writer regretted that he was unable to make it to the General's funeral, but matters of state demanded his attention. The General was a comrade who would never be forgotten by his friends or the People of Vietnam. The letter was signed: General Võ Nguyên Giáp, former Supreme Commander of the People's Army of Vietnam.

The family felt such pride in this bronze man. Would you prefer it if I had given you a comparable idol? I could have – my research did yield some documents about your Ông Cố. I might not have been able to give you a bronze bust, but there are other kinds of statues, the kind made to remember victims. But they are so often lacking in substance. Take the Vietnam Veterans Memorial wall in Washington, DC, a three-metre high slab listing the names of each one of America's 58,320 casualties. The memorial is not without its virtues – the names of the dead are listed without distinction of race or rank or manner of death, and there is no doubt a certain solemnity and grandeur in the mildly reflective slabs of black granite that taper off to each side, back into the earth. But its monumentality comes at the cost of its humanity. Only those looking for specific names – a son, a brother, a father, a lover – do any mourning at the wall, and in that case they bring with them much more – a whole remembered life – which they then take away again, together with a rubbing of a name on tracing paper, a photo of a hand touching the looked-for entry. For the rest, the wall is only a blank screen on which to project abstract ideas – the nation, sacrifice, folly, the Cold War, death.

Worse still, at least on this measure – the measure of humanity – is The Other Vietnam Memorial, by the American artist Chris Burden, a four-metre-high steel, aluminium and etched-copper-plate sculpture arranged like a giant Rolodex on its side. Its copper sheets are etched with three million Vietnamese names, representative of the war dead during America's involvement, and obviously a response to the official memorial – a response and, to my mind, a capitulation. For while the memorial in Washington features the real names of the dead,

Burden's counter-sculpture used a basic catalogue of four thousand Vietnamese names to generate the otherwise nameless three million, a number that is itself only an estimate, unlike the precise accounting of the 58,320. No one had bothered to do the same for the Vietnamese – not even the Vietnamese.

So not even the grieving can find anything real, anything to hold on to, at The Other Vietnam Memorial. There is just the Big Idea. And the Big Idea is not, as it seems at first, anything to do with the dead, still uncounted, still unnamed Vietnamese, but everything to do with America – with American memory and American glory – for it was the Big Idea of America that was at stake there. The two monuments are sectarian, rather than interfaith: both sides believed in the promise of America. The dead Vietnamese were only a weapon to be wielded by the faithful who felt that the promise had been broken against the faithful who felt that it had been honoured – was still being honoured.

There is something of the impersonality of the Big Idea about the way your Ông Cố is remembered in the documents I found. As if he were being reduced to a slab of black granite. There is the text that set me off on my quest for fame and glory: three paragraphs in an Amnesty International newsletter. There, he is a lawyer, a father, a non-Communist intellectual, and a prisoner of conscience.

I have wondered whether this might be enough. Certainly for you – how much do you need to know about a man you never met? Perhaps it should be enough for me too. It attests to his work, to his love of his family, to his innocence. You could make a fine memorial out of that. I think many in our family already have.

But lately I have been imagining a different kind of monument. I've mentioned it to you already – the house with many rooms. The many rooms have many windows. From each window you see the same world, but differently. I don't mean that you see a different part of the same world, though that is true as well. I mean that each window has its own mood, its own light and its own time. You experience the world differently from each window. So from one window you might see the main street, Boulevard Gambetta, and the angle of the window means you get the morning light, so you go to this window first thing, when the world hasn't yet found its colours, and this is how you see your Ông Cố, an indistinct figure in the gloaming, skinny, with the frame of a boy, a body with enthusiasm and will but no experience, and so a body that can withstand the extreme predicament in which it finds itself: hungry, starving, and pulling down the boulevard a wooden cart stacked with fresh corpses.

As the light brightens you can start to make out the figures huddled together beneath the banyan trees that shade the footpaths. You see a woman dragging herself on her stomach across the cobblestones to join them. It has been like that for days, as if some unnatural force compels the dying to hobble and stumble towards the same tree, the same patch of footpath, to sit propped up against each other or just to lie together on the dusty ground. You see the skinny boy who will become your Ông Cố leave the cart and approach one of these groupings, curled up against the gates of the racecourse pavilion. You see him bending over, going through pockets, keeping an eye out for shoes. Beyond the gates, the grand building with the sweeping staircase and painted dome crouches like a tomb. The boy works slowly in the rising heat, carrying bodies to the cart one at a time with another boy. You see him covering the bodies with a worn old mat, but their arms and legs poke out like dried, withered branches. The sun crests the opera house and the light sharpens: you see weeping sores on ankles and wrists, a cockroach skittling out of a gaping mouth, a woman's body leaning against the gate, still clutching a bundle against her chest, you see your Ông Cố pulling back the cloth to reveal a tiny wrinkled head, you see that the baby is still alive, still curled up against its mother, still trying to suckle at her empty breast.

There is something a little hysterical about golden morning light – it is too much, it is light to get carried away in. Which isn't to say that what you see from this window is untrue: there were many books in Thich's bookstore that told me about rice shortages and armed guards outside silos, about the long parade of the dying who dragged themselves to Hà Nội to die, about the pits coated with quicklime into which the bodies were tipped by the cartload, like dirt from a wheelbarrow, about the one in ten northerners who died in the famine, more than a million people, none of them shot or bombed, about whole families who went home after the rice crop failed and shut their doors and lay down to die together, about the dead who littered the same market lanes where the well-off continued to play bầu cua cá cọp, laughing and shouting even as the hungry picked at their discarded peels and wrapping leaves, about the French and Japanese soldiers who guarded concrete silos full of uneaten rice while the world around them fell apart, about the American bombers blowing up the train lines supplying the North with weapons and fuel and rice from the surplus-producing South, about men fighting each other over taro bulbs and discarded bran, food fit for pigs, about fathers who abandoned their younger children, the ones who couldn't work, locking their doors and throwing stones to chase them away, about the poor who ate banana roots, boiled and shaped into small, fist-sized balls, and who wore straightened hay tied around their waists with banana rope, about the stampedes at the back gates of charitable households, about how the skin of the thronging hungry flaked off and covered those handing out kitchen scraps in scales as white as the frangipani petals that adorned those wealthy walled gardens, the sweet fragrance of the petals mixing with, but never masking, the putrid, rotting odour that got into clothes and stayed there no matter how hard one scrubbed.

So there is nothing untrue in what you saw of your Ông Cố through that first window. It really happened like that. And yet – the light is untrustworthy. The light casts doubt and, anyway, you've never even heard of this famine. How could such things happen without producing a ripple in history? Could it be that these million lives are too insignificant to leave a mark? But no – that thought is too distasteful.

You move to another window, one looking south, onto the back of another grand home. It is a steadying view, stately and measured. Often enough there is nothing much to see here at all. It is a window for overcast days, for staring out unseeing at the dull grey world as you lose yourself in your own, brightly coloured daydreams. And occasionally you see activity in the other house. You see your Ông Cố, a man now, always in a dark suit, bent over piles of paper in a busy office. You see him taking the stage at a press conference and fielding questions from the assembled journalists. It all looks like a movie about the government – any government. The window, like all the windows in the house of many rooms, is unglazed, and when the southerly wind is blowing, as it is now, snatches of conversation waft up to you. You hear his voice, a deep boom. You hear him answering questions about Agent Orange: No, he says, it's just a herbicide, a defoliant to get rid of trees. It mimics the plant's hormones, he says, to interfere with their metabolism. There's no evidence at all that 2,4,5–trichlorophenoxyacetic acid caused malformations. Nothing to link it to disabled babies, missing limbs, paralysis, blindness, miscarriages, cardiovascular disease, diabetes, cancer, porphyria, endometriosis, decreased testosterone or chloracne.

The funny thing about the light on overcast days in Hà Nội – or in Sài Gòn, for that matter, where your Ông Cố was a press secretary for the Southern regime propped up by the American war machine – is that the light is so diffused, it is as if it has no source at all, as if the world were a photo studio, perfectly, evenly lit. It is light for television, as when the cameras arrive for a particularly important press conference, when your Ông Cố has heavy make-up put on his face, and the lights are so bright that he sweats – but it all looks great on the screen, they tell him. It is also the light for judgment. Evenly distributed, steady. It is a light for seeing things as they really are.

Or at least we might think so. In this light, from this window, you might wonder, as I have, what your Ông Cố was doing, being a propagandist for – for what, exactly?

When I was younger, and dabbling in university politics, I had imagined the worst. I spent my time with people who kept portraits of Chairman Mao and Hồ Chí Minh above their boarded-up fireplaces, who read *The Coming Insurrection* and blockaded Immigration Department deportations from detention centres. For a while they squatted a row of terrace houses owned but left vacant by the university, and even though I was living with my parents – your Ong Bà Nội – at the time, I would sit in on squat committee meetings, feeling like a fraud, thinking I was learning how to see the world as it really was – to see beyond the world, to the oppressive truth that lay behind the rendered-brick facade, whether that was the corporatisation of the neoliberal university or the creation of a pliable, disposable, migrant workforce. I learnt to critique, which really just means that I learnt to judge.

Only later did I come to understand that this was a paranoid way of looking. But that was years later. At the time, I spent days reading about Mỹ Lai, about the 504 Vietnamese villagers – including a one-year-old baby – murdered in cold blood by US soldiers on a single day, about how I ought to have been calling it Sơn Mỹ, about the museum built on the remains of the village, with an outdoor mosaic dripping with giant drops of red blood and the sculpture of a mother holding her dead child in one hand and raising her other fist in defiance. Reading about the massacre, I began to imagine that your Ông Cố must have defended even this. That when the Western journalists began asking questions about the rumours of a cover-up, he denied everything, until denial was no longer tenable. Then, I imagined, he would have started to mitigate, to justify – I listened on YouTube to the 'Battle Hymn of Lieutenant Calley' and I imagined your Ông Cố singing to the press corps: The soldier that's alive is the only one can fight, and, The only one in sight that you're sure is not a VC is your buddy on the right.

I'm ashamed now of such imaginings. Who am I to judge him? Still, whenever I look out of that particular window in the house with many rooms, the light tempts me to wonder: how could he have done it? There is no such thing as having no choice – I don't believe in that. Not for me, and not for you. For others, perhaps, in the abstract – the poor have no choice, the racialised have no choice, the gendered have no choice, the abused have no choice, the chemically imbalanced have no choice. When I am feeling particularly objective – after a bracing reading group on *Capital*, say – I might even believe that the rich and powerful have no choice, that they are buffeted by the winds of social forces as much as anyone else. But for you and for me, and for your Ông Cố, I claim the privilege of choosing, and being judged for our choosing. Is there any privilege more bourgeois, or more precious? If nothing else I want to leave you this consolation, that your choosing matters. And for your choosing to matter, so must his.

So you see, everything appears so clearly through this window, and the view gives strength and reality to your moral convictions. But as soon as you move away, everything is foggy once again. And, after all, you find that you must move, that the vision from one window, even as convincing as this one is, is not enough. Look: through this narrow aperture, little more than a weak source of light for this otherwise gloomy hallway, through here you see, materialising out of the early morning mist, your Bà Cố, in the formal uniform of a nurse at a Catholic clinic, walking along cobblestones in a French provincial town. You see that there is still something of the girl who wore a frangipani in her hair. It's in the corners of her mouth – the way they are poised to turn upwards, even now, on this grim morning, if only circumstances would give her the slightest pretext. But nothing amusing presents itself. Instead, you watch as she goes into the clinic, you see how patient she is with the old French people, how she holds

the hand of the man with pneumonia because no one else has come
to see him. You see how she ignores his vitriol, often racial. She holds
his hand while his last breaths rattle out of him. She calls the family
of another patient, whose children and grandchildren have all moved
to the south and the west, and stretches the phone cord as far as it will
go so that the old woman can hear their voices, and she, your Bà Cố,
translates the woman's facial expressions for the anxious family – yes,
she can hear you, yes, she recognises your voice, she opened her eyes
as soon as you spoke – no, I don't think she remembers that – say
more, she is smiling now.

Move on now, to the middle of the house of many rooms. There
is a light well there, a two metre by two metre cavity sunk through all
three levels of the house. The four walls of the light well are unglazed
but instead barred with thin iron rods that are beginning to rust. In the
light well, through the bars, you see a man – almost a skeleton, so thin
that he could probably slip the chains from around his ankles. There is
nothing between you and the rich, deep smell of week-old faeces and
urine, so you keep your distance. You do not want to press your face
against the bars to get a better look. Which is just as well, because the
skeleton is speaking to a rat.

The skeleton is explaining to the rat that he is in this predicament –
solitary confinement, that is – because of a weakness for fortune-
telling. It's this place, says the skeleton. They built it according to the
old sacred geometry. The hexagram. Heaven knows why. What kind
of French architect reads the *Book of Changes*? The other prisoners
crowded around as I threw down the yarrow stalks and consulted
the oracle.

The rat shakes its head. That's no good, sir. Shows a lack of
moral fibre. These superstitions – ghosts, the fifteenth stair, God, the
number four. Goes against the material dialectic.

The skeleton smiles. Dumb as an ox, he says. Sometimes I feel like
I've had no choice at all in my life, that I'm a drop in an ocean that

overwhelms me, rolling me to unknown shores. That's how I imagine fate: like a wave I can see coming, but that I can do nothing about. And other times I think my life has been nothing but choices, an endless nightmare of deciding.

Probably you will not want to linger here, in the middle of the house. There is something grotesque about this view. Too inward looking, perhaps. Still, I am always thinking of it. I think that the image really is too reductive, victimising, gratuitous – basically that it's tacky. It's the kind of detail that a bad thriller writer, a sentimentalist or a national treasure might linger upon to give gravitas to their book. But then I think that this really did happen to your Ông Cố. He really was chained to a wall. And if that really happened, then how can it not be at the heart of things? What can we do? Wall off this light well? Brick it up? It would help with the smell, I suppose. But you would still hear his voice, going on and on to the rat about the Nation, and Fate, and God. And there would be a curious discrepancy in the dimensions of the house. A missing bit that more discerning visitors would notice as a non-alignment of measurements – if the dining room ends here, and the study starts there, what is in between? What lies behind the bricks? Clearly they were put up in haste, and not by any bricklayer, judging by the way the mortar has leaked out, dripping down the wall in unpleasant stains. What had to be hidden away with such haste?

But what if we made the wall into something else? Think of the Vietnam Veterans Memorial wall, and The Other Vietnam Memorial. Think of how black granite and copper were transformed by a simple listing of names. Couldn't we do the same with these bricks? Only, this would not be a partisan list, nor one generated by a computer. Were they nameless, these peasants who died in the famine, who died from French American Russian Chinese bombs, who died in muddy ditches in Mỹ Lai and Huế, who died in dungeons in Hà Nội's Maison Centrale, on Côn Đảo and in Chí Hoà?

Of course not. But their names – as opposed to their lives – are expensive. It would take a lot of time – and a lot of money – to find all those names. Still, it could be done, more or less. Someone would have to go to each ancestral village, and there to each family temple, and look at the family trees kept at those temples, and speak to the people who keep the tree and the temple.

There is enough memory in those places to transform our brick wall into a monument. But the memories won't last forever; eventually the old people who keep them will have all died off. I saw that for myself when I was living in Hà Nội and decided to go to our ancestral village – to our quê hồn. In all the chaos of the wars, my great aunts and uncles had moved around so much that they no longer knew where our quê hồn was. Father and Mother are buried just outside Hà Nội, they would say to me sadly, but that is not where our ancestors are.

Then, one day, among the histories of forgotten peoples on the third floor of Thich's bookstore, I came across a thick book of family genealogies. It was laid out in the traditional style, with each genealogy preceded by a short paragraph describing the location of that family's quê hồn. Flicking through the book, I soon came across a stack of —— families, the pages half a thumbnail thick. Eventually, I found one that matched what I knew of your Ông Cố's father and grandparents. The entry about the quê hồn read:

The —— family come from a hamlet called Hung-Xa, which is part of a commune of the same name, in Ý-Yên province, Nam Định district. From the city of Nam Định to the village it is 27 kilometres: first go to Nguyễn, then 500 metres further, on the right, is a road towards the village. Go over the bridge and enter the hamlet. The —— family temple is 200 metres on the left.

When I showed the document to the General's son, he burst into life. He was on the phone, calling a driver, telling his wife to arrange for flowers, his son to get ceremonial fruit, while he and I went through a cupboard of gifts – souvenirs from the family's many overseas trips.

He settled for an array of Longhorns merchandise – my second cousin had gone to the University of Texas to do an undergraduate degree in business management. Then we were all piling into a minibus, which swerved and honked its way through Hà Nội traffic and onto the truck-laden highway that sped away southward, to Nam Định City.

It was only once we were out in the countryside that the General's son said, So, your books are good for something after all! He laughed, and then, suddenly becoming sober, he continued, Everything was so mixed up by the war. My father left home so young – it was too dangerous for him to write home, in case his letters were intercepted. It was nearly ten years before he saw his parents again. By then everyone had moved around so much – and it did not do, in those days, to dwell too much on ancestry, on the old ways. One must be ultra vigilant, and never more so than at the beginning of a revolution – that is what my father would always say. It was better to leave no doubt, in those early decades, about one's commitment to the new order – to the glorious future. So you see, nephew, with one thing and another, there was no chance to visit, and, over time, especially once his parents passed, and then he passed – well, he said, stopping abruptly. You see how it happened.

After a couple of hours, and multiple stops along the way to ask for directions, we were there. A hamlet of concrete houses built in the middle of rice paddies. Stray dogs chased ducks through the narrow lanes. Villagers came out to see what this minibus full of strangers wanted. The General's son explained, We're looking for the —— family temple. The locals pointed in contradictory directions. Apparently there were five different —— temples in the hamlet. Finally, someone produced an ancient man, who took us by foot to the right house.

When we arrived, another ancient came out and spoke to the General's son. They conferred and compared notes, tracing back their ancestors, each one nodding at the familiar names. Finally, the match was confirmed – we were a long-lost branch, the sons and daughters and grandsons and granddaughters of the Primary Ancestor's eldest grandson.

More ——s materialised from neighbouring houses, bearing trays of food and cups of tea. We exchanged gifts and then were ushered to the surprisingly new-looking family temple on the roof of the main residence. The General's son handed over a thick wad of cash. For temple upkeep, he said. The Longhorns memorabilia and fruit were passed along too. Someone jammed a Longhorns cap on the ancient one's head. Someone else gave me incense sticks to hold and pushed me forward, bidding me to pay respects; expectant smiles gave way to clapping motions, head bowing. I followed their lead and everyone was very happy, patting me on the back. Others pressed their hands together as well, and we all prayed to the Primary Ancestor, and I wondered if my grandparents would count this as apostasy.

For lunch, the Hung-Xa ——s killed a dozen ducks in honour of the occasion, and produced a vat of their homemade liquor, which was the colour of rust and tasted like turpentine. After eating, we all walked out of the village into the paddy fields, where the Primary Ancestor was buried. Someone gave me a phone and told me to call my father – your Ông Nội – in Australia. Feeling swept along by an irresistible momentum, I keyed in his number and handed over the phone. My father answered the unknown number tentatively, Hello? But there was no such tentativeness on the part of either the Hung-Xa ——s or the Hà Nội ——s, for the phone was on speaker and everyone was weighing in at once.

Your son, he found our quê hồn —

— we're there now, at Hung-Xa —

— you again, in America —

— or is it Australia? —

— should be here yourself —

— he's a good son —

— haven't done this yourself —

— so happy, it's been so long —

— your father would be proud —

— must come visit, anytime —

Forgotten in all the excitement, I wandered over to the tomb of the Primary Ancestor. It was painted bright yellow, a startling colour against the soft green rice paddies around us. I stepped past some water buffalo shit to get closer to the tomb, and further away from the hubbub. I tried to make myself feel something for the ancient spirit before me, but I could summon only a vague sense of wonder at the idea that, for as long as local memory could stretch back, our relations had been buried in this little rural cemetery. But that wonderment faded as soon as it arrived – for the local memory stopped at your Ông Cố.

(Now, writing to you about this pilgrimage, I notice two things: first, that I was feeling a kind of envy for these Hung-Xa ——s, rooted as they were in that place. So this, I half-thought to myself, is what it would look like to belong, to have a home. Second, and in total contradiction of the first – these Hung-Xa ——s were hardly flourishing. My half-formed envy was further diluted with pity, or condescension. My suspicion was that the Christian missionaries, soldiers and merchants who had passed through this village and so many others around the globe had remade the world in their own image, so that wealth and privilege accrued to the restless and rootless. That I am writing this letter to you at all is directly tied to our being so uprooted: had we remained in Hung-Xa, there would be no need for such a letter, nor would I know how to begin.)

At the family temple, an entire wall was taken up by a family tree. Our stunted branch ended with your Ông Cố and his siblings, against whose names there were no marriages recorded, no children remembered, but only question marks. I supposed they would try to fill in that branch now that we had found each other.

To make the brick wall in the middle of the house of many rooms – the one walling off the light well – into a monument, we would simply have to pay the same sort of visit to every village and every family temple of the dead. We would have to pay particular attention to where the family trees have withered into question marks. We would have to speak to the ancients to find out what they remember.

But to go and do that in every village – what's more, to go and speak to those who have left, for Hà Nội or HCMC, or San Jose or Springvale, but who nevertheless have memories of the dead – would cost a fortune. The venture would have to be bankrolled by an eccentric and extraordinarily wealthy individual – say, David Tran, the owner and inventor of the famous brand of sriracha, the one with the rooster on the bottle, who named his company Huey Fong, after the freighter that carried 3318 refugees out of Vietnam in December 1978, including Tran himself, a former ARVN major. Because there is no chance that a government would ever spend such an extravagant amount on such a folly. But isn't that the point? Instead of building a hospital or a university, to spend so much on a useless thing – mightn't that have the power to actually move us? A devotion to the dead so total that its very uselessness makes us stop and wonder? Isn't that what art is?

The problem is that all these bricks would be too heavy. The house of many rooms would start to slide back into the swamp under all that weight. You would have to keep climbing the stairs to get away from the mud coming through the foundations, under the doors, spiralling around the walled-up well, from which you can still hear the muffled voice of your Ông Cố talking about the Caravelle Manifesto, about Nguyễn Văn Thuận, who was going to be Pope one day, even as you climb all the way up into the attic, where you can look out at the swamp from under the eaves of the house, at the rising surface that gets closer the longer you stay, which you do – stay – because where else could you go now that the mud, mixed in with the remains of the dead whose names adorn the heavy brick wall, has cut off all exits, so that your choices are to stay and watch or jump and drown, which is to say that this is what I can hand over to you – a borrowed view, due to be returned any second now, as soon as the house finally collapses under the weight of the monument constructed within it.

The attic provides a fleeting vision that is, nevertheless, in the moments before it is gone forever, heavy with possibility: not your Ông Bà Cố as young lovers, nor even in the prime of their lives, but at the end – you see your Ông Cố on his hospital deathbed, patting the space next to him with a withered, wrinkled hand for your Bà Cố to come sit next to him. You see not only the end but after the end – his plain gravestone in the small cemetery in Boissy-Saint-Léger, just down the lane from the parish church, a cemetery that backs onto the forest of Grosbois, a miraculous patch of pines and oaks – miraculous if you have just come from the train station, or the housing projects behind the station, where black and brown boys tussle on miniature gravel pitches to be the next Zidane or Kanté. In the forest behind the cemetery you can be alone for miles of well-kept paths, except, perhaps, for the occasional deer, which are said to still live in the forest – once the best hunting ground in all of the French Empire. Here you will see us – your Bà Cố helped along by your mother while I carry you on my front – winding our way through the gravestones.

Love always,
Papa

27

Sitting for the last time in Simons' office, I hand him a paper copy of my thesis. It begins with Viet Thanh Nguyen's description of an abandoned cemetery for fallen soldiers of the losing side, in the Republic of Việt Nam, on the outskirts of the city formerly known as Sài Gòn. The gravestones have been defaced, the memorial statue of a soldier gazing across the highway has been torn down, the grass is overgrown. This sort of deliberate forgetting also begets a kind of remembering, writes Nguyen, sometimes thought of as a haunting.

So it's a ghost story, says Simons.

The typical Anamite is fundamentally ghostly, I say. They haunt community events, dressed in the colours of the fallen regime, waving the yellow-and-red striped flags; they speak about the old enemy, The Communists. I feel a little sorry for them, but mostly because to me they always seemed so absurd, handing out leaflets at a food fair at the Queen Vic Market, protesting against SBS's decision to broadcast Vietnamese news from Vietnam, collecting funds for pro-democracy movements based in the diaspora. They are Antigone's reverse-image: they, too, are motivated by a mad love, a love beyond all reason; they, too, wish to keep alive something lost. But where Antigone is a tragic hero, they are only tragicomic. No one is particularly interested in hearing from the losers of a forty-year-ago war, one that has surely exhausted the public imagination in countless books and films about 'Nam.

Sometimes I am less charitable, I say. Just before we left for Cambridge, I heard that the local Anamite association had stymied plans for an exchange program at our local primary school because of their opposition to any formal links with Vietnam. We lived in a suburb in the west of Melbourne that had historically been a Vietnamese enclave, and the local school had the only remaining Vietnamese bilingual program in the state. But as the area became less Vietnamese the gentrifying white parents wanted their kids to learn a more useful language, like Mandarin or French. A writer friend – a reformed Anamite herself, who overcame her parents' prejudices and decided to 'go back' in her late twenties, and who has been campaigning for the program to stay – wrote to me that the local Anamites would rather that the program die than support any relationship with The Communists – even if that relationship was as trivial as an exchange between two primary schools. So it's likely that, if we return to Australia, Edith will not learn Vietnamese in the school at the end of our street. And, if I'm honest, I find myself hoping for more forgetting – hoping that the Anamites who gather at the RSL beside the school every 30 April will be consigned even more quickly to oblivion.

But is that what will happen, asks Simons. It sounds as if you are in danger of naturalising this process, as if memories always tend towards decay. But the opposite is very often true. What's to stop your Anamites from assembling the material and political support to not only avoid oblivion but to congeal, like a blood clot in the veins?

That is why the thesis looks at the ghosts of the famine, I say. I try to work out why famine ghosts are so much rarer than the ghosts of the wars – why they do not turn up in popular novels and films. I find them only in the most obscure places, like the books I found in Thich's bookstore. There is, for instance, a book of pre-revolutionary writing, in which I find an article by Nghiêm Xuân Yêm, which says: All through the sixty years of French colonisation our people have always been hungry. They were not hungry to the degree that they had to starve in such numbers that their corpses were thrown up in piles as they are now. But they have always been hungry, so hungry that their bodies were scrawny and stunted; so hungry that no sooner had they finished with one meal than they started worrying about the next; and so hungry that the whole population had not a moment of free time to think of anything besides the problem of survival.

What I find interesting about that, says Simons, is the suggestion that the body itself can be a site of memory. In your earlier drafts, you often made the classic Cartesian separation of mind from body. Which led you to an excessive focus on mental processes of remembering.

I tell Simons about the Hanoian cab driver who had told me laughingly that my well-fed body marked me out as a Việt Kiều. Simons laughs too.

When I read about the forgotten famine, I say, I always find that the most vivid testimonies are about what people were forced to eat in their desperation: rats, pig feed, human flesh. They are almost never about the not-eating itself.

There is something quite Catholic about that, says Simons, this connection between memory and the food that passes through our mouths. There are Proust's madeleines, of course. An echo of the bread with which Christ asked his disciples to remember him.

I must have heard many hundreds of times, I say, the priest intoning the words as he broke the Eucharist: do this in memory of me. Memory is fleshy. I can still taste the wafer, the way it stuck slightly to the roof of my mouth. What did I learn from that weekly meal? Apart from the patience and discipline to sit still through that interminable hour – one trick was to read the weekly newsletter back-to-front, an A4 sheet folded to create four pages, filled with death notices, hymns for the week and a précis of the homily. Apart from that, I learnt that the spirit, like memory, is fleshy too. For that was God, or God's son, that I was pushing around with the tip of my tongue as I walked back up the aisle, that I swallowed as I knelt at our pew.

And if memory and the spirit are both bodily matters, says Simons, then so too is forgiveness – which, if nothing else, is when memory is moved by the spirit. He gets up from his seat and opens up his laptop, which has been sitting on the sideboard, next to an array of spirits – mostly Scotch, from what I can see. On the laptop, Simons brings up a clip from what I think I recognise as the 2002 biopic about Derrida. We watch the scene together: Derrida is visiting the prison on Robben Island in South Africa where Nelson Mandela was imprisoned by the apartheid regime. At one point, the white-haired philosopher, in his suit and tie, stands in a fluorescently lit corridor with the bland and antiseptic feel of a hospital. A man gestures to a point offscreen and says, This is the cell where President Mandela slept eighteen years. To which Derrida asks, How much? And the man says again, Eighteen years. Then the camera pans left and we watch as Derrida shakes his head in disbelief and peers through the metal bars, like any of the many tourists that come here to – what? Pay their respects? Gawk? Learn about history? I am reminded of myself, peering at Chí Hoà from the street in HCMC, mentally shaking my head and thinking, Ten years. The tour guide goes on: there was no water facility in the cell, no toilet. The toilet was a bucket. The tourist nods his head, still looking at the cell.

The clip ends, but another one is already beginning, chosen by the site's algorithm: the film has moved on, to Derrida speaking at a South African university on the topic of pure forgiveness. In the clip, Derrida begins by asking whether we forgive some*one* for some transgression, or whether we forgive someone some*thing* they have done. Do we forgive the who or the what?

The video cuts to the end of the lecture, when a student, sitting sideways on one of the desks in the terraced amphitheatre, launches into a challenge that feels staged – not rehearsed, exactly, but perhaps premeditated, and certainly performed for the benefit of the room if not the cameras. The challenger points out that Derrida is here as a white, Western male, that he is speaking to a white audience who form the class of former oppressors in the old regime, and that he has chosen to speak to this audience about unconditional forgiveness. What ideological function, asks the student, is being served by telling this audience – who are all, Derrida included, guilty, one way or another – not to repent or to seek forgiveness, because that would ruin the possibility of pure forgiveness? Isn't that a demand that oppressed people forgive without expecting repentance?

One can understand her anger, says Simons. But you will probably recall Viet Thanh Nguyen's line that too much remembering and too much forgetting are both fatal. In the end, it is a matter of learning how to live. That is what Derrida says we have to learn from speaking with ghosts. And it is for us to live with what they have to say, even if that means that we have to bear what cannot be borne.

If the typical Anamite is ghostly, I begin to say, unsure, feeling my way, then I am certainly not typical. Too fleshy, for one thing. We both laugh. But maybe that's the point, I say. To give flesh to the spirit. To be an atypical Anamite – an Anamite without the haunting. I do share at least one thing with them: I, too, am a loser. Winners of wars have no need for Anam, or any of the other provinces of the diasporic time-place. Look at Vietnam today. There is a street, in Đà Nẵng, named after Trần Đức Thảo. Now that he is safely dead, he can be rehabilitated. That is how victors remember: they name streets after harmless idols. Losers – Anamites – have to remember differently. There is much more risk to our way of remembering, precisely because we have no power. The stakes are higher, because our remembering – our imagining – is trying to do what we could not do on the battlefield, in parliament, in the streets. We're trying to reverse our losses, which runs the risk of making each loss deeper. Ghostliness, haunting, paralysis – these are all ways of mitigating that risk, of avoiding it. But what if there were a way to live with the risk? To keep moving with it?

You remind me, says Simons, of Peter Benenson, the founder of Amnesty International. Less than a year after the founding, Benenson wrote a memorandum which, I think, comes closer to revealing the truth about the human-rights movement than anything in the reams of academic scholarship that has been produced about it in the years since. Benenson's memorandum says, The real martyrs prefer to suffer, and the real saints are no worse off in prison than elsewhere on this earth. The point of the prisoner of conscience campaign, says Benenson – says Simons, half-smiling – is not to bring people out of prison but to free the men and women imprisoned by cynicism and doubt.

I think once again of my grandfather talking to me about forgiveness. He had not, I realise now, been talking only of his captors. He had had in mind all the people at the death-day celebration I attended at the General's house in Hà Nội – his brothers and sisters, their children, the drunk men in the olive-green uniforms, even the General himself, whose name had been Minh, and then became Sơn, now immortalised in bronze. So my grandfather chose to learn how to live, I say.

28

Walking home from Simons' office, I cut through Coe Fen, where cows doze under the trees, and tourists chase after swans and their cygnets for a photo. Near Mill Pond, I have a presentiment of an ending – or a feeling that I will later think of as the beginning of an end: perhaps it is here that I finally make my decision. Or perhaps not. The true course of my mind remains opaque, open only to inaccurate reconstruction after the fact.

Actually, to say that this is a reconstruction is misleading. I am not a forensic psychologist. The best I can offer is a *representation* of my thinking. The re- is crucial: this is a re-presentation, a transformation of the thing being presented – not a mirror but a map. And just as the map is not the territory, no representation of my thinking will ever be my thinking. That distinction escaped me before, when, hoping to achieve fidelity, I drew maps of my thinking with me at the centre, sitting at a desk, the whole universe revolving around my thinking I: a positively pre-Copernican cartography, not to mention pre-Freudian.

But if a map is no more and no less than a useful fiction, if all re-presentation is in one way or another false, then it is just as well to spread the map out over the territory – to link my thoughts to the physical landscape, not because it really happened that way, but to enforce some discipline over that which is too unruly to be held, to behold. A map is not, in this instance, an archive – it is not, as I had previously thought, a record of where my mind has been – but instead a travel guide, a handbook for how to get to where I am going. Or, if I'm feeling expansive, I could say that the map precedes the territory.

So, in drawing this map, I am not setting down what I thought and when I thought it, but instead I am forming my thoughts as if for the first time: passing the Granta and turning up Newnham Road, the sense lingers that this will be the last time I will see all this. I walk by the parked coaches waiting for the day-trippers to clamber back on for the return drive to London. Perhaps it is because I am thinking of endings that I imagine another ending; certainly my mood is wistful, receptive to the quiet that I find, once more, on the path beside Queens Road, looking out over the river and colleges beyond. At the same time, it is a mood for raw nerves, for mistrust and misgivings, for envy of the picnickers and the joggers in their blank, blithe contentment, a mood for knocking expensive cameras out of hands and colour co-ordinated tour hats off heads, for wonder at the sheer stupidity of years of fingers rubbing away You Are Here markers on information-board maps, a mood for vacillating between wanting to sever myself from these apparently carefree people and joining them, between following duty and pursuing happiness, between remembering and forgetting; most of all it is a creative mood, a fecund one, a mood to feel the wellsprings overflowing, the ego inflating, a mood for remembering *and* forgetting, for making things up – in a word, an Anamite mood: into this multitudinous quiet I pour a scene not shown in Great Uncle's home video.

My grandfather and his brother, the General, meeting again, at last. I imagine them sitting in awkward, high-backed chairs, speaking of trivial things: the price of food at the markets, the health of their siblings, their preferences in liquor (vodka for the General, cognac for my grandfather), the names and ages of their many children.

Things not said but understood: that true forgiveness, the kind prayed for, must be of something unforgivable. That forgiveness is therefore impossible. That forgiveness must come without or regardless of repentance, and that to say, I forgive you, is to kill forgiveness. For it is the divine (God for my grandfather, History for the General), through its human agents, that forgives. The proper formula: You are forgiven. They both understood, therefore, that forgiveness had little to do with either of them as individual men, or even as brothers. Forgiveness, being impossible, was possible only through a state of grace.

On the other side of the gated entrance to the St John's playing fields, I think of how such a scene, had it really happened, would have changed nothing and everything. I think of them, the same brothers who had set out together to change the world, sitting in the high-ceilinged room of the Continental (newly refurbished by the state, which was itself renovating, letting in more light, or reorganising deckchairs, depending on your point of view: Đổi Mới, the Vietnamese version of glasnost and perestroika), the venue a special arrangement of the General's to mark the occasion – his little brother's release from prison after ten years. Arranged, I imagine, at no little cost to himself, in the form of favours called in and the loss of prestige, perhaps even the loss of some trust, in associating himself, however briefly, with an undesirable. Yes, a high-risk encounter. So mightn't I take a risk, too, and imagine them saying more to each other – a confrontation: where were you, we made a pact, such waste, such folly; or joy and pride: look, our children, they live and prosper, we wanted adventure, and didn't we find it? But no. It is impossible. Such words could not have been said. And I am tired – tired of remembering, of imagining. Enough. As a child hits a cricket ball with a dull thwack, I think, this is as far as I will go: they were drinking from a bottle of vodka – direct from Moscow, a gift from a colleague – and speaking of nothing in particular.

29

I open our front door to find Lauren and Edith waiting for me. Papa! shouts Edith, both hands raised as high as they can go. Hooray! She claps. Behind them I see that Lauren has put up bunting. On the kitchen table are the expensive anchovies I like and a bowl of crisps. The martini glasses are chilling in the freezer, she says. Congratulations – all done.

That night, once Edith is asleep – at least, we assume so – we sit in the kitchen with the baby monitor switched off, drinking. Lauren flicks through the pages I have had cheaply bound by the student union's print shop. Even your love is researched, she says, laughing. You took Barthes' *A Lover's Discourse* as a manual.

It is literally, I say, an A–Z.

Magnetised fingers, the stars were shining, an accidental touch. All taken —

— transposed? —

— from Barthes, without acknowledgement.

Ghosts come back to tell you how to live. Well – these are my ghosts. Or should I say that my ghosts spoke through these others – through these poets and philosophers and saints. 'If it weren't for books I would have been good', 'before the world had found its colours'.

Don't tell me. All someone else?

All research, yes. Teresa of Avila, and Jean Anouilh's Antigone, respectively.

And us, Edith and I – we're in here too, aren't we?

You are.

Are we research too, then?

Or it's the other way around. I wrote all this to learn how to live with you, with us.

And have you been successful?

Listen, I say, finishing my drink. Let's not stay here. I'll find another way to pay back my parents. Let's go home.

30

More mail – electronic, this time, attaching a new video from Great Uncle. This one is a mash-up of *Có một lần trở lại*, the video I'd seen at Great Uncle's house, after the peacock showing, and more recent footage, shot a couple of years after my grandfather died, on the occasion of my grandmother's first visit to Hà Nội since 1954. This video sets up a series of mirror scenes: my grandfather, skeletal, sitting with Eldest Great Aunt and Great Uncle and the rest of the family, sipping from tumblers of Mackinlay's Whisky; my grandmother, in her best pearls, posing with Eldest Great Aunt and Great Uncle and the General's son at a restaurant owned by one of my father's cousins, before them the goat slaughtered in my grandmother's honour; my grandfather on the red bridge to Tortoise Island; my grandmother at Văn Miếu, the Temple of Literature, looking at the stones inscribed with the names and successes of long-dead scholars; my grandfather standing before the tomb of his parents; my grandmother walking down Trần Hưng Đạo, the Boulevard Gambetta that had once been.

Last September, when Lauren and I stopped by Boissy on our way to Cambridge, my grandmother told us that going home – that's what she called it – had made her feel at peace for the first time in years. After Hà Nội, she'd gone on to Sài Gòn, where she stayed in a convent. There, the young nuns cooked for her, cleaned her room, and talked to her in Tiếng Việt. In return, she paid what was really quite a modest fee – actually, the money came from her children – which

helped support the orphanage attached to the convent. I could have
stayed there the rest of my years, she said to us. Why hadn't she gone
sooner, then? I had to wait, she said, I could not have gone back while
your grandfather was still alive.

Watching the video, I think of how all the old people in the
posed stills looked the same as each other. They wore the same
clothes, probably used the same hair dye. Yet they had once been on
opposing sides of a bitter, brutal struggle. Not just as bystanders, but as
active, passionate protagonists. They had imagined better worlds and
put their bodies on the line to bring those worlds into being. Neither
world came to be: their plans went awry, as all plans do. Now those
bodies they offered up are in more or less the same state of decay. Their
imagined worlds have converged into this one, disappointing to all.
So what, in the end, had been the difference?

A'

Dear Edith,

Your mother often says that my letters to her were written for myself. Not that I've written her a real letter in years. Now, if I'm away, as I was when you were a month old, I send photos of my breakfast and she sends back photos of you asleep in our bed. I send photos of the frangipanis in the car park of the Broome motel where I'm staying, and she sends me a short video of a woman stealing pot plants from the mall in Footscray. I text her to complain about all the shops in Perth being closed after five, and she sends me a link to a review in the *London Review of Books*. It goes back and forth like that when we're away from each other now, all day and into the night. It was different when I was younger, before you were born. When I was living in Hà Nội, I sent her handwritten letters in which I got carried away. When I got home she said that the letters were nice, that some of the images in them had even been beautiful, but that the words hadn't been written for her.

Which is to say that I got carried away in my last letter to you. So, to put it in simpler terms: the ground beneath us is not firm. Not here in Cambridge, which, just like Hà Nội, is reclaimed swampland. Here it was monks and scholars who clawed back territory from the fen to build the university – destroying, in the process, an indigenous culture. From Hung-Xa to Cambridge to Footscray – for all their differences, you'll find that all these places are sinking back into the mud in one way or another. I mean that none of these places is – can be – home.

They could only become home through a forgetting so total that it would be a kind of amnesia.

I doubt that you will be drawn to Cambridge or to Hung-Xa anyway. But perhaps you will be tempted to think of Footscray or Melbourne or Australia as home. True – day-to-day, the ground there can seem firm enough, concreted all over as it is. And concrete does help with forgetting. No doubt you know many of these amnesiacs, who can live on stolen land without any anxiety. Perhaps you are even envious of them, and wish your parents had just let you be. After all, what kind of parents wouldn't want the best for their children? And what could be better than a home?

Sorry – I don't mean to be so cynical. Of course, I want you to be happy – and with that must come a place to be. Look, I don't think you will spend every day tortured by this – I certainly am not. Most days I am no different to the other amnesiacs; I have to make a concerted effort to rouse myself to care. Everything about the world around encourages us to be numb, and that is not new. One of the reasons I wanted you to know about your paternal great-grandparents – your Ông Bà Cố – is that they struggled against the numbness, they tried to feel things, to live.

What I want to say to you is this – even if you do not take up that struggle yourself, there will be times when your feelings will be roused. You more than some of your classmates, whose whiteness protects them. Sometimes you will be reminded, quite involuntarily, about what kind of place this is, and I want you to be ready. You might see, for instance, an old pub overlooking the train tracks in Footscray, and find on its side faded white letters spelling out 'ANA Australian Natives Association Friendly Society'. Then, on a visit to the Immigration Museum, you'll see that 'natives' does not mean what you thought it did: you'll see an aluminium and brass medal commissioned in 1910 by the ANA, and on the medal an outline of Australia with the inscription WHITE AUSTRALIA, and around that, a brass circle, inscribed AUSTRALIA FOR THE AUSTRALIANS.

Maybe the closest place we have to a home is Paris. I don't mean the Paris of the Champs-Elysées, or the Paris of Montmartre or the Sorbonne, nor even the Paris that Edward Said described as a capital famous for cosmopolitan exiles – I mean the other city that Said also described, the one where unknown men and women spent years of miserable loneliness: Vietnamese, Algerians, Cambodians, Lebanese, Senegalese, Peruvians. That is, the Paris that is not really Paris at all, but the banlieues like the one where your Ông Bà Cô lived with their eldest daughter in a too-small apartment. The apartment where your Ông Bà Cô told me about their many houses. Sometimes I thought that that telling might itself be a home: for a long time I dreamed that I could take those stories and write a home for you – a place that was yours, a country to which you could say you belong. That I would be able to give you a book and say, here – here is where your ancestors are buried, here are your roots. But the past is not a home.

Your Ông Cô tried to tell me that. I did not understand what he meant at the time. But looking back over my notes from our conversations, I found that he had once read out a passage to me, written by a twelfth-century monk from Saxony, Hugo of Saint Victor:

It is, therefore, a source of great virtue for the practised mind to learn, bit by bit, first to change about invisible and transitory things, so that afterwards it may be able to leave them behind altogether. The man who finds his homeland sweet is still a tender beginner; he to whom every soil is as his native one is already strong; but he is perfect to whom the entire world is as a foreign land. The tender soul has fixed his love on one spot in the world; the strong man has extended his love to all places; the perfect man has extinguished his.

In my notes, after faithfully transcribing the passage, I had appended my own annotation: ???. I see now that the same ??? is repeated throughout my notebooks recording my conversations with your Ông Cô, most often following some remark about Catholic theology. And it is only by following the thread of my own incomprehension that

I begin to piece together what he meant. He often spoke of the Societas Peregrinus, or the Peregrine Society, a Catholic lay association for whom he served as secretary for some years in the late nineties and early 2000s. The society organises pilgrimages – more like walking tours, really – through southern France, Spain, and North Africa. The peregrines, as members of the society are known, wander in silence through these arid interior landscapes that sit just beyond the Mediterranean coast, only speaking after sunset at the pensions where they stay the nights. Before he got too old, that is how your Ông Cô spent his time: organising the itineraries, corresponding with peregrines, and selecting the readings for their nightly discussion groups.

Well – that is not strictly true. For a long time, that is what I wanted to believe. I don't know why. As if his suffering had not already been enough without some Biblical wandering through deserts. Truth is, they didn't really walk. The Societas Peregrinus is a society of fantasists. Their pilgrimages take place entirely on the phone. The only desert they've crossed is the one Milan Kundera called the desert of organised forgetting; in his stories of exiles desperately trying to resist erasure, Kundera showed just how much can be at stake in a world where official memory is to be the only memory, every intimacy to be forgotten and every countervailing fact to be erased: notebooks from an old love affair can be worth dying for, and an undoctored photo can be revolutionary. But his characters are all heroes, or anti-heroes – at any rate, they're individuals. And one cannot cross the desert on one's own. That is something the peregrines got right, even if it all started off as a joke, as a way of getting your Ông Cô to speak after he got back from prison. But the thing is, it worked. It got him talking. It got him imagining. And then it spread – other people wanted to imagine themselves walking too. Actual exiles, like your Ông Cô, and then, eventually, those who simply felt exiled in one way or another. And maybe that is enough – the wanting to walk, together.

One of the readings that keeps recurring in my notebooks – each time marked ???, as if each time your Ông Cố recited it I was as bemused as the first time, learning nothing – was from Saint Augustine:

There is perfection and perfection. One can be perfect in travelling but not yet be perfect in arriving. The perfect traveller starts well, walks well, holds to the way, but, while still a traveller, does not yet arrive at the goal. And yet the traveller who walks, and walks on the way, is walking somewhere, trying to arrive at some destination.

I imagine the two of us walking – you, a young woman, and me, not yet old – through the Edwardian garden at the top of Footscray Park. The rising sun is well clear of the racecourse across the river now, and it shines through the palms and ferns to bathe us in light. A third joins us – your Ông Cố – and I ask him whether the better translation for peregrinus is sojourner or traveller. He says he prefers stranger. Because, he says, it reminds me that I do not belong – not in Chí Hoà and not in Boissy, not in Hà Nội and not here in your imagining.

It's true, he says, that some people still live traditionally. They still live at home, and I cannot speak for them. No doubt it is better that way, to have roots in firm ground. But that is not possible for most of us – the ground has been ripped away, or we were born into mud. It can be a source of great sadness. In Laon, for many years, I could not accept that I was a stranger even in my place of safety and sanctuary. I had spent those ten years in Chí Hoà dreaming of a homecoming. But whenever I did believe I belonged – when I believed in Sài Gòn and the Republic of Vietnam – that was when I did things that I came to regret. When I helped to rip the ground from beneath others. So there is solace in being a stranger, too. If I belong not here but to the City of God, then how unfamiliar – and therefore, full of wonder – everything is. How strange the light that comes off the steel and glass city in the distance, at the end of this river! How strange your faces – one I knew only as a boy, and the other only in visions!

Volo ut sis,

Papa

B'

Lauren and Edith are at the playground in Histon Road park, just around the corner from the house that will soon no longer be our house. I am sitting in our living room, surrounded by the suitcases and boxes that once again contain all our possessions, ready to be shipped and flown to the other side of the world – to Footscray, the concrete, post-industrial and formerly working-class inner-city suburb that's home to junkies and craft-beer enthusiasts, to yo-pros and retired ARVN soldiers, to young families and anarcho-syndicalists, and to every wave of postwar migration to Melbourne – including, but not limited to, Italians, Greeks, Albanians, Macedonians, Chinese, Vietnamese, Cambodians, Lebanese, Ethiopians, Eritreans, Sudanese and South Sudanese.

Sealing up the last box with packing tape, I wait for Lauren and Edith to return from the park, and remember yesterday's punt up the river towards Grantchester. Exams finished, and thesis handed in, we had finally done what we had talked about doing all year – we had hired a punt from the college and, with Lauren and Edith sitting side by side on the cushions, I had used the long pole to push us along the silty river, past Clare and Kings and Queens, through the lock and the fen, where we passed cows grazing on the riverbank, and then out into the meadows, where Edith dipped her hands into the water at passing ducks and, once, a mother swan escorting her fluffy grey cygnets downriver. I was surprisingly adept at punting, at using the

pole to steer us around other punts – and, on occasion, to push us away
from the riverbank – at ducking below the low bridges and at giving
the pole a sharp pull to get it out of the riverbed mud. At last this
seemed like a kind of happiness, I thought, watching Edith splashing
her hands and pulling them out to stare in wonder at their wetness,
laughing hysterically when her mother played peek-a-boo.

And now we are going to return to the house that had been our
first rental together, the hallway of which we had repainted when we'd
moved in because it had been left half-painted orange, the renovator
seemingly having run out of patience or paint. The house where I'd
spent an autumn and a winter digging up the ex-industrial, lead-paint-
soaked backyard in order to install a tiny square of instant turf and
raised garden beds for summer tomatoes. I wonder if any of that work
has survived our time away, or whether the subletters have retreated
into the house, leaving the garden to be reclaimed by Footscray.

But why should the past need redemption? Lauren asked me that
just before taking Edith to the park, after reading again the first page
of my thesis, which I left lying on the dining room table. She'd read
the whole thing before I'd handed it in. She had picked up the usual
errors, but hadn't made any substantive comments – I suppose I'd given
it to her too late for that. I didn't have an answer for her right away.

When they get back from the park, I think I will say, I'm not
sure we can redeem the past. We can return potential to it, but that's
not the same thing. We have to take responsibility for the past, for
the places we are and have been and will be – even when, or especially
when, those times and places don't belong to us. Responsibility without
redemption. That's the rub.

It is an answer derived from the last bit of reading I managed
to do in a Cambridge library, in the days after my assessments were
complete. Lauren had wanted to do a long video call with her parents,
to show them Edith's new words, so I had gone for a walk in the early
summer sun. Inevitably, I had ended up under the leafy canopy of

Burrell's Walk, passing the iron gates to the University Library. On a whim, I had gone in, through the revolving doors, which had been stopped open to let the air in, and on up the stairs into the library proper. There, I had decided to look up that Walter Benjamin quote, the one that Lauren had once told me as we walked to Grantchester: What research has established can be modified by remembrance. It seemed that the line had come from his mammoth *Arcades Project*, an unfinished, thousand-page collage of material about the iron- and glass-covered shopping arcades of Paris. The manuscript had been hidden by Benjamin's friend Georges Bataille in a closed archive in the National Library, after Benjamin had to flee the Nazi occupation of Paris, only to die by suicide on the Spanish border when his travelling party was refused permission to cross. The manuscript was later assembled nearly sixty years after Benjamin's death by the German philosopher Rolf Tiedemann, followed by an English translation published by Harvard University Press, a copy of which I find on the fifth floor of the library's North Front.

I pull the tome from the shelf and flick through to page 471, where I read the passage in its proper context for the first time, and I see that Benjamin had been responding to Max Horkheimer's pessimistic thoughts about the partial incompleteness of history, namely, that past injustice, past harm, past suffering – those negatives of history – are irreparable, everlasting, complete, whereas the justice practised, the joys, the works (of art, of politics) – those positives of history – are subject to the iron law of decay, of the transience of all things, and so are incomplete. It is this thesis which Benjamin corrects with a line of thinking that is theological – an article of faith, you could say – in the quotation that I finally read in full: What research has established can be modified by remembrance. Remembrance can make the incomplete (happiness) complete, and the complete (pain) incomplete.

C'

(If I think of them now, after all of this walking and talking, this writing and reading, this imagining and remembering, two people are thrown into relief, their outlines showing like clay figures against the mud in which so many others are trying, and failing, to resist the ebb and flow of forgetting. Both are elderly and Vietnamese and live in an apartment outside Paris with their eldest daughter. They have been together sixty years, through two wars, and many separations. They speak to me, in a mix of Vietnamese, French and a smattering of English, of suffering, loss, exile, forgiveness and redemption. They are always laughing, with each other and at me, pinching, touching, feeding me, looking at me, shaking their heads and chastising me, praising my plumpness and my height and my grades. They say to me over and over again, We want you to be. And also, Eat up, Why aren't you eating, Finished already? And just now, thinking of them, I remember the visit she and I paid him when he was on his deathbed, in a clean, beige room in a public hospital a train and a bus away from their daughter's apartment. I remember the way he patted the side of the bed for my grandmother to come sit by him, and how when I asked them once again about the story, expecting them to tell me the usual things, they chose instead to sing, something they had never done before, an old jazz standard about having your dreams come true, *I remember you* . . . I think of that song, and their wrinkled smiles as they finished. I imagine him lingering a little longer, long enough for them to have said, together, Your daughter, she has the family nose. Her mother's eyes – but that nose, that is ours. And then, You must visit more often. When will you come back?)

ACKNOWLEDGEMENTS

This novel was written on the unceded lands of the Wurundjeri Woiwurrung and Bunurong peoples of the Kulin Nation.

I have been writing different versions of this work for over a decade. In that time, many people and institutions have helped me to imagine, write and rewrite this book – far too many to name here. An incomplete list of thanks, then:

Creative Victoria for a Development Grant and the Australia Council of the Arts for an ArtStart Grant, which allowed me to work on a first draft.

The Wheeler Centre Hot Desk Fellowship, the Asialink Arts Residency in Hanoi, Truong and co at Bookworm in Hanoi, the Emerging Writers Festival—Ubud Writers & Readers Festival residency across Indonesia, RMIT's McCraith House Writer's Residencies in Dromana, Sanjay Fernandes, Carla dal Forno and Sally in Castlemaine – all for giving me the time and space to rework subsequent drafts.

Kent MacCarter at *Cordite Poetry Review* for publishing an early version of my meditations on Jacques Derrida and Trần Đức Thảo. Sam Cooney, Elizabeth Bryer and Dženana Vucic for your comments and encouragement on an early fragment – with particular thanks to Sam for helping me find my title. Elena Gomez and Alison Evans for awarding me the Victorian Premier's Literary Award for an Unpublished Manuscript. Sheila Ngọc Phạm for our conversations about home, and for publishing an extract from *Anam* on diaCRITICS.org. Leah Jing McIntosh and *Liminal* for producing a video extract for the Beijing Bookfair.

Michael Green, Ellena Savage and Rebecca Harkins-Cross, for your close reading and your friendship – all that a writer could wish for. Danish Sheikh, for our walks through locked-down Melbourne. Jinghua Qian for revealing to me the history of the Australian Natives Association in your essay on migrant labour. Maria Tumarkin for your support over the years, and for modelling how to live a writer's life. Nam Le for an astute and generous eleventh-hour reading.

Clare Forster, my Australian agent, for championing this book. Karolina Sutton, for finding a home for it in the UK. Thanks also to Benjamin Paz, Sabhbh Curran, Amelia Atlas and Katie McGowan.

Ravi Mirchandani at Picador UK, for recognising a fellow hybrid. Meredith Curnow and Johannes Jakob for the care and rigour with which you have shepherded this novel into the world. Bella Arnott-Hoare, Bek Chereshsky and all the team at PRH Australia for getting this book to readers. Emma Schwarcz for a perceptive proofread, and Laura Thomas for a wonderful cover.

Craig and Gina for the little desk at Shoreham.

Bà Nội, Bác Tâm, Chú Trí, Cô Tú, Cô La, Cô Trinh, Cô Diệu và tất cả gia đình ở Pháp – cảm ơn, merci, for your love sustained over the oceans, and for all our conversations – I have tried to honour your words and lives in this novel.

My brothers, Pierre and Damien. And Bố Mẹ, for everything. None of this would be possible without you.

Catherine, for your arrows of longing for the other shore, which have made me a better writer, and a better person, than I could have imagined. Léa and Louis, for being. Volo ut sis.

A NOTE ON SOURCES

This novel converses with, borrows from, remembers and forgets many traditions. Some of those traditions, and some of the authors and texts comprising those traditions, are embedded in the text. Others are only alluded to. A comprehensive list of all my sources is neither possible nor desirable: one of the concerns of this novel is how we deal with our inheritances, literary or otherwise. A comprehensive list – or itemised bill – is no substitute for working through what is to be received, and what is to be passed on, nor can it decide how much of that is to be made explicit, and how much to be submerged. Still, for those curious about how this novel was composed, a lengthier note is available on the Penguin Random House Australia website, and on my personal website at andredao.com.

André Dao is a Melbourne-based writer, editor and artist. *Anam* won the 2021 Victorian Premier's Literary Award for an Unpublished Manuscript. His writing has appeared in *Meanjin*, *Sydney Review of Books*, *Griffith Review*, *The Monthly*, *The Lifted Brow*, *Cordite*, *The Saturday Paper*, *New Philosopher*, *Arena Magazine*, *Asia Literary Review* and elsewhere.